Sorrel
in
Scarlet

Peter Vialls

Dedication

This book is dedicated to my mother,
who supported my crimes against literature
from an early age,
but who did not live to see Sorrel fly.

Chapter One

Any landing you can walk away from is a good one.

This wasn't.

I crawled out of the wreckage of the dead triplane, grabbing at the jasq to take that, at least, with me as I twisted out of the ripped canvas and broken spars. Blood was oozing from the gash in my side, and from the gash in my head, and probably from the other gashes I hadn't spotted yet.

Merik was dead. A branch had skewered him cleanly through the heart. His face had a look of surprised annoyance. I howled obscenities at the lafquassing scarlet trees that had wrenched the aeroplane into the ground and killed my friend, and more obscenities at Wrack, wherever he might be. I use too much foul language at the best of times - Tolly always complained that I couldn't complete a sentence without saying 'volg' or 'lafquas' - but now I discovered just how wide a vocabulary of swear-words I possessed. The volging lafquass had followed us down, scorching the wings, buffeting us with his passage, tearing the little triplane apart piece by piece. I hoped the lafquass had hit this impossible jungle down here, too, torn his own wings to shreds.

I had the jasq in my grip, squirming in my uninjured hand like a sack of porridge as I squeezed it. My head was spinning. But I had the jasq, and if Wrack wanted it he would have to come down here with us... With me.

The heat was extraordinary, worse than the hot springs at Werintar. Spiralling over two miles down, Wrack sniping at the aeroplane every yard, I hadn't had time to be aware of the rise in temperature. Up in the air over the surface, I needed the fur in the flying suit, or I would freeze in flight. Down here I was poaching in my jacket. Sweat was dripping from my forehead. I pulled the jacket up to see my side - a branch had ripped through my breeches, and through me, and I needed to see how badly I was hurt. Volg it! I needed Merik. He knew far more medicine than I did. There were trees all round me, leaves blood red. Red vegetation? And everything was soaking wet. The humidity was unreal. I blinked droplets of sweat out of my eyes and flicked another drop off my nose.

I peeled the jacket off my good side, and tried to ease the sticky leather away from my other half. I needed to put down the jasq, but the volging thing would ooze away if I let go of it. And I had been through too much to let it go. Wrack was not having it back.

I glanced around. The canopy above me was thick like a woven red mat. He had to be able to see the rip in the trees where we had crashed, but I doubted even he could land without tearing his own wings apart. Good. I wanted the volg to suffer.

I gently undid my breeches and eased them down enough to look at the gash over my hip, and the world promptly went crimson. More crimson, that is. I could feel the blood pulsing from the wound in my side, and the pain was like a dozen saws along my ribs. Blunt ones, at that. I hadn't managed to get to my feet since getting out of the triplane, but even on my knees I felt as though I was going to collapse. I had to stop the bleeding. The wound was killing me. The ground was soft, matted with fallen leaves, wet with condensation. I thought I had seen some sort of snake writhe away from the crash, but now there was no sign of anything more than insects, buzzing around me, drawn by the smell of lunch - my blood. I hoped that none of them were poisonous, but I had more serious concerns. I could see the injury. The branch had gored me below the ribcage. My vision was swimming. I, on the other hand, was drowning. I knew enough to know that I was dying, losing blood, and with a potentially fatal wound in my guts. The damage needed to be cleansed and the opening sewn up.

And all I had was a wrecked triplane, the torn clothes I would be standing up in if I could stand, and an empty knife sheath on my lower leg.

I was twenty-seven years old. I didn't want to die. There were so many things I still wanted to do. Good food. Fine wines. Men I wanted to bed. I wanted to climb the Red Tower in Darshaal. I wanted to see an ice worm. Take the steam train over the Grand Bridge at Juldressi. Maybe even have children.

And I was dying in this impossible red jungle more than two miles down at the base of the Chasm, under those permanent clouds. I wanted to tell people what was down here. So much for the theories that there was a vast ocean down here, or that the Chasm went down to the centre of the world.

I wanted to see Wrack's face as I told him what I had done with his jasq. Fat chance of that now. I should have thrown it from the aeroplane before we crashed. But the volging creatures were pretty well indestructible, and he would have found it. It squirmed in my grip. Red despair snarled through my veins and pumped out of the gaping wound in my side. I had enjoyed watching Wrack bleed when I cut the jasq out of his arm. Sweet revenge. He would heal eventually - I had, when he did it to me.

The old scar on my left upper arm itched again. I was too weak to scratch at it. I was all alone in this dimly-lit red jungle, clutching at my side to try to stop the blood flowing. Fat, iridescent flies were buzzing around me, wanting to drink my blood. Fear was clutching at my chest, tightening my heart.

The jasq squeezed through my fingers, trying to escape, the gelatinous blue creature crawling across my flesh, a cruel parody of my own long-dead jasq. I would never cast spells again. I stared at the blue mush in my grip, remembering Wrack's gritted teeth as I carved it out of his bicep. He hadn't screamed. I had, when he robbed me of *my* jasq. I looked at the amoeboid, remembering how mine had knitted the clean cut Kelvar had made in my arm when he first gave it to me, remembering that a jasq could repair a great deal of harm.

The idea was madness, raw and bloody in my thoughts. This was Wrack's jasq, not mine. Mine was gone. No one could have two jasqs. Everyone knew that a second jasq would poison you, kill you in agony, react against the first jasq's taint.

Except that this jasq was not attuned to human stock. It was Wrack's. How human was he? I was dying, my vision fading. A jasq could repair a lot of damage. If it killed me, because it rejected me from my first jasq - well, I was dying anyway. Or if it did nothing, because it was not attuned to humans... what did I lose?

I pressed the squirming ameoboid against the bloody wound in my side. It flowed into the gash, greedily slurping at the living tissue, its blue pallor suffusing with crimson. Pain flared within the wound - I tried to whisper an obscenity, but I hurt too much. I had lost the gamble. Fear clamped into my stomach - I would die in this red hell. I was dying now. My vision blurred, lit in scarlet, and I felt all consciousness flee.

I was aware of the heat. I was burning, my mouth the taste of a pan boiled dry, my skin prickling. There were shapes around me, low growling voices in a tongue that should mean something... but didn't. It didn't sound good, though. I could not focus. My eyes were rolling in my head, lids too heavy to open fully. Everything was blurred, flowing as though the world itself was half-melted. Hot hands on me, at first just pulling off my leather flying helmet, but then tugging at my shirt, at my breeches. My body raged with fire, and I was glad to feel rough hands peeling my sodden shirt from me, even though the wet air was no cooler. I groaned a demand for cold - my only reply was more of the harsh language. The smell of hot, sweating bodies. There were hands on my bare skin, exploring. Too hot. All I could see was colour, shifting and changing like oil on water, red and scarlet and vermilion mixing with ivory and emerald green, amber eyes and yellow teeth. More hands on me, rolling me like a rag doll. Faces swirling, faces with tusks and yellow eyes, harsh, cruel amusement in them. Vague accounts of monsters from the other side of the world or from old stories mixed with bitter memories of capture. Sound drifting in and out of clarity. Rough earth squishing under my back. Pain in my side, but no longer the agony I was feeling before. I wanted to close my eyes and sleep, but the hands were insistent, invasive. More tugging at my semi-conscious body, efforts to drag me to my feet. The world swayed around me. Memories of Wrack manhandling me slid through my nightmares, and I felt a silent scream of fury building inside me. For so long I had crushed my rage. I tried to focus on the dark red face in front of mine, but everything was vague except my anger, which was boiling. Part of me wanted to kill Wrack. Tear out his throat. Hard fingers tightened around my arm. The rage was roiling through my veins as it had so many times, impotent, all powers lost, and I screeched through my burning dry throat as I thrashed from side to side. My thoughts were full of blood, remembering Wrack bleeding as my dagger carved into his arm, enjoying his gasp of agony.

Something caught the side of my body, below my ribs, and the pain was intolerable. I tried to scream, the colour red all that I could see. I wanted to escape, or to fight. Ancient memories, from years before, flooded my thoughts, and I reached for something long lost. For a moment, the world was a blaze of colour, a different, yet familiar, place. I clutched at the scarlet near me, knowing I wanted to fight. Everything was vague and swimming, moving and swirling. I could still, as though at a distance, feel hot hands on me. More immediate was the agonising pain in my side. I swept the brilliant colour in a circle round me, and then the pain took me. I screamed, and I was barely aware that there were other screams from around me. Agony, scorching through my veins and blazing behind my eyes, was all that I was aware of. I had never felt such torture, even in Wrack's clutches. I had to get out of the realm, retreat away from the anguish. I had wanted to return to the realm so badly and now it was hurting me. I would have wept but my eyes were burning. I wrenched myself back, away from the impossible brightness of the other place.

Everything went dark, back to the dull ruddy place I had been before, except that now there was the crackle of hot orange fire. I felt the flames blazing out around me. More screams. My sight was purple and yellow, the ground swaying under me, the smell of burning flesh in my nostrils. I knew that smell - vague memories of Wrack snarled through my mind's eye, and more anger surged within me like an unstoppable tidal bore. I heard the crackle of flames and then a roar, more fire flaring a distance away, but the men who had been dragging me off were gone. The fever roared within my ears, drowning any cries from elsewhere... drowning my own moans. I could feel the flames on my bare skin... or was that just the heat of my burning flesh? I stumbled, unable to stay on my feet. There had been water, I thought, but everything was swaying, smoke swirling above me, my eyes blurred again. Two drunken steps, a slope; I rolled down the incline, feeling impacts on my outstretched legs, and then felt a sodden splash into a layer of blessedly cool liquid. Only a few inches deep, but lower than the temperature of my boiling blood. Mud under the back of my head, my eyes looking up at branches that waved and shook. Were those wings above me? I imagined something sinuous, soaring beyond the thick canopy of the jungle, black against the orange clouds. I tried to shout a curse, but the effort was too great. My anger had failed me. I slid into dark, dream-infested unconsciousness.

Voices in my ears, hauling me out of the darkness. I groaned and rolled over, wanting to sleep, only to find my mouth and nose filled with water. I spluttered and tried to sit up, my nose sore from the warm fluid filling it, my eyes blinking. I was in soft gloom, two shimmering lights only a few feet away, held by shapes that moved like men. I was in six inches of water and six more inches of ooze, my body mostly naked apart from the mat of dead leaves and mud smeared across me, and the torn fragments of my clothes. My thoughts were clearing. I was still hot, but now the heat felt natural, rather than the fever burn I had had before. I could still smell smoke and the taint of roasted meat.

One of the shimmering lights lifted closer, illuminating the man who leaned over me, his fair skin and fair hair lit by the lantern that was its source. A man... a human. A real person, impossibly - how could there be people down here? He was wearing what looked like a short dark blue leather kilt - no fashion sense, whoever he was - and a leather harness with a sword over his back. His skin was pale, almost white, unnaturally pallid. His hair was golden blond, and I felt a rush of envy. I had always wanted to be blonde, like Shenli or like this man. His face was calm and concerned, his voice level and friendly. Unfortunately, I couldn't understand a word of his strange tongue. I pulled myself to my feet, and the jungle swayed around me. He put out a hand to steady me, and I took it gratefully.

"I'm Sorrel" I said. Not the greatest of first lines, but I was still not really myself. He was looking me up and down, his eyes lingering for just a moment on my breasts. I'm not unused to being naked, and I'm in good physical shape, but I felt a rush of irritation at his attention, and scowled fiercely, pulling my hand from his. He grinned, and I felt the ire growing. My side pulsed in sympathy - I looked down to where the jasq was half-hidden in the mud and mulch sticking to my hip. The creature had already grown into the wound, a blue scab inside my skin. I shivered despite the heat, and the man facing me reached to take my arm again. I shook away his proffered assistance, glaring at him, and stumbled, my foot tangling in a shrub protruding from the marshy water. The pale man spoke again in a low, calming voice, gesturing off to one side. I could see nothing but darkness in the direction he indicated. To be fair, there was nothing but darkness all around us, just the two lights the men were holding. Only the blond man near me was clearly visible - there were two other men a little further back, equally pale-skinned, in similar skimpy garb. Not so surprising in this heat. Their eyes were on me, too. I could feel anger flowering in my blood. I needed a weapon. I had been helpless for too long!

One of the other men said something, his voice low and worried. The only word that meant anything was "graalur". I stepped back further, my feet squelching in the marsh in which I stood, and repeated the word, questioningly, my fever memories snarling at me.

The blond man nodded at me, and pointed up the slope to the left of me. "Graalur" he replied, nodding again. "Skal ragga tathrioki graalur, belid."

More gibberish. Graalur were black legends, monsters, goblins from the far ends of the world. The stories I'd heard about them were travellers' tales, talking of them pillaging and raiding - were there such creatures here? Unclear memories of feverish struggles tiptoed through my thoughts. My head was spinning, but I needed to know what was nightmare and what was real. I reached out and seized the lantern, ignoring the blond man's protest, before pushing past him and his friends and scrambled up the shallow slope down which I had rolled... how many hours ago? The climb was hard, my legs not moving properly, as though something was tangled round them.

At the top the lantern revealed a scene of carnage. Five figures lay still on the red mulch, contorted in death, flies crawling across the remains, a low, intense buzz telling of their activity. Beyond them I could just barely make out the remains of the triplane in the dim illumination, canvas wings scorched and blackened, the spars burned to ashes. Merik's funeral pyre. I could see from here that the fuel from the tank had turned the tripe into an inferno, leaving the aeroplane a charred ruin. I felt tears sting my eyes. Perhaps it was a result of the smoke I could smell in the air. I would not weep. No.

Hands gently took hold of my shoulders. I ripped free of the blond man's grip, and walked forward. The flies buzzed away angrily as I leaned down to look at the corpses, lifting the light to show them clearly. Something slid away into the darkness, long and sinuous on too many legs. The bodies had been torched, the fat burned from the bones, but there was enough left to see the remains of dark red skin, the tusks, the burly muscled bodies… and the pointed ears. Almost human. I glanced down one of the bodies, his loincloth lost or discarded. Yes, in some ways very human, if large. The graalur of the pulp stories were bogeymen, a delicious thrill of vicarious danger, spicy tales of ravaging and derring-do in exotic distant lands. These… these were brutal savages, all too much flesh and blood. If the fire had not roasted them, I had no doubt that my fate would have been grim. How could they be here? Next someone would say that there were still elves, too.

That thought made me shiver in earnest.

I looked up at the trees above the dead creatures. The lantern's faint radiance was not enough to show the rent in the canopy above me through which we had tumbled. I gazed around at the fire-scorched ground. I had a vague memory of sliding into the magerealm, of using sorcery to blast the graalur. Or had that been a fever dream? Memories of jagged agony returned, too, and I shuddered, not wanting to think what that meant.

The blond man spoke at my shoulder, his voice concerned. I ignored him, picking up my jacket. It had a pattern of flames across the brown leather, and the gash in the side was black with dry gore. Flies had been working, building their own civilisations in my spilt blood. I flapped it hard to knock off the insect eggs, before bending down and scrubbing the tough hide on the charred earth to remove some of the ordure. The insects buzzed in protest at the end of their dreams of empire.

The blond man had been looking at the ruins of the aeroplane. Now he was just waiting, his two friends at his back. He was keeping them away, giving me time. I felt a faint tinge of gratitude for his forbearance as I pulled the jacket around my shoulders, fastening it closed. Having my jacket back helped a lot - I felt almost myself again. I lifted the lantern from where I had put it down on the ground, looking down at my breeches. They were torn, no more than shreds around my legs. They were several yards beyond repair. I realised what it was that had been tangling my efforts to walk. I tugged at them and flung the remnants aside. My boots had been dropped a few feet away. I picked one up, and something moved within it. I dropped it hastily, and something small and scaly writhed out of it and slithered away. I grimaced, checked the boot again, carefully, before putting it on, and more warily picked the other boot up. It was unoccupied. I had my boots, my underwear and my jacket. I picked up the unpleasant curved blade of one of the graalur. I felt it gingerly. Not desperately sharp. The metal looked like bronze, lighter than I had expected, and probably less strong. Wonderful. But at least it was a sword, and having one in my hand again made me feel a bit more human. I hadn't been the world's greatest swordswoman in the war, but I could handle a blade pretty well.

I turned back to the waiting man, feeling a touch more confident than I had been an hour ago.

"All right, blondie. Lead on."

One of the others, dark hair and bearded, gestured, clearly unhappy about me having the sword. I glowered at him and hefted the blade, making it clear that they were not taking it from me without a serious fight. The blond man nodded and snapped some kind of command at the others. Grudgingly, they turned to move off. The blond man held out his hand towards me, inviting me to follow. Odds were that I was walking into more trouble, but the alternative was staying here, in the midst of the jungle. And it would be here that Wrack would be looking for me. I paused for a moment, looking over to where the remnants of the triplane enshrined Merik's remains. I thought about trying to bury his body. No – Merik would not have been unhappy about his body ending in cleansing fire. And I hadn't got the tools to extract his remains from the impromptu pyre. I swallowed, my throat closed with a grief I couldn't voice, and headed after the unknown men.

Two dim lanterns, unknown terrain and three men moving at speed. A recipe for a broken ankle or a painful fall. Fortunately, I didn't suffer either - quite. Blondie's bearded friend was setting a strong pace, and I was struggling to keep up. The two lanterns shed little useful light, and all I could see were the dark hulks of trees and the flicker of scarlet leaves; most of my effort went into watching my footing against the gnarled roots, tangled vines and uneven, mushy ground across which we strode. This was a landscape quite unlike the wildlands of the surface, with pine trees and coarse scrub through the snow – this was lush, rampant and vigorous life, red in branch and leaf. Occasionally I saw the twin points of eyes reflecting back the lantern-light, or shapes writhing away from our passage, but nothing dared to approach us. I was acutely aware of the chitterings and shrieks of the jungle night, which told me that we were by no means alone out here. As we walked, the men muttered between themselves, all three of them glancing back on occasions to see if I was still with them. The dark bearded man scowled every time he looked at me. I made a point of scowling back.

Despite the deep night darkness, the air was still bubblingly hot, steam rising from the soft, wet earth. My body was drenched in sweat and droplets of moisture from the air. When I did stumble and my hands sank into the ground I could feel how warm the soil was.

I wanted an opportunity to catch up with Blondie, try to talk to him somehow. Find out something about this land, about these people. There were people down here, people like me. Trees, a jungle. How could that be? The Chasm was supposed to be bottomless. Or else drowned in a mile of deep water. The stories said it had been created when the world had been devastated in an ancient sorcerous war that was almost a myth. I'd heard of half a dozen aeroplanes that had vanished into the Chasm – I hadn't heard of anyone returning. Not a thought that improved my optimism.

Blondie wasn't going to stop to talk. No chance. His two friends weren't giving us any time. I hefted the sword and hacked at a liana that had tried to garotte me, taking out my irritation on the scarlet vegetation. I was glad of my leather jacket for protection and modesty, but I was perspiring inside it. I knew that I already stank abominably, and sweating hard wasn't helping.

I don't think I'm ever going to forget that first night-time journey through the scarlet jungles of the Chasm, starting in surprise at every shadow and seeing strangeness in every pool of light the lanterns spread. All around me towering trees, not one remotely akin to the pines and sycamores of the surface. Dripping foliage with leaves ranging from small to bed-sheets, in shapes from needles to dinner-plates. The smell of damp heat, wet soil, of rampant growth and sour decay. And always movement, eyes, the myriad denizens of this deep world watching my passage in terror or with hunger, sometimes both.

I wasn't much of a wilderness girl – I preferred the stone-clad pavements of the cities or the short grass of the aerodrome. If I wanted to travel I could fly, or else take a train or one of the new steamcars that were breaking down on more and more of the roads throughout Sendaal. Jungle treks weren't my idea of a good night out.

I needed to think, to decide what I was going to do. Merik was dead. I was alone down here, the triplane was a hopeless wreck, and Wrack was out there somewhere. I should have killed him when I had the chance. If I had, Merik would still be alive. Guilt and misery clawed at my stomach, old despairs rising in my throat. No one knew where I was. I hadn't believed Wrack could recover so fast. We should have been safely into Belkani aerodrome in two hours, not veering off course over the gaping canyon to try to escape Wrack's wrath. I could feel the muscles of my jaw grinding my teeth together. He had been trying to force us down. All common sense said that he wouldn't flame the triplane over the Chasm. But he had, his callous ruthlessness driving us into the morass of cloud. And I had been too stubborn to turn back and land… too scared to fall into his clutches again.

Another reason to kill Wrack next time. I felt my scarlet fury like an old friend seething inside me, crushing out my depression. I concentrated on hacking at the red vegetation as I went past, imagining it was Wrack's neck, letting the anger burn.

I was trying to get some grasp on the geography, but even with my eyes better adjusted to the darkness, all I could see was the tangle of virulent jungle. At first I was really pleased when I saw a flicker of flames to one side of us. The three men obviously saw them too, and there was a staccato exchange of conversation between them. Their tone told me that there was something awry. Again I cursed that I did not understand what was being said. Blondie snarled an order, and the four of us headed towards the flames.

Within a few dozen paces I had some idea of what was there. I was not a stranger to the ravages of war, so I had a nasty suspicion of what I would see. We burst out from under the leaf canopy into the wreckage of a cluster of stone and wooden houses set within an open area of land. My attention was caught by the gigantic spire of rock on one side of the village, climbing hundreds of feet above us, the village nestling in its shadow. As I looked at the village itself, I saw that the buildings were broken ghosts. A few still smouldered, low flickering fires consuming the remaining timber. Most structures had already burned out, thatched roofs torched and timber frames charred, stone walls crumbling. Those that had not been set afire had been shattered asunder as though some gigantic beast had trampled them. That was when the stench hit me. The village was a charnel-field, strewn with the bitter remnants of the inhabitants. Uncooked meat and charcoaled buildings. I had no doubts as to what I was seeing. I gagged, and jabbered a protest at the three men. Blondie turned, his face grim, and lifted his lantern, illuminating enough to show the devastation. They had not known of this, and their bleak tones and drawn faces told me that the victims of this assault had been their friends. I tried to look at my three companions, rather than the scene they were examining. This was not their home village, of that I was sure after only a few moments. They were not moving to look at the individual bodies, or to search for loved ones who might be amongst the dead.

And dead there were. Despite my efforts not to look, the light from the lanterns was enough that I saw the bodies of children and old people, hacked down without mercy, of men and women in the contorted tangle of those who had died fighting. This had been a very recent tragedy; it had to be less than a day since this village was put to the sword. Some of the bodies were heavy-set, the bloody skin much darker than the pale humans. The graalur had not had the assault all their own way.

Blondie and Dark-beard were moving through the ruins, looking to see if there were any survivors. The place had been looted, that seemed obvious. A savage, brutal raid by the graalur. I still found it difficult to believe that I was seeing the bodies of goblins from my childhood stories.

After only a short exploration of the field of the dead Blondie growled a terse comment. The other two replied in kind, equally grimly, and then turned away from the wreckage. I felt only relief when we plunged back into the jungle, even though the stench of the slaughterfield clung to us like a sadistic lover for too many hundreds of yards. I could see all three men stiff and grim, not meeting each others' eyes or mine. I wondered if this had been their original goal, but there was no way I could have asked, even if I had wanted to.

We had trekked for no more than another hour, as far as I could judge it, before I had the opportunity to put my new sword to use. We were climbing slightly, angling up the side of a ridge. I fancied I could hear the sound of water rushing somewhere ahead. The jungle was still thick around us, its own orchestra still in good voice. My feet were growing sore inside the boots, and I was ravenously hungry. After the slaughtered village, the thought of food had turned my stomach, but now I was regaining my usual appetite. I gritted my teeth. I was feeling feverish again, hunger and exhaustion coiling around my thoughts and making my vision swim, when one of the men ahead cried out. I peered forward through the gloom, the note of alarm in the man's voice clear enough. I tightened my grip on the hilt of the blade, and something surged out of the undergrowth straight at me.

Chapter Two

I recognised the acrid odour as the grathk flung itself at me, long neck extended, orange beak wide. The grathk was *big!* The ones I had tangled with on the surface were only about two or three feet long - bad enough when there's more than one, I can tell you - but this one was almost twice as big, and equally fierce. Tolly always reckoned they were insane, attacking savagely until they were hacked to pieces. This one was just as psychotic. Instinct took over and I thrust the sword low under its charge, trying to jam the blade's point into its throat. My blade took it in the neck, as I intended, and there was a gush of dark, foul-smelling blood, but the grathk was not stopping. Its blue-purple scales glistened in the dim light, the two heavy claws of its legs scrabbling at the earth as it tried to get to me with its snapping beak, despite the blade in its jugular. I could feel the bronze bending as I tried to hold it back. The heavy beak was a foot wide, and if it closed on my arm I would lose it. If it closed on my throat, I'd be dead. And it didn't want to die! I tried to twist the sword, afraid the metal would break. I was filthy anyway from the mud I had awakened in, but the grathk's blood was even worse. It hopped forwards again - I threw myself backwards, keeping my grip on the hilt, letting it come over me, hoping the claws wouldn't connect. I pulled my legs up and kicked it hard in the chest, trying to fling it backwards. It felt like kicking an engine block - the impact jolted me back onto a lump in the ground, and for an instant I thought I'd broken my back. The grathk squealed, the high-pitched squeak that always sounded so ridiculous coming from the savage lizard-birds, and it toppled backwards, its tiny forelegs waving pathetically as the long neck lashed back and forth, spraying blood everywhere. I scrambled to my feet and hacked at the neck, taking the head off the brute. It continued to twitch and kick, the body not realising the head was gone.

Ahead of me, I heard shouts and more grathk squeals. I staggered forward. One of the men was down, a grathk snapping at his body sadistically. I couldn't see which man it was, nor where the others were. I dived forward and hacked at the grathk, catching the volging lafquass by surprise. My first blow caught it in the side, and barely got through the blue scales. I swore as it spun round. They were amazingly agile on their two powerful legs. It lunged at me, beak open in anticipation. The beak raked across my side, the leather of the jacket preventing it carving a ravine in my ribs. I mentally praised my sense in putting up with the heat and leaving the jacket on, and hacked at the grathk's head. It felt good to let rip at something. I was snarling in battle-lust. It swung its head into the blade. Dumb cluck. Blood spurted from the cut in its skull, but - typical of my luck - it didn't stop. The beak snapped down on the blade, and I thought the bronze would crack. I shoved hard, feeling the strength of the bird's muscles, and it opened its beak again, more blood frothing around the mouth. Nothing in the way of a fatal blow. It leaped upwards, and I dived sideways. Grathks on the surface could jump up to four feet vertically. This one jumped higher than me, and I'm five foot six. It came slamming down, missing me by three feet. It might be fast, but I was faster. I sliced at a scrawny leg, hoping to cripple it. Missed completely. No score to either of us. I twisted to the right, feinting. The dumb bird was stupid enough to follow the motion, and I ducked under its bite to cut home at its neck. The blade caught the grathk cleanly, and carved deep. Not deep enough to decapitate it, but enough to have worried it if it was smart enough to worry. Which, of course, it wasn't. It was bleeding profusely from the neck wound, staggering slightly. So was I, for the record, but I wasn't seriously injured.

It was then that I realised that actually I was bleeding quite a lot from a ragged wound on my left hand. I hadn't felt it, but I must have fallen onto something sharp. A branch or something, from the look of it. I didn't have time to worry - or else I was as dumb a cluck as the grathk. It was stamping, swinging its head, spitting blood to the left and right in the process. I could tell that it was dying, but it wasn't going quietly. It lunged at me again; I dodged to the right, hacking wildly in the hopes of keeping it back until it did the decent thing and expired. My foot caught a half-buried stone, and I fell backwards uncontrollably, hitting the ground much harder than I would have wanted. My head slammed into the hard earth, and for a few moments I could see blinding lights in front of me. Fury surged in my thoughts. I was not going to die here at the beak of some overgrown chicken! I swiped madly with the sword, kicking with my feet. One boot connected and I kicked again, hard. I blinked, trying to clear my vision, and something heavy slammed into me. Hot fluid sluiced across my face; the smell was appalling, the taste of the quantity that went into my mouth worse, like liquid manure. I kicked and shoved instinctively to get the grathk off me, my sword slicing randomly. The grathk was twisting and squirming against me, but I could not feel its beak connecting. I heaved harder, and the body slid sideways, suddenly still. I dragged my hand across my face, smearing the corpse's blood everywhere but clearing my eyes.

The grathk was dead, sprawled beside me. I felt weak, anger leeching out of me the same way my blood was escaping. I slapped my right hand over the wound on my left, trying to quell the blood loss until I could bandage it properly. I felt bruised and sore all over, particularly the small of my back and my left thigh. I didn't remember being hit there, but I could see a dark red graze all across the skin.

Blondie was walking back towards me. He didn't look much better than I felt. He knelt beside the man my second grathk had savaged, looking down at him worriedly. A hand to his neck - a motion I recognised all too well. But then a smile, and he nodded at me, saying something in that unknown language of his. I wished I could *talk* to him! I felt irritation surge in me at the unfairness of the universe. At least the other man was alive. I pulled myself to my feet. I needed something to bandage my hand. Blondie was treating the other man's wounds - he was not in good state, but he was better off than the grathk. I walked over slowly, and saw the dark bearded man making his way towards us. He had blood-stains on his arm and his kilt was torn, but he looked in reasonable shape. He came over and looked at me coldly. From across the way Blondie said something firmly. Dark-beard raised an eyebrow, and replied, his voice somewhat warmer. I grinned at him. He responded by turning away and walking off. So much for proffered friendship.

He bent down and pulled some leaves off a shrub to one side of the path we had been following. He walked back, nodded at my wounded hand, pushed my other hand aside and pressed the leaves against the injury. To my surprise, the blood-flow lessened, the wound scabbing as I watched. He cracked a small smile. Maybe this was the start of a beautiful friendship after all.

I was perspiring heavily, my heart still pounding painfully in my chest. The volging canyon was so squuming hot! It had no right to be so warm in the time before sunrise.

The sky was brightening... a little. Perhaps it was dawn. Blondie had managed to get the injured man to his feet. He gesticulated towards the top of the ridge, and Dark-beard nudged me onwards. I complied, despite the fact that I was beginning to feel as though I had been drained dry. I was desperately thirsty, and the jasq in my side was pulsing uncomfortably. My own jasq had never done that. I wished I knew what was happening.

The top of the rise, and my legs were telling me I was not going any further. I just hoped it was only downhill from here. Blondie turned back and grinned. I'm sure he was just trying to be reassuring, but in the growing dawn light it was more like a skull's amusement. I looked at the way ahead of us. Forty feet below us white water sparkled indistinctly, and the roar of the rapids battered at my ears. A narrow rope bridge spanned the gorge. Dark-beard was waiting for me, lantern in hand. Blondie gestured. I didn't know if I could do it. Heights don't worry me - I'm a flyer, after all - but the thought of walking across that single rope, with a rope on each side... I wasn't sure I had the strength.

Blondie gestured again. It was definitely getting brighter. I had two shadows.

Hunh?

I looked back, towards where the sun was rising.

Or not.

Above us was the solid ceiling of clouds, still pretty much as dark and enclosing as they had ever been. Perhaps they were glowing slightly, not quite as black as an hour ago. The light was not coming from there. From this height I could see across the valley out of which we had just climbed. Laid out like a red carpet was the jungle, a few openings in the canopy hinting at the presence of more villages. Towering above the leaves a mile away I could see a far taller tree, dark, rough bark, with a cluster of bulbous gourds growing from the upper branches like grapes. The gourds were glowing brightly, shedding brilliant light across the scarlet jungle. The tree had to be three hundred feet high, each of the gourds between ten and twenty feet across. And they shone like sunlight.

I stared around. On the far side of the gorge, a good two or three miles away, I could see another tree of gourds, equally bright. I stared at a bunch of the glowing fruit. Not as bright as the sun, then - I could look at it without hurting my eyes. I adjusted my estimate of its brightness. Looking across the roof of the jungle, I could see the rock spire that had bounded the village. We must have come at least two miles in the last hour, mostly uphill. No wonder my feet hurt. There were other spires, too, climbing half-way to the clouds, and beyond them a faint, distant dark wall that seemed to climb to the sky, too. The edge of the canyon. It looked terrifyingly distant, and impossibly high. There were more lights glowing in the middle distance, rising above the jungle. I also fancied I could see the glitter of light on water, a lake or a wide river dozens of miles away. I shivered, trying to grasp the size of the Chasm, and I looked back at the impossible tree as it shone brilliantly.

Blondie could see where I was looking, and caught my gaze. He gestured at the brilliant light and said something in a matter of fact tone. I gritted my teeth, angry yet again that I couldn't understand a volging word he was saying. He pointed at the rope bridge again.

"Volging lafquass, Blondie!" I swore. "You expect me to cross *that?*" Knowing that he couldn't understand me only added to my vituperation.

There was nowhere else for me to go. I just had to find the strength and get on with it. I scowled at Blondie again, and stepped onto the bridge.

Believe me, I'd much rather be in an aeroplane at ten thousand feet than on a fragile rope bridge forty feet over a churning river. The spray from the rapids meant the ropes were slick, and as I moved over the rapids the roar of the water became deafening. The universe is fundamentally unfair – all that water, and I couldn't do anything to quench my thirst. The growing light from the trees made the peril clearer. That didn't help. I held the rope tightly, and walked steadily, slowly, watching my footing. If the rope was stretched a foot above the ground, I'd have crossed it without a second thought. Yeah. But when all that's supporting you over a lethal drop is a set of three ropes that look like they've been here for centuries it feels far more unsettling.

Half way over, I glanced back. Blondie was not far behind, assisting the injured man. Two of them together? Blondie was braver than I was. Despite myself, I felt ashamed of my own nerves. I strode faster, wanting to get off the bridge before the other two put too much weight on it.

Dark-beard was waiting for me. He assisted me off the end of the bridge. I would have brushed aside his aid, but I was realising just how exhausted I was. I dreaded the thought that we had further to go to… well, to wherever it was we were going.

Half a mile more felt like ten leagues. It wasn't all downhill, either. Instead of jungle, the ground was craggy, our route weaving between monoliths of granite, like the tumbled ruins of a giant's fortress. More of the crimson vegetation festooned the rockery, mostly mosses and grasses. I was concluding that Blondie was a callous volging bastard when I realised that the crags and vegetation were giving way to more artfully crafted stonework. Ancient, solid blocks of cut stone, swathed in burgundy plants. I was beginning to realise how many different shades of red there actually were. I could kill for a glimpse of honest greenery. Blondie called out something, and two figures appeared atop one of the slabs of masonry towering over us. Spears pointed in our direction for a moment, and then we were gestured to pass.

The camp beyond nestled in a relatively level area, with cliffs rising on two sides, a stream tumbling down rocks into a pool at one end. The ruins of old stonework formed buttresses on the other two sides. The makeshift encampment lurking within it would be relatively defensible. Canvas and skin tents mingled with makeshift huts of jungle timber and rushes to provide shelter for people. Forty or fifty tired, dishevelled men, women and children, most virtually naked, only strips of cloth and leather about them. Refugees. The look is universal, whether down here in the depths of the Chasm or up on the surface. It looked so like some of the camps from the… from my war. Sad eyed children were hustled away from us by bleak, worried women. Bitter men, helpless after the turmoil of a retreat or a flight. The major difference between this camp and the ones I had been in was that the inhabitants weren't fighting over any fur or shred of blanket that might keep them warm. I still wasn't used to the heat down here, and the place smelt rank, the warmth making the people stink nearly as badly as I did, but it was probably better than struggling to survive in the bitter surface snow.

Blondie and Dark-beard were ushering their injured friend into one of the nearest huts. Other people were talking with them, and I could guess from their tone that they were reporting the destruction of the village.

I stood by the entrance, forgotten by everyone, and eyed the camp more carefully. They had not been here long at all - the structures looked recent, semi-finished. But the surroundings... now those were much, much older. I blinked, working out what I was seeing. Lloruk work. The shaping of the stones, the carvings mostly smothered by plum-red moss. Swirls and coils, knot-work and scales, and the stylised, vertically slit eyes that were the mark of the primordial saurian-folk. In a couple of places there were coils and spikes of dark metal, too, embedded in the stonework in artful patterns that almost seemed to make sense, until I looked at them more closely. I had seen pictures of lloruk ruins in books, historical texts I had read at school, before the war. Why should I be surprised at the presence of lloruk remains in this canyon? Their war had caused the devastation of which the Chasm was one example. I just hadn't thought that there could be anything left down here.

I realised someone was gazing at me. Blondie had come back, and was watching me, noting my interest, I gestured at the nearest carving.

"Lloruk" I said simply.

He nodded in agreement. "Lloruk" he echoed back at me. "Old ruins."

I blinked, and then realised that he was speaking in the ancient lloruk tongue. I had had the volging thing drummed into me when I was a child - a mark of erudition, my teacher had called it, back when our lords and masters allowed us humans to learn more than basics. A dead language, not used by anyone apart from a few scholars with nothing better to do. And yet here it was being used by a savage in the depths of the Chasm.

I hadn't used the lloruk tongue for ten eventful years. How much could I remember? I let the sibilant syllables of the language echo in my mind, and responded. "Old. No lloruk now."

Blondie's face broke into a vestigial grin. "You speak the lloruk tongue" he said, stating the volging obvious. I was so glad to be able to talk to him, albeit in my halting and half-forgotten school-girl vocabulary, that I did not protest.

A few people had gathered around us. A man with tattoos on his face was talking vociferously - and incomprehensibly - to Darkbeard. A tall, pretty, fair-haired woman walked up to us, saying something to Blondie, and I caught her expression when she glanced sidelong at me. Jealous. Ho hum. I glared back at her. I hadn't been chasing Blondie, and I didn't need grief from his woman.

An older man was at my elbow, saying something utterly meaningless. I glared at him, too, and said, firmly, "Talk in lloruk." At least I hope that's what I said. My teacher at Telmarak School had done a good job of etching the language into my skull, but it had been a long time ago. I hadn't had a need for it since I addressed the headmaster in lloruk at the leaving ceremony, proving I had got a decent grip of the tongue. Ten years. It felt like a lifetime.

The older man nodded. He had greying, receding hair, a sparse beard, and a bright expression. I christened him 'Grey'.

"I'm Tulher." So much for my nickname. "Darhath and I verulnarch the camp together." Veruln- what? Verul was ruler in lloruk. Govern, perhaps. Darhath? Tulher was already continuing. I struggled to keep a grip on his words. "Which town are you from?"

He was eyeing me, running his eyes up and down. I bit back a comment - I couldn't instantly remember my lloruk swearwords, unfortunately. I fixed his gaze. "I'm Sorrel. I came from the surface."

His expression was blank, uncomprehending. Join the club, Tulher. Before he could respond, though, the woman who had been talking to Blondie was at his elbow. She looked at me; even in this heat, her expression was icy. "There is a water for washing" she rasped.

I began to bridle, then realised that actually the idea was extremely appealing. I had been wishing I was upwind of myself for some considerable time. I wanted to say "Lead on", but had to settle for "I follow you."

A vigorous scrub down in the warm, clear water of the pool to which she led me left me feeling almost human again. I was surprised how warm the water was - I had nervously expected the sort of icy mountain streams we had on the surface, but it was pleasant, warm enough to be comfortable, not far off body temperature. The blonde stood, making sure none of the camp's inhabitants made the most of me being naked. Mostly I suspected she was making sure Blondie didn't get too near me. I can spot a jealous woman at fifty paces. I rubbed my hair, wishing I had some soap, glad yet again that I kept the dark locks cut short. Long hair is hopeless under a flying helmet. Getting it soaked like this would only make it curl even more unmanageably, though.

Once I'd got the blood, mud, ordure, gore, leaves, filth and general yuk off me, I took the opportunity to examine the jasq. The dark blue scab occupied a substantial fraction of my side below the ribs. I ran my hand down it; it was smooth, not unlike my own skin apart from the colour. If Wrack wanted it back he'd have to cut it out of me. Hmmm. I'd better not give him *that* idea - he'd enjoy it. A nasty corner of my mind replied "like I did." I shouted it down. Yes, I'd enjoyed it. I had no regrets. Wrack had deserved it. How it was part of me, now, I did not know - all rational logic said that my feverish decision to claim the jasq had been lethal madness.

But it had worked.

I felt it again, with no new rush of comprehension. It was growing into me, just as my original jasq had. And that meant… the temptation to reach sideways to the other realm was for a moment intense, and then I slid down into the water, soaking myself thoroughly as I thought about what I was going to do. I was tired, hungry, aching in more than a dozen places - this was not the time to experiment. A twisted memory of agony after the crash convinced me I did not want to try it yet. The risks… all common sense told me I ought to be dead already. I was in no shape to compound that risk. And there was no hurry. There was no way Wrack could use it now – was there? I shivered, despite the warm water. Wrack was not going to be happy. It was only a matter of time before he found me.

I was not scared of Wrack. Honest I wasn't. The scar on my upper arm itched. I scratched it roughly.

26

Memories told me I was lying to myself. I ignored them, grinding my teeth together hard, and attacked my flying jacket. It did not fare well; the leather was not coming clean easily, and the pale fur and lining were sodden before I was satisfied it was fit to wear again. I had bought it at considerable cost to replace the one I lost after Wrack brought me down during the war. I did not intend to lose another expensive jacket. The woman was watching. I lifted the jacket up, and water poured from the seams. She grinned. Bitch.

"I need something to wear" I said harshly. She nodded, and walked round the rough wattle screen that masked the pool. This was obviously the main bathing area for the camp; the water flowed down over a tumble of stones into the pool, and poured out into a trickling brook that headed further down. I just hoped it wasn't used for drinking water anywhere below. I felt better than I had been in hours. I was also aware how tired and hungry I was.

The woman returned, and tossed a bundle of dark blue straps to me. I stared at the garment. Using the word in the widest sense, unlike the clothing, which was narrow bits of cloth on a leather harness. My first instinct was anger at the stupid clothing... but then I looked at the woman, and realised that her own garb wasn't much different. In this wet heat, leather made some sort of sense, with softer cloth to cover more sensitive bits of skin. Anything more substantial and I'd bake. I shrugged into the harness, and cinched it tight around me with the small bronze buckles, smoothing down the short excuse for a skirt around my waist. Better than some of the things I'd had to wear at Wrack's.

The woman inspected me. I looked her up and down, too. More muscles than most women I knew on the surface. Hard faced, the lines of care in her features. She had lived already. So what? So had I.

"Name Kelhene" she said simply. It occurred to me that her Iloruk might be worse than mine. I gave her my name, and bluntly asked if there was food.

Water to drown my thirst, and food - not desperately substantial, but anything was welcome - and then a place to curl up on softish grass - well, something that looked sort of like red grass - to one side of the camp. The place was abuzz with noise and clamour, people talking, arguing, haggling, flirting, shouting at children and each other - all the usual activities of humans in groups. I was too tired to care, despite it being mid-morning. The jasq was still warm, throbbing slightly, and the bruises and cuts all over me stung, but most of all I couldn't keep my burning eyes open. I slid into a bleak slumber. My dreams were tangled mixtures of Wrack, falling aeroplanes, scarlet trees and glowing lanterns. I did not sleep easily, despite my fatigue.

Chapter Three

Tulher and Blondie - no, get used to calling him Darhath - were both looking at me in disbelief. Blon - Darhath's blue eyes were hard and suspicious. Above our heads was the solid ceiling of cloud, unchanged, unyielding. And I had come down from above it. I suppose I could understand their doubts. I gestured again, spreading my arms instinctively. It didn't help that there was no word in Iloruk for an aeroplane.

"Three fixed wings, one above the other, and a... a..." Volg it, how did I explain a propeller, let alone the engine? "...a thing on the front that turns fast, pulling the winged box through the air so that it flies." All right, so it sounded improbable to *me*, and I'd flown them ever since the aerodrome got its first delivery of Malagan biplanes, two years before the war started.

"This... *machine*... where is it?"

I grimaced, and explained it again to Tulher. Darhath was slightly more satisfied; he at least had seen the wreckage of the triplane, albeit in the dark and at a distance.

"From the surface, all we can see in the Chasm is a sea of cloud" I added. "Sometimes we see flashes of lightning, but we don't know what's down here. The stories tell of its creation in the elf-Iloruk war, but that was over two thousand years ago."

Tulher shook his head. "We have stories about lands beyond the sky, but they're fairy stories. Myths of water that becomes glass, and clouds that fall from the sky and coat the land with white fur." He half-smiled. "The elf-Iloruk war - that's something else we have stories about."

I grimaced, and sipped the hot, spicy drink I had been given. The light blue mug had a smart glaze and an attractive abstract pattern in yellow. It also had chips in the rim, evidence of hard use. These refugees had brought some of their goods with them, but their escape had not been easy. Across the camp, I could hear a child shrieking in protest, and a woman's tired efforts to calm the brat. "We had no idea there were people at the base of the canyon." I responded shortly. "I don't know what else there is down here." I gestured at the stonework. "Are there still lloruk here?"

There was a cool pause, and I wondered what I had said. Tulher drew in a breath, and then nodded. Sometimes the simplest motions can be the most chilling.

I couldn't ignore the horrible thought that Tulher's response awakened in me. I looked at them both and asked one word. "Elves?"

Both shook their heads, and I felt myself relax, but only a little. The idea that there were lloruk down here, improbable as it sounded, was bad enough.

Not that lloruk were my problem. I needed to get back to the surface. I still had work to do – courier and observation duties by day, and by night... I had a jasq back. If that meant what I hoped it did, then I could do far more within the Firebirds now. Always assuming the raid on Wrack's mansion had not brought the wrath of the other Lords down on my friends. I shook my head, dispelling the dark fears crawling around my thoughts, and looked at Darhath. "How can I climb to the surface?"

Tulher answered first, shaking his head firmly. He gestured to the left, and I followed his gaze. All I could see were the cliff walls to one side, rising up thirty or forty feet from the edge of the camp. "You can't climb the walls of the world" he answered plainly.

I got to my feet and looked upwards, trying to see past the tops of the cliffs. They weren't that steep, at this stage. "How close are the walls?"

"About ninety miles from here" Darhath replied slowly. There was a yell from the far side of the camp, and people began making their way over. I'd already found out that the ramshackle building at which they were gathering was the communal kitchen - I'd had a rather thin breakfast there an hour before. My thoughts were still with the walls.

"Can they be climbed?"

Darhath's turn to shake his head. "No one ever has, to my knowledge. There is no path - how could there be?"

"Stairs? A tunnel into the side of the canyon, angling upwards? I can't believe you haven't tried to reach the surface!"

Tulher laughed. "Why? The surface is cold, too cold to live any more. There is no life or warmth up there. And it is impossibly high."

I put my hands on my hips and canted my head sideways, looking at him sternly. "Squuming lafquass, Tulher. *I* come from up there. There's plenty of life on the surface."

"So you say."

"I need to get back home!" I wailed. I realised with growing shame that there were tears in my eyes. I missed Tolly and Verin and Kemal and - volg it - I even missed Shenli. All the Flying Corps. The war might be over, but we still had work to do. Mail and urgent messages to deliver, areas to observe, even the occasional passenger. We had feared the Lords would close down the aerodrome after the war, but our little aeroplanes still had uses, and Tolly and the Marshall had justified us continuing to fly. Dragons couldn't be everywhere – our ramshackle collection of fliers patrolled the northern edges of Sendaal, giving early warning of ursoid incursions or grathk flocks. I had a purpose up there. I had friends.

And I had the Firebirds.

Darhath put a hand on my shoulder. I shook it off, angrily, and rounded on him, telling him to leave me alone. All right, so I used somewhat richer language than that. A few hours had been enough for me to dredge up from my memory some lloruk swearwords, picked up illicitly after lessons or in whispered conversations in class in a school that no longer existed. I didn't need Darhath's sympathy! I stalked away and made for the kitchen tent.

I stopped before I reached it, and paused. This place was struggling to survive. I had no right to their food. Hell, they'd taken me in without any good reason. They could have left me to rot in the jungle. I owed them some thanks, not my ever-present anger.

I needed to go back and make my peace with Darhath. It wasn't his fault that I was stranded down here.

Fine thoughts. I don't do apologies.

I looked round. Tulher and Darhath were watching me, worried faces and wide eyes. I almost laughed at them.

Twenty paces back, and I sat down, facing them again. Typical Sorrel. Act first, think about what to say later. I gestured around me, giving me time to put a question into my fast-improving lloruk.

"What caused all this? Who are you fighting? The graalur?"

Tulher looked at me levelly. "You really don't know anything, do you?" he asked quietly.

I looked at him and raised my eyebrows. Wrack could raise just one eyebrow - very stylish, very effective. I wished I could do that.

Darhath chuckled, but there was little humour in his tone. "If she has fallen from the sky, how would she know?"

Tulher took a deep breath. "The enemy we face is the graalur – that is who we are fighting. We've lost nine of the Solani towns in the last two months, and we've had to flee in the face of their advance. But they are not the minds behind the attacks – they are being controlled." He held my gaze, making sure I understood what he was saying. "The true enemy is the lloruk."

I took a slow, careful breath. Beings from deepest myth, one side in the most devastating war the world had ever known. They had been gone from the surface for two millennia. The idea that they were here, now, and waging a brutal war against the humans of the Chasm was almost beyond belief... except that Darhath and Tulher were so clearly deadly serious.

"The Solani occupy most of the land between the rocklands of the Neldar Ridge and the edge of the Helkin Expanse" he explained. "The graalur hit suddenly and hard, far better organised than they had been before. They took Cangedran, Zarilas and Belgran before we had any chance to fight back. Enslaved the people they took alive, but more than half of the population were killed." I could picture burning towns, the dead sprawled across the cobbled streets where they fell, the grim survivors chained and whipped to make them march. Perhaps my pictures weren't a true image of the fallen settlements, but I had seen the aftermath of the fall of Trakomar. Tulher's words evoked memories I did not want to recall. "We tried to fight back, but we were too few, and too disorganised."

Darhath took up the saga. "We asked for help, but it was already too late. The remaining towns didn't stand a chance. We were in Muranon when the graalur

32

attacked. We gathered some of the survivors here, but we're outnumbered and in no shape to offer a real fight to the graalur and the lloruk sorcerers."

Tulher nodded. "We wanted to flee into the Eski lands, the other side of the gorge, but they refused to allow us to come into their region. Their minister, Norghlin, fell out with my predecessor over the rights to a copper mine, and now they seem to think our misfortunes are amusing. That's why we're stranded here."

Darhath scowled grimly. "That may have changed now. That settlement we saw burned out – that's the north-western boundary of the Eski lands. They'd been keeping a watch on us, making sure we didn't try to move into their territory."

Tulher shrugged. "Maybe they'll be more willing to aid us now the lloruk have come south and started on them."

His bleak amusement was punctuated by a shout from one of the guards atop the outcroppings of rock overlooking the encampment. She was gesturing, pointing upwards with a spear, indicating a dot against the grey clouds. A dot that was approaching, wings outstretched. I stared up into the sky, my heart in my mouth, guessing what I was seeing. Wrack had found me. He had sensed the jasq, and it had called him to it. He had come to cut it out of me again. I was on my feet, backing away, my heart hammering in my chest as the shape swooped low over the camp.

But it wasn't Wrack.

The flyer had long, sinuous necks, wide wings, two tails lashing. Two heads gazing down at us. It looked like a creature out of some of my more colourful nightmares. It had pale silver-blue scales and horns extending from the back of each head, four limbs tucked up tightly against its underbelly. Its eyes were bright green, startling against the cloud-blue body. Missiles were already flying up from the camp - I had not seen the ballista at the far edge of the depression in which the camp nestled, but now the netting and leafy branches that had disguised it had been hastily pulled aside, and the crew manning the weapon were trying to bring it to bear. A second bolt flew from the dark, battered wooden frame, and missed the circling horror by too many yards. The creature swung around and swept downwards. One of the heads spat, and something slammed into the ground a foot from the ballista, smoking as it splashed. A man cried out, bare skin burning where a droplet had caught him. Fortunately the brute was no better a shot than the ballista crew, or the weapon would be a ruin by now.

Darhath had seized a spear and flung it expertly - and inaccurately - at the flying fiend. Good throw, but it had already turned. Typical of ground troops firing bows at flying enemies - they never aimed far enough ahead. They didn't understand the speed of a flyer. If I had my sorcery, I could slam a burst of fire into it that would put paid to its depredations. I had a jasq again - I just hadn't had the time - no, be honest, Sorrel, I hadn't yet had the courage to see if it meant I could cast magic. Now I had no choice. I let myself feel for the jasq's senses, and slid into the magerealm.

For a moment I thought I was seeing the brilliant colours of the other world, and then someone charged past me, running hard to grab at a spear leaning on the side of a tent, jolting me in his passage, and I was back in the Chasm. The other realm was gone - I couldn't concentrate enough to hold it. I'd forgotten how hard I had found trying to see the magerealm when I was first learning sorcery. The jasq was throbbing painfully, too, and my head was hurting, but I didn't have time to think about that. Someone else was yelling near me, and I abandoned the effort. Even so, I was glowing inwardly - the new jasq meant I had a chance of using magic again.

Just not now. Other people were yelling and flinging weaponry. Near me, a burly man with an injured face had a large crossbow. The horror swooped round again, and spat another gob of acid. I cringed automatically, but it went nowhere near me. The man it hit screamed and flung himself to the ground, trying to scrub it off his bare skin. Poor bastard. I dived over to the crossbowman and gestured at him. I could see he was aiming too close.

"Let me!" I shouted, and reached for the bow. "I can hit it!"

I was yelling in lloruk - he looked at me blankly, and shouted something in his own tongue, swinging the crossbow to bear. The winged brute was moving again. He didn't have a chance. The shot missed by a mile. I swore at him expertly, and grabbed at the crossbow. He snarled obscenities back - amazing how curses translate so easily - and pulled the bow back, reloading competently. Probably just as well - hauling the heavy bow back might well have been beyond my strength. I reached out, making it clear that I wanted a shot. He glowered at me, and the brute swept low again. More missiles flew from the camp, and the ballista this time only missed by a foot. One spear actually hit it, and bounced off the scaled hide. It needed a crossbow bolt, not just thrown spears. It spat again, and this time the acid caught the ballista. They were starting to reload it, and the crank hissed. I heard the bow arms crunch as the tension was released again, amidst the screams of the crew. I snarled at the bowman, and grabbed at the cocked weapon - not a wise thing to do, actually, but it worked. He relinquished the bow and I swept it up, judging the speed of the bat-beast as it swept around. I wished I knew where it was vulnerable. The throat had to be a good guess, but it had two. And the underbelly looked pretty well armoured. A bolt would just go right through a wing membrane, without doing much damage. Eyes? Chance of hitting it in the eye was non-existent. I was hesitating. Stupid. Make a decision, girl! It spat again, and I heard the bowman snarl angrily as the gob of acid caught one of the tents. Two women scrambled out, screaming. I mirrored the bowman's anger as I watched the creature soar round. I lifted the bow, matching the beast's speed, and fired ahead, into its line of flight.

The bolt flew true, and slammed into the left throat, driving home. Beside me the bowman yelled in triumph. The beast's injured neck reared up, and other people were shouting in relief. I thrust the bow back into the burly crossbowman's hands, and he struggled to reload it in haste. But the beast was not going to wait for me to shoot it again. It bellowed, a honking snort of pain, and began to beat away to the head of the valley. More missiles followed, missing widely.

The crossbowman turned to me and nodded, gesturing and saying something firmly. I could recognise approbation. Darhath and Tulher were moving through the camp, trying to help the wounded and clear the damage. Darhath turned and gestured with his hand to me approvingly.

I grinned. It felt good to have done something effective. I handed the crossbow back, and made my way over to the ballista, to see if I could help repair the crank.

Over the next couple of hours I began to realise just how much trouble the people here were in. I had been right to worry about their food. The store behind the kitchen was threadbare. The bronze jars contained enough food for two more days. But they also had five injured people, and no medicines or apothecaries. One of the women was six months pregnant, two of the children in the camp had no parents, two more of the people were elderly and infirm. They could not hope to travel quickly, particularly if they took the ballista with them again. They had brought it from their town of Muranon so they had something to defend themselves. They had needed four olgreks to pull the thing along on its crude, unsprung wheels. The attack of the snarq (as I had been told it was called) showed that even with it they were vulnerable to aerial assault. Hunting and foraging parties were out trying to bring back food, but the territory around the camp was barren. Only by crossing the gorge into the Eski territory could they reach a good source of food, and the jungle was a dangerous place to look for victuals. If the graalur were encroaching from their camps to the north, increasing the risks greatly, it would become almost impossible for any but the most capable hunters to forage. The only two candidates currently were Darhath and Korhus. (I was starting to learn names. Korhus was the man I'd called dark-beard).

And that meant leaving the camp with no capable guards. Gelhdin, the burly crossbowman I had tussled with, was in his fifties, and had an injured leg to go with his wounded face. He had been a carpenter in Muranon – most people here were from there. He had been sanding down a set of chairs two weeks before – now he was having to wield a crossbow. The ballista-crew had no training, and were guessing at how to hit their targets. And Shardhla, the only experienced soldier in the camp, and apparently the only survivor of the Muranon militia, was the woman who was pregnant.

Volg it, I didn't want to get involved! This wasn't my fight! What I needed to do was to head for the nearest wall at the edge of the canyon. Whatever Darhath and Tulher might say, I couldn't believe that it was entirely unscaleable anywhere. I was a good climber. There had to be a way up. It was just that no one from down here had ever tried. Less than a hundred miles, Darhath had indicated. And then the surface would be only two and a bit miles at most away from me. All right, two miles straight up, but with a rope, a bag of supplies and some warm clothing for when I got up to the cloud level I could do it.

I didn't want to think about what would happen if I fell. Volg it, if I had a rope I'd make lafquassing certain I didn't fall!

A two mile climb.

Don't think about it, Sorrel. Just do it. Stop and camp and rest every chance I got. Just keep climbing. The first stage was to reach the wall and see what I was facing. See if it was practical, despite the doomsayers. A hundred miles. I could do it in a week.

I didn't need to take any of the supplies from here – I could forage as I travelled. I wasn't a great fan of being in the wilds, but after the fall of Trakomar I had been helping the refugees survive in the woods west of the town. I had become quite good at finding something edible before I finally got a chance to get back to the aerodrome. I just hoped the plants down here weren't too different. I hoped they could spare one length of rope. And I'd like to have something to make into breeches. Not that needlecraft was my strong point – I'd always relied on one of the tailors in town for clothing.

Across the camp, a child started to cry. She was only five or six. Her mother was fussing over her, trying to pull tangles out of her hair with a makeshift comb.

I walked slowly, looking at the camp. The stonework was old, Iloruk workmanship, carved with swirls and spirals, in places inlaid for no obvious reason with strips and twists of dark metal and a few semi-precious stones. The pillars around the entrance were decorated with ovals and spines, the patterns sinister and uneven. Chips in the stones showed where efforts to remove the strange decorations had been unsuccessful.

The camp could use a decent fighter. If I did say so myself, I could wield a sword pretty well. And if their efforts against the snarq were anything to go by, they needed someone who knew how to deal with flying menaces. One of the men at the ballista, who had fair Iloruk, had told me the snarqs often worked for the graalur, as scouts and assailants. The odds were that the camp would face a graalur raid within forty-eight hours. If I could relearn sorcery, that would be a major benefit to the camp - I hadn't seen anyone here who had a jasq. I owed them something - they had taken me in, when they had no need to.

But I wanted to get back to the Corps! If I *had* got my sorcery back, it would make me a far more valuable and effective pilot. Anyhow, I needed to tell Tolly what had happened to the triplane. And to Merik. He deserved that much. Frankly, he deserved far better. The Corps could ill-afford the loss of the triplane. One sixth of our surviving air force. And persuading the Marshall that we needed the funds for a new aeroplane was not easy. Maybe I didn't want to return to the surface, after all. Facing Tolly would be difficult. He never shouted at us, but his quiet disapproval cut far deeper than immediate anger.

I could be useful here. Perhaps more useful than back at the aerodrome, flying the same patrol runs week in, week out, looking out for incursions or for people running - no, I didn't want to think about it. Which only left the Firebirds. Without me, I doubted my little band would have the courage to carry on. And we were pretty much the only group standing against the Lords. Not that our jobs were achieving anything. Too small scale... dare I admit it now to myself, too petty. The raid on Wrack had been our biggest effort... and it had ended in disaster.

I looked across at Darhath, trying to imagine him in his old life as an olgrek herder. He had owned forty of the brutes – he had been an important man in Muranon. And now he was trying to help a pathetic gaggle of refugees, all but six of his old charges lost to the graalur. He was giving orders, trying to improve our defences, but he paused long enough to give me an encouraging smile. I responded in kind. He was directing his people, sending them scuttling around the camp, keeping them busy. Too busy to worry. But I could still feel the air of underlying panic. Everyone was scared. With good reason - there was little chance that we could hold the camp against a serious assault. At best, we would block the entrance and be besieged. And there was far too little food here for us to hold out for long.

Us? I looked at the camp again. Yes, us. My people, on the surface, had lost in their bid to break free of our slavery to Wrack's kind. The war was over, and I couldn't change that. The graalur - they would make Darhath's people slaves, like we were. Perhaps down here I could help prevent it happening in the first place.

Why do I always end up siding with the underdog?

Chapter Four

Four long days. No graalur. No assault. Perhaps the snarq hadn't survived to fly back and tell the graalur where we were.

And maybe we'd have a visit from the Silver Elf with rose wine for the men, silk dresses for the women and painted wooden and tin toys for the children. Get real, Sorrel.

I hate waiting. Everyone was edgy. Darhath had broken up five fights in four days, one of them with knives. Tulher had caught two groups trying to steal food, preparatory to sneaking away. One of them had been Shardhla and her man.

The Valley was as well defended as we could achieve. Watchers on the heights, the ballista moved so that it could fire through the entrance if need be, stockpiles of food and missiles, makeshift armour being sewn together frantically out of spare leather (mostly tanned olgrek hides). Four days had given us a chance to be ready. It was also destroying our morale, waiting for an assault we probably couldn't win. I was getting to loathe the sight of the people here. Volg it, despite my grand words to myself, this really wasn't my fight!

All I was doing was eating supplies that they needed for their own people. I didn't belong here, and if Kelhene glowered at me once more I was going to break her neck. She seemed to think that every time I so much as looked at Darhath I was trying to steal him from her. She obviously felt deeply insecure about him, probably with good reason. I'd mentally catalogued her as a spoilt bitch, demanding her own way and not thinking about anyone else.

Gelhdin snapped angrily at me, and I tried to concentrate. The burly crossbowman was trying to teach me the veredraan tongue, so that I could talk to everyone, instead of just the few who spoke lloruk. I'm usually not too bad at learning new things, but I couldn't concentrate. We were atop one of the taller chunks of rock around the valley, watching for the oncoming army. In the space below us, Darhath was arguing with two of the women about something. Probably food for the children. Everyone was on half rations, and the smaller children were grizzling constantly. We didn't dare send too many people to forage for food, in case they were absent when the graalur came. We needed every combatant we could get. Volg it, we needed to know when the attack would come!

My eyes scanned the badlands. You could hide an army in the rifts and openings between the outcrops of rock. I'd seen a snarq wheeling some distance away in the early morning, but since then there had been nothing moving. And it was so volging hot!

Gelhdin snarled an obscenity, the veredraan equivalent of 'volg'. That word at least I knew. I shook my head. "I'm sorry, Gelhdin" I replied in my halting veredraan. "I hate… hate… " volg it, what was the word? "Waiting" I finished lamely in lloruk. Gelhdin shook his head and gave me the veredraan equivalent. His lloruk wasn't much better than my veredraan.

I was surprised how much of the lloruk tongue had stuck. At school I had hated it, and had cursed the teachers for making us learn a useless language. Then, the only reason for learning it was to be "cultured". A way for the school to prove it was sophisticated and classy. Which was one of the many reasons Kabal had decided that his humans were getting above themselves. The school had been only one casualty, but that had been after I had left. More bitter memories. Telmarak School was never going to teach lloruk to any more children.

We'd spent much of my first evening debating whether to move. The question was where to go. The gorge poured south through the rocklands, chuckling sixty miles to a vast lake that sounded more like an inland sea. There was a lloruk city on the coast, there. To our west, beyond the badlands were the Solani plains, verdant land which Darhath's people had farmed for centuries. Beyond those was a more barren region, the Helgin Expanse, and the Chasm wall rose from the far side. It was the nearest wall – less than a hundred miles. If I wanted to get back to the surface, I had a long walk ahead of me.

The other way, east across the gorge, lay through the jungle, populated on this edge by the Eski people. Deep, swampy jungle filled the valleys beyond the Eski lands and carpeted the hills for over a hundred miles to the east, and beyond that were the Valadril cities, including Jajruuk and Maladzaal. The Valadril were yet a third human group and equally unfriendly. This was reminding me unpleasantly of the rivalries between Darshaal and Werintar on the surface, which had been a significant reason for the failure of our revolt.

The only other direction was north. The gorge cut through the land like a fracture in the floor of the Chasm, with another Iloruk city, Luthvara, to the west of it, and a cluster of human cities, Daryan, Tolgrail and Falnaul to the east, sprawled between the mountains that clawed at the clouds to the north of the jungle. North of them were more human cities, but the names were just noise in my ears by then. The people at Daryan and Tolgrail were relatively friendly, as far as I could gather, but between us and them lay Jurujnai, which was a jungle area controlled by more graalur. All in all, the territory did not give us many choices. If we'd known the graalur weren't going to attack for days, Darhath would have got the group moving, probably making for Jajruuk. But we'd assumed an assault in hours. Being caught travelling through the jungle by a graalur militia would have been disastrous. So we'd dug in, tried to make us able to withstand an assault, hoping to flee once we'd driven off the first wave.

And we were still waiting.

I was frustrated and fed up. I hated killing time doing nothing. During my war, on the surface, I had ended up in more than one fight with other members of the flying corps or other soldiers, because I had got wound up waiting for an attack. The worst had been the siege of Trakomar. This felt just like it.

The first two days had been all right. I had flirted with Darhath, much to Kelhene's irritation, and I had done something useful, helping bolster the defences.

The afternoon of that second day, though, I had finally taken the plunge and tried to use my sorcery. It was nearly two years since Wrack carved my jasq out of me and drowned it in acid. It had meant I was no longer a sorceress, and there had been no chance of me regaining my magic. But now I had a new jasq, against all probability. I hadn't made a serious attempt to call on my sorcery since wakening with the jasq growing in me. I had finally decided to find out if I could use Wrack's jasq fully.

I had twisted sideways, just as I always had done, prompting the jasq as I did to take me into the realm. If you've never had a jasq I can't explain it more clearly –

it's like turning a corner without actually moving.

For a moment, just for a moment, I could see the blaze of colour that was the magerealm, coruscating rivers of blazing light in every hue of the rainbow, and more. I could hear the soft wind-whisper of the magic flowing within the other land. I could taste it, though I had never understood where the citric sensation in my mouth came from. I was using the jasq's strange, unearthly senses, tasting the strangeness that was at the heart of magic. I could not believe how badly I had missed seeing that place.

It was gone again, and I was on my knees, gasping, agony wrenching through my side. The jasq hurt as though I had twisted a knife inside it. I clutched at myself, rasping for breath. What the volg was *that*? Darhath and Gelhdin were gathering round me, asking what was wrong. They had not seen what I was doing – only another mage, in the realm, can see a sorcerer move into it. But they had seen me collapse.

The pain faded. I looked up at them in dismay. I gasped some kind of explanation that left both men looking completely blank. The magerealm had been there. I had seen it clearly for the first time since Wrack's jasq grew into me - and it had hurt like hell. I'd never felt that sort of pain from my original jasq. Was this the rejection-poison, catching up with me belatedly? My heart had pounded painfully in my chest, terror seething just below the surface. The pain had faded, though, sliding away. Did I dare try that again? I had so badly wanted to believe it was possible for me to use sorcery again. To hope for it, and for that hope to have been dashed, was worse than the despair I had felt after Wrack mutilated me. I had hugged myself, angry that Wrack's spectre was stretching forth to deny me again. I was not going to let him beat me. I had slid back into the mage-world.

For a moment it stubbornly refused to reappear, and I had a horrible thought that I had burned it out of me, that the pain had told me I could not return. Darhath was demanding that I talk to him, tell him what was wrong. I ignored him and tried harder. And then it was shimmering around me, the sound hissing in my ears - and the pain scythed into my side, the jasq hammering needles into my body. I almost yelled - but I wasn't quite that soft. The magelight was shining around me, and I struggled to see the other land. I could see what my hands had become here, glittering spindles of blue light that I recognised. Was the pain fading? I couldn't bear it. I slid out again, and the pain slowly flowed away. I took some slow, deep breaths, my hand massaging the blue scab in my side. I was not going to let this beat me!

Third attempt. The pain, just as bad as before. This time I did cry out as I tumbled out of the realm, and felt the rough ground rasping against my cheek. The world was topsy-turvy, and my body felt as though molten silver had been poured over me. I slid my gaze out from the jasq's perceptions hastily, hoping the pain would fade again. My sight was scarlet for a moment, but then, blessed relief, the pain slid away.

I had known then that my sorcery was gone. I could not endure that agony for more than a few moments. And I shivered as I wondered what damage it meant the realm or the jasq was doing to my body.

I had been in a foul mood for the rest of that day, and for most of the next. Can you blame me? I had dreamed that I could have sorcery again, against all reason. My hopes had been raised so much that to have them shattered again was ten times worse than never having the dream at all. Worse still, there had been nothing useful for me to do except to wait for an attack that hadn't yet materialized.

Now, I was just standing around at a loose end, wishing there had been more breakfast. Volging lafquass. I looked at the people in the camp, unsure if I should be throwing in my lot with them after all. I wondered again if I should have got moving instead of staying here – make for the wall of the Chasm and climb out. I wasn't doing anything useful here. We didn't even know if the graalur were coming at all. Volg it, if only I had an aeroplane! Fly over the area, find the graalur if they were there, maybe drop a rock or two on a few of the enemy as I went, and then return and confirm the state of play. Easy.

Like I said, Sorrel, get real. The Silver Elf wasn't going to bring me a triplane.

On the other hand… I looked more keenly around. I was getting a reasonable grip of the geography down here. About two miles north-west a spire of rock that had to be four hundred feet or more high pointed rudely at the clouds. From the height of the spire I might be able to see something useful. I could be at the base of the spire in an hour, no more than two hours to climb… I was scrambling down to talk to Darhath while poor old Gelhdin, game leg and all, was still demanding to know what was up.

I was half way towards Darhath when someone took hold of my shoulder and spun me round to face her. Her voice was dangerously soft, the veredraan words poisonous. "Darhath's been my man for four years." It was Darhath's woman, Kelhene. "If you carry on trying to steal him from me, I'll rip your lungs out."

It took a few moments for her words to sink in. I was looking at Darhath, right enough, but that didn't mean I was chasing him. The volging woman was accusing me of trying to seduce her man! I rounded on the fair-haired woman, anger boiling to the fore, the frustrations and uncertainties of four long days seething to the surface within me. "Listen, you volging squum! I'm not interested in that lafquassing blond!" I was shouting. She snarled an obscenity in response, and swung a fist at me. It caught me on the side of my face, barely connecting with any force as I ducked sideways. I lashed out in response, punching at her chin and missing completely as she dodged neatly. I swore again and kicked – I never worried about fighting dirty. My foot connected with her hip and she was flung sideways. I leapt onto her, pushing her down onto the rough ground, and grabbed one of her wrists, shoving it down hard so that she couldn't claw at my face with it. Her other hand clenched tightly and struck my shoulder with bruising force. I thrust one knee into her stomach and she choked.

Hands grabbed me from behind, hauling me off Kelhene, grabbing my arms and lifting me bodily between them. I snarled angrily at the squumers trying to stop me beating the living daylights out of her. She hauled herself to her feet and dived at me, taking advantage of the thugs holding me still. Typical volger, needing others to hold me still because she couldn't face me on her own. I kicked hard with both feet, catching her squarely and flinging her back onto her backside satisfyingly.

Darhath and a man whose name I didn't know had hold of Kelhene. Gelhdin and Korhus had hold of me. My harness had come adrift in the fight. I wrenched my arms free of their grip and pulled the clothing straight. Volg it, I should have kept my flying jacket on!

"What the volg are you doing, Sorrel?" Darhath demanded. "Why did you attack Kelhene?"

"Me?" I replied, outraged, my anger still bubbling white-hot. "That volging lafquass started it!"

"It's all her fault" Kelhene retorted. "She was..."

"Volg off!" I snarled. "You deserved everything you got!"

Darhath shook his head. "I'd expected better of both of you" he began.

Kelhene snarled an obscenity. "Sorrel's been trouble ever since she got here" she snapped.

I saw red again and flung myself at her, intending to kick her teeth out of the other side of her head. Gelhdin and Korhus spoiled my fun, seizing me before I got to her. I kicked out at them but they blocked every blow.

"Stop that!" Darhath bellowed. More than half the camp were gathered around us, watching the entertainment. "Sorrel, that's enough of that!"

"Volg off!" I swore, adding a couple of other choice epithets about Darhath's character and the nature of his woman. I could see he was rattled at the vehemence of my words, but I didn't care. I was angry and wound up. Kelhene's accusation that I was trouble had hit deeper than I wanted to admit. I'd intended to try to help them – if that was the way they thought of me, I'd be better off out of here. My words tumbled out, settling my intent as I ranted. "I'm not staying in this squum-hole any longer than I have to!" I was drifting between lloruk and veredraan, but Kelhene and Darhath were getting the general drift. "I'm leaving, and I hope I don't see any of you losers again!"

I turned and walked away. Feet pounded behind me - Kelhene tried to grab at my arm. I shoved her hard, grinning harshly as she stumbled sideways. Darhath was running towards us, yelling something. I ignored his protests, and stalked away. I needed supplies and equipment. I'd already gained some grasp of the geography. Ten minutes to gather what I needed, and I'd be out of here.

Chapter Five

Late morning. I was already crossing what Tulher had called the Neldar Ridge - assuming I had correctly understood the directions I had been given. I was getting used to the heat down here. Either that, or I was getting so used to being drenched in sweat that I wasn't noticing it any more. The clothing Kelhene had given me would have been more practical in this heat than my leather jacket, but I still preferred the benefit of the jacket as armour. From all accounts, I was in territory now that had been completely over-run by the graalur. The people at the valley had fled away from these lands, and I was going into the heart of the occupied region. Typical Sorrel, doing the stupidest thing possible. I was glad of the sword I carried. The grathk-hide belt holding my battered jacket together sported various loops intended as blade sheaths. I would have been glad of another knife as well, but the sword would have to do. And I even had a rope over my shoulder.

There had been enough arguments about that. The rope was one of the items brought with them from Muranon, tightly-wound hemp (or the Chasm's equivalent). I had no hope of climbing out of the Chasm without it, but they could ill-afford to lose it. I supposed I should have been grateful.

Darhath had tried to persuade me to stay. Volg it, he had almost begged. If Kelhene hadn't been standing nearby glaring at me, his imprecations might have worked. Trouble was, he wasn't bad looking, in a pale and rather exotic sort of way. From the way the men in the camp had been looking at me, I suspected that I was just as strangely exotic to them. My skin was far darker than any of theirs, half-way to the graalur dark red. And I hadn't seen anyone with hair as near to black as mine. Most of them had blue eyes, a few had brown. I was the only hazel-eyed person in the camp.

Kelhene's obvious dislike had been enough to maintain my resolve. I'd gruffly said my thanks for their aid, and for the food and clothing, and I'd promised to head back if I saw a graalur force coming their way.

By now, not for the first time, I was regretting my hasty flare of temper. Was it really right to abandon them? I could go back and apologise.

With my tail between my legs.

No, actually, I couldn't. No way was I doing that. I don't do apologies. I ground my teeth together and kept walking. I didn't really owe them anything. Anyhow, I could do them far more good by getting out of the Chasm, going back to the aerodrome and stealing another aeroplane. With a triplane I could turn the tables on the graalur without a doubt. See what they were doing, direct the ground forces, maybe drop a few stones on them. From a hundred feet a rock the size of two fists becomes a dangerous weapon. Even without magic I could do a lot of damage from the air. It was a good image, and lent a spring to my step.

The terrain was bleak, tumbled rock, reminding me irresistibly of some old sketches I had seen of the region round the Lulvantal volcano after it erupted. That had been nearly four hundred years ago, before the Shentrini uprising, and it had left cold rivers of grey stone that had turned the once-fertile lands around it into wasteland. This landscape had the same look of congealed granite, but far older, with red vegetation managing to grow from the flanks of the outcrops.

Tulher had sketched the area so far as he knew it, giving me some more picture of the geography, and warned me of the likely threats in my path. Rather a lot, frankly. I was forming the opinion that the Chasm was a distinctly unfriendly place. Grathks, graalur, wild olgreks and snarqs I knew. Ruzdrools, inskiirs and adjaliks meant nothing. Vrusks I knew and didn't fear, assuming they weren't twice the size and viciousness of the ones I knew. The good news was that he hadn't mentioned dragons… no, I wasn't even going to think about that.

Even the smaller denizens of this strange countryside were peculiar. As I'd trekked up a red grassy hill I'd spotted some dark blue lumps grazing near holes in the ground. I'd tagged them as rabbits. When I got closer to one, I realised it had a shell like a tortoise. It then astonished me by bolting for the nearest rabbit-hole at a speed that made rabbits look geriatric. The shell was segmented, so it moved across its back. It made me wonder what the local carnivores were like.

Travelling on my own was madness, frankly. But I needed to get back to where I belonged. To somewhere that I could have some effective defences against

Wrack. Down here… no. Put one foot in front of the other, keep your eyes alert, keep moving. Don't think. Don't remember. I was going home. That was all that mattered. Back to the aerodrome. Back to Dragonhead Tavern, and drink half the lads under the table and a survivor into bed. Visit that tailor on Coronet Way, buy that dark blue dress I'd looked at - really surprise Tolly and Saldrin at the next dance by looking like a woman. Go visit dad. Maybe he'd even recognise me. Borrow an olgrek, ride over to Werintar, get a jehanish meal for a change.

Ninety miles. And then two, maybe three miles straight up.

And once I had a triplane I could come back, salve my conscience and strafe some graalur.

A stand of odd-looking plants caught my eye. They had twisted, widespread leaves and small green gourds hung suspended from the branches – the first real green I'd seen in ages. I looked around for the nearest lantern tree, wondering if this was a lantern sapling. I'd become used to seeing the brilliant glowing lights - I hadn't yet got close to one to see it properly. I was even almost getting used to having two or three shadows at any time. I walked a little closer, and then recoiled. There was something about it, a stench or a miasma, that was utterly revolting. My jasq was thumping in my side, as though it did not like the plant either. I retreated from the growth and nicknamed the thing a giant hagweed – it smelt even worse than the hagweeds that grew on the surface, but it seemed to me that everything down here that mimicked surface dwellers was bigger or stronger or more foul than its surface counterparts. Anyway, it almost looked like a hagweed, sort of, apart from the gourds. Not that I'm an expert on plants, I would add.

There was a scream from ahead of me. High-pitched, fear, not pain. A woman, terrified, or furiously angry. My hand caught the sword-hilt without conscious thought, and I ran forward. The rough rocky hills I was crossing should - if the people in the camp were right - give way to farmland in a few miles. No sign of that at the moment. This was wilderness, just wiry red bushes and gnarly crimson grass, unforgiving and desolate. And everywhere ancient chunks of sandstone worn by the rain and the wind into crazy columns and outcroppings rising out of the scrubland. A maze of broken pathways and tumbled rubble. And somewhere in this natural labyrinth was a woman in lethal peril.

Another scream, echoing through the rocks. She was still alive and able to indicate her emotions. Oh, and summon anything nasty within half a mile. Not to mention me. North, if my compass directions were right. Volg it, I missed the sun! The clouds above glowed a little by day, so that you could tell when the sun was up, but the solid grey above me gave no indication of where the sun actually was. The Chasm ran virtually north to south - four thousand miles long, four hundred wide for most of its length. I needed to head west to get to the nearer wall.

I headed north, trying to find something easily climbable.

The next outcropping was a jumble of fallen slabs, like a child's tumbled building blocks. I went up it hand over hand, only swearing once when an apparently solid chunk of stone came loose in my grip and almost sent me tumbling. Only thirty feet down, and that over jagged rocks. No trouble.

Atop the stones I could see all around me - except that the crags were full of narrow ravines and pathways that could comfortably hide an army. And standing where I was I would be visible to anyone even glancing upwards within a mile, and vulnerable to arrows, slings and sorcery. Not that I'd seen any magic here. Darhath hadn't mentioned any mages - not that I had been in the mood to ask. Maybe sorcery was unknown. On the other hand, they supposedly had lloruk down here, and the lloruk had been some of the greatest sorcerers in the world. Two thousand years ago, anyway. I still wasn't convinced that they were really here now.

A third shriek. Close, too. I took the best guess at the direction and started scrambling down, getting off the skyline. Can you call it a skyline when there's no sky behind you? Thinking about it, I began to realise that perhaps I hadn't been as visible as I had imagined.

A yell, deeper, gruffer. I could identify that sound. Graalur. Why wasn't I surprised? Where were they?

Jump down, into a grassy dell between two boulders. I scrambled sideways, between the rocks, and into a clearer area, rough ground almost devoid even of the coarse red grass. There were graalur there, all right. Three burly males, advancing, blades in hand. Their intended victim was a woman, backed against an outcrop of stone. She was clearly the one I had heard scream. Looking at her stance, I suspected it had been a shriek of rage rather than terror. She was grabbing hold of a fist-sized rock - there was a sword on the ground a few feet from her, and a nasty wound on her right forearm. Every picture tells a tale. The graalur did not look worried - why should they?

She was clad just in a strip of cloth across her breasts and a breech-clout below her waist. No doubt what the three graalur intended with her. One of the graalur had a whip, the second one a loop of rope. Slavers.

They outnumbered me, and they looked confident and lethal. If I was right, they didn't intend to kill the woman. I didn't know her. And it wasn't my fight. Why should I care what the graalur did to her? I just wanted to get to the walls and climb out of the Chasm. They didn't know I was here. No reason for me to get involved.

One of them lashed out, using the flat of his blade, catching the woman on her wounded arm as she tried instinctively to block the blow. She cried out and flung the rock she had in her left hand. It clipped the graalur on the right, bouncing off his shoulder, but he just laughed. Tough guy. I knew the sort. I'd faced thugs like them in the war. Never show an injury or a weakness, however much it hurt, and outface the enemy. Volg it, I'd used similar tactics myself. The woman snarled an obscenity, her voice hoarse - I didn't know the words, but I could identify the sentiment. I was just standing there. I either had to walk away, or get involved and probably end up suffering the same fate as the graalur intended for the woman. Not to mention being enslaved myself.

Not a chance of that. No way was I going to be a slave again. All logic said I should leave, abandon the woman to her fate.

One of the graalur snarled something, a callous leer on his face. I couldn't understand the words, but I knew exactly what he was telling the woman he was going to do to her. I'd heard just that tone before. I wasn't going to stand by and watch. Anger over-rode logic. I grabbed a chunk of stone the size of both my fists together, and looked at the three graalur. The one on the left had no helmet. Idiot. I drew back my arm and flung the rock with all my strength. If I got this wrong, I'd have three of them against me.

I got it wrong.

Chapter Six

The graalur moved at the last moment, striking low at the woman. My stone caught his shoulder rather than the back of his head. It broke his blow at his intended victim, but did nothing else of any use. He spun, snarling a warning at the others. No point trying that again. Three to one. Oops.

The graalur in the middle had a crested helmet and a smart leather harness. Oh, and the whip. He ran across the open space towards me, yelling a war cry, or else telling me to surrender. Fat chance. As he approached, he flung the whip to one side and drew his sword. Big deal - I had a sword, too. I waited, my sword in my hand.

The graalur nearest the woman took a grab at his original victim. She kicked, savagely, trying to catch him between his legs. Good for her. Okay, she missed, but it was a good try. Made him back off. The third graalur was following Crested Helmet towards me. I needed to down one of them quickly.

Crested Helmet reached the rock I was standing on. I was four feet above him. Only an idiot would jump down, abandoning the benefit of height. I waited till Crest got within a few feet, and leapt. Always do the unexpected.

My boot caught him under the chin, and he staggered backwards. I hacked viciously, slicing at his left arm, as I hit the ground with both feet. I'd rather have taken out his sword arm, but any injury would do. Four feet is nothing - it jarred a little, but I landed cleanly.

There was a yell from the woman. I turned automatically, and the third graalur's lunge scraped over the leather of my jacket rather than connecting. She had been warning me of his assault. Crest was bleeding from the wound to his arm, but did not look out of it. Rats. Move, Sorrel! I rolled sideways, ducking under Crest's blow and getting away from Three, before hacking wildly at Crest's right side. He blocked the blow cleanly, swords clashing together, sparks where they met. He was between me and Three - I only had one to worry about for a moment, and he was injured. I wasn't.

He did his best to correct that, lunging once and then again at me. I parried the first strike and dived away from the second. Useless volg! Missed by a mile!

He twisted the blade, and I realised, too late, that the second lunge had been a feint. He brought the sword sideways, into my path, and I felt it cut across my bare thigh. Lafquassing volg! Only a slight cut, not a deep wound like I'd done to him, but bad enough. It meant I needed to finish this quickly, before I lost too much blood. The jasq was warm in my side. I wished I could have used sorcery. A moment in the magerealm and I could have immolated one of the graalur. Never mind regrets and bitterness now. Concentrate on using this sword properly. The woman was shrieking again. Definitely rage, not fear. Not my problem. I had two of the volgs to deal with. Crest was grinning, tusks gleaming against the brick-red skin. I limped back, making the wound look far worse. He approached, still blocking Three. For small mercies... I stumbled as I backed away, falling backwards, and incidentally letting him get a good view of the top of my thighs under the jacket. The idiot fell for it, gawping at me for just a moment too long. My blade caught him under the chin, the point transfixing his grin and plunging into his brain. Not that he had much of a brain to start with. His grin became a gurgle, and then a death-rattle as I wrenched the blade out.

Three was moving round, more warily. I could feel hot blood on my leg. Crest was toppling to the ground. I ignored his death - I'd killed men before. And Three was no longer grinning. He had dropped into a fighting stance, his expression hard. He was no longer thinking about taking me captive. The other woman had gone silent, and I wondered fleetingly what had become of her. If I could deal with Three, I'd try and help her.

Three took an experimental swing, trying to gauge my skill. I let him almost pink me. Lull him into false confidence. The blow came closer than I had intended, and I only just managed to parry his strike. Volg it, he was fast! I had a nasty suspicion that I was lulling him into a realistic feeling of confidence. He struck again, and only the leather of my jacket saved me. At least he wasn't wearing any armour. If I could connect I could do him some damage.

If.

His next blow was low and twisting, beautifully timed and controlled. Volg it, the squumer was good! I brought my sword up, catching his motion, barely edging it aside and leaving myself with no way to hack back. I retreated, trying to remember where Crest's body was - the last thing I wanted was to fall over him. Three, of course, wanted nothing else for me. He was grinning, breathing fast, the sword moving in small circles as he bore down upon me. And somewhere there was the other graalur - it didn't sound as though the woman was keeping him occupied. I was in trouble. Again.

Three lunged suddenly. I had expected it - he could see I was almost on top of Crest. His plan was to push me backwards or make me jump back, and fall on the body. Good tactic. Unluckily for Three, I'd been banking on his trying it. I flung myself sideways, instead, letting his blow go right over me, extending his reach. Leaving him vulnerable under his arm. I thrust my sword home, catching him cleanly. His turn to scream.

Volg it, he was almost as fast as Wrack! He turned sideways, pulling away so that the blow only went in a few inches, not getting anywhere near his heart. It was going to bleed, and must hurt like hell, but it was not a fatal wound. And I was down, rolling on the stony ground, seriously disadvantaged. If the blow had gone home as I had intended, it wouldn't have mattered, but now he had me where he wanted me.

He knew it. He kicked out, low and hard, catching me in the ribs. I gasped in pain, winded, knowing I was helpless. I was trying to roll away, but the loss of my air left me unable to move fast enough, let alone get to my feet. He was standing over me - he could finish me with a single thrust, and my leather jacket was not going to save me now. I hadn't even got the wind to swear at my killer.

The graalur grinned down at me, and kicked again. Hunh? His boot connected with my wrist, and I managed to find enough wind to gasp in pain. The sword fell from my numbed hand, and he laughed, tusks clear in his open mouth. He was drooling, looking down at me. I tried to lash out with my foot, hoping to put him down. He was playing with me, and I didn't want to die like that.

Not surprisingly, he blocked the blow with ease. He was no fool. He'd expected it. He responded with another kick, this time at my head. Volging slaver! He thought he could make some loot out of me. I'd half-expected him to go for my head - I pulled back, managing to lessen the impact. It still left me seeing stars and feeling queazy. Second time I'd been hit in the head this week. Not healthy. I slumped back, letting my eyes close. If he was smart he'd kick me in the head again to make sure I wasn't lying doggo.

He wasn't quite that smart. I obviously did a good job of looking unconscious.

The jasq was throbbing again, painfully. On the other hand, in comparison to the other pains I was suffering, it was a mere bagatelle.

I waited for something to happen. Nothing did. I warily opened an eye a crack, to try to see what he was doing. Bandaging his wound, of course. I'd given him a nasty stab-wound. My head was still splitting, but I wasn't going to get another chance. He was a few feet from me, strapping a grimy grey pad of cloth under his leather harness to cover the wound. Underarm wounds are difficult to strap up.

My sword was feet away, and I wouldn't reach it before he saw the movement. His own sword was on the ground beside him, also out of reach. And from my poor vantage point on the ground I couldn't see the final graalur or the woman. Not a good position.

If I could find a loose rock… there's always a loose rock when you're walking, lurking and waiting malevolently to twist your ankle. But when you actually need one, when your life depends on it, the ground is as smooth and rock-less as a ballroom floor. I had to act quickly, before he was ready to come and deal with me.

I rolled sideways, flinging myself at him bodily, going for his sword. If I could get it, he'd be unarmed. Good theory. Big if. He saw me move - he'd obviously been half-watching me while he was patching himself up. He grabbed for his sword before I was within a foot of him. I slammed into his legs, trying to take him down - and there was a new shriek, a different timbre to anything I'd heard before. The graalur and I tumbled onto the ground, both of us equally distracted as a new participant joined the fray.

The creature was at least seven feet long, small bat wings behind its neck beating wildly to lift the gigantic head away from the ground as the dozen spindly legs carried the snake-body towards us. This thing was never meant to fly, but the wings enabled it to rear up well above my head, even if I had been standing. The sleek, brilliantly-coloured blue and scarlet hide was rippling as it flung itself at us. The head divided where its mouth should have been into a cluster of long, writhing violet tentacles, each tipped with a vicious-looking spine. It did not appear to have any eyes, but it was homing in upon us without any difficulty.

The graalur spun, and hacked at the three-foot tentacles as they lashed at him. I couldn't fault him for courage - I just flung myself away, leaving him to face the monstrosity. I had no idea what this thing was - it could be a ruzdrool or an inskiir, or even an adjalik. Frankly, I didn't care. I snatched up Crest's sword - he wouldn't be needing it again - and turned.

The graalur had carved away half the nightmare's tentacles, but it had struck home effectively with the rest. The graalur was bleeding profusely from wounds in his left shoulder and the side of his face, and one of the tentacles was embedded in his left forearm. He was weakening visibly. The creature was pumping out dark blue ichor from the wounded head, and he hacked at the side of its neck desperately. He was crying out in anger and pain. If I intervened I might be able to defeat it and save him. All common sense, however, told me to get the volg out of there.

I got the volg out of there.

By the time I had scrambled to the top of the rocks, and turned to look down into the open area where we had fought, it was all over. The graalur was down, and the wounded tentacled thing was tearing at his flesh with its surviving tentacles, ripping out chunks of meat and neatly carrying them to the maw at the centre of the head. It was no longer bleeding, despite the deep gashes in its neck and the loss of half its tentacles. I wondered if it would simply regrow them. I didn't really care. It was no longer interested in me.

What I couldn't see was the woman or the final graalur. The woman might have escaped in the confusion, been chased away by the graalur... or else the slaver had simply grabbed her and carried her off. In the grip of just one thug, the woman might have a chance. I needn't feel any obligation to help. I needed to patch myself up.

I realised belatedly how hot the jasq was in my side. It was pulsing, pumping blood around my body. The wound in my thigh had already scabbed over, miraculously. My original jasq had grown warm when it was healing injuries – Wrack's jasq seemed to do the same, but to a far greater extent. It also seemed to heal me far more effectively than my original jasq had done. I might have no hope of using sorcery, but the new jasq had probably saved my life three times already. I wasn't complaining. I hadn't got anything suitable to place over the wound, so I would just have to be careful not to let it open again. It hadn't been as deep as I had feared. My head hurt abominably, but there wasn't much I could do about that except hope the jasq could assist in that direction, too. It was still thumping, suggesting that it was doing something. I wish I knew more about jasqs. My old jasq had never pulsed like this, or got as hot as this one had become. On the other hand, my old jasq had been in my upper arm, not against my gut.

I ran my hands over my scalp carefully, making sure I wasn't bleeding anywhere else, and then headed slowly in the direction that was my best guess as to where the woman had gone, with or without graalur captor.

Two hours later, and I could really do with some food. I had a waterskin, which fortunately had survived the brush with the graalur, but food I would have to forage for. I was still heading north, but I was coming down off the Neldar Ridge into the farmlands beyond. If the reports from the camp were anything to go by, this whole area was over-run by one or other of the two local clans of graalur. This was the region that Darhath's people came from, in the main. Around fifty square miles of good agricultural land, until the graalur had laid waste to it.

I had seen few signs that the graalur or the woman had passed this way. The best evidence I had was a short length of tattered cloth which could be one of the rags the woman had been wearing. There was a road – frankly, no more than a track, compared to the smooth, engineered highways of the surface – along the spine of the ridge, and any logic said that had to be the route they would take. Trouble was, I had no idea where it led to, or even any certainty of which direction I should follow. I preferred to keep roughly aligned with the direction I had been following when I reached the road, and hoped to find some sign that I was right in my guess.

I had decided that if I had seen no sign of them in another hour, I would abandon the hunt. I was no tracker. Volg it, I was a pilot! I'd made that decision an hour ago. I ought by rights to head back onto my planned path, make for the wall of the Canyon.

But I couldn't do it. I couldn't just give up on the girl. All right, so I didn't know her. But I couldn't leave her in the hands of the graalur, to be a slave. I had an extremely good idea what slavery would be like for her.

A shout from ahead of me gave me new strength. That was a graalur voice. I pounded along the track, throwing caution to the winds. I'd recovered my strength, and I felt more human again. The jasq wasn't so warm. I hoped that was a good sign.

Another fifty yards, and I stopped in dismay. I had finally reached the edge of the ridge.

Below, the road wound down from the crag onto a patchwork of cultivated fields divided by narrow drainage ditches. People were working amidst the crops near me, picking the fruits off an orgy of writhing red vines which wound around a forest of poles. Each triangle of pale poles had a vine clambering up it, tangling the poles together, with long, narrow pods hanging from them. The people had baskets, and guarding them, ensuring they worked without pause, were a number of graalur. It was a guard I had heard, probably ordering one of the men to work faster. He was sprawled on the ground - the graalur had clearly cuffed him across the head, and now he kicked him. The slave lurched to his feet, and tried to return to his task. The man was ageing, his hair grey and sparse, ribs visible under the tight skin. He staggered, and fell again. The graalur who had kicked him shouted a gutteral command. The man struggled to get up. The graalur stalked over – and without any warning thrust forward with his sword, taking the slave in the throat. He was dead before his body slid to the ground. It had happened so fast that I had not had any chance to intervene. The slaves were crying out in horror and anger, but the other graalur were moving forwards, whips and swords ready. Any slave rebellion died stillborn, and the slaves turned back to their tasks, working faster, the object lesson still spreading blood into the soil. I was on my feet, my grip tight on my sword, fury seething in my veins, my teeth gritted. For a moment I was ready to throw myself at the guards and hack some of them down… but cold sense slowed my action, bound my feet to the rocks. There were around thirty slaves picking the crop, and eight graalur. The slaves were unarmed, naturally. Not good odds. All I could do would be to add to the corpse-count.

I bit back my rage. I could do nothing to help the slaves. And after all my pursuit, the woman I had tried to help was nowhere in sight. She could be anywhere.

She could be a slave.

I sat down on the rocky promontory overlooking the fields. There were stone buildings, still showing the marks of relatively recent conflict, a few hundred yards away. A couple of miles away there was another farm just barely visible, and a road – well, a track, anyway – leading towards it. To the west, barely visible at the distance, I could see what had to be the ruins of a substantial town – from what I had been told, I was pretty sure that it was Muranon, home of most of the refugees I had abandoned.

There were more graalur busying themselves - or more accurately busying their slaves - in the cobbled yard onto which the nearby buildings faced. There had to be thirty graalur in the area in total, and at least four times that number of slaves. I had no chance of achieving anything here. All I would do was end up as a slave myself. And I had no doubts that enslavement would be unpleasant and probably terminal - I would not be an obedient slave, and the graalur were unlikely to put up with me the way Wrack had. There had been more than one occasion when I had lashed out at Wrack – he had simply hit me back, whereas most slavemasters would have had me whipped or worse for such effrontery. Before our revolt, I had seen enough examples of the brutality of the lords or their guards, beating a peasant who dared disobey them. I had no doubt these graalur were no different. I glowered down at the slaves and their overseers, not really caring that if anyone looked up they would see me.

A sudden hammer-blow of sound from immediately above me shook me out of my fugue. The landscape was for an instant lit in actinic white as the sky exploded. The lightning had to be right overhead - there had been no delay between the light and the sound. The sky was almost black in the aftermath - could it be night-time already? No, it was barely afternoon.

Something slammed into my leg. And then two more. Raindrops, but big ones, heavy and solid, splashing against me. The impacts were almost painfully hard. In moments, the clouds had opened, and the rain was pounding the ground. The impacts were actually painful, now. I had never been in a rainstorm like it - the sky was looming over me, it seemed only a few yards above the ridge, and the water was flinging itself downwards, turning the ground into a sea of churning, bouncing raindrops. And the noise of the downpour was incessant and deafening, the constant pummelling against my bare legs and head growing seriously painful. I was going to have bruises all over if I didn't find cover.

What cover? I had seen no caves or openings in the rocks I had crossed recently. No trees growing nearby - the nearest stand of trees had to be quarter of a mile away, across the fields. The slaves and the graalur were already running, struggling with the three-quarter full baskets. They were making for the buildings, obviously. If I stayed in this… I scrambled down the treacherous, sodden rockface, rivulets of water spraying around me as I made for the ground. Another crackle of lightning lit the sky, illuminating me clearly, but no one was looking in my direction. I joined the headlong race for the nearest building. The slaves, both men and women, were wearing loincloths and little else. In my leather jacket, with my sword, waterskin and rope, I stood out like a rose among daisies. I'd better hope the graalur didn't know much about flowers. This rain - I couldn't stay outside in it; I had no options.

Two hundred yards, and a roof over my head for the first time since I crashed in the Chasm. Considering how strange this deep world was, the buildings were remarkably straightforward. This could have been an old farm anywhere in Sendaal - heavy stone walls, rough-cut, with wooden beams supporting dark slates against which the rain was hammering at a volume that drowned out any chance of talk.

Not that there was anyone to talk to - fortunately. The slaves had been bustled into a large, open chamber, probably a barracks for them. I had thronged with the slaves until I was under cover, but now I was lurking in the covered colonnade that surrounded the farm's inner courtyard. The farm had quite a collection of structures, including a stone tower and half a dozen outbuildings. The main building looked pretty ancient – three or four hundred years old, at a guess, if the crumbling stonework was anything to go by – but it had clearly been extended and expanded on a number of occasions. The colonnade was relatively new, and so was the tower, which contained a couple of bored-looking graalur sheltering out of the rain, who were being entirely derelict in their duty as look-outs. Just as well. There was a glowing point of fire almost by the mouth of one of the two – I peered cautiously up towards them, trying to work out what it was, but without success. I filed it away as a mystery. One of the newer outbuildings was the slave barracks, and a couple of others looked like stable-blocks. The nearest definitely was, as evidenced by an olgrek leaning out of the stall at the end and clucking at the falling rain. I was more interested in the building nearest the main farmhouse, which I very much hoped was a storehouse. I was ravenous. I'd briefly wondered about taking off my jacket and going in with the slaves, but any graalur overseer worth her salt should spot me. My darker skin would be a dead giveaway. Anyhow, I'd be surprised if the slaves had enough food to share, and what they did have probably wouldn't be very nice. No, I'd much rather steal from the graalur.

Tiptoe around the colonnade. No one else was moving - not surprising in this downpour. If this was normal rain round here, I'd need a steel umbrella. I realised that something was faintly tugging at me, calling me to it. I could feel a need, as though it was some kind of hunger for me. Not malevolent, but demanding. The direction of the strange pull would take me beyond the farmhouse. I was curious, unsure what it was I was feeling, not even certain that I was feeling anything real at all. I kept moving, letting it guide me. Passing the low building alongside the one I'd mentally identified as a store, I heard low graalur voices and the sounds of rattling dice. All soldiers are the same, whatever skin colour or race. I tagged that as a barracks, and warily crept past it.

The door of the store was unlocked, slightly to my surprise. Odds were my identification was wrong. I couldn't believe the graalur officers could leave their thuggish minions with free rein in the larder. I could hear a low moaning sound from the darkness within. Was this a prison? Then a louder groan, and a husky graalur voice growling something. I took another couple of steps - to one side of the chamber a female graalur was moaning on her back on a low bed, thighs locked behind the thrusting hips of a burly male graalur. She was clutching at his back, encouraging his vigorous attentions to her. There are worse ways to occupy a rainy afternoon. There were a dozen more bunks along the wall - this was actually the graalur barracks, then. The one with the group gambling was evidently something else. Volg it! I could really use some food.

I retreated cautiously, and looked around the courtyard. Almost certainly there was a kitchen in the main building. Equally probably, it would be occupied. Maybe just slaves, more likely some sneaky graalur raiding the pantry. Another good pastime on a wet afternoon.

I gazed around the colonnade. Base of the tower. Slave barracks. Stable. Gambling den. Graalur barracks. Main house. The strange attraction I had felt tugging at me would take me onwards, into or even past the farmhouse. No easy way I could do that. And I was more interested in finding something to eat. On the far side of the colonnade there were another two low buildings. One I'd assumed, from the wide doorway, contained farm wagons or similar. The other?

Nothing ventured, no food gained. I put my head down and scuttled across the front of the main house, below the level of the windows, hoping the guards in the tower were not looking my way. I slunk into the shadow in the corner of the colonnade by the mysterious door, and lurked for a few minutes. No hue and cry, just more rain. Good. I gingerly tried the door.

It was locked. Goodie! I was really optimistic that this was the food store. Of course, it also meant I couldn't get in. I experimented with the lock for a few moments, wondering if I could pick it, but the lock was better than I had expected, a complex brass affair with more than one pin inside, just as sophisticated as those I had struggled with on the surface when I had engaged in nefarious activities after the war, usually without success there, either. Darhath's people were not as primitive as they had first seemed. I swore under my breath. I needed to get something to eat. Of course, this might not even be the storehouse, but it looked a likely candidate. I had to get the door open.

I gritted my teeth. I had been telling myself that I could not try using sorcery again. I didn't know how great the risk would be. But starving or being too weak to fight off graalur would be far more deadly. I only needed to find a fireflow. A fragment of liquid flame should be enough to burn out the lock.

Did I dare try?

Sometimes it's better not to stop and think. I tensed my muscles to resist the pain that was coming, and I slid into the realm.

Chapter Seven

Torrents of colour all round me, the eternal hiss of the realm in my ears. I didn't have time to use finesse. I reached for the nearest column of flowing sorcery, violet and cream in the unending torrent pouring upwards and sideways, and swept a tiny fraction of its power into a jet that roared through the hole I had ripped between the realms. I heard the tone of the windsong change as I pulled the flow where I wanted it. I was already sliding out of the realm again before I realised that it was not hurting.

I was looking out at the grey, rainy land under its permanent blanket of cloud again as the shower of raw sorcery flared in the real world and carved into the door, blazing brilliantly for a moment as it melted the brass lock.

The light faded, and I glanced around, worried that the sudden crimson and violet glow would have alerted someone. But no one was looking at the rain - if anyone noticed a sudden flicker of light, they probably assumed it was just another flash of lightning. I stood facing the door for a moment more, my hand exploring the jasq in my side. It was thumping, but I was not in the agony I had felt before. I wanted to shout out in joyous abandon, but I wasn't quite that suicidal. I had used sorcery! And it hadn't hurt! Perhaps that first burst of pain in the camp had been a one-off, just a single instance as the jasq got used to me. I wanted to go back into the magerealm, explore it again. On the other hand, I was dangerously visible. I couldn't stand here all afternoon. Besides, I was ravenous, and with luck there would be abundance within. I pushed the door open, and walked into the store-room.

Abundance. Oh, yes. The place was stacked high, shelves groaning, more food than I could have imagined in one place. Barrels of flour and ale, sacks of amber and gold vegetables, crates of yellow fruit. Baskets of bread, jars of conserve and pickles. More food than this farm had any right to have stockpiled.

All right, so I wasn't thinking. I was tired. It didn't occur to me, then, to wonder why there was such an extraordinary mass of food. I was too busy being hungry. I could feel my mouth watering and the sound of my stomach making demands was drowning out the drumming of the rain. Using sorcery always had left me famished - my old jasq needed sustenance after shifting me into its realm, and leeched goodness from my body. I suspected that Wrack's jasq would do the same, but in spades. I closed the door behind me, and without contemplating the reasons for the plenty I set about endeavouring to demolish the entire contents of the stores single-handed.

Half an hour sufficed - just about - to satisfy my hunger. When I first learned sorcery, before the war, my jasq had drained me more than once. My tutor, Kelvar, had warned me that I would need to eat to replenish my strength. Now I was having to get used to Wrack's version, which seemed ten times as voracious. I didn't care – I could cast magic again.

The rain still had not stopped, but I had learned to ignore the deafening rattle on the slates above me – either that, or the constant volume had finally deafened me. It would not be long before someone noticed the damage to the store-room door. My only hope was that the graalur would assume it was one of their own who had done it, to steal food. All common sense said that I should head east again, make for the wall of the Canyon. There was no realistic chance of finding the dark-skinned woman I had come hunting. I could not take on the entire mass of the graalur single-handed, even with my dubious scope at magic. I parcelled up a bundle of food in a sack I had purloined - I had no idea when I would get a chance to find food again - and crept out of the store.

The sky was almost black, and the downpour, though lessened, was still continuing. There was no sign of any light from the lantern trees I'd seen, and beyond the farm buildings there was only wet darkness. The vague sense of something drawing me on had faded – I wondered if I had dreamt it. The only illumination came from yellow glow-stones embedded in the tower and slung in a couple of places in the colonnade. I struggled to resist a deep yawn. Where was I going to go? Did I want to risk the rain even now? I yawned again, realising how tired I really was, and I paused. Would I be better resting up tonight here? I'd worked out that the Chasm was not a healthy region. At least in the farm I'd be safe from animals and creatures. All I'd have to worry about was the graalur.

I'd identified a couple of stables. I headed for the nearer one warily, a more solid shadow creeping through the shadows. The door was unlocked, and there was no sign of a guard. Most likely all I had to worry about was a slave stable-hand. It didn't smell right, though. For a start, the main door was wider than that of any stable I knew. And the roof - something was not right about that, either. The beams did not stretch all the way across the stable - the one near me had been cut recently. Butchering things came naturally to graalur, but they had to be really short of things to kill if they chose to hack apart a roof.

Something stirred in the straw spread over the floor. It was dark in here - no helpful lanterns to show me what I was facing. I ducked into the shadows and tried to make out the bulk nestling in front of me.

It suddenly raised a head, and large, emerald green eyes were looking my way. Moments later, a second pair of eyes were also peering towards me. I really, really hoped it had poor night vision. I guessed what I was looking at. A large wing twitched, confirming my very nasty belief. I was confident that I had killed one head of the snarq I shot at; this had to be a different snarq. Which meant it had two fully-functioning and lethal acid-spitting heads. And it was looking my way. Someone in the camp had said the brutes sometimes served the graalur. Just my luck to find a tame one. I stood very still, and waited, wishing I didn't need to breathe.

One of the heads lowered into the straw, and then the other settled down as well. Phew. Slowly, cautiously, stepping gingerly so as not to knock into anything at all, not even a piece of straw, I tiptoed backwards like a frightened mouse creeping away from a dozing owl.

Did I really want to stay the night here after all, I wondered as I eased back to the colonnade. The logic was fine, but I didn't like the bed partner in that stable. After I had a fling with Lorgren, Tolly joked I'd sleep with anyone. I was going to prove his calumny false tonight. Best to try the other stable.

This one was far more comfortable. Really, it was no different to a stable on the surface, with stalls containing nervous olgreks scratching and clucking. Unlike the ones I was used to, these had sleek, scaled hides, rather than warm fur. Hardly surprising in this heat. Otherwise, though, they were very little different - solid haunches from which the two heavy legs stretched down to the ground, the wide body, and the long neck with the beaked head. The tail was the major difference; instead of the furred length of the surface breed, these olgreks' tails split into two near the end.

I didn't spend too long observing the olgreks. As soon as I got into the stable, I pulled off my hot, sweaty jacket and kicked off my boots before diving into an empty stall and burrowing into the straw. That, at least, seemed little different to the stuff that I had played in as a child at the farm where my grandfather worked, if slightly different in hue - this stuff was more orange than gold. It even smelt the same. With the straw soft under me and around me, hiding me from sight, I risked closing my eyes for a few minutes.

I slept fitfully. I knew I was in the heart of enemy territory, and I had a pretty good idea of what capture would bring. I did not settle, instead stirring at any sound or hint of movement. Straw is supposed to be comfortable. It wasn't, that night. Strands stuck into me like needles. They got caught in my ears, in my mouth, and elsewhere that got extremely uncomfortable. And the volging olgreks wouldn't shut up! I felt like shouting at them. By the time the Chasm grew lighter, I wanted to kill them. Before it was really light enough to see I was on my feet again.

The sky was bereft of rain. It wasn't clear, of course – the clouds were as solid as ever. I had grown almost used to the impervious sky. Despite my brave thoughts yesterday, the idea of flying under that solid ceiling did not greatly appeal. Clouds may look fluffy to you groundlings – to a pilot they are lethal, all-enveloping patches of darkness that regularly hide nasty, vicious things like mountains.

I crept out of the stable, barely avoiding tripping over a plough that had not been put away properly, and tiptoed quietly as a stalking tabitha towards the edge of the concourse. My plan to was to move on, head west towards the wall of the Chasm. Fate, on the other hand, had other ideas. I had only just emerged when I heard the sound of an angry graalur swearing crudely, followed by a sudden soft impact and a cry. There was a burly warrior at the entrance to the store, and beside him a human slave. I could make perfect sense of the conversation, despite it being in a dialect that meant nothing to me. The graalur was blaming the slave for the damaged lock and the pilfered contents of the chamber. The pale young man was going to be punished, probably harshly, for my crime.

I wonder now if history would have been different had the young man not been well-made and nearly naked, with curly fair hair and fear in his blue eyes. As I peered round the corner at the cruel scene the graalur slammed a fist into the lad's stomach. The slave crumpled to the ground, and the graalur drew back a booted foot and kicked him in the face. He cried out in pain, blood streaming from his nose. The graalur swung his foot again, but I was already moving. One graalur, one of me, and an attractive man in distress. I've read too many of the pulp magazines Verin enjoyed. Usually in those it was a pretty woman needing rescuing from the brute, but the effect was the same – a hero doesn't pause when an attractive member of the opposite sex is in peril. My footsteps were enough for the graalur to turn as I charged towards him like an irate bull. All the better – it meant my fist connected squarely with his chin.

Which was where it all went wrong. In the stories, I would have laid the graalur out, seized the gorgeous prize, and we would have fled out into the wilderness, to find somewhere safe, exchange life stories, and probably engage in a steamy, passionate liaison to our joint satisfaction and no long-term commitment.

But the graalur didn't go down. Instead, he grunted in rage and swung back at me. I dodged, fortunately – close to, I could see that he was built like a steam wrecking-machine and had a punch to match – but he did not abandon the effort. He also bellowed a challenge, which saw fit to summon every graalur within a mile. Worst of all, my handsome hunk scrambled away and fled without a backward glance. So much for gratitude.

Believe me, it didn't take me long to decide that discretion was the better part of stupidity. But even that brief pause for thought was too long. As I turned to retreat, I found my route blocked by half a dozen grinning warriors, their eyes exploring me. The graalur I had punched was behind me, and seized me roughly. He got both my elbows in his stomach for his pains, and stumbled backwards for a moment. I would have felt much better for the success if I hadn't been surrounded by graalur. I tried to scramble away, but there was nowhere for me to run, and one of the graalur had a sword at my stomach. He prodded me with it, and laughed again. Volg it, I had been a fool to leap in!

I knew what awaited me. Interrogation, probably rape, and then enslavement. One of the graalur grabbed my hair, pulled me to face him. Two more made short work of removing my weapons, before they tugged at my flying jacket, peeling it off my shoulders. I protested, but they were stronger than I was. The only remotely positive thing was that they stopped there, rather than stripping off my harness, too. I had a nasty suspicion that they were saving that entertainment for later.

They dragged me out of the colonnade, growling orders in the unknown tongue. Unfortunately it seemed the graalur didn't speak veredraa, and my lengthy efforts to learn it were now of little benefit.

The smell of frying bacon as I walked into the house filled my mouth with saliva. We were going into the kitchen, and I was hungry again, despite my repast last night. If they were going to give me breakfast it might be worth being captured. I glanced around at the graalur with the sword at my back – my sword, I noted with irritation – and said "Breakfast?" in a querying tone of voice, this time in lloruk. Of course, most likely they couldn't speak lloruk. My old school reckoned that knowing the lloruk tongue was a sign of erudition and good breeding.

These were evidently erudite, well-bred graalur. The one with my sword replied harshly in clear, recognisable lloruk "Not for you. Walk!"

All right, so they were *evil*, erudite, well-bred graalur. I stopped in the centre of the kitchen, and turned round, ignoring the blade prodding at me. "No breakfast, no walk."

For my pains, I got a hard slap across the side of the head. I almost made a swing back, but one of the other graalur grabbed my arm and shoved me hard towards the door into the body of the house. To my surprise, the third graalur shoved a piece of soft doughy stuff into my hand. I didn't argue - I was too hungry. The stuff tasted good - filling and sweet. By the time I had finished it I was being propelled through another door. The farmhouse had been ransacked at some time, that was clear enough. Most of the doors had been poorly repaired where they had been hacked or smashed open, and there were dark stains on the smooth planked floor that I didn't intend to investigate. There was a corridor, with an open door and a fat, grinning, waiting graalur at the end. From the insignia on the harness the brute was wearing, I was about to face someone in a position of authority. Lucky me.

I was pushed roughly into the presence of the graalur officer. The chamber had once been a smart day room. The furniture was broken and the floor scratched - there had been a lethal fight in there at some time. My escorts pushed me in, draped my jacket over one of the chairs, and then stood back, close enough to ensure I wouldn't try anything clever, but giving me space to stand straight and confront my interrogator.

The graalur was female, grossly fat, middle-aged, and ugly. Now I could see her garb clearly, it was obviously poorly cared for and filthy. Her insignia was ornate, but not substantial – my suspicion was that I was in front of the equivalent of a sergeant-major, or similar rank, rather than a commissioned officer (always assuming the graalur had such sophistications). Hanging out of her mouth was a dirty cream tube, only a couple of inches long, which glowed like an ember at the end. She looked me up and down, and barked a question in their tongue. I looked into her yellow-green eyes and shook my head firmly.

"If you want to talk to me, talk in lloruk. I don't speak the other language."

The graalur's eyes widened slightly. She nodded, and sat back onto the damaged table behind her.

"Where are you from?"

"The sky." No reason to lie.

Something slammed into me from behind, and I doubled up, gasping in pain. One of my two escorts had hit me in the kidneys with a clenched fist. The one with my sword, no less. I really didn't like him. I dubbed him Snapper – short for "sword napper" - so I had some kind of handle for him. I was still moaning from his low blow as the female graalur took hold of my chin and lifted my head to look into my eyes. I was close enough to smell her - not pleasant. She obviously hadn't heard of bathing, and the tube in her mouth smelt awful, like burning tyres. "Which clan of humans do you belong to?"

I glared at her. I wasn't really afraid. This heavy-set woman in the decorated harness was not prepossessing. She clearly considered herself important. I had dealt with far more capable sergeant-majors in my time. Tolly would have put her in her place with a few calm, even words.

"Answer, or they hit you again!" she shouted, her face almost in mine, the strange little cylinder twitching in the corner of her mouth. Oh, the temptation to head-butt her! I resisted the desire, not without difficulty, and simply stood there, looking at her levelly.

"I come from above the clouds. I came in a flying machine. I am not one of the human clans of the Canyon."

She gestured. I sensed Snapper behind me moving, and I stepped aside smartly. His blow did not connect. I laughed, dodging and turning so I was facing all three of them. "Look, I answered your question, graalur! Call your dogs off!"

She scowled, her face contorted as though she was drinking vinegar. She took hold of the cylinder at the corner of her mouth between two fingers and drew in a breath through it – the end glowed more brightly. And then she leaned towards me and breathed smoke at me, as if she was some kind of dragon. I stared at her in astonishment as she snarled at me and demanded "Tell the truth, slave!"

I stepped back, trying not to inhale the foul smoke. I picked up my jacket and put it on. Strange how much it helped to have it round me again. Then I walked over to a chair lying on its side by the far wall, picked it up and settled myself into it, stretching out my legs. I'd have liked to put my feet up, but there was nothing obvious in reach. "I am." Simple, blunt, honest. Snapper was growing angry. His red skin was almost purple and he moved towards me, clearly intending me harm. He obviously didn't like uppity prisoners. I tensed my muscles, ready to leap aside. I'd make them work to inflict bruises on me.

"Don't lie, scum!" Snapper snarled. "You're one of the group from the Grihl Valley! Admit it!" He stepped closer, his fists clenched. "You're here to stop the attack – aren't you!?"

Maybe my shock showed in my face. I had no doubts who the group in Grihl Valley were. Somewhat to my surprise, the female officer snapped at Snapper, glaring at her minion angrily. I was glad I wasn't in Snapper's boots. The woman's voice was deceptively soft, a slight rasp emphasising the gutturals. "The prisoner did not need to know of that." Snapper cringed. The officer gestured - one of the other graalur lashed out at the unfortunate thug viciously with a fist, and he fell, gasping for a moment. The female graalur did not watch the punishment being inflicted - her eyes were on me, studying me coldly. "What use can you be to me?" Her voice was hard and final – I could tell without a doubt that my answer to the query would determine my fate. If I was not of any significant use to her, she would enjoy watching her minions torturing me, assuming she didn't decide to join in. On the other hand, did I really want to be of use to this fat officer? What could I do to be useful?

Squum that! I was asking myself the wrong question. The critical issue was whether this lafquass could be useful to *me*. She was less than two paces from me, and her only weapon looked to be a long knife in an open sheath at her belt. I had let her shout at me for too long. I let my eyes flicker past the woman's right shoulder. Just a fractional move, nothing so obvious as telling her to look behind her. Enough for an experienced soldier to think there was something there. She turned instinctively – I grabbed for the blade at her belt, jerking the slightly curved bronze out of the sheath and against her neck in a swift, smooth movement. At the same moment I slid my other arm around part of the vast expanse of her waist, dragging her to me – or more accurately me to her, so that her fat, flabby chest was pressed against mine. Not a pleasant experience – she really wasn't my type.

The ogress was already moving, reacting to my assault, but her attempt to respond ceased as she felt the edge of her own knife against her throat. I just hoped she didn't assume she had too much blubber to be at risk from the blade. "Not a move!" I snarled at Snapper, who had responded two heartbeats too slowly to my lunge. "Or your sergeant gets demoted to corpse!"

I felt the graalur's muscles tauten under her dark red skin; to my surprise, the fat female felt as strong as a Werintar wrestler. If I gave her any opportunity to break free she would grab it – and me, probably. But Snapper was unsure of himself, and gave his sergeant no excuse to try to fight. She growled reluctantly at her men to stay back.

"Through the door" I growled in the woman's ear, trying to make her twist round so that she had her back to me, to make it easier to walk with her in my grip. She turned after a moment's encouragement with the blade, a fine red line showing

71

on her neck. She was not struggling now, and moved slowly as I directed her. This was too easy. She had to be about to try something. I hauled at her, shoving her bulk ahead of me out of the interrogation room. If she refused to walk I would have no way of moving her – I just hoped the threat of the blade at her thick neck was enough. Her graalur thugs did not dare to protest or intervene. The burly female moved slowly, trying to impede my passage. Her muscles tensed against me, and I sensed her right arm lifting up to where my hand held the blade. I hissed in her ear, warning her that I knew what she was about, and she desisted.

Into the hallway of the farm building. I glanced through the open doorway of the adjoining chamber as I dragged the sergeant with me, and then paused to take a second look.

Four spires rose from the floor, each curving inwards and narrowing to points like the tusks of some primordial monster.. Between them some kind of tracery, formed of glittering crystals of amber and sapphire bound by silver wires. It ought to be beautiful, but the curves and twists were asymmetrical, the angles and curves disturbing. My jasq was thumping like a hammer, as though something in that room was clutching at it. Somehow I knew that the shape in the gutted, otherwise empty space was important, but I had absolutely no idea why.

I slid into the magerealm, curiosity over-riding any vestige of common sense I might pretend to possess. The light was brilliant, glaring around me, coils and jets of iridescence flowing in impossible patterns that baulked at symmetry or gravity and churned around me. The realm hissed softly at me, but there was still no pain. It felt good to be using magic. Again I felt the sense of something tugging at me, away and to the east. A dark haze almost against me had to be the sergeant's vast body, virtually non-existent within the realm – she most certainly did not have a jasq. Beyond it – there was something else, a figure of angles and impossibly hard edges which had to be the tusked structure, and an emerald haze further out – somehow I suspected that the tusks were the cause of that eerie glow.

Something else moved in the realm, a clutch of spines and gems in gold and blue amidst the lambent fire, a form I could translate without too much difficulty into picturing as a man, but a man with an impossibly long neck and a diamond head with glittering silver eyes – eyes that were staring at me directly. There was something here, something unlike anything else I had seen in the magerealm before, something alive. Something that could see me, too. A presence that spoke to me somehow of power and malevolence.

The sergeant was twisting against me, trying to loosen my grip. I didn't have time to rubberneck. I slid out of the realm and looked around hastily, breaking the hideous fascination of the thing in the room. Whatever it was I was seeing in the realm was beyond the chamber I was looking into, and I didn't want to go that way.

I wrenched at my hostage, hauling her around, pushing her back towards where the graalur had brought me into the farmhouse through the kitchen. I belatedly saw two graalur ahead of me, blocking my passage. I snarled an impolite request for them to get out of the way, my attention upon them – and the fat sergeant finally made her move, demonstrating to me just how she managed to maintain her authority over the graalur thugs around her.

Chapter Eight

One moment I was growling at the graalur, the next moment I was flying through the air to slam into the wall, the knife spinning out of my grip to clatter against the smooth stone wall of the farmhouse. I still don't really know how the sergeant did it – a sudden twist of her body, using my own movement to fling me over her shoulder as she wrenched my right arm to yank the blade away from her throat. I can recognise that it took a lot of courage to act as she did – at the time, though, I was too busy being dazed and bruised to appreciate the artistry of her action. Instead I had three graalur seizing me and pinning me down, kicking and pummelling me until any fight I had within me was beaten from my body.

The graalur hauled me to my feet and back into the interrogation chamber before I was unconscious, and it was the sergeant's turn to snarl at me threateningly. My head had hit the stone wall hard, and I was still blinking away bright flashes of light from my vision. My bruises had bruises, and I could taste the blood seeping from the corner of my mouth where a graalur boot had caught me.

The sergeant stood facing me. Behind me Snapper and another of the thugs had my arms twisted up behind my back, agonisingly. The ogress glared at me, all trace of the calm officer flushed from her obese face by red anger.

"You are going to suffer for a long time" she rasped, spittle foaming at the corner of her mouth. Her smoke-breathing cylinder had vanished ages ago. She slapped me across the face with deliberate viciousness, and then she coldly and in detail outlined exactly what she and each of her men were going to do to me. Suffice it to say that it didn't involve wine, flowers and chocolates, and was not planned with my good health in mind. I was still suffering from a spinning head and a myriad range of aches and pains across much of my body. My jasq was hot, pounding away in my side. I doubted it would be able to heal the damage that the vengeful sergeant intended to inflict upon me.

She was barking instructions to her men, and I was trying to get a grip on myself to be able to fight back, when another graalur waddled in from the direction of the tusk chamber, full of an evident sense of self-importance.

"You got orders to leave her alone" the newcomer grunted. If I had been in fit state to do so, I would have raised my eyebrows in surprise. I had no doubt that the sergeant was not the senior figure here, but I wasn't aware of anyone else being aware of my existence.

The sergeant looked equally non-plussed, and deeply disappointed. She demanded a reason why, but my saviour was already giving it. "The Proctor says she is of interest. That he wants to study her once he has finished his current task."

Now it was the sergeant's turn to look abashed. Who or whatever this Proctor was, he had a dramatically powerful authority over all of the graalur. Mere mention of his demand was enough that the sergeant's twisted plans came to a sudden halt. Instead, I was dragged hastily through into a side room, and flung to the bare planked floor. A few minutes sufficed to bind my wrists and ankles, while they secured the room. The door slammed shut, the sound of the impact like a thunderclap, and then I vaguely heard the fat woman ordering her squad back to work. She had another of the smoke cylinders in her mouth, the end glowing balefully, and she took the time to tell me that my punishment was only delayed, not cancelled, breathing foul smoke in my general direction as she did so. I lay back on the floor, drained by everything that had gone on, and closed my eyes, wondering how long it would be before the Proctor came to see me.

I don't know how long I lay there, recuperating slowly. All I know is that I felt considerably more human after a little sleep. I also knew that I really didn't fancy sticking around for the entertainment of the sergeant or her thugs. There was a narrow window that I had seen one of the guards locking as they bound me, and outside it was still daylight. Of course, with the unchanging lantern trees, that could mean I had slept for five minutes or eight hours.

They had lashed my wrists and my ankles together with a length of rope, but they had left me my jacket... and I had my jasq. As yet, the mysterious Proctor had not come to investigate me, but that might be only a matter of moments away. The bare stone walls around me had once been a storeroom of some form – there were well-made wooden shelves stretching the full length of two walls, and a cluster of empty barrels in one corner. A pantry, I suspected, already gutted by the graalur.

I slid into the magerealm again, far more warily this time. I suspected that the Proctor was the blue and gold figure who had gazed at me however long before, last time I had delved into the other world. I did not want to come to the Proctor's attentions again.

The realm blazed, bright as always. I could sense the strange tusked shape looming only a few yards away; I kept my gaze averted, hoping not to become obtrusive here, in case the Proctor was nearby. A fireflow trickled only a couple of feet from where I lay, my own spindles and globes shimmering amber and amethyst in the brilliance. I was bound, unable to move my limbs more than a fraction, but in the magerealm such motions can be magnified exponentially, if you know what you are doing. A really capable mage can draw upon a flow up to quarter of a mile or more away. I had nowhere near such skill, even when I was using my magic daily, but for this purpose I only needed to move a fragment of fire a tiny distance.

The flow was caught by an amber spindle, and slid smoothly and almost silently towards my shape. This was going to hurt for real, I knew, even if the magerealm finally liked me. I yanked it through before I could change my mind, and the fire sizzled against the ropes and against the skin of my wrists.

I jerked my wrists apart violently, as much to get away from the flame as to break the scorched cord. For a brief moment the room was lit brightly, and I held my breath, waiting for a guard outside to call out in alarm.

Silence reigned. The nearest shouts were from the window – there had to be a work-party busy a few hundred yards away, and a graalur overseer was exhorting them to more effort. I undid the bonds around my ankles, and got to my feet, a little unsteadily. Now all I had to do was to get out of the farm and get away.

Through the window I could see wide, rolling fields, the glow of two lantern trees shining to give the illusion of daylight. The window faced west, which was the direction in which I had been planning to head, across the patchwork of fields through the abandoned or conquered towns that I understood dotted the plain.

Seventy or more miles to the west was the wall of the world. Even from here I fancied I could see the dark line of the wall in the distance. Almost certainly just fancy, but I wanted to believe I could already see it through the hazy atmosphere.

My gaze shifted away from the distant horizon, and my heart tightened in my chest. I was looking across a stretch of land I had not seen before. Scattered across the landscape to the north-west were dozens – no, hundreds – of dirty leather cones, each more than the height of a man, each wrapped around a tripod of wooden staves. Tents. Standing or lolling in the vicinity were graalur. Lots of graalur. An army of graalur. The force that was going to slaughter the valley folk.

I stared at them, and my stomach felt as though it was full of lead. My mouth was dry, and I felt sick. I needed to warn Darhath what was coming. The Grihl Valley, that was what the graalur had called their camp. I tried to tally the numbers. My first subjective guess had to be in the right order – there were hundreds of tents, each home to three or four graalur, at a guess. More if they were friendly with each other – which I doubted, actually. Not that lack of friendship would stop their commanders pushing them into close proximity. It might make them more bad-tempered... make them fight harder. Six hundred soldiers, at my best guess. No wonder the farm had been stockpiling rations.

I had stormed out on Darhath and the others. I didn't have to go back and fight with them, and probably die with them against that throng. I could head for the wall and climb out of this hot hell. Ignore their fate completely.

Except that I couldn't do that. Volg it, they had taken me in. Saved my life, probably. And they were decent people. All right, even including Kelhene. I couldn't just leave them to be slaughtered. I had to get back there. Warn them. Get them out of there.

If it came to it, fight with them. My sword and my magic could make a difference. Not enough of a difference, mind you... but I had to try. I couldn't just abandon them.

I glanced back at the door. Odds were there were graalur in the farmhouse who would see me blast open the door; the alarm would be raised, and I might well have serious trouble getting away. I turned to the window, exploring it slowly with my eyes. A simple stone wall, with the window topped by a plain, solid lintel. Below the window, more stone blocks, another wide slab providing a support for the window-frame. The opening was only two feet wide, and the small glass panes were set into a solid wooden frame, locked by an elegant brass padlock. Even if I could open the window, it was less than two feet square – it would be a tight squeeze getting out through it. On the other hand, there was no one immediately visible outside. The work party I had heard was obscured by a stand of bushes. If I was quick and quiet... I grinned mirthlessly, and slid back into the realm again.

Traceries of fire and water were easy to spot. Earth-flows and air squalls are more difficult to identify within the realm. Sometimes the hardest things to see are the artefacts from the real world. People are just vague shadows, at best, unless they have a magerealm presence, too. Objects vary. Metals usually show clearly, almost as solid as in our side. Wood is as insubstantial as people. Stone, though, is sometimes clear enough... and can be manipulated. There was a pale red mosaic directly in front of me, a torrent of earth flowing across it. I reached out, spindles growing as I concentrated upon the task in hand, and I wrenched at the blocks below the window.

My hope was that I could tear open enough space without causing too much noise. The last time I had tried a stunt like this, years before, when I was trying to get into one of Mondi's storehouses to steal supplies, the racket had been atrocious, and I had had to run like a rabbit. I hoped I had learned something from that escapade about technique.

A block shifted slightly – I nudged it again, pushing it forward slightly, and then repeated the effort with another one. If I could persuade the majority of the stones to stay together, and simply move the entire chunk of wall sideways and outwards, the task might just be done in relative silence.

This, of course, assumed that the Proctor didn't notice my efforts. When I had been tussling with the sergeant, though, there had been alarums and excursions throughout the farmhouse, and the Proctor could not have failed to be aware that something was going on. This time, if I was lucky, he might be asleep, or about other business, or not paying any attention to the realm.

There's a cliché about fortune favouring the bold. Let me tell you, from bitter experience, it seldom works.

But this time it did. It took me over quarter of an hour, and by the time I slid out of the realm I was drenched in sweat – well, all right, *more* drenched in sweat, and feeling somewhat weak at the knees. Hungry again, too. The volging lafquasses hadn't bothered to provide me with any food whilst I was in durance vile. I can cope with being a prisoner far better on a full stomach.

A narrow opening in the wall below the window. Three feet high, a foot wide, and all supported by the lintel and the window above. Genius, if I do say so who shouldn't. I slipped out through the gap, and wondered about putting the blocks back. Make them really worried about how I got out of a locked room.

No – I didn't have the time or the strength. And this corner of the building was relatively sheltered. With a little luck, no one would walk past and notice the opening for hours.

Where to go now? I had to get back to the camp – to the Grihl Valley. I was completely on the wrong side of the farm. The safest option was to creep south, along the wall of the farm, and sneak back the way I came. But something was drawing me northwards, towards the work-party still busy beyond the bushes. That same summons, insistent and compelling. My curiosity was piqued by it, even if I could resist the urge itself. The taste of the demand seemed to mean something, but I couldn't work out what. I think now that part of me somehow knew the source of that summons. I still wonder, sometimes, what would have happened had I ignored it.

Tolly always complained that I was too impulsive. He's right. I pushed my way through the bushes, glad enough of my jacket to protect me from the spiky red branches. The growths were dense enough to hide me from casual glance – I was able to ease forward to where I could see the people beyond.

Not that the first figures I saw really count as people. Graalur, swaggering in their leather trappings. I was beginning to realise this smoke-breathing vice was pretty wide-spread amongst them – a couple of the thugs had cylinders with glowing tips in their mouths. All were carrying whips and staves to keep order. And the subjects of those tools were working within the circle of guards, heaving at timbers, building wooden structures in the open area north of the farm. Not houses, no. These were pens, whether for animals or slaves was unclear. A pit was being carved out of the ground on one side. Seating along two edges of the pit hinted at the intended purpose of the construction. And the slaves... I gritted my teeth to stop myself blundering into the clearing and hacking at the graalur. Five dozen or more people, mostly nude or nearly so, whip-scars and ribs visible through the grime on their pale skins, staggering as they struggled with the tasks allotted to them. As soon as one fell, the whips fell, too, the graalur taking delight in punishing any hint of weakness. Men, women, even children were being driven to the edge of endurance to build this arena. I was unarmed, vastly outnumbered - there had to be fifteen graalur watching the slaves. I could do nothing except curse volubly under my breath. I had no idea what had drawn me here, but this was where the compulsion had brought me. To watch the graalur abusing and hurting slaves. And I couldn't do anything about it. Even with sorcery, there was no chance of me striking them all down before the alarm was raised, and the army to the north would not grant us any mercy. Whatever this compulsion had been, and it was still singing to me, it apparently had a cruel streak within it.

A child, no more than ten, was struggling to try to move a heavy block of stone. A graalur snapped an order at it - I couldn't tell if the child was male or female - and the child snapped back, frustration and fatigue writ across its face. The graalur scowled and lifted her whip without a pause, catching the child across its bare upper body with a stinging, savage blow.

A heavily-tanned slave man, his right arm in a makeshift sling, was a few yards from the pair, He turned, seeing the unequal match, and stormed over, yelling what was clearly a demand at the graalur to stop.

The graalur turned on the man, flailing the whip at him. His body was lined with red stripes where he had been the victim of such treatment before. He glared at the graalur, ignoring the blows, and snarled an order at the child. The kid promptly, and sensibly, fled.

The graalur was striking at the man again. I was staring at him. I was lurking at the edge of the construction field, skulking in a bush covered with dense red leaves. He was only a dozen yards from where I was standing. He could not be here. There was absolutely no way that the graalur could possibly have enslaved him, no prospect of him being a captive victim unable to prevent the strokes of a whip across his back. And yet I had no doubt. Even with the marks on his dark body, the growth of dark beard on his face, the grime and the rags, he was unmistakeable.

Wrack.

Chapter Nine

I stared at Wrack, emotions tangling themselves into knots in my stomach. I had forgotten just how imposing he was, physically. I had hated him. I still did hate him. The scar on my arm ached on occasions; the scars in my emotions hurt more.

And yet the sight of him also stirred feelings in my body. A tightness in my throat, a warmth in my stomach. During the months at his mansion I had been his slave. I had hated him for the way he had humiliated me. He had beaten me when I fought him, treated me as an abject thing to abuse and vilify in front of his friends. But there had also been times when he had shown hints of compassion, almost of kindness – not that those times ever seemed to last. I had always been aware of his presence, of his physical strength. Seeing him now felt like mingled ice and fire in my veins.

The jasq had drawn me right to him. Bound us together with a connection that I already feared would be harder to break than the bindings Wrack had used at his mansion. I realised that I was gritting my teeth as I stared at him.

The graalur struck at him again, and I winced in sympathy as the whip carved another bloody streak in Wrack's lean flesh. He gasped in pain, but the child had fled. He had achieved his intent, now he was taking his punishment for it. He lifted his head in defiance - and as he turned his head slightly, his emerald eyes met mine. I saw his eyes widen, recognition flowering in his hard, striking face, and I felt the jasq in my side reaching out to its original master.

Wrack's face changed. No longer the stolid, bleak mask. There was amazement, then a rush of pleasure. At the sight of me? No, his eyes said this was something else. Suddenly his expression contained his old confidence, and then as the graalur lashed at him again I saw the surge of the hot anger that had caused me enough pain when I was his prisoner. Not aimed at me this time. Relief washed over me - I hadn't realised that I was still scared of him.

The jasq in my side was thumping like a wildly beaten drum. It felt as though there was a strand of fire stretching between me and Wrack now. He was shouting in triumph, and he snatched the whip from the startled graalur. I realised that I was grinning, watching his sudden burst of violence. I was glad I wasn't that graalur. He kicked out, hard, catching the guard in her stomach. She crumpled, crying out in pain. Other graalur were coming running, some with staves or whips, others with drawn swords. There were a dozen of them, and he was all on his own.

I almost felt sorry for them.

As they approached him, I could see that at last Wrack's body was changing, the skin growing gnarled, his neck extending. His legs were growing more muscular, claws extending from his toes. His tail was growing out from his spine, stretching out to balance him as he stood proudly. His head was elongating, growing the long, fierce muzzle and sprouting the four ivory horns that grew back from his head. His left arm had drawn back, the skin forming between his body and the limb. His other arm… he was wearing a sling. He flung it to one side, but the damage was clearly serious. His left wing was strong and spreading wide, but his right wing was sprawling across the ground, unable to give him any lift. I felt absurd dismay. He was magnificent, but he was crippled. As every moment passed his skin mottled with more of the dark red scales that were his hallmark. He turned on the graalur. They had all paused in their advance, shaken at the sudden transformation, staring at the dragon standing on its hind legs before them, nine feet tall and every inch in control. Wrack drew in his breath and then roared, his deep, dragonish voice echoing around the construction site.

"Run!" he bellowed. Half of the graalur needed no second bidding. Five, though, stood their ground. Two, braver or more stupid than their comrades, moved forward, swords drawn. Wrack laughed, that deep braying amusement that foretold sudden, violent death for his enemies. I had heard that more than once. It still put a shiver up my spine. Wrack swayed backwards slightly as the graalur charged. I felt the jasq hot in my side in sympathy as Wrack opened his jaws wide, and breathed harshly. A spear of orange fire tore from his throat, hammering into the advancing graalur like a red-hot sledgehammer. The two graalur screamed as their bodies were charred, dying in a few moments of agony. I could smell their burning flesh. More people were screaming, now, the slaves fleeing in terror, too.

Wrack turned, his eyes seeking the graalur. Most of the guards were running, now. The two who did not run without delay screamed for a few moments before they died, fire blazing around their bodies. I was transfixed, watching the dragon as he stood, master of all he surveyed, only his broken wing limiting his power.

To the west I heard a bell start to clang, the repeating sound slightly flat as it rang out, being swiftly repeated by more bells, each a slightly different note. Voices were being raised in concern. It would only be a matter of moments before the massed ranks to the west headed our way.

Wrack turned, his eyes scanning the bushes. He was looking for me. All my instincts told me to run. I tightened my teeth together and got to my feet, pushing through the undergrowth until I was standing directly in front of him. If he breathed, I would be charcoal. Even in his draconic form, I could see the healing wound on his unbroken arm. I had carved the jasq out of his flesh there. He had every reason to want to punish me for that. Just as I had had every reason to want to hurt him, too.

His diamond-tipped tail was swinging back and forth behind him, dark wings closed against his body, as he stood silently and stared at me.

"Wrack, you idiot!" I snarled. "That's an army of graalur over there – and they're heading this way. Move your arse and get out of here!"

I gestured eloquently towards the graalur force, invisible through the copse of shrubs, and indicated the dark, heavy rocks that formed the border of the farmlands – they also formed a bulwark against the oncoming tide of soldiers. "Up there – quickly!"

I realised as I shouted at him that Wrack was going to argue – the line of his long, dragonish jaw showed his anger and his refusal to take orders from anyone, let alone me. I had seen that expression too many times before. To the west of us we heard distant, but approaching shouts and clamour. Wrack glowered, looking at the outcroppings I intended us to climb. Get to the top, and the pursuit would be slowed considerably. If we couldn't get to the top, we would be most definitely between a rock and a very hard place.

Wrack followed my gaze. "Want me to climb *that?*" he roared. "With a broken wing? Just how stupid are you, Sorrel?"

I looked back at him, and shivered. For once, much as I hated to admit it, he was right. There was just no way he could hope to climb the escarpment at the edge of the plains. The graalur had to be only a few hundred yards away. We were trapped. The graalur would overwhelm us – the only question would be how many we could kill before they got us.

Wrack was turning his head, and I felt the jasq pummel inside me, thumping in time with Wrack's heartbeat. His body shrank in upon itself, the muzzle flowing back into his human face, the wings drawing back into his skin as the wing-struts melded into arms and hands, his claws retracting and the scales becoming tanned skin again. I've seen Wrack change more times than I care to remember, but I still find it an amazing sight. Back in human form he was nude, but I didn't have time to admire the view. He was no longer in dragon form. Our one significant weapon against the graalur, aside from my magic, was gone. I stared at him in disbelief as he grabbed at the discarded sling from the ground.

"Move, idiot!" he shouted as he straightened up. Even in human form, he had an impressive roar. I stared at him blankly. He snatched at my hand, dragging me after him as he turned and ran.

Behind us I could hear the graalur hammering the ground with their feet as they stormed towards us. Wrack was hauling us almost directly north, along the rough, rocky ground below the face of the escarpment, as though he had some idea where he was going. It would only be moments before the graalur burst through the undergrowth and caught sight of us – and then we would be in real trouble. I chanced a momentary glance over my shoulder – half a dozen dark-skinned figures were hacking their way through the shrubs and yelling as they spotted us. We had a lead of perhaps two hundred yards, and nowhere to run to.

Hard, uneven ground is no fun to run across. Even in boots, it slams at your feet with every bound, and it is rough enough to send you tumbling into a hard landing. And scrub is far less welcoming than grass. Trouble was, the graalur seemed to have no difficulty pursuing us over it. Slowly and surely they were gaining on us. I was recognising the major disadvantage of my leather jacket - I was roasting in it, and it was making me tire more quickly. It and my boots were the only links I still had left with the surface - I didn't want to abandon it.

Wrack glanced over his shoulder and yelled at me to run faster. He had longer legs than I did, but I didn't have enough spare breath in my lungs to point this out. I chanced a glance over my shoulder - one graalur had got to within fifty paces. We were in real trouble. I looked ahead of me again, and jumped hastily, only evading a clump of the foul-smelling hagweed gourd-plants by dumb luck. My fellow fugitive was gaining ground on me. I spared some breath to curse and tried to run faster. I was only glad the graalur nearest to us hadn't brought bows.

Ahead of us there were more bushes, and some kind of dip in the ground. Wrack turned, looking back at me as I struggled to match his pace across the uneven ground. I threw myself after him recklessly, trying to stay well ahead of our hunters. When will I learn not to be so unwise? At his feet there was - nothing. I came to a juddering halt only a few inches from the edge. Below - some way below - I could see water glittering. The gorge we were facing was about forty feet wide. No way to cross it. A stream fell in a graceful arc from the far bank into the water below. I looked across at Wrack in dismayed horror, and began to expostulate. All right, swear. Same difference. Wrack was holding his injured arm, and gestured downwards at the churning water below.

"How brave are you, Sorrel?" he growled.

"You what?" I answered intelligently.

"We jump."

Sometimes I really think I'd have been better off finding a nice, safe career. Something like juggling scorpions or gargling with broken glass. I could hear the sound of boots, yells of anger, and muffled movement behind us. No time to have doubts. I grabbed his hand - no way was I doing this on my own - and nodded. "Go!"

We jumped.

Chapter Ten

When you hit it from thirty feet above, water feels like solid rock. I had pointed my feet down, hoping to make it easier to carve into the river. It felt like I broke every toe. If I hadn't had my boots, I probably would have done.

The water was warm - I don't think the Chasm has heard the word "cold". It was deep, too - I went well under the surface, and began to kick desperately to drag myself up to the top of the water. I'd lost my grip on Wrack's hand as we dropped - I think he pulled his hand free. For a long moment I wondered if I was going to surface. I'd taken a lungful of air just before we hit the water, but it still felt like the wrong side of forever before my head broke out from under the waves and I could take a gasping breath. Water was pouring down from the stream above us, showering over our heads, but frankly that was the least of my concerns. My boots were full of water – while I had been extremely grateful for their presence until now, I had no doubt that they would be a serious liability in the river. I didn't even have seconds to make a decision – I kicked wildly, feeling them loosen around my feet and slide to the bed of the river. Good boots, too – I already suspected that I was going to miss them. Wrack was already swimming with the current, hampered by his injured arm, heading downstream.

Something hit the water only feet from me, a resounding splash dousing me thoroughly. A boulder, I'd guess. They'd found something to throw at us. It meant they weren't trying to take me alive. I wasn't sure if that was bad news or a relief. I would have shouted some insults at them, but I didn't want another mouthful of water. Common sense said I ought to abandon my jacket as well as my boots. Equally common sense derided this as foolish in the extreme, and told me to keep struggling and keep my head above water. I started thrashing along the water, trying to go with the flow. Not that difficult, really. Just as well - my skills at swimming come from a few feeble efforts in the Werintar hot springs and a couple of summer days in the south, in the Furulyeer Ocean, years ago when I was little, before Kabal imposed restrictions on travel.

Wrack was letting the current take him, using it to carry him away from the yells and insults from the graalur massing along the lip of the precipice. I made rather ineffectual efforts to manoeuvre through the churning, fast-flowing river, and nearly drowned myself. Forget style, Sorrel - concentrate on moving through the water. I was vaguely aware that we had even higher walls ahead of us – the gorge flowed into a deep ravine within the escarpment.

A few yards behind me there was another resounding wallop as something big and heavy plunged into the water. I assumed it was a boulder, until a tusked face broke the surface two yards to my right. Gave me an incentive to kick out with my feet. The right foot connected with a soft belly – he needed to get into better shape. The graalur 'ooofed' and went under again. I doubted that he would drown, but it ought to bring an end to his intended pursuit. Could have been worse for him – I was right that I was going to regret losing my boots. I grinned, and took a mouthful of water as a wave or a ripple rolled over my head. My turn to splutter and gasp.

But then my feet hit something solid. My poor toes felt like I hated them. The river was shallower, here, without the pouring water from the stream opposite to dig the channel deeper. Perhaps I could have hung onto my boots. I cursed mentally. On the other hand, I was glad to be able to reach firm ground. I gratefully tried bouncing along the bottom of the river, and promptly found my feet getting tangled in something that was trying to drown me again. Weeds of some sort, probably. Psychopathic ones, at that. They were wrapping around my left foot with great gusto and considerable skill. I yanked hard, and to my great relief the vegetation released me. I tried swimming again, and looked around. The river channel was heading between vast outcrops of rock - we were deep within the gorge, and the high walls on each side of us looked distinctly unclimbable, at least from a wet start.

Wrack yelled, and swung his uninjured arm towards the edge of the gorge, water splashing around him as he did so. The roar of the surging water was deafening, and I could barely hear his shouts. The river was angling round to the left, and the twisting current was flinging him towards the rock-face on the outer edge of the curve. He was already making for a narrow culvert where the river was carrying him, and he was gesturing at me to follow. I intended to head after him - I would not be sorry to get out of the water.

Something burst from the water feet away from me. Tusks, dark red skin, amber eyes, unfriendly visage. The graalur I kicked in the stomach. Oops. He didn't seem pleased to see me. I should have kicked harder. I lashed out, but he was expecting it and dived away. It's not easy kicking in the water - like fighting in custard. The first time I'd caught him by surprise. No chance of that again. He turned, grinning harshly. I had the distinct impression he didn't have my best interests at heart. He struck out at me. He had a sword! That wasn't fighting fair! I ducked, and the blade missed by some distance, but that wasn't much consolation. I tried to swim, letting the current pull me away from him. The river wasn't particularly wide, and the current was growing faster as the walls narrowed, but the graalur obviously could swim like a fish. A fish with a steel barb. I wished he had armour, too - it might have drowned him. No such luck, just a leather kilt. My flying jacket was somewhat the worse for wear and was full of water. It slowed me down and did nothing for my swimming style. The graalur leaped after me, and his hands gripped my right leg. I promptly went under and got another lungful of water. The graalur was on top of me, pushing me down, making sure I couldn't get a breath. My kicks and struggles seemed to hit nothing but water, and my chest and throat were burning with agony. If I could not break the squumer's grip, I was going to drown.

My throat and my lungs were raw, and I needed to take a breath, but I knew that if I did I would never take another. My vision was blurring, and the graalur's grip felt like a sadistic vice. I punched and elbowed, but he seemed to be made of water himself - I could not make an impact upon him, and I needed to breathe.

We slammed into something hard. A protruding rock was my prime suspect. I had been lucky - the graalur, above and to one side of me, took the worst of the impact and went limp in my arms. I shoved upwards to the surface, gasped and choked and coughed, spluttering water out of my lungs. I kept my grip on the graalur, swinging round so that I was straddling him, keeping him under the water, reversing our previous position. We were already past the rock that had hit the graalur, still tumbling through the white rapids. I needed to release the brute and grab onto something. Not a chance if the graalur was still alive - I didn't want to face him if he tried to drown me again. I tried to look ahead, and realised that there was another big chunk of unfriendly stone directly ahead of us. I wrenched the unresisting shape of the graalur into its path and kicked off hard, letting the current finish the job on the creature, turning back to see the graalur slam lethally into the outcropping and then vanish into the spray.

I swept past the executioner rock, looking around desperately for a place to get out of the gorge. Not a chance. Steep stone on each side, implacable boulders strewn throughout the waters ahead of me. I had dealt with the brute just in time - a few seconds longer, and we would both have been chewing granite. I struggled to swim sideways. The river was too deep here to reach the bottom. I had no idea what had become of Wrack – he was already out of sight, back upstream. I just hoped he had managed to get out of the water. If at all possible, I needed to get out on the same bank.

Not that there was any chance of that at present. The torrent was fast-moving. My biggest fear was that the rapids would turn into a waterfall. I fancied I could hear a roar approaching, but frankly over the growl of the rapids I wouldn't have heard a cataract until I was tumbling over the top of it. I needed to get out of the river. At least the water wasn't cold - I hadn't really got used to the idea that a mountain cascade might be warm. My poor old flying jacket was sodden, pulling me down. I was not going to abandon it, whatever the risk.

The seething, chattering water was full of rocks. I was ducking and swimming, weaving between them, half-relying on the current to evade them, too busy dog-fighting with slabs of igneous stone to be able to look for a way out. And all the time I was travelling downriver, carried by the current further from the graalur, from the encampment – and from Wrack.

My reactions were slowing. I pushed off to sidestep one boulder, only to catch my shoulder on another. The impact *hurt*, volg it! My jacket absorbed most of the damage, but I fancied I saw a faint red tracery swept away by the spray. There was a blur to my left - I pushed away from it, kicking with my bare feet. Now I was glad I hadn't been wearing my boots – they would have dragged in the water and I might not have pushed in time. As it was, a wall of granite hissed past me, close enough for me to kiss it. Not that I did. I'm not that desperate for a relationship. There were more, smaller rocks just lurking under the water beyond, white with spray leaping to avoid them. I drove away from them, and found myself in the lee of a massive outcropping of water-weathered grey-black stone jutting into the course of the river. For a moment the river was no longer carrying me onwards. I could feel the ache in both thighs and calves from keeping myself swimming. My legs could not go on for much longer. The jasq in my side felt red-hot. My lungs still burned from the water I had breathed. There was a shelf of rock in the lee – I grabbed it with both pain-filled arms and hugged it like a drowning pilot. By the time I had hauled myself onto its jagged peak, mostly out of the water at last, I could barely feel any part of my body that didn't hurt. My eyes were stinging, my lungs burned, and my muscles were complaining. I was growing deaf from the constant, implacable roar of the water around me.

I looked up the side of the gorge. Wrack, volg him, looked to have found a relatively easy niche to clamber up. Me, I just had a relatively sheer cliff-face. I eyed it, and then wondered if the light was dimming. I had no idea what time it was. For a moment I panicked, terrified of being stuck at the foot of this cliff in the dark. I slid into the magerealm, intent on dragging out a fireflow to ensure I didn't end up in midnight gloom.

And then I was back in the comparative gloom of the real world, stuck on the rock in a cascading river, and I was on my knees, gasping, agony wrenching through my side. The jasq hurt as though I had twisted a serrated knife inside it. I clutched at myself, rasping for breath, tears in my eyes as much from disappointment as from the pain. It was hurting again. A lot. The jasq slowly withdrew its knives from my side, my mouth tasting of lemons, and I clutched at the rock under me to ensure I didn't slide back into the rapids.

I sat like that for a long time. I was crying. I don't often shed tears, but this... it was so unfair! I had been able to use sorcery again! I had been free of the pain! I had been... near Wrack.

I gritted my teeth, unable to believe what I was thinking. What it meant, if I was right... no. No, it couldn't be.

I was looking up at the cliff as I ruminated. I couldn't use sorcery to get me up the cliff. I was a good climber. It wasn't the worst rock-face I'd struggled with. And I was fed up with the roar of the water. Bare feet were often better than boots for footholds. All right, so *wet* bare feet may not be a good idea, but I didn't actually have a towel down here. I pulled myself to my feet. The jasq might have savaged me just now, but it was still hot and feverish, undoing the damage I had suffered in the water. I was ready to go.

The first foothold is always the hardest – that's what the man who taught me to climb properly always said. Lying bastard. The third, fourth, tenth and seventeenth were the hardest. Oh, and all the rest.

Actually, it wasn't that bad a climb. The granite was broken and pitted, with numerous hand and foot holds. Only forty feet. I probably could have done it in the dark. Not that I wanted to try.

Top of the cliff. Brooding jungle only a few yards from me. No weapons, no food, no idea of what's around here, no boots or leggings, just a jacket and underwear. No obvious bandages for my sore and scratched arms. Volg it, just for once the universe ought to owe me a favour!

I wasn't sure how long I'd been walking. It felt like an hour, but I couldn't have made more than quarter of a mile on the difficult, tricksy edge of the gorge. I'd lost count of the number of times I'd been forced to cling onto untrustworthy branches and hug strange, red trees to avoid toppliing back into the current below. My feet hurt - I'd cut them a couple of times on thorns on the ground, despite the leaves I'd tied around them - and there was still no sign of Wrack. What there was, instead, was a large, unfriendly plant. No way was I going near it. Eight feet high, twenty feet wide, scarlet tendrils rearing up, two orange bell-shaped flowers that were turning restlessly. Not in the breeze, no - there was almost no wind. This thing was moving itself. Daffodils weren't supposed to do things like that. And it stretched out almost to the edge of the gorge. I wasn't going to risk sneaking past it and ending up falling back into the water. No, the better option was to creep into the jungle. Ease my way through the trees and avoid anything else that might want me to be its lunch-date.

I was ravenously hungry. I could have eaten the killer daffodil if it hadn't been moving. Twenty feet into the jungle, I could see dark blue berries on a bush. Only twenty more feet into the undergrowth. All right, so they might be deadly poisonous. I bit into one gingerly. Juicy, tart, like a sharp pear. I waited to see if my stomach would complain. It did, demanding more. I obliged. Not the best lunch (nearer supper, frankly), but very welcome.

I moved onwards, paralleling the gorge, to get past the killer daffodil. I was making assumptions - perhaps I was maligning the plant, and it was cultured, friendly and vegetarian - but I didn't care to take the chance.

Another fifty yards, and I was skirting an outcropping of rock, maybe forty feet high, extending to the gorge edge and into the jungle. I was realising that I might have a bigger detour than I had intended. I really didn't want to waste time. Climb the outcrop? Why not? I pushed through the cream grasses growing up at the edge of the granite, and began to climb.

Not too bad, this one. Lots of handholds, stuff I could dig my toes into. Ten minutes and I was on top of the world.

To the south-west, across the gorge, I could see a spire. There was a good chance that that was the one near to the Grihl Valley. Maybe another mile along the gorge. South of that a thin wisp of smoke. The camp? Or else the remnants of the camp after a raid. I gritted my teeth, not wanting to consider that possibility. To the east of me, red jungle sprawled across the wide valley, a couple of lantern trees and some more spires breaking the canopy. Smoke rising from three or four places, suggesting settlements of some kind. Almost certainly graalur controlled. Not healthy. The nearest looked like some kind of town, only a couple of miles from me, but the crimson leaves obscured any structures. I turned, wondering if I could spot the gash in the jungle where I had crashed, but there was nothing obvious I could identify.

And then I felt something tugging at me. I turned, looking along the gorge from my vantage point. A single figure, walking warily at the edge of the gorge, looking down into the churning waters as often as he looked ahead of him. If he turned his head a fraction, he could not help but see me. I dropped to my knees, unable to take my eyes from him.

Did I want to see him again?

The call caught at me again, demanding, needing, urgent and desperate. He lifted his eyes, scanning the jungle, and I met his gaze. There never had been any choice. I walked to the edge of the granite and scrambled down, silently, not even thinking about hand-holds or what would happen if I slipped. I'm pretty sure I scraped one hand raw on the way down – the jasq grew warm, starting work on the latest damage I had done to myself. I ignored it, concentrating on reaching the ground.

Wrack was standing there amidst the trees at the base of the rock, waiting, his green eyes upon me. We were alone together. Just him and me. Just like old times. There was a loose stone in the cliff-face beside me – I took hold of it tightly before I turned to face him.

"Hello, Wrack. I didn't expect to find you a slave."

He snarled at me, anger in every muscle of his body. I half-expected him to change his form, take on his dragon shape and blast me with fire. I stared at him, daring him to do so. He stepped a little closer, close enough that I could smell his sweat.

He growled, so deep that it seemed to resonate in my ribcage. "You lafquas, Sorrel. You evil squumer."

I took a step back, unable to hold his gaze. "I only did to you what you did to me."

He looked older, somehow, even than when Merik and I had broken into his bedroom. When I first knew him, before the war, in those long weeks when he had watched me learning sorcery at his mansion, I had thought him old. I had only been a girl, then, only just twenty. He had been over thirty. Now he was forty, and for the first time he looked it.

I stood facing him, my heart beating a retreat in my breastbone. Part of me - quite a lot of me - wanted to run. I could see the mending scar in his unbroken arm. I had promised myself, days before, that if I met Wrack again I would put a knife in him for killing Merik. Trouble was, I didn't have a knife. Volg it! I doubted my chunk of stone would be any good. I hefted it, and looked at it contemplatively before looking back at him. He glanced down at it in my hand. He simply raised an eyebrow, anger hovering behind his eyes, waiting for me to attack. I grimaced back. "You really think I'm stupid enough to attack you, Wrack?"

He didn't bother to answer, simply shrugging.

I smiled. "I'll wait until you turn your back, instead."

He wasn't amused. He took three swift paces to me, taking no notice of my weapon. His left hand reached out, clutching at my shoulder fiercely, pulling me round to face him. I should have slammed the stone into his head without a moment's hesitation.

I hesitated. His glare scorched into my eyes, his grip tight, his face close to mine. "Ought to kill you now" he hissed, his breath warm against my face. "Going to enjoy punishing you."

I glared back and thrust upward with my knee, hard. I guessed that he was half-expecting it - he twisted his thigh to block the blow, but it still connected. He winced, and shifted his grip until it was against my throat, tightening to choke me. Obvious and crude, Wrack. I slammed my head forward, catching his nose. There was a satisfying crunch – he shoved me backwards, a spurt of crimson at his nostrils. I hefted the stone, grinning savagely. Blood was streaming from his nose. He was ignoring it.

"Sort your nose out, Wrack. You're a mess."

For a moment I thought he was going to transform. Instead, he shrugged, and bent down to rip a wide red leaf off the tree nearest to us. The soft foliage was enough to block the bleeding and mop up the sanguine stream down his chest.

While he was cleaning himself up, his attention away from me for a moment, I took the chance I had, and I slid into the magerealm like a swimmer into a cool, welcoming pool of water.

Except that this water was acid, with a side-helping of knife-blades. I stumbled backwards out of the realm, my face streaming with tears, my stomach leaden. I had been so sure. Confident that if I was near Wrack I would be able to use sorcery.

Instead I had plunged into the same pain, if not even more, that I had suffered before. I sat down on the ground, bitterness seething just under the surface of my thoughts. I had no idea, now, why the jasq was hurting me again.

Wrack looked over at me. I had only been in the realm for a moment, and I had almost bitten my tongue holding back a cry of pain. I did not know if he had sensed my sudden immersion in agony. I hoped he hadn't – I didn't want to concede any weakness in front of him, let alone admit that I couldn't work sorcery.

He was still holding the bruised leaf to his nose. His voice was muffled by it, but proved by his words that he had not recognised my sudden despair. His words, though, had a strange resonance with my thoughts.

"Give me back my jasq or I'll tear your head open, Sorrel."

I laughed, despite my misery. I had been waiting for this. For once, once only, I felt superior to him. I could deny him and there was nothing he could do. I pulled the jacket up to expose my hip, showing him the dark bruise-blue stain on my side wordlessly. He stared at me and then reached forward, letting his hand slide over the dry surface of the jasq far more gently and lovingly than he ever caressed me. His eyes lifted to mine.

"How?"

I shrugged. "I was dying. Wounded after you made our triplane crash. It was the only chance I had."

He stared at me, expressions changing as his face shifted. I could see the thoughts scrambling through his mind. Two or three times he was going to speak, but in the end he simply shook his head. "Could just find a knife and cut it out of you again."

I leaned against the tree and smiled sweetly. "You're not that stupid."

He paused, half way between a scowl and invective. The chance of his surviving reclaiming the jasq with my blood in it was even lower than my chance of having claimed it in the first place. He knew that. He didn't want to accept it, but I knew him well enough to know he wouldn't roll those dice.

It was nearly a minute before he turned away from me again. I could see the anger boiling within him. I wanted to turn on my heels and run, old terrors crawling up inside my throat as I watched him rage. It was not the first time I had seen him angry like this. The last time had been just two weeks before I escaped. I had smashed a goblet deliberately, one that he liked. Some sentimental value, I suspected. He had hurt me that evening; I still had the bruises when I got to the aerodrome. Afterwards, for once, he had been contrite about what he had done to me (perhaps because I hadn't managed, for a change, to give as good as I got). He had allowed me a little more freedom, mostly out of guilt, and I had used it to get away, the train carrying me out of his lands and out of his influence.

I was too proud to let him see that he still scared me. He studied me for a few moments, hot fury lurking in the curve of his lips.

"How did you find me?" His voice was deceptively calm.

"You drew me. You and the jasq."

He nodded, and then lunged at me, grabbing my arm painfully and twisting it hard before I had a chance to struggle. It felt as though he was dislocating my elbow. As he pulled me against him he glowered down into my face. "You're bound to me, Sorrel. My jasq... this time I am not going to let you get away!"

"I'm not your slave any more, Wrack!" I could shout as well as he could. "You can do what you squuming like! Now I know what drew me to you, I can make sure I always head directly away from wherever you are. I hope I never see your muzzle again!"

His face was close to mine. "So that's it, is it, Sorrel? Come back to gloat? Laugh at me and then leave me to rot?" He shoved me down onto my knees, his grip on my arm agonising. I tried to punch him with my other arm but he dodged easily.

"I hope you do rot!" I snarled back, trying to break his grip, and I managed to free one foot enough to kick his shin hard. He howled in anger, more than pain, but his grip lessened enough for me to wrench free, albeit with enough damage to my elbow and shoulder that my vision blurred with involuntary tears. The jasq was burning in my side, throbbing hard. Wrack scrambled back, and I saw him bare his teeth. I knew that face. He was about to change.

"No!" I bellowed. "Human to human, Wrack! Or are you too scared to face me in this form?"

I thought for a moment he would ignore me. His eyes were narrowed with bitter hatred, but he paused for a moment. Once again his voice was dangerously quiet. "Could sense you, too, Sorrel. Could feel that something was coming. You can try and run if you want to, but I'll be on your tail."

His intensity was terrifying. I believed him. I knew Wrack well enough. Once he became obsessed with something, he would not give up. I scowled at him. "Why, Wrack? Aren't there other women for you? Or is it because I beat you this time?" I stalked closer, tense, ready to leap back if he grabbed at me again. "Give it up, Wrack! Once your wing heals, go back home. Forget this – there's no way you can have your jasq back! You're just going to have to learn to live without it – like I did!"

His face was thunderous, and I realised that the smouldering anger was ablaze again. He lashed out with his good arm – I dodged fast and kicked at him. He twisted sideways and grabbed at my wrist. I kicked again, this time catching his kneecap. I wished I had harder toes – I might have broken his knee to go with his broken arm. He cried out in pain, and I pulled free. He swung his other leg at me, ignoring the pain in the knee I'd kicked, and caught the back of my legs, sweeping them out from under me. I fell heavily, gasping with pain as I slammed into the roots below me. He flung himself on top of me, grabbing at my throat again. I bit at his hand and tasted blood. He backhanded me, slamming my head against a hard knot of wood. Stars and flashes, thumping pain, and he had one of my wrists pinned above my head, the weight of his body holding me down. I glanced past him and snarled "Graalur!"

He struggled to his feet, turning wildly, grabbing at a tree branch as an impromptu weapon. I was surprised at the alarm on his face. I scrambled back, pulling myself on my backside until I could get to my feet. He turned back, confusion turning to comprehension.

"Crying wolf is stupid, even for you, Sorrel" he rasped.

"I didn't expect it to work" I replied honestly. "I didn't think you'd be so worried about them."

He lifted the branch a fraction, pointing it at me. Not much of a threat, frankly. I knew Wrack well enough. If he actually intended to attack me, he would prefer to use his bare hands.

Or transform.

"Not going to be a slave again, Sorrel" he hissed.

"No fun, is it?" I taunted.

His eyes slid away from mine. "Didn't treat you the way the graalur do."

I glared at him, forcing him to look at me. "It was still slavery, Wrack. I was still your possession. Just a *thing* you owned."

"Not the same" he insisted.

"Wasn't it?" I asked softly.

For a moment he paused, and I thought – or just kidded myself – that I saw some understanding, at last, of what he had put me through. But then he shook his head and rasped "No."

I looked at him curiously and raised my eyebrows. "So why did you put up with it so long?"

He froze, his green eyes locked into mine, disbelief in his expression. After a pause, he spoke. His voice was quiet, a slow drawl of growing comprehension. "You don't know, do you?"

I just glowered at him. I didn't know how to answer.

He turned away, got to his feet and started walking towards the jungle. He glanced back over his shoulder. "Come on."

I stood there truculently, feet firmly planted on the ground. Like a three-year old, my mind whispered sardonically. I ignored it.

"Want to stay here and wait for some graalur to catch you?" he asked. "They'll be far harsher with you than I ever was."

I canted my head to one side. "Want to bet? Maybe I prefer them to you."

"Don't be stupid" he answered matter-of-factly. "Now move."

I shook my head. "I'm going my way." I gestured vaguely in the direction of the Grihl Valley. "I have friends a few miles that way."

He lifted his eyes back to mine. "And will they be friendly to *me*?"

I grinned evilly. "Why should I care? You go wherever you want – just leave me alone!"

His voice was soft. "Can't let you go, Sorrel."

I turned round and stood facing him, hands on hips. "Volg off, Wrack! Isn't it time some other woman had to put up with you?"

"You cut my jasq out of me and now you bear it."

I didn't reply. He was stating the obvious. That was always a bad sign.

"I need my jasq to be able to transform."

I stopped dead, Wrack's words slamming into me like a crashing triplane. He had been an indifferent mage, nowhere near as capable as I had become. I had thought that taking his jasq would simply prevent him working sorcery. I had never thought, never imagined that the jasq had any connection to his dragonish state. It felt as though I had stalled at ten thousand feet, nothing but empty air beneath me, as the implications of what he was saying took shape in my thoughts.

I looked across at him. "But you just did transform..."

He took a slow breath. "After you hacked the jasq out of me, I learned something. Don't need the jasq to be within me to change. Only has to be close to me, within thirty or forty feet, but if it's close enough then I can change. After you walked out, leaving me bleeding, I managed to change before you were too far away. Came after you."

"I hadn't thought without your jasq you'd recover fast enough to give chase."

"Changed as you left the mansion. Found I couldn't change back. That's why I had to stop you. My dragon form is strong, it fights well, but I have no hands. I am so limited in that guise!"

I never expected to feel sorry for Wrack about his dragon form. Volg it, I didn't feel sorry for him even so! I ignored his plaintive efforts to win my pity and kept walking, trying to blot out the thoughts churning in my head. What all this meant was that he *couldn't* let me go. He had to enslave me again. Once again it was him or me.

This time I *had* to kill him.

Chapter Eleven

Wrack matched his pace to mine, walking just behind me. I ignored him, concentrating on maintaining my footing as I stalked between the red foliage of the dense jungle. After I escaped Wrack's mansion, I had thought my emotional turmoils were over. Now it felt like I was in a flat spin with a dead engine.

"So what happened to you?" Wrack asked evenly. I didn't answer. He knew what I was feeling.

Another few hundred yards, another opening gambit. "What happened to your co-pilot?"

I shivered. For a moment I almost lost control. It would be so easy to turn round and shout at him. Satisfying, too. But I had decided to freeze him out. I kept moving.

We were making our way along the side of the valley, staying parallel to the river gorge as it chattered and roared to our left. If we managed to keep up our current pace, I thought we ought to reach Darhath and his people by the evening. Assuming that the graalur hadn't already launched their assault and wiped them out. Volg it, I needed to get back there sooner! A nasty corner of my thoughts commented drily that having Wrack there would help more. At the moment, he was following my footsteps. Did I really want him coming after me?

More words from behind me. "Came down in the jungle. Couldn't get through the trees, so I changed in the air, where your aeroplane had ripped through the trees, leaving a gap." He paused, an edge of remembered pain entering his voice. "Got it wrong. Was trying to reach you where you'd crashed." He was only a few feet behind me. I made sure he knew I was ignoring him. He growled something under his breath. Good – I was irritating him. Maybe he'd give up.

No such luck. He resumed his tale. "Knocked unconscious by the impact. Broke my arm. Got caught by a gang of graalur. By the time I knew what was going on, was too far from you to be able to change." There was a note in his voice

– he had not relished his time as a slave. Good. "Couldn't make them understand me – didn't think to try the Iloruk tongue then – they took me to their camp. Found out later they'd sent a patrol to see if there was anyone else in the area. I was afraid they'd find you."

Liar. He'd hoped they'd bring me back to him so that he could change. I concentrated on ignoring him strongly, watching my footing in my virtually-bare feet. I brushed a branch to one side and hoped it would spring back into Wrack's face. From the oath behind me, it had connected. I grinned edgily and kept moving.

We were climbing, now, making our way up the gorge. By the time we reached the top of the ridge, I was sweating heavily, tiny bright orange flies buzzing around me as they endeavoured to feast on the salt on my skin. Yet again I thought about discarding my poor, battered flying jacket, for the sake of being less boiled. No. It was my only link to home (apart from the dragon behind me, a malicious imp in my skull pointed out caustically). The trees were thinning out, and we came into a clearer patch of land. I needed to take a break, and slid onto the ground after first checking for anything that might decide to bite or sting me. The nearest likely assailants were a vermilion bramble bush with sadistic spines and another of the revolting giant hagweed gourds – but both were around eight feet away, and probably out of range. I settled down, ignoring the aches in my feet and my calves. Wrack settled down near me. I turned away. Yes, it was petty, but it was about the only means I had to express my feelings.

He spoke again. "Sorrel, for volg's sake talk to me! What the squum does it achieve to shut me out?" He was only a foot behind me, his breath hot on my neck. He was losing his temper. I remembered him shouting at one of the male slaves at the mansion like this because he had been insolent. He ended up hitting the slave. Broke two of his ribs, because the slave dared to answer him back.

I was tired, hungry and thirsty. I spun round and shoved Wrack hard with both hands. For once I actually caught him by surprise – he toppled over, landing on his back like a felled sycamore, arms like branches trying to break the fall. I heard another cry of pain from him as his broken arm suffered. He snarled in rage and flung himself at me again.

I'd been expecting it. I dived sideways, letting his momentum carry him past me, towards the bramble. I shoved at him as he went, encouraging his embrace of the thorns. He cried out, and I scrambled back to the edge of the clearing.

"Keep following me, Wrack, and you'll get more of the same!" All right, so it wasn't the most polished speech, but it made my feelings clear.

He got to his feet slowly, red scratches oozing on his face and his upper body. At least I had my jacket to protect me. His face was livid, fist clenched and his teeth bared like a mastiff. For a moment I thought he was about to change. I had no way of taking on his dragon form, even injured as it was. He walked forward slowly, not rushing in stupidly. Wrack learns. Unfortunately.

"Ought to break *your* arm, let you know how it feels" he growled.

"Cripple us both?" I taunted. "That's really dumb, even for you."

He paused in his advance, and grinned, sudden amusement breaking through the anger. I took a breath, taken aback.

"Us?" he repeated. "Glad to know you accept we're together." He smiled more, obviously seeing my expression, and then he lunged, grabbing my wrist tightly, yanking me towards him. I'm quick, but Wrack's faster. Before I could react I was looking up into his face. I tried to jab at his eyes with my free hand, but he turned his upper body to evade the blow and twisted the arm he was holding viciously. I felt tears in my eyes – for a moment it hurt as much as the magerealm had. He could see the pain in my face. He liked it.

"Try that again and I *will* break your arm" he rasped. I didn't grace the threat with a reaction.

"If we're going to reach the Grihl Valley before nightfall, we need to get moving."

"And what then?" His expression was cold. "You intend to stay in the Chasm the rest of your life?"

"Don't be so stupid" I retorted hotly. "My plan is to scale the wall. I'm a good climber. Are you?" I added sweetly.

"Once my arm is healed I can fly out" he snapped with understandable irritation. All right, so mine had been a stupid comment, but I enjoy needling Wrack. "Could help you climb" he added.

"Until you're healed we need somewhere to hole up" I said quietly. Part of me was screaming about what I was saying. Did I really want to work with him? What did I think would happen when we reached the surface? He needed me – did I need him? I'd been rolling such thoughts around in my skull for the last hour, and I was still no nearer an answer. I turned away from him and gathered my bearings. The gorge was still to our left. If there was any justice, the rope bridge I had crossed on my first night in the Canyon should be no more than another mile ahead of us.

It was nearer two miles. My feet were agony, now – not helped by the fact that I had unwarily trodden on a piece of shattered bone half-embedded in the ground. The sharp edge of the cracked shoulder-blade had hurt considerably. The only compensation was that the shard of bone made a makeshift axe. If we were attacked again, I wasn't completely defenceless. Wrack had eyed me when I hefted the weapon in my hand. I had simply shrugged and left him to wonder what I intended to do with it.

I was nervously eyeing the nearest lantern tree, trying to decide if it was starting to darken, when I at last saw a spindly structure stretched out over the gorge. I didn't realise how good a few tatty strands of rope could look.

"You trusted *that?*" Wrack murmured beside me. "Never doubted your courage, Sorrel, but your sanity worries me."

I laughed, and then realized that I was feeling genuine amusement at his words. I squared my shoulders, and walked onto the bridge. It swayed like a drunken snake, but I had crossed it before without injury. I moved warily across it, trying to keep my balance. Having virtually bare feet made it somewhat easier to keep my footing. Behind me I could feel Wrack's eyes following my progress. I wasn't sure if he would try to follow me. My suspicion was that he wouldn't dare let himself be left behind. With his broken arm, it would not be an easy crossing. A great deal of me wanted him to be too scared. Was this really a chance for me to lose him?

Of course not. Once I was across safely, he looked across the gorge at my face, and then he took a tight grip on the rope on the right, and started across. I shifted my makeshift axe in my grip. He was very trusting. I could cut the ropes, send him plunging into the gorge. The odds were against him surviving the fall. Even if he tried to change, he would not be in dragon form before he hit the water or the rocks at the base of the ravine. If he did change fast enough, his broken wing would prevent him flying.

My eyes met his. He knew precisely what I was thinking.

I didn't need him. And I wouldn't let him enslave me. This would be my best chance to deal with him.

Except... if the graalur were yet to attack, Wrack's presence could tip the odds in our favour. I cared about the Grihl Valley people. I shifted the axe in my grip a fraction. Wrack's expression shifted slightly – alarm? Resignation to his fate? Sorrow? He was trying to cross faster. I had to act now, or not at all.

I lowered the bleached bone, and turned away. We still had some distance to travel, and it was getting dark. I heard Wrack scramble off the bridge, and his feet thumped the ground as he stalked towards me.

"Why didn't you cut the ropes?" he asked quietly from only a few feet behind me.

I shrugged. "Why did you cross when you knew what I could do?"

His head tilted slightly, his expression almost unreadable. "Needed to know what you *would* do."

I laughed, but this time without real amusement. "And you worry about *my* sanity?"

Abruptly the space where we stood near the edge of the gorge was plunged into darkness. The cool glow of the nearest lantern tree had been extinguished like a crushed firefly. Wrack snarled an imprecation. "Hope you know where we're trying to get to, Sorrel."

So did I, but I didn't say so aloud. I reached out to where Wrack had been standing and took hold of his hand. "Come on" I urged. Trusting to my memory I headed for the opening in the granite around us, and headed into the badlands.

Four wrong turns, and over an hour to travel half a mile. Wrack was grumbling, as were my fingers which had been barked raw against unforgiving stone many times more than I wanted. I had thought I could recognise the way into the camp. It was more luck that led me to it than any skill at navigation.

Not that I wanted to see it when we finally found ourselves within the boundary.

The camp was dead. Between the high walls there was virtually no light, just the ghostly flicker of the guttering remnants of a single fire. The dead lay where they had been cut down, bodies already beginning to rot, the stench nauseating. I heard Wrack muttering oaths behind me. It took all my self-control to make my way to the fire, weaving between the bodies. The blaze had been alight for many hours, devouring what once had been the kitchen. I dropped my makeshift axe and wrenched a piece of broken wood from the ground before thrusting it into the embers, holding it there until it caught fire. A crude torch, but enough to light the scene of carnage. More illumination than I truly wanted, but I needed to be able to see to identify the victims.

Gelhdin was on his back, his throat and chest black. Insects were crawling across his eyes, already beginning the task of demolishing his mortal clay. So far, there was no sign that any larger predators or scavengers had found the charnel ground. It would only be a matter of time, though. I did not fancy facing any of the big predators I had encountered so far.

Tulher was clutching the spear that had impaled him. I didn't look any more closely at him – the spear had not been the only wound he had taken. Shardhla – I felt my tears welling up. The pregnant soldier had died trying to protect her unborn baby. She had been unable to save either of them. I snarled angry adjectives and lifted the torch higher, trying to count.

Twenty-four bodies. Three of them children. Six looked to be graalur – they had not had the battle all their own way.

The camp had contained around fifty people. What had happened to the rest? I could not find Darhath, Kelhene or Korhus among the dead. Had the others escaped? The structures in the camp had been wrecked. The ballista was a smoking ruin, the huts burned to the ground. I went back into the shell that had been the kitchen. The wisps of fire that had illuminated the slaughter-field had guttered out – my torch was our only surviving illumination.

106

The supplies were spilt over the rock, fouled and wasted. Graalur work. The surviving refugees would not have left anything that was salvageable. I checked more carefully, trying not to think about what this meant.

In a fold of rock in the wall there were small collections of herbs and condiments, collected painstakingly to give the limited food some flavour. Any survivors would have carried them with them.

Which meant that no one had escaped. I took a deep breath, trying to unblock the tightness in my throat.

Wrack's hand settled on my shoulder. I jumped, and he made soothing noises. I snapped an obscenity, and stormed out into the open air.

"No one's left, Sorrel." His voice was gentle, trying to be placatory. I turned and gesticulated at him – a crude signal involving two fingers and a blunt indication. I held the torch high and walked across the camp. I should have been here! If I'd been here... if I had been here I'd have been captured, too. Or killed. Wrack, as usual, was right. There was no one left.

The whistle of a missile hurtling through the air straight at me proved us both wrong.

Chapter Twelve

Something slammed into me, and I staggered backwards. A heavy stone had hit me squarely in the stomach. Once again my jacket had saved me from serious harm. I dived for cover as another stone slammed into the ground where I had been standing. Someone, in the darkness beyond the glow of my torch was yelling something about ghouls and gloating. A woman's voice. My torch had gone spinning away to land on the ground a dozen feet from me. It was hissing on the ground, and then it went out, the flame extinguished.

We were in total blackness, as though a cloak of velvet had been flung over us. Behind me I could hear Wrack's voice, demanding to know what I was doing. I was rather glad when his irritation stopped suddenly, only a thump and a cry of pain explaining his silence. The rock thrower had a good aim. I moved slowly along the ground, trying to creep soundlessly towards my assailant. I already had a suspicion who she was. I was going to enjoy tackling her.

Another thump, only a few feet from where I had reached. She hadn't got a good enough ear to tell where I was. I grinned mirthlessly into the darkness, and then closed my lips hastily, in case my teeth gleamed brightly enough to reveal me. No stone hit me – there wasn't even enough light down here to reflect off a bright surface. Either that, or my teeth were filthy. Possibly the latter, I conceded.

Wrack's voice. "We aren't your enemies! We aren't graalur!"

"I know one of you" the voice retorted. "Come back to gloat now you've led the graalur to us." Her words were followed by the faint hiss of a missile which clacked against rock loudly. Wrack swore. It must have been close. She was a good shot.

Ten more cautious paces. She had to be nearby, now. Come on, Wrack. Make her speak again.

"Sorrel? You all right?" No way was I answering that. Was Kelhene going to be stupid enough to respond?

No such luck. I strained my ears, hoping I could hear her move or breathe. More likely she would hear me – the jasq was pounding in my side loud enough to be heard half way across the canyon. I froze, wondering what I was feeling... and the camp was suddenly full of blindingly brilliant red-orange fire. I was blinking away tears, but Kelhene was only feet from me, her arm raised to block the awesome glare. By the kitchen Wrack was in dragon form, a demonic shape in the sudden hell-hues, fire scorching from his jaws to bathe a rock and some already charred wood. I dived forward, catching Kelhene around the waist and slamming her to the ground. She was crying out in anger and hatred, one hand catching at my hair. I swung my head forward, catching her on the bottom of her face. Squuming lafquas, she had a hard jaw! My head was ringing from the impact, but she was moaning, her eyes glazing over. I grabbed her by the throat and tried to dash her head against the ground.

Strong, clawed hands pulled me off my semi-conscious victim. "Volg it, Sorrel, what do you think you're doing?"

"She tried to brain us with rocks!" I snapped back at Wrack. She was moaning and trying to sit up. My attempt to kick her was foiled by Wrack hauling me away like a recalcitrant child. I'd forgotten just how strong he was in his draconic form.

"You just wanted to gloat!" she retorted harshly in veredraa.

"Have you two quite finished?" Wrack growled, his lloruk sibilant in the breeze. I saw Kelhene look at Wrack properly for the first time. Standing facing us, lit from behind by the fire he had started, he looked terrifyingly impressive, like a troll from one of the fairy tales. I saw Kelhene blanch and try to inch away. I walked over to him and shoved him in the chest with one hand, as much as anything so that Kelhene could see that I had the measure of him.

"This is between me and her" I replied coldly. "Keep out of it."

"What *are* you?" she whispered, sliding into lloruk. Her attention was on Wrack, not me.

"A dragon" he replied. He was stating the obvious again. Ho hum. "What happened here?"

"Her friends attacked us" she hissed. "Wiped us out. Dragged off survivors as slaves."

"The graalur aren't my friends" I answered fiercely. "Are you really so stupid as to think I was working with them?"

She snarled something in veredraa and flung herself at me, fingers like claws.

Wrack grabbed her before I had a chance to claw back at her. With his whole wing he blocked my responding charge. "Any more of this and I'll burn you both!" he roared, his deep timbre echoing around the camp like thunder.

I backed off. Kelhene was still in his grip, her eyes wide. For once he had some other woman to menace. Good. She deserved it.

"Sorrel, calm down. As for you, any more trouble and I'll tighten my grip." Kelhene stopped struggling. "Who are you?"

"I'm Kelhene. Darhath – one of the leaders of the camp – was my man."

Wrack slowly released his grip on her, his eyes moving restlessly between the two of us. "Have you finished trying to kill each other?"

I grinned widely. "No."

Wrack's shoulders slumped slightly. Even in dragon form I could see the frustration in his stance.

"What do you want with me?" Kelhene complained.

"Came to find out what had happened to you" Wrack replied simply. "You started throwing rocks at us."

"I thought she was helping the graalur" Kelhene explained, trying unsuccessfully to sound reasonable. I opened my mouth to express my views on her perceptions, but Wrack turned his head, looking down his muzzle at me quellingly. I shrugged and turned away.

Wrack made a low growl in his throat. "How many of you have they captured?"

"Over twenty" she whispered. I could hear the despair in her voice. "There were more than two hundred graalur in the attack, and two snarqs. We didn't stand a chance."

I looked back at Kelhene, hearing the misery in her voice.

"So many?" Wrack mused. "Must have wanted you all badly."

"They were looking for something. A jasq. I heard the word used half a dozen times by the graalur after they had won. No one knew what they wanted."

Despite the warmth of the air, I froze inside. Jasq. It was a word from the Iloruk

110

tongue, unchanged for centuries. I couldn't hope this was a misunderstanding arising from language differences. And I was as sure as I could be that I was the only person with a jasq down here. Wrack was looking across at me. "Sorrel?"

I shook my head warningly. I didn't want to tell Kelhene that it was me they had been looking for. The shape I saw in the magerealm.   Something that knew about jasqs... that knew what I had. The Proctor had wanted me preserved. Told the graalur about me. Insisted they caught me.

No! They'd been planning the assault on the valley before I ever got to the farm! The force had been there before they knew anything about me! It wasn't my fault!

"You knew about this" Kelhene rasped accusingly, her eyes reading the signs from my stance, my expression. I was never a good liar, even if I didn't open my mouth. "They were looking for *you*!"

I turned away, unable to meet her eyes. Behind me, Wrack growled some platitude about me not knowing what they would do. I felt my jasq pound, and realised he was returning to human form.

I looked round at Kelhene. "I'm sorry" I muttered. "I didn't know they would come looking for me. They were going to attack here anyway – I didn't mean to make things worse."

Kelhene stared at me, her eyes wide and brilliant with unshed tears. She opened her mouth for a moment, but no sound emerged.

"Where have they taken them?" Wrack asked quietly. Her eyes turned to him, but she still did not answer for a time. Then at last she dropped her gaze.

"Ilkadala."

I raised my eyebrows. Either it was an obscenity or a name. I suspected the latter. At our puzzled expressions, she added "The Iloruk city. I followed them for a few miles, but then I came back to see what I could salvage."

"Where is it?" I demanded.

Again she lifted her eyes to Wrack's. Apparently she trusted him more than she did me. "South-east" she answered. "About forty miles."

I nodded. I remembered the road I had seen as I trekked away from the valley originally. "We can do that in a day, if we hurry. We might catch them up before they reach it."

Wrack looked between us. His expression said, louder than words, that he thought we were both deranged. "They aren't our people" he growled. Kelhene's expression mirrored mine.

"They're my friends, Wrack! They took me in – and me being here made things worse. I can't just abandon them!"

Wrack drew himself up taller and grimaced at me. "Not my fight."

I shrugged. "Then go. I don't need you."

He raised an eyebrow, not bothering to put his response into words.

I raised my eyebrows in return. Two could play at that game. "Who rescued you, Wrack?"

"All I needed was your presence... the presence of my jasq." He stood, looming over me.

I grinned savagely, no humour in the grimace, and gestured to my stomach. "Here it is" I snarled. "You want it, you try to take it. Or else you come with me."

His face hardened, his teeth clenching before he spoke. "Maybe just rip it out of you" he growled. He twitched fingers that could in a moment become claws.

I held his gaze, daring him to do it.

Kelhene was looking between us, not understanding our exchange. I didn't bother to enlighten her.

"I'm going to Ilkadala" I said harshly, my eyes not leaving his. Volg it, he didn't need to blink, and I had to. "If you want my presence, you'd better come with us."

For a moment I thought he would argue more. His eyes lingered on the set of my jaw and my clenched fists. "Must be as dumb as you are" was all he said.

Chapter Thirteen

My estimate of a day's travel had been wildly optimistic, of course.

We rested – restlessly - a few hundred yards from the ruined camp. None of us had wanted to sleep with the dead around us. By dawn, we were all wakeful, eager to move on.

The badlands do not make a good road. It took until well into the afternoon (so far as I could judge time – I sorely missed the movement of the sun) to reach the highway I had encountered the first time. We would be heading the other way along it, not back towards the farm but south towards this Iloruk city. I had taken some boots off one of the dead graalur, so at least I now had something to protect my feet – I had not even considered taking footwear from one of our own dead – but even with them I was growing footsore and irritable by the time we reached the track. It didn't help that Kelhene seemed to be making eyes at Wrack, helping him get a grip on the veredraan tongue and flirting with him as she did so. So much for any loyalty to Darhath. She told us that the graalur had searched the women roughly after they were captured, which was something the graalur had enjoyed a lot more than their victims. Kelhene had been hiding (surprise, surprise). Once they were sure the jasq-woman was not there, they had marched their prisoners off. They had identified Darhath as the leader, and Kelhene said grimly that she had heard he would get special treatment, whatever that meant.

They were many hours ahead of us, but escorting slaves should slow them down. With luck, they would be camping before they reached their city, and then – well, I didn't know quite what we would do, but at least we had a dragon on our side. Probably. No, be fair, Sorrel, Wrack loathed the graalur more than I did. He wouldn't side with them.

Once we were out of the badlands, the terrain around us did improve. We passed a number of settlements, ranging from small farms to a couple of substantial villages, and another distant town. Flindraan, according to Kelhene. It had been seized by the graalur more than a year ago. Their rate of advance against the human settlements was slow, but relentless. Two of the farms were hard at work, slaves labouring in the heat at the direction of graalur masters. This was thoroughly conquered territory. We crept past them, keeping off the road and in undergrowth so that they did not detect our passage. The first village was a ruin, long since burned out. I saw Kelhene looking away from it, her eyes unsteady with unshed tears. I didn't dare ask her if it was her home. I'd either get tears or anger, and I couldn't take either. I remembered seeing the ruins of Ulvaraan, in Malgarin, after Mondi torched the village from the air. The villagers had not paid the full tithe she demanded, and she had burned the village to the ground. The charred remains had been left untouched as a warning to other communities – I had a dark suspicion that this had been left in the same way. Old rage bubbled in my thoughts, and I felt my teeth grinding together. The second village was in better shape. People were on the streets, buying and selling, chatting, even flirting. The graalur overseers were very obviously a familiar and accepted presence. Given time, people can get used to anything, even slavery.

Not that I had any doubt what the graalur mastery meant. Most of the faces had the drawn, wary look that I had known since childhood – the permanent fear that a lord would look upon you with disfavour. Which would lead to a beating, a rape, torture or a killing. Never feeling safe. Never knowing when the next blow or whip would fall. Add to that the ever-present sight of the masters. Graalur, down here. On the surface the guards were human, but the crests on their helms and the colour of their tabards made their allegiance clear enough. Most had been no better than the lords themselves. I felt my jaw grow tight, my fingernails biting into my clenching hands as I remembered. As a child, growing up in Starron's lands, I had understood that we were just property, with no redress against the whims of the dragon lords. That knowledge had fostered a deep, unrelenting loathing of our masters, a sense of injustice that had been fuelled by the increasing harshness of some of the dragonlords. It had made me quick to join the fledgling revolt when it began.

What had surprised me was how many of the guards, whom I had loathed and despised almost more than I hated the dragons, changed sides and fought alongside us. Down here, though, from idle comments I overheard Kelhene say to Wrack, it was clear there was no prospect of such a sea-change in the servants of the Iloruk. Cold hate churned in my stomach and I scowled instinctively at the graalur, remembering belatedly to drop my gaze so they did not see my expression.

Getting round the occupied villages without being noticed slowed us down more. By the time the lantern trees began to go out, we were still significantly more than a dozen miles from the Iloruk city, as far as Kelhene could judge. Travelling on the Iloruk road had improved our pace, but not enough to catch up. The occasional presence of patrols we had to evade had not helped. I suggested that we keep going, but Wrack was the first to protest.

"Need to be in good shape when we reach the city. Not a good idea to be tired."

I wondered if Kelhene would argue. She had been setting a hard pace for much of the day, sweat cutting complicated paths down the dust across her back as she forged ahead of us. She had also been ignoring me, so it hadn't been all bad.

Around us, the road was pushing through increasing growth, plants towering in extraordinary bursts of different shades of crimson, mixed with occasional yellows and the odd greens of the giant hagweed. The air was full of strange and exotic scents, cloying in my nose and throat.

We were past most of the farms, now, and the ground was rising towards a high ridge. A stream was chortling under a low stone bridge that looked like it had been lurking there for centuries, and I pointed to an open area near where the stream formed a small pool. Wrack shook his head. "Going to be teeming with insects" he pointed out. Being that we had been irritated by glittering, sneaky bugs throughout the day, the thought of facing a throng of them did not appeal. "Do better over there."

There was a hard outcropping of grey stone, a remnant of the badlands we had escaped, like a pustule on the rich verdant red. It was about fifty yards from the road, above the bridge, with no prospect of soft rest about it. Both Kelhene and I together protested. Unusual for us to agree on anything.

Kelhene picked a third direction, directly away from the road at right angles. "I suggest we try over there."

I automatically shook my head. "There's nowhere to camp in that direction."

Kelhene spun and glowered at me. "You're an expert on this area, are you? I doubt that!" she rasped. "I think there's a clearer area that way."

Wrack chuckled. "You saying you know this area, Kelhene? Or is that just a guess?"

Kelhene turned her actinic gaze onto Wrack. Unfortunately for her, he was immune, as I knew all too well. He shrugged, and set off in precisely the opposite direction to Kelhene's proposal. "Coming?" he asked over his shoulder.

I shrugged. "Might as well" I replied coolly, amused at Kelhene's discomforture. She looked at us both despairingly, and then followed grudgingly.

By the time Wrack found a suitable camp, we were deep into darkness. We were all tired and hungry, but food was not on the agenda. Wrack said he would keep the first watch. I didn't argue, and curled up on the least hard patch of ground to sleep, after making sure that Kelhene wasn't going to annoy Wrack.

I woke, mostly because someone was nudging me in the ribs with his toe. "Your watch, Sorrel" Wrack growled. I was enveloped in velvet black. I could not see Wrack, nor anything else – no moonlight, no stars, nothing. I knew there was a blanket of solid cloud above us and red trees on each side, but there was no hint of either. I would have appreciated a fire, but it would have been visible in this darkscape for miles, and the Chasm was, as always, too warm to need such a luxury. I mumbled something about being awake, and stumbled to my feet.

Wrack paused beside me. "Stop harassing Kelhene, Sorrel" he murmured. "If I didn't know better I'd wonder if you were the jealous type."

I snarled invective at the suggestion. He thought *I* was jealous that Kelhene was chasing him? I caustically told him he was wrong in absolutely every particular. He sighed, and I felt him squeeze my shoulder, either companionably or out of irritation. I pulled away; he sighed again, and stalked into the murk to settle down across the camp from Kelhene. I really didn't understand what was going through his head. Maybe dragons just couldn't comprehend humans. I paced warily around the edge of our clearing, feeling my way, working out what, if anything, I could perceive. I couldn't do much good as a watch-woman if there was no light.

I could hear Wrack settling down. A tree tried to poke me in the eye with a low branch, and I bit back a curse. This was hopeless. There was nothing useful I could do, except stand still and listen.

The soft whisper of a breeze. The occasional rustle of leaves. The sudden rasp of a creature's call. I was no woods-woman. I had no idea what had generated that low coughing sound. It could be a frightened rabbit, or else the leader of a pack of wolves about to launch themselves at us. Or else some other strange and nightmarish monstrosity that had escaped from some twisted imagination to come and devour us slowly. I'm good at inventing terrors to worry about in the dark.

I couldn't even judge the passage of time. Had I been on watch for an hour or for three? Was it Kelhene's turn yet? I dearly wanted to go and kick her awake. I was still sweating, feeling the droplets trickling down my back. I really wished that for once the canyon could cool down a bit.

A light blossomed to my left. I almost shouted. It was brilliant, blinding, the sudden radiance scorching my straining eyes. I stared towards it, about to kick the other two awake, before realising that it was very distant through the trees. A spike pointing at the sky, a needle stabbing at the clouds that it was bathing in colour. It flared radiantly like a frozen fire, yellow-orange, then changing to violet and then blue, before vanishing again, leaving the clearing even blacker. Had I really seen that strange outburst of luminance? How near had it been? My instinct was that it was far away, with trees and branches between us and it. If it was close, then we could be in trouble. I strained my eyes towards it, wondering if it would shine again.

I had almost given up, when my eyes were assailed again. Another blaze, almost the same as the first, except that this started in vivid emerald green before flaming into blue and then violet, and then into deep, burning red, painting the trees round me with blood. It was definitely some distance from us, and the spike must be at least eighty feet tall, if not higher, for us to see it.

Darkness again. The forest was still growling, chirruping and soughing. I growled back at it, and waited. No more midnight excitement, though. The distant finger remained lifeless. I gave up and went to kick Kelhene awake.

117

My dreams were lit up by a mysterious spire, glowing balefully.

It did not surprise me that the spike was visible in daylight. Above the trees it rose as if to hold up the sky, seeming even taller than the lantern trees that were lighting the landscape, a crystal stiletto threatening the clouds. The tower had to be two miles away, but it dominated the horizon as we got moving. Kelhene dug up some roots which were hard to chew, bitter of taste and did not fill the belly. Pretty pointless, really. She said they were the only sustenance she could find. I reckoned she just wanted to make us suffer.

The road was sloping downwards slightly, the spike directly in our path. I gestured at it, describing what I had seen in the night. Kelhene had seen similar flares, and seemed unimpressed. "Lloruk work" she said shortly.

And then the ground twitched beneath our feet. All around me, the red grass was vibrating as though we were on the surface of a tambourine. I flung out my hands to stay stable, crying out in alarm, and then the motion was gone. The land seemed as solid as it had been a minute before... but I stood in alarm for a moment longer, all confidence in the certainty of the solid earth stripped from me. Wrack looked equally shaken, but Kelhene seemed unflustered.

"Earthquake" she said in a matter-of-fact tone. "We get them now and then. Don't you have them on the surface?"

I shook my head, but Wrack nodded. "Not in our region" he replied. "But in other areas. Lulvantri, Furdintaal... and there was a big quake sixty years ago in Maalrech. Nearly destroyed the town of Durgnerri."

Vague memories from school surfaced. "Also the fall of Malurtrin's walls" I said slowly. "At the time the Belkiri said it was a miracle."

Wrack nodded. "Almost certainly an earthquake. The Belkiri were lucky. All logic says they should have lost that siege."

Kelhene looked between us blankly. "Ancient history" I explained. "Two rival cities, a long siege. The Belkiri claimed they won with divine help."

Wrack chuckled. "And the Malurtrin survivors said they used forbidden elven sorcery."

Kelhene looked alarmed. "Did they?"

I shook my head. "It was in 1330-something. Eight hundred years ago. They didn't understand about earthquakes then."

Kelhene asked about the history of the surface lands. Wrack and I struggled to remember anything of the tangled events of the last thousand years. The dragon lords extending their grip over Sendaal, Darshaali warlords and the Strianni empire that spanned a third of the world before it disintegrated. An entirely unsuccessful attempt to explain the industrial revolution and the advent of iron – Kelhene just looked at us blankly, not grasping anything we were trying to describe. It was easier to tell her about Varlish raiders from across the ocean, the Shentrini uprising and the Werin peace accord. By unstated agreement, neither Wrack nor I talked about our war. Some things were too close, too raw. The stories took our thoughts away from the drudgery of the trek, but I don't think Kelhene learned much of any use to her about the world we came from.

By my estimate we had walked two more miles, and there seemed no end to the forest. The road here was obviously well-travelled. Twice we had to duck into the trees as a loaded wagon drawn by a pair of olgreks trundled past. The needle was taller, easily visible through the canopy of trees, but now there were more spines clawing at the sky to each side of the big one. In daylight they were glittering crystals of sapphire and emerald, diamond and agate. The trees thinned, and at last I could look out and see the lloruk city properly, sprawled alongside the forest. It looked like a sculpture spun from molten glass. There were towers of gem and crystal, blue and silver and amber. Narrow bridges soared between them like wings. Thinner spires rose within the structures, the entire focus at the heart of the city being the gigantic spike that I had seen in the night. It rose towards the clouds, lording itself over the rest of the city, walkways and bridges leading always towards its might. My estimate had been wrong. It was over four hundred and fifty feet high, twice as tall as any other structure, and it couldn't be less than fifty feet wide at its lowest point where it emerged from a surrounding sea of low buildings. A gossamer thread ran from near the top of the spire out across the sky, soaring above the lesser towers in the city and going off into the wide expanse of air beyond.

We were still quarter of a mile from the edge of the city. We had all paused at the edge of the trees, staring at the sprawl of glittering gems that was Ilkadala. I had no idea how long it had shone there – I could see no signs of age within its heights. It could have been a year or a millennium old. There were tiny figures moving amidst the shards of glass, crossing the bridges and climbing narrow stairs that twisted round the spires like string on a bobbin. The road led towards the city, with no obvious cover that would disguise our progress. Ilkadala had to be up to a mile across. At a rough estimate there were a thousand buildings. Our friends could be anywhere within that maze of crystal. Our chances of finding them were infinitesimal.

I shook my head despairingly, voicing my feelings.

Kelhene turned on me savagely. "So you intend to abandon them, then?" she snapped. "Give up? Walk away and leave them to the lloruk?"

Wrack tried to make some conciliatory murmur, and Kelhene turned on him, still bitter. I was staring at the nearest way into the city, trying to make sense of what I could see. The guards, needless to say, were more graalur. Passing along the paths near the entrance were humans, in the ubiquitous leather skirts that everyone in the Chasm seemed to wear. Wagons and cargoes were being transported in and out of the city, the bustle of trade that was common to every culture and race. But I could see nothing that could be lloruk anywhere. My eyes are pretty good, and though we were a long way away I was sure I could have seen these mythical beings if they were by the entrance. I looked across at Kelhene.

"There are graalur guarding the city."

She nodded curtly at the statement of the obvious. I persevered, gesturing at the distant human figures. "And the humans?"

"Slaves, of course" she replied.

"Lots of slaves in the city?" I hazarded. At her irritated nod, I grinned. I knew what we could do.

It was not as easy as I had hoped. By night, the city glowed. Every building seemed to shimmer in some shade of bright. So much for my hopes of sneaking in through the darkness. On the other hand, as we neared the edge of the city, the flickering glamours in violet, blue and scarlet, orange and vermilion made our faces unrecognisable even to each other. The graalur were alert enough, though, looking around suspiciously. Kelhene solved that concern in a few moments, unhooking half her harness to leave herself topless. That kept the attention of the graalur guards we passed. They were more interested in ogling her than worrying about her reason for using their entrance. Not that Wrack was averse to admiring Kelhene's curves – I saw him eyeing her sidelong as we strode onto the city streets.

My attentions were on the extraordinary structures around us. At a distance the city had been eye-catching; close to, it was even more impressive. Knife-like towers of milky glass and marble, gold veins glittering in the light gleaming from the walls. Soaring spires, narrow bridges between them at dangerous heights, platforms extending out to give high vantage points. Walkways of smooth white stone with occasional blue markers that meant nothing to me embedded into the ground. I still couldn't hazard a guess as to how old the city really was.

It was well into the night, and the streets were still bustling. Most of the pedestrians were human slaves, busy about their unknown tasks. Some were carrying packages or bundles, others hurrying from place to place with no obvious purpose. Most wore harnesses and kilts like ours, but some were virtually nude. Their eyes were dull, downcast, no interest in us as they passed. More alarming were the graalur patrols, gangs each of three strutting warriors who acted as though they owned the city. Perhaps they did – I had still seen no sign of the supposed lloruk overlords who were the alleged masters of the city. If this was their metropolis, there were very few of them occupying it. Two graalur patrols eyed us suspiciously (or else were just admiring Kelhene) – I was afraid they would demand to know who we were, but no questions were forthcoming. I was relieved that I had persuaded the other two that carrying any weapons would be a recipe for discovery – there was no way we could have hidden even a small knife from the graalur scrutiny. I wished I could have worn my leather jacket, but it would have stood out like a coal in snow. I had stashed it at the edge of the jungle – I just hoped I could find it when we emerged. I felt naked without it, mostly because I was, virtually.

Not all the inhabitants were human or graalur. Other creatures were more startling sights. One kind were bird-men, winged with feathers that spread from shoulder to fingertip, their heads beaked. Their chests were gigantic, their lower limbs atrophied so that they walked stiffly on splayed feet. Kelhene whispered to us that they were creations of the Iloruk, used to carry messages when the skywires (whatever they were) were too slow. Another creature that caused me to shiver at its passage was an emaciated, almost skeletal figure, human in basic form save that two pairs of arms grew from its shoulders, and it had only a single dark red eye in its forehead. Even Kelhene quaked at the sight of its pale blue skin stretched tight across its features. What we did not see were any Iloruk, and I became more certain that the famed rulers of the Chasm were not really here at all.

Our goal was not to hunt unhumans but to find the people from the Valley. My plan, such as it had been, had been to walk in openly and march through the city as if we had the right to be there until we saw something to guide us to them. I had not understood just how vast and complex Ilkadala was. Towers rose around us. I could not even hazard a guess as to the purpose of most of them. When I could make an identification, it was speculation at best – one tower might be a refectory, if the mouth-watering smells from within could be believed. Another looked like some kind of cart-store, with a wide door and a smooth slope to give easy access, but no obvious stable near it to harness the wagons. The pathways wound and wriggled between the spires, no visible reason to their patterns. Everywhere there were protrusions and outcroppings of glass that jutted into the ways, glittering with light and sharp edges that made no sense. Occasionally patterns swirled within the crystal – my suspicion was that the twisting shapes in vivid blue were akin to writing, and would be clear to the city's unhuman occupants. To us, they were the source of headaches if we watched them churn and move for too long.

"This is hopeless" Kelhene whispered after we had walked for nearly an hour. "We've no chance of finding anyone in this!"

Wrack glowered at her, impatient at her despair. "Has to be something we can spot" he growled.

I was beginning to agree with Kelhene. We were standing near yet another spire, its ribbed sides rising perpendicular to the ground. There was a doorway into it, the opening a truncated diamond. A slave was emerging, clad in a loincloth only. I stepped boldly into her path. "Where are the new slaves?" I asked bluntly in lloruk.

The woman looked at me. She had to be no more than twenty. She also looked scared. "Please" she murmured. "I have done nothing wrong. I do as I am told."

Beside me Kelhene muttered something confused. I took the woman by the arm. "All I need to know is where to find the slaves they have brought in recently" I said firmly. My mastery of the lloruk tongue had improved vastly in the last few days. The slave-woman shook her head again, still fearful. "I do not know" she answered.

Wrack muttered something coarse. I let the woman go, and moved on, keeping my eyes peeled.

We asked two more slaves, with similar lack of response. I was beginning to concur that this was quite hopeless. Kelhene was scowling, and I felt that every graalur that walked past us was about to seize us. Wrack was sweeping his eyes across the streets, his muscles taut under his skin.

The fourth slave I questioned was more forthcoming.

"They would have been taken to the chambers below the tormel tower" she answered. She was older than the last slave I'd questioned, in her fifties, her bare skin lined by age and ill-use – I had no doubt that most of the white lines on her body were scars from being whipped. I looked at her blankly, stumbling over thanks, before asking her how to find the tormel tower, trying not to mispronounce the unfamiliar word. She looked at me with some surprise, but obediently pointed along one of the pathways to our right.

"That way" she hissed. "The third tower... the silver diamonds." She pulled out of my grip and stumbled swiftly along a different path to that she had pointed out to us, not waiting for a moment. Wrack raised his eyebrow. I just shrugged. We had an indication of where to go.

The slave-woman's description of the silver diamonds led us straight to our goal. The third tower's dark blue translucent glass was encircled by two bands of silver lozenges that were extruded out of the smooth surface. The doorway was another truncated diamond... and a female graalur stood guard, a short staff in her grip. Kelhene's bared attributes were unlikely to hold her attention. I murmured a suggestion to Wrack about what might catch her interest, trying without much success to keep a straight face. He was not amused. Kelhene glared at us.

"This is no time for stupid jokes, Sorrel! How do we get past that guard, assuming this is the right place?"

"Anything you can do from the magerealm, Sorrel?" Wrack asked quietly.

I looked at the solidly-built graalur and thought briefly. Did I really want to delve into the magerealm? The thought of the likely pain chilled me. I shook my head briefly to the other two. "We don't need to" I whispered back. There was no one else in the immediate area. I gestured at the woman. "Three of us, one of her. Speed and surprise."

Kelhene blanched, but Wrack was in agreement. I suspected that the chance to take physical action was much of the reason for him accepting my proposal. He walked forward, and we had to traipse after him to avoid being left standing like lost children. This was my plan – I was not letting him take the lead. I strode past him, and as I reached the graalur woman, I inclined my head to her. "We need to knock you out" I said firmly. She looked at me blankly, and I slammed my fist into her stomach – hard.

She gasped and doubled over, and Wrack's fist was underneath her chin as her head came down. The second blow swung her up again, and Kelhene and I seized her arms, dragging her backwards bodily into the tower she had been guarding. Clean, swift, almost silent. Inside the door the chamber filled the full interior of the tower, lit by the same glowing glass. Spiral stairs rose around the inside, but otherwise the chamber was empty. The graalur was only semi-conscious – once we were out of sight from the doorway I let her slump to the ground. Then I kicked her in the head, hard. Pretty savage, but I did not want her raising the alarm – and the alternative was to kill her. I wasn't going to kill even a graalur if I didn't need to.

Kelhene reached for the short staff the guard had been holding. "Careful of this" she growled. "If this hits you with the gem alight, it'll hurt or even paralyse."

I hadn't even seen the dull red gem in the end of the rod. "Now you tell us!" I griped.

"You didn't give me a chance!" Kelhene remonstrated.

Wrack snarled at us to be silent. "Where now?" he asked. I shook my head to say I didn't know, looking around for some indications of what this tower was. Wrack didn't wait. "This way" he said dictatorially. He had spotted a dark opening in the floor, and was already making his way downwards. I shrugged at Kelhene, and followed.

The ramp angled round and down, at a far steeper gradient than I found comfortable. The walls were pale, unglowing stone, unlike the misty glass of the walls above the surface. From below there was a deep, monotonous pounding sound, a single slow thudding. If the drumming had been a double-beat, I would have feared we were hearing some gigantic heart beat. As it was, it sounded more like a mechanical pump.

The only light apart from the glow from the surface glass was a dull blue luminance crawling up the slope from the chamber below. Wrack slowed, flattening himself against the wall to reduce the chance of the occupants of the area seeing him, before peering around warily. Wrack having to be cautious, worrying about force majeure - I was mildly amused. After a moment he turned and beckoned before moving forwards. I walked down, glad to be off the steep slope, into the invitingly empty area.

The room we were invading was circular, the same width as the tower above us. More diamond doorways, apparently devoid of doors, opened in five places around its circumference. In the floor, five round holes were covered by frosted glass, each hole accompanied by a marble pillar topped with tiny dull coloured stones and a minute forest of black metal spikes. From the ceiling hung down around a dozen segmented tubes of dull blue metal, each nearly long enough to reach the patterned mosaic floor.

There was no obvious source for the dull beat that thudded almost painfully around us. I could feel its rhythm reverberating within my chest-bone. I could not even tell if it came from the side or from below us, though I suspected the latter. The chamber was alien, its purpose incomprehensible; I could finally believe that the mysterious lloruk existed to use this apparatus for strange and nightmarish purposes.

Kelhene was behind me, and she whispered something in astonishment. I raised my eyebrows. "Seen anything like this before? It mean anything to you?"

She shook her head. "The lloruk use machines and impossible objects – no way we can understand them."

Wrack growled something about madness from the elf-lloruk war. I shivered, remembering stories from childhood about the strange machines that the two races had used in their cataclysmic conflict. If this strangeness down here was akin to the stories – but we didn't have time to rubberneck.

"Anything particular catching your eye?" I asked brusquely.

She gestured at the opening on our left. "The passages – they look to go on forever!"

I hadn't even looked through any of the doorways. I remedied the omission, studying the way she was indicating. Kelhene was right – there was a tunnel heading directly away from us, with openings off it, but no visible end. I looked across our chamber – the opening nearly opposite me seemed the same. We would have to check down each of them.

A twitch of movement to one side of me was the first warning that the city had its own plans for us.

Chapter Fourteen

Wrack was looking at one of the pillars, and then knelt to peer through the grainy white glass of the floor. As he did so, I saw one of the segmented tubes twitch, and then coil sideways towards him, about to grip him around his neck. After an instant staring at the impossibly-moving inanimate object, I yelled a warning and ducked hastily, as the tube nearest to me decided to copy its fellow.

I didn't have time to worry about Wrack or Kelhene. I flung myself flat as a tentacle endeavoured to throttle me. It hissed through the space my head had occupied an instant before, and I instinctively lashed out at it with my fist, wishing I had a sword. I connected – the metal was warm and smooth, but it was also hard. My knuckles stung from the impact, but the tentacle drew back. Behind me Kelhene was crying out – she had not moved so fast, and a tentacle had tightened around her stomach, lifting her off the ground. She swiped at it with the staff in her hand – another tentacle struck, winding round her arm, and the staff went flying, slamming into the ground only a couple of feet from me, the red gem glowing balefully. I twisted to avoid it – another tentacle scraped across my stomach. My movement had thrown off its attempt to grapple me. I glanced around hastily. Wrack was lurking in a doorway, two tentacles waving in his general direction, unable to reach him but ensuring he did not venture out. Kelhene was right off the ground, two tentacles tangling her tightly. Three more tentacles were questing for me. I rolled again, throwing off their efforts, hoping I could persuade them to tangle each other. No such luck. The limbs were being directed by more than just instinct. I wished I knew how they could see – none of them appeared to have any eyes or other senses.

I rolled again, but this time one of the tentacles wrapped around my left ankle. It yanked hard, pulling me sideways. I grabbed desperately for the staff Kelhene had thrown. A second tentacle clawed at my right arm, and I felt myself hauled bodily off the ground, twisting sideways. The staff was only a few inches from my left hand in this ungainly posture – I lunged, seizing it. The gem had become dull, lifeless. I tried to turn my head to see Kelhene, but I could not move enough in the tightening grip of the tentacles.

"Kelhene!" I bellowed. "How do I turn on the staff?!"

"Slide the central ring towards the gem!" she yelled back from behind and above me. Central ring? There was an unpleasant thumping sound from the right, and Wrack cried out. I was hanging upside down, and trying to concentrate on the staff. Yet another tentacle was trying to pull my arm away from my face, while I could feel something sliding across my breasts in a fashion that would have earned it a stinging slap in the face if it had been a man. My hand was holding the staff by the middle, right on the central ring. I couldn't bring my other hand anywhere near it to change my grip. If I stopped clutching it as the tentacles whirled me around again I was likely to lose it, and it was the only hope of escape that I could perceive. I took a desperate risk and loosened my grip, letting it slide through my hand until I could shove at the central ring with my thumb. Volg it, the thing was stiff! It suddenly gave, sliding a short distance before clicking into another position – and the gem flared into life.

The tentacles lurched, and I suddenly felt the one around my ankle release. I swung downwards, only supported by the two tangling my arms, expecting to hit the floor hard.

No floor below me. Instead, I was dropping into one of the dark holes that had previously been covered by glass. The covering had vanished mysteriously. I clutched at the tentacle across my chest with my right hand as my arms were released, stopping my fall for a moment – I lunged with the glowing gem at the tentacle that had previously been holding my left arm. I connected – there was a smell of hot metal, but the tentacle seemed undamaged. The tentacle I was holding onto straightened – I began to slide down it as though it was a greasy pole, neatly into the dark opening beneath me.

I flung the staff, red gem still gleaming dully, until it slammed into one of the pedestals. I didn't have time to see the result – more importantly to me, it meant I had both hands free. I grabbed at the tentacle with my newly-free hand, halting my descent. The glass had slid into a recess in the edge of the pit – I yanked my leg up and jammed my foot into the opening, levering myself up and out. A tentacle endeavoured to shove me back down – this wasn't a greasy pole, it was a merciless lance. I rolled under its blow and wound up almost tumbling onto the staff. I pulled away hastily to avoid blasting myself with its gem, and the tentacle that had been striking at me struck my back. I gasped in pain and twisted round, grabbing the offender in both hands before hauling it bodily so that its end hit the staff.

There was a satisfying crackle of fire, and the tentacle jerked away, just like a man touching a red hot iron. I seized the staff by its middle and dived for the opening where Wrack had been lurking. Two more tentacles lashed out – both missed by a mile. I'm good at dodging.

Wrack grabbed me, hauling me into the dubious cover of the side passage. I grinned at him wanly, avoiding spiking him with the crimson gem.

"Thought you were going the same way as Kelhene" he growled.

I shook my head. "Not a chance" I said firmly. "If I'd got caught, you'd have had to rescue me – no way was I going to need rescuing by you."

He glared at me. The tentacles had slid back into their original, flaccid state, trying to look harmless and welcoming. Not good actors, those tentacles. The deep beat was unchanged, which I thought was probably a good thing. No alarms sounding, which surprised me – not that I was complaining. From one of the glassed-over pits I could hear a knocking – Kelhene, trying to get out. I looked at Wrack levelly.

"Any bright ideas?" I asked without further levity. He shook his head grimly.

I looked further down the corridor where we were lurking. Openings on each side, but the main length was dead straight, with no end in sight. The walls were glowing glass, pale violet in colour. What that meant I had no clue about, nor about where to go.

I looked back at the main chamber. I could try burning out the tentacles with fire from the magerealm. It didn't appeal as a plan. No certainty it would work, and I did not like the idea of going into the realm. No, this called for subtlety and sneakiness. Not originally my strong points, but I had learned a lot in Wrack's mansion. I whispered a brief outline of the plan to Wrack – I wasn't sure if I needed to worry about the tentacles hearing my intentions, but I didn't want to take the chance. From his expression, he wasn't impressed. Tough. I didn't give him a chance to object or to suggest anything better.

Four wary steps to the edge of Kelhene's prison. Two tentacles were hanging down near it, doubtless the ones that had molested her. I was walking very slowly, almost on tiptoe. What would make them come alive? I had the staff ready. My hope was that even if they were not destroyed by its touch they would try and avoid it. Two more steps. Walking softly seemed to be keeping the tentacles from reacting. Beside the frosted glass disc there was a small silver wheel – I just hoped I was right in guessing its purpose.

I slid down onto my haunches, and gingerly reached for the wheel. Wrack was waiting for me – as I stretched out my hand, he moved into the chamber, gesticulating obscenely at the tentacles. His motion caught their attention, and kept them from focussing upon me. I tried to turn the wheel, watching Wrack diving into safety as the tentacles endeavoured to grope his nether regions. It might be fun for them if they succeeded, but Wrack obviously didn't want to play.

The wheel did not turn. It seemed stiff and solid. I squeezed harder, trying to twist it. It did not budge. I restrained the temptation to swear and tried turning it the other way. It moved smoothly, easily, and the glass began to slide to one side. The trouble was, the tentacles suddenly decided that molesting me might be more fun than going after Wrack. The two nearest ones swung towards me, the tips twitching like eels out of water. I ducked sideways, trying to finish opening Kelhene's prison. Wrack was yelling something, his deep baritone rumbling. I didn't have time to worry about him. One tentacle raked across my shoulder. I rolled, letting its embrace grasp thin air. The other was trying to intercept me or, if that failed, drive me towards a third tentacle. I flung myself flat and almost toppled into Kelhene's abode. She was trying to climb the walls, without obvious success. The chamber beneath the glass was smooth-sided and quite deep. She would need a rope. I thrust upwards with the staff, hoping to incapacitate a tentacle. I had no compunction about using a crippled enemy as a ladder for a friend – or even for Kelhene.

My attempt to clobber the groping metal tendril missed completely, mostly because another tentacle had taken the opportunity to sneak up on me and tangle around my throat. I panicked, gasping for breath as it squeezed, for a moment feeling I was in serious trouble. I lashed at it wildly, catching it squarely with the gem on the staff. More luck than judgement, I had to accept, but it worked. The tentacle smoked and stopped throttling me. I hauled on it, and it stretched. I swept it into the pit while hastily evading another. Kelhene called some variant on thanks. I was too busy to take note.

Wrack was duelling with two tentacles. I was more concerned with my original assailant, which had resumed its efforts to entangle me. I stabbed at it with the staff, and it reared back in alarm. Nice to know I could frighten it. I glanced round hastily – Wrack had grabbed both his enemies, and was trying to knot them together, with noticeable lack of success. Kelhene was most of the way out of her prison, but her rope was starting to twitch. I bellowed at her to move her arse. My own opponent lashed at my face – I clipped it smartly with the side of the staff, which it ignored. I ducked again, and found myself teetering on the edge of an opening that hadn't been there before. Another of the glass circles had slid aside sneakily. The tentacle swiped at me – I grabbed at it, using it to regain my balance. It reciprocated by coiling around my arm. I shoved the gem against it, and it smoked satisfyingly, the grip loosening enough for me to wrench myself free. Kelhene was diving for a doorway, two tentacles wriggling in pursuit. Wrack was backed into a corner, edging around the wall towards a different opening. I eyed my opposition, dangling limp, and made for Wrack. Two quick jabs with my staff incapacitated one of his threats, and he grabbed at the other, swinging on it to dive into Kelhene's retreat. I flung myself forwards across the floor, below the level of the tentacle that I had stunned previously which wanted to re-enter the fray. It scraped across my shoulders, but could not get a purchase before I was beyond its reach.

We stood, gasping for breath, sweating a small ocean, but briefly jubilant.

"What now?" Kelhene asked quietly, shattering our glee. "They must know we're here."

Wrack chuckled deep in his chest. "Unless they're deaf. Let them come!"

I grinned at him. He oozed optimism. I could have hugged him, but he would doubtless have got the wrong idea. I looked down our corridor. "Let's see what's down here."

I fancied that I could already hear the sound of feet on the stairs leading down into the main chamber. I turned, trying to be resolute. I was beginning to feel somewhat trapped, despite Wrack's apparent confidence. We hadn't seen another way out, and the lloruk obviously knew their way around this place. If there was another way down, there would be guards there, too.

Wrack was having to duck as we made our way along the corridor. The roof was barely six feet high, and even Kelhene, two inches taller than me, was lowering her head warily.

The first two openings led to empty chambers. Cells, I suspected aloud. Kelhene and Wrack did not disagree. The third opening was more unpleasant. Six oblong slabs, formed of some coppery metal, each about three foot high and large enough to lay a human body upon them. Two of them had such a cargo. Both male, both nude… both dead. Skin even paler than was the norm down here, eyes open and staring. For a mercy, I did not recognise either of them, but Kelhene cried out, gesturing at the man on the furthest slab.

"That's Elvhion!" I could see tears welling in her eyes. Wrack slid a comforting arm around her shoulders. I felt for a pulse, but I was rightly pessimistic. There was no sign of injury or indication of the cause of death. The hieroglyphics on the walls of the chamber meant nothing to me, and apparently nothing to Kelhene either. I motioned her towards the doorway, and Wrack edged her out of that grim mortuary.

The next chamber contained a morass of strange structures – narrow tubes of green and purple crystal containing flowing blue liquid that tangled like mating snakes, tall pillars of red copper into which the tubes nosed and emerged, discs of black and silver apparently suspended in mid-air. There was an acrid, chemical tang to the air. My jasq was itching in my side, and I felt a deep unease at the contents of this room. Some deviltry was being worked here, far more twisted, I suspected, than the mere corpses of men next door.

Wrack was shaking his head. "Haven't time to waste with this junk" he growled. I could see the worry-lines on his forehead. We all knew the lloruk would be upon us in minutes at most.

Kelhene was already moving into the next chamber. I took one last look at the bubbling fluids in the spaghetti of tubing. As I turned away, though, my jasq was aching more. There was a copper vat on one corner of the chamber, the size of a large barrel, with a glass top. I peered inside, half-expecting to find another body. Instead, the vat was half-full of an unpleasant-looking amber liquid, and within the juice were half a dozen purple slimes, each the size of a fist. They were moving, their shapes changing as they oozed through their medium. An acidic smell hit me, the foul stench tearing at my throat, and then I felt my jasq shivering within my side. It was not the same impact as when Wrack changed, more a feeling of gut-wrenching nausea, worse than the hangover I had had after Merik's thirtieth birthday party. I retched, my skin crawling as though my entire body was immersed in the foul vat in front of me.

Strong hands hauled me away from the vat and into the corridor. Wrack was gazing down at me, demanding to know what was wrong. I was still gasping, trying to recover my breath, but the nausea into which I had plunged had receded. Not gone, no, but it was no longer the demand to empty my stomach that had been incapacitating me moments before.

More questions. I shook my head. I couldn't just lie here. I still felt somewhat uneasy in my stomach, but the need to move was more critical. I struggled upright, feeling as though my legs were made of the spaghetti of the piping. Wrack was staring at me, demanding to know what had happened. I spluttered something about the tank being foul. I wished I had just one of the grenades Gandruli and Vebrish had been working on – vicious things that turned ordinary flares into lethal weapons. I wouldn't hesitate to use one to destroy that vat and the chamber round it. Wrack put his hand to the side of my head – I brushed his fingers aside irritably.

Kelhene's cry of triumph put paid to Wrack's concerns about me. She was gesturing from the opening on the far side of the corridor, peering through a grill inset into a metal door. "I've found them!" she exclaimed, her face alight with relief. Her expression changed as she saw me. I suspected I looked as bad as I felt.

Wrack nudged me towards Kelhene. I gritted my teeth and silently told the contents of my stomach to stay put, and followed them. The doorway was hedged around with glyphs that doubtless told the lloruk about the contents of the room beyond. The door itself was solid brass, with rivets and the narrow opening through which Wrack was peering now. No lock or handle, though. I looked blearily at Wrack, not trusting myself to speak much yet. Wrack was shoving at the door, trying to force it open. It looked as obdurate as a stone wall. Kelhene was pushing at the hieroglyphics, seeing if they were some kind of concealed lock. They obviously weren't. I touched the door experimentally. It felt like brass as well as looking like it. No way would it open without the correct key... and there was no keyhole or other indication. Possibly one of the mechanisms in the tube room, or back in the tentacle chamber would do it. The chance of finding it was negligible. I wondered about trying the staff, before realising that I was no longer holding it. I must have dropped it when the nausea hit me. I wondered briefly about going looking for it again, but it could be anywhere in the tubes chamber. I didn't want to go back in there. Not for anything. Anyhow, I didn't think the gem on the staff was likely to do anything useful against a solid brass door.

Kelhene's face was bleak as she struggled with the door. To be so close and yet to be unable to release them – it was just the sort of cruelty that seemed to typify the lloruk. I glanced over my shoulder, wondering what had become of the graalur guards, why we were not already being hunted. My stomach still felt as though a swarm of butterflies were having violent sex inside it. Fun for them, but not for me.

Wrack turned to me. "You all right, Sorrel?" I nodded, not risking saying anything. He seemed satisfied with that. I was dreading what he was going to say next, because I was already asking myself the same question in my head. I heard him ask it. I didn't answer. We couldn't leave Darhath and the others trapped in this appalling place, and we wouldn't have another chance to get in here. The only hope we had of getting them out was if I could do something through the magerealm.

I just didn't know if I had the courage.

Wrack gripped me tighter. "Come on, Sorrel" he growled. "Get on with it! Ought to be able to tear that open with sorcery."

"The magerealm. It hurts when I use the jasq" I stuttered. "Hurts a lot."

"What?" His surprise and alarm was genuine and intense, if monosyllabic. I

134

repeated what I had said. Wrack spun me round to face him. "Why the volg didn't you tell me this before?" he demanded.

Kelhene snarled something behind us, telling us we were running out of time. She had to be right – the graalur, or something worse, would come hunting us any moment.

"Talk about this later" Wrack growled. "I'll change, use fire to burn the door."

I shook my head. "Don't be an idiot. The corridor's too small for you to change, let alone breathe fire. You'd toast us all."

"We need to do something now" Kelhene snapped.

I couldn't do it. I couldn't take that pain again. I had no idea if I was hurting my body in the real world, now... I just couldn't.

I felt Wrack grip my shoulder gently, his warm body close behind me, supporting me. Kelhene was looking at me uncertainly.

"Come on, Sorrel" Wrack murmured. "You can do it." I leant back against his body, strangely glad to feel him there, unable to tell him that I couldn't do it. Kelhene was staring at me like a sad puppy, willing me to do something for her friends and for her lover. Wrack's hands were on my shoulders, holding me securely.

I couldn't let them down. I couldn't abandon Darhath and the others. I had come this far to get them out. Could I really face the pain again? I turned my head briefly to look up at Wrack. His expression was a mixture of worry and uncertainty. I had been half-expecting him to be demanding that I use the magerealm. If he had been, it would have been easier to refuse. Arguing with Wrack came naturally. But this – he was actually concerned for me, waiting for my choice. Time was ticking past, and the lloruk or their guards had to be getting close. I had to make a decision. I had to stop dithering.

I closed my eyes, clenched my teeth and my fists, and slid into the realm.

Chapter Fifteen

The realm was brighter than I had ever seen it, and it was nothing but hard, angular silver edges. In front of me I could just about make out the shape of the people, just shadows and spines. Across, to one side of me, there was something violet and horrible, nauseating even at over fifteen feet. There were more of the violet obscenities further back. I could feel myself cringing away from them, fear and loathing sweeping across me like an icy shower. Directly in front of me was a glittering red lattice. That had to be the door. Nothing flowing, nothing like the realm that I was used to. How could I breach that geometric pattern quickly, before the pain caught me? I needed time to decide what to do. I wrenched at the zigzag of the door before tumbling out of the realm to escape the pain... that was not there.

I stood for a moment, confused, and then slid back into the other region again, my eyes adjusting to the brilliance. There was no pain! I could have shouted for joy, relief and exultation sending my spirit soaring. There was no pain. The magerealm was not hurting me... this time.

This wasn't the first time it had been painless, only for the agony to reappear the next time I ventured into the brilliance. I realised belatedly that my happiness was probably misplaced. I had work to do, anyhow.

I slammed forward with a fist – just a blue spindle, here – and tore at the lattice more scientifically, trying to rip a hole in it big enough to get through. The etched zigzags that were the door already had a blemish where I had struck at it the first time. I wrenched at the geometry more, carving deeper weals into its mathematical precision, hoping that I was actually achieving something in the real world. Half a minute sufficed to rip the scarlet lattice into twisted fragments, and then I slid back into reality.

There was a large, ragged rip in the brass door, rent as though it had been cardboard. I admired my handiwork. The Grihl Valley people were already scrambling cautiously through the opening I had torn, evading the lethal lacerated edges. My spirits lifted as I saw familiar faces scrambling out of durance vile. Helinhus, who had manned the bolt-thrower. Veldhra, one of the kitchen team – I vaguely recalled that she had been a musician before Muranon fell. Eldhor, who never seemed to smile. Others who I recognised but couldn't name – the small, dumpy woman who worked with Veldhra; the red-haired woman and the tall, dark-haired young man who always seemed to be glued together; the woman with the white hair, despite only seeming to be my age; and a score of others. And there was Darhath, being led out of the cell by Kelhene.

Now all we had to do was get out of this foul place. My momentary high seeped into the floor. We had to face the tentacle chamber again, and there would be guards soon. We had got so far, but we hadn't a hope of getting out of here past those tentacles again, with more than twenty of us. I caught at Wrack's arm as he confidently called to our rescuees to get moving.

"The tentacle chamber..." I began.

"Not going that way" he replied with a grin. "Stairs at the other end of the corridor."

Stairs? Up or down? I didn't have time to ask. Someone had clearly been busy while I had been ripping open the door. We were all moving hastily along the tunnel like frightened rats. Too many people round me to see much. I grinned at the people round me – some of them responded similarly.

At the end, a small chamber, barely large enough for four people to stand in, no obvious purpose to it, on one side of the corridor, and glassy stairs leading up on the other. Good. I didn't like being stuck underground like a mole. A full storey – then yells from the people in the lead. Wrack bawled something about climbing more. I hoped he had some idea what he was doing, but I doubted it. I had by now reached the ground floor chamber, and the steel-blue metal door from this foyer was shivering as it was hammered against hard. No way out here. I was feeling trapped again, and I clenched my teeth to try to drive out the feelings. The stairs went on up. I didn't need a picture painting. I followed the fleeing valley folk further up the stairs. Odds were we were in another of the city spires. Going up wasn't likely to lead us to an easy way out, but it was better than facing Iloruk and guards.

Another floor, another closed door, more stairs. Climbing was hard work. I was glad I was reasonably fit. I straightened my shoulders and pushed myself harder. Some of the others were already looking rather worn. I was gaining on some of them, nearing Helinhus and another bearded man whose name I ought to know, but had forgotten. They seemed to be the leaders of our flight. The next landing gave me a chance to push my way into the lead, only Wrack staying with me.

This circular room occupied the entire floor of the spire we were climbing. Walls of semi-transparent glass, a floor of mosaic in a coloured pattern of sky blue and vermilion that made my eyes water with the clash of hues. Either the lloruk sense of colour was greatly different from ours, or the locals had appalling taste. I suspected the latter. There were half a dozen human slaves, and a pair of alarmed bird-people retreating hastily across a narrow bridge that led to the neighbouring tower. There were five bridges leading off this floor. The escaping birds had firmly closed the brass door they had fled through, and I made a small mental bet that it was bolted from the far side. That left four options, or else the stairs on upwards.

I gestured to Wrack. "Pick a bridge!"

He was weighing up the situation, too. He pointed to the bridge opposite the one the birds had taken. "Looks like the best chance – no one going anywhere near that way to raise the alarm."

The view was brightening as the lantern trees in the middle distance glowed with the local equivalent of dawn. I was looking across the city, trying to get a picture of the other spires. I could see a fine black thread high above the streets, stretching from the wide, tall spire at the far end of the bridge nearest to us. This had to be the gigantic spire that I had seen as we approached the city. I remembered a comment Kelhene had made when we were searching, and that triggered a memory of a conversation with Darhath when we had been awaiting the graalur attack. It felt like a month ago. He had said something about skywires that the lloruk used to travel from city to city. He was standing a few feet from me, staring blankly, Kelhene holding his arm. I pushed past a couple of people and grabbed his other arm. "Darhath! Is that the skywire thing you told me about?"

He turned slowly, his expression still blank. His eyes were empty, like windows into a deserted room. I stared at him. "Darhath?"

He did not reply. Kelhene was shaking her head. "He was like this when we found him" she whispered.

"What happened to him?" I asked automatically, before shaking my head. "We don't have time. Kelhene, is that the skywire there?"

She followed my gaze, and nodded. "I think so. Why?"

"Can we operate it?"

Her expression told me that I had said something entirely impossible. "It's a lloruk thing. We can't make it work."

Her words drenched my optimism for a moment. If we couldn't make it work, we'd be trapped there instead of here. Higher up. Nowhere to go. On the other hand, I was a flyer, a sorceress and I had a basic grasp of mechanics. Could this skywire be any more difficult to handle than a triplane? I grinned briefly at the thought, ignoring the faint stab of pain in my side. Either I had a stitch, or my jasq was complaining. I crossed my fingers that it was the former. "Everyone! This way!"

The bridge was only a couple of feet wide, cantilevered out from the side of the tower. It was made entirely of the clearest glass, as though we would be walking on air. The only concession to our height above the ground was the presence of a glass wall on the left side of the bridge, perhaps three feet high. It would provide something to hold. On the other side... I didn't want to try flying without my aeroplane. I would stay close to the left. I gestured at everyone. "Follow me across!"

Then, after taking a deep breath, I began to walk. I'm not afraid of heights – I'm a pilot – but even I found it unnerving to be treading apparently on nothingness. I just hoped my example would encourage the others to follow me. Glancing down didn't trouble me greatly – I was used to seeing the ground spread out far below me, streets bustling with early risers who at the moment seemed quite unaware of the drama unfolding up here.

I was three quarters of the way across when one of the city guard graalur, bejewelled black harness tight across his broad red shoulders, ventured onto the bridge from the far side. He was carrying one of the gem staffs, glowing brightly even in the dawn light, and he looked quite happy to use it, tusks bared in what was either a grin or a threat.

I couldn't retreat – too many nervous people behind me. I had heard protests and voices of alarm behind me as I had begun to cross. "Back off, graalur" I snarled. "Unless you want to try actually walking on air."

"*You* back off" he answered, unimaginatively. Graalur, I would guess, aren't noted for witty repartee. "You can't come into this tower."

Looking beyond him I could see a similar chamber to the one I had just vacated. There was some kind of structure inside, but no sign of any other occupants. That explained the graalur's decision to take his place on the bridge. If we got there, he would have been seriously outnumbered. Here, he could hold the bridge potentially against us all. I wished I still had a staff of my own. His gem shone red for danger. He looked confident, solidly built, and ready to tip me off the bridge without a second thought.

I heard Wrack snarl something from further back along the bridge. For a moment I wondered about following his advice, but I rejected it an instant later. No way was I going into the magerealm to take this guard out. If the pain returned, it was guaranteed to tip me over. I had to do something fast. Fighting the graalur on this bridge might be madness, but sometimes unexpected insanity was the only answer.

I raised both hands and walked two steps forwards. "All right, I surrend..." - and then I kicked, hard, at the graalur's left ankle. My blow connected, and I grabbed at the low parapet on my left. The graalur's foot went out from under him and he toppled sideways. He instinctively reached for the parapet with his right hand... which was encumbered with the staff. By the time he had released the staff it was too late and he had missed the wall, tumbling sideways off the edge of the bridge. He howled in terror as he fell. I didn't want to watch him drop. The staff tumbled after him. I hauled myself upright again and hastily finished the trek across the bridge, into the spire beyond. A small part of me was telling myself that I had had no choice, but I still didn't like killing a guard, who was just doing his duty, in such a terrifying fashion.

The chamber I ran into was empty, alarmed slaves having already fled our approach. A less eye-damaging mosaic, too, but my attention was taken by the structure that rose almost to the roof of the high chamber. Four ivory tusks rising from the outer corners, curving inwards and sharpening to points which almost touched under the ornately (some would say garishly) painted ceiling. Between the horns an extraordinary and intricate tracery of blue, silver and gold gems and wires glittered in the light. There was a tension in the air that spoke of power within this strange edifice. I had seen something like it before, albeit a quarter the size, in the farm beyond the Grihl Valley. That had been strange and intriguing. This... this was awe-inspiring. Not malevolent, somehow, but it gripped me. It was doing something important, of that I felt sure. What, however, I had no idea.

Not that I had time to examine it in detail. I could definitely hear the sound of feet coming up the smooth stairs from below that wound up to one side of the chamber. A flight below us at the moment, but we'd have company soon. There were some large, ornate wooden seats at the edge of this room – I yelled at the first couple of people off the bridge after me to lend me a hand. The chairs were heavy, but they were also the right size to tumble down the stairs noisily. I heard shouts of alarm and cries of pain after the first one went crashing down, and left my two assistants to struggle with the next couple, waiting a few moments to bag some new victims. I was confident that the furniture onslaught would keep the guards below at bay. I made for the stairs up, taking them two at a time. Behind me my motley rabble of fugitives hastened in my wake.

Another floor. This was nearly as interesting as the chamber below, and far more comprehensible. We wound along a narrow track hugging the edge wall of the tower. The floor in the middle was a map, a relief built up from the tiles, coloured and incredibly detailed. I could see Ilkadala, recognisable to me after only the short time I had been within it, glowing white at the centre of the room. I could even determine the tower we were climbing. I squinted, wondering if some strange magic would enable me to see us within the chamber, but there was nothing so extraordinary. To one side a second Iloruk city shone pale blue in crystal and glass, and beyond that, almost at the far wall, a third, this time in violet. There was a fourth, too, but that did not shine – the towers and streets were black and charred, as though melted by dragonfire. Between the crystal cities hills and lantern trees loomed in miniature, with the lacy webs of the skywires between them. I paused, astonished. I might not be able to see people in the city, but there were dark specks moving, gliding smoothly along the wires. As I looked more closely I could see faint coloured shimmers hovering alongside each fleck, different colours and symbols limning each of the moving skyboats. If I was right in my identification of where we were, the skywire here led half way across the Rift towards the pale blue Iloruk city.

The person behind me prodded me, eager to keep moving, and I reluctantly hurried onwards, trying to explore the map with my eyes as I passed. Some of the skyboats were flanked by symbols in pale blue, others in violet or white, yet more were in reds and amber, greens and darker blues. I couldn't try to work out the meaning of the symbols before I was climbing yet another flight of glassy stairs. If this was the Iloruk route to the skywire, they were much fitter than I had previously given them credit for.

The chamber above contained two skyboats, resting on their sides as a handful of human slaves patched and painted. They looked at us incuriously, and then turned back to their duties as though we were not there. The hulls were dark red, twenty feet long and eight feet wide, flat-bottomed with what seemed like five curving masts growing up from each side of the hull to meet, supporting an inverted keel that ran along the centreline of the structure, eight feet above the body of the vessel. On top of the keel there were a line of metal rods, each topped with a dull metal sphere a foot or more across, making me think of a line of pins on a stand. I could not see how the thing was propelled, let alone steered or braked. There was no obvious place for a pilot to sit.

The stairs led ever upwards. I hoped I was right in my guesses about the skywire. This next flight seemed to last twice as long as each of the previous ones, but it suddenly opened out into the open air. I was standing on a wide platform, easily bigger than the chambers below us. There were no handrails or defences against the elements. If the wind blew hard, it would be a long and eventually terminal drop.

At the far side, there was a narrow, six-sided tower rising up above the roof, a walkway extending from a closed door in the hexagon onto the rooftop. The tower looked too small to be a useful room, or a place for guards to lurk. I turned my attention to the rest of my surroundings.

At the centre of the platform a solid stone pillar, five feet across, rose more than another dozen feet. I gazed at the skywire that it supported. The wire was spun from a bundle of narrower cables, wound together to build a wire than had to be three feet thick. On one side, the cable ran down at an angle, stretching down vertiginously to an anchor point on the ground far below. On the other side of the pillar the skywire began its long journey towards the next lloruk city. From my brief sight of the map two floors below, it passed through half a dozen stone columns or lantern trees before it reached its goal. Before it reached the first such spire, though, dimly visible in the distance, there were a cluster of orange spheres floating above the wire, lifting its bulk. At this range the balls looked like a child's marbles impossibly hanging in the air. In reality, though, each globe must be twenty yards across. I stared at the line of the cable cutting the sky in half. Hanging from it over the platform, ready to travel, was another of the skyboats, the keel directly below the cable, the spheres I had seen on the ones below somehow embedded inside what had to be a tube, not a solid wire. I could guess that in some means the spheres must turn to let the vessel move. A small stepladder led to one of the openings in the side of the hull, and I made for it, yelling at the people behind me to follow. I just hoped the boat would hold us all.

I clambered up the steps, climbing into the gently-swaying craft, only to stop dead. Standing on the deck of the craft stood a tall, slender shape, serpentine neck swaying sideways as jewelled sapphire eyes held my gaze.

I was face to face with a lloruk.

Chapter Sixteen

A smoothly-scaled amber tail scraped across the wooden deck. The lloruk's arms were thin, multiply-jointed, with slender, supple fingers. Long, rich blue robes shrouded most of its body; the golden-scaled neck rose from the top of the robe and was at least a foot long, topped with a diamond-shaped head of the same hue. The virtually-lipless mouth opened. It had a forked tongue to go with the rest of the snake-shape. I had never seen one before, but I knew the descriptions from the old tales.

The lloruk stood, head moving from side to side, tongue flickering between half-open cream lips. I obviously wasn't the cargo it was expecting. "What are you doing here?" it asked softly in the lloruk tongue, and then its eyes widened as more of us scrambled in behind me.

"Hijacking this ship" I answered cheerfully, and walked towards it menacingly. I was completely unarmed, but there were enough people behind me to give weight to my words. "Try anything and we'll throw you overboard."

It backed away - it had a weird, overly-graceful motion, like a dancer. Its gem eyes were fixed upon me. There was a faint hint of cinnamon in the air. It opened its mouth to speak, tongue flicking between its lips, but then grew silent as the skyboat filled swiftly with our numbers. I looked back along the vessel – there were seats lining each edge of the hull, and wooden plinths in the centre. I guessed that it was large enough to take us all – just. I suspected we wouldn't all be able to breathe in at the same moment. I just hoped that the skywire could support our weight. There was no hint of any other skyboat on the roof, nor any indication of how one might appear. It meant we didn't fear immediate pursuit, always assuming that we could get this boat moving. I looked back at the lloruk, who was clearly contemplating diving over the side before we left the safety of the tower.

"Don't try it" I said conversationally. "Now, get this thing moving."

"And if I do not?" it asked sibilantly.

I grinned maliciously. "Can lloruk fly?" A casual wave towards the edge of the tower made sure the lloruk understood my meaning. It nodded calmly, apparently unconcerned by my unsubtle threat.

Something twisted below my ribs, and I realised that the jasq was throbbing as if it were raging with anger. I slid instinctively into the magerealm, realising as I did so what was happening. The lloruk was using sorcery. I didn't have time to try to figure it out - the lloruk was clawing at the flows of light, channelling them together into a binding rope that would entangle and befuddle me, even if it did not burn me. I snarled in fury, and grabbed at the flows. The lloruk had far more skill in this realm than I could have mustered, even when I had been a sorceress previously. But I did not need any skill, here. All I needed to do was to confound the serpent's efforts. During the war I had stood against enemy mages a good many times, and demolishing someone else's magerealm structures was something I could do well.

I swept my mage-arm through the lloruk's structure, twisting my motion to tangle the flows into chaos. There was a blaze of green and orange that engulfed the shadow, and I knew my efforts had not been in vain. I slid out of the realm, my heart and my jasq both thumping, my mouth tasting of lemons. The lloruk was shaking its head, whether in disbelief or to try to see what was going on I neither knew nor cared. I seized the lloruk – its skin was dry and smooth, almost rubbery, not the slimy coils I had expected. The lloruk was gasping and hissing like a punctured tyre, and I chuckled at its astonishment and discomfiture.

"Try that again and I will throw you over the side!" I threatened grandly.

"You are the human we were told of" it said weakly, words slipping through its narrow lips. "You have a jasq. How can this be?"

"I'm just awkward that way" I replied absently.

"You are a contradiction with known lore" hissed the lloruk. I struggled to understand its fluid lloruk language. "Humans cannot have jasqs!"

I laughed. "I like doing impossible things. Now, are you going to move this boat, or learn to fly?"

It turned away from me with abrupt alacrity, moving to the prow, reaching to a small brass wheel just to one side. I realised that I had no way of knowing if its actions were obedience or would plunge us into capture or destruction, and I began

145

to regret my hasty demand, watching the snakeman's swaying torso and delicate hands like a hawk. The lloruk only turned the wheel a small amount, and there was a sudden, eerie whistle. The boat slid into motion, swaying slightly as it began to traverse the skywire. It seemed it was obeying me.

Behind us the roof was suddenly thronged with oncoming graalur, armed with gem-staffs. Three were emerging impossibly from the tiny hexagon tower – I presumed they had been lurking there after all, awaiting reinforcements – but most had evidently come up the stairs. No obvious missile weapons, fortunately. We were moving incredibly slowly, and one of the guards grabbed the forlornly-abandoned stepladder, jumping up it to seize the thick cable, pursuing us hand over hand. She had a staff in a holster at her waist, and a savage grin on her face. She was twenty feet behind us, and would catch us in a dozen seconds at our present rate. I shoved the lloruk aside, ignoring its hissed protest, and spun the wheel a full turn, hoping I was guessing rightly. The skyboat lurched, and its forward motion increased dramatically, bouncing on the wire. There was a terrified yell from behind – the bounce on the cable had jolted the graalur loose. She fell, grabbing at the edge of the tower as she passed it, catching with one hand. Two others leapt to her assistance, and she was hauled to safety. I grinned gleefully, relief flooding my tired body as we swept away from pursuit at the speed of a fast runner. We were still over the city, and by no means out of trouble, but it felt good to be in the sky, even in a thing like this. Up on the surface the Furulyin had been building 'flying boats' for ten years, but they had been nothing like this!

It took us less than three minutes to escape the city, gliding over the streets distantly below us. It took me those minutes to get used to the motion of the carriak (as Korhus told me it was called). The hull swayed from side to side, tilting slightly forward as it hung under the wire, the spheres invisible to us above the keel. It was moving downhill at present towards the distant balloons of gas that were lifting the wire ahead of us. I was not sure what was propelling the craft along the wire – I could see no sails and no obvious engine. The motion was by no means silent – the spheres growled as they rolled along the inner surface of the cable, and the wind whispered around us. The pedestrians below us ignored what was obviously a familiar sight to them, unaware that this was a stolen skyboat. The city nestled beside a wide lake of grey water, a slight swell stirring the surface. I stared over the side, gazing back to see if there was any apparent pursuit. As yet, there was nothing on the roof of the tower from which we had departed except confused-looking graalur. There could be no easy pursuit below the skywire now that we were over water, mists coiling over the lake. I was again relieved that I had a comfortable head for heights. It was not unknown for a pilot to find altitudes alarming – I remembered Geller, early in our training in the sturdy Malagan biplanes, confessing that he did not dare to look down at the ground once he was over about two hundred feet. He was still a good flyer, but we regularly teased him about it. He would have hated this. We were well over a hundred feet up, and the carriak felt solid and dependable, but we were not in control of it. Geller could cope with the sky so long as he could decide where and how he travelled.

Once we were clear of the city, I turned back to see how our escapees were doing. Fortunately, the carriak wasn't quite as crowded as I had thought – there was more space than at first appeared. Korhus had pushed his way to the front, his dark beard not obscuring the broad smile on his face. He hugged me – I was startled at the display of emotion from him. Others from the Valley were equally keen to express their gratitude, but Darhath was not among them. I eased through the throng of pleasantries, concerned to see Darhath seated at one side of the carriak, apparently uninterested in the events around him. I glanced forward once to check someone was keeping a weather eye on our lloruk, and made my way back to where Darhath was gazing evenly at Kelhene. She turned and nodded at me as I reached them.

"Darhath?" I said conversationally. He turned, his eyes taking me in, but he still did not reply. "Darhath?" I asked again, slightly surprised at his lack of response. Kelhene shook her head.

"He won't answer" she said softly, a catch in her voice, and I realised that she had been crying. "He's not really there any more."

I was tired from the struggle within Ilkadala, and my side had started aching. I didn't need any more mysteries or strangeness. "What's wrong?" I demanded, perhaps a little more harshly than I should have done.

Kelhene gestured to his left arm. I had been vaguely aware of a purple bruise below his shoulder. I looked more closely, before recoiling. It was not a bruise. Embedded in his skin he had a purple lump, glistening slightly as though it was coated in slime. There was the merest hint of a pulse beating within the left side of it, and it was growing into his flesh like... like a jasq. I found myself looking down at the blue stain in my own side. It was a jasq, or something akin to it. I reached out to touch it, remembering the purple slimes I had seen in a chamber under the tower.

Before my hand had even contacted the purple skin, my own jasq was awash with nausea. By the time my finger had confirmed the slick, rubbery surface I was struggling to retain what little was left in my stomach. Kelhene and another of the Grihl Valley people pulled me to a seat, as I gasped for breath. My mouth tasted as though I had eaten rotting meat. My tongue felt dry. My side... I didn't want to think what my jasq was doing to me. I clutched at it, desperately wanting it to stop making me sick. I had never experienced this in the real world. I was badly scared, terrified that some damage I had done to myself in the magerealm was coming home to roost. I wasn't even in the magerealm! It wasn't fair! Why was it doing this? I glared at Darhath, feeling angry that he wasn't the smiling, vibrantly alive man he had been.

I blinked the tears out of my eyes and shook my head. People were demanding to know what was wrong. I ignored them – I didn't know myself, so how could I answer their questions? Volg it, I *liked* Darhath. I wouldn't try to steal him from Kelhene, but if he had been a free man I'd have been tempted. Now, looking at him, I was repulsed by him.

By him, or by the thing in his arm? The nausea was receding again, slowly, but the feeling of revulsion was as strong as ever. I got to my feet unsteadily. I wasn't sure if that was me, or the swaying of the carriak. Hands took hold of my arms, trying to stop me falling. I ignored their help and faced Kelhene.

"What happened to him?"

It was Veldhra who answered, indicating the obscenity in his arm. "The lloruk cut him. Put that into his arm. It seemed to grow into him!" I realised that she was near to breaking point herself, and I squeezed her arm reassuringly, urging her to go on. "Since then... he's been a zombie. He doesn't talk or do anything

148

independently – he has to be told what to do, and he doesn't really listen to any of us at all!" She gestured savagely towards the silent snakeman at the prow of our vessel. "But he'll jump to it when ordered by one of *them*!"

I stared at Veldhra in disbelieving horror, and then looked back at Darhath. "When did they do this to him?"

"The day after they got us to the city. Only a day or so ago. I keep hoping he'll wake up out of it!"

I shuddered, and then I saw Kelhene's expression. This was her man, turned into a husk by the lloruk obscenity. I could understand why she looked so devastated. To have thought that her man was safe, back with her, and then to find him like this. Behind me, one of the other escapees muttered something darkly. I only caught a couple of words, something about others being done the same way. I glanced round. I knew the woman's face, but not her name. "Say that again" I demanded.

"I heard two of the lloruk talking" she mumbled, almost guilty at the admission of what she had overheard. "They said that since the larisq worked, they'd use it on more of us. Keep us docile." In her voice the last word sounded like an oath. I could feel anger surging in my veins. What the lloruk had done to Darhath was appalling. I only hoped that I could carve the repulsive not-quite-jasq out of his flesh as easily as I had ripped out Wrack's. "Docile"! My first instinct was to fling the lloruk on board the carriak over the side – see how docile it found *me*! I was already storming forward to grab hold of the volging lafquass when a little more common sense managed to insinuate itself through my thick skull. By the time I reached the snakeman I was almost in control of myself again.

Almost. I lashed out, punching the volger on the snout hard. It staggered backwards against the rail of the skyboat, lifting its hands in an attempt to block further blows. An unsuccessful attempt, I might add. I slammed my other fist into its stomach, and it doubled up, enabling me to hammer its jaw again. It hissed in pain, cowering in front of me.

Other hands were holding me back, or I'd have kicked it while it cowered.

"Why?" I demanded. "Why the larisqs?" I was assuming the woman had heard the name correctly. From the lloruk's reaction, she had.

149

"They are none of my doing!" it protested, crawling sideways along the deck away from me. "Do not hit me any more!"

I took a step closer, shrugging off the hands holding me. I suspect I looked pretty terrifying. Good.

"You lloruk did that to Darhath!" I pointed wildly behind me. "Are you planning to do that to all the humans? Is that your plan?"

"Not my plan" the lloruk whimpered. I lifted my foot to kick at it, and it cringed. I let my foot slide to the deck again. My anger was still burning, but it had cooled a little. I couldn't kick it while it was on the floor. It would have felt like stamping on an injured tabitha.

"Get up" I snarled. Fingers tightened on my shoulders. Wrack was behind me, calming and even-tempered. I didn't want even temper. I wanted answers. "Tell me about the larisqs – quickly!"

It hissed, and then glared at Wrack. "Do not let her hurt me!" it begged.

Wrack smiled evenly. The effect was chilling. "Think I could stop her? Safer to tell her what she wants to know. Might calm her down. A bit."

The lloruk scowled at him. There was a long, pregnant pause. I kept my eyes fixed on it, glaring into its gaze. After a good two dozen heartbeats I took a menacing pace forward. The lloruk tried to step back, and banged its back painfully against the side of the deck. I hoped it was painful, anyway. Its head swayed from side to side, and then, quietly, it began to speak.

*　　　　　*　　　　　*

I was standing at the stern, looking back towards Ilkadala. Far back along the skywire there was another dark dot, at least a mile or more away. I rubbed my side as I ruminated. The jasq still gave me a faint queasiness. I was getting more worried that I had done something serious to it.

Our pursuers were not gaining on us. On the other hand, our carriak was trundling along the skywire at its maximum pace. I'd experimented with the brass wheel that controlled our conveyance, and it would not go any faster. The lloruk's story was hideous. I was determined to do something about the larisqs. Trouble was, at the moment I had absolutely no idea what. Unfortunately, our captive didn't really know much about them itself. It said it disliked them, too, somewhat to my surprise.

The city was still just visible, but we would be out of sight of it soon. I sighed, and made my way back to the bows, where our snakeman captive was still lurking. It flinched every time I looked at it. I couldn't see any bruises on its scales, but the way it carried itself suggested that I had left some painful marks in its psyche. I looked away from it, unsure if I felt guilty for frightening it so badly, but I had needed to know. The obscenity in Darhath's arm was a jasq. Not something like one, not a near relative – it was a jasq. And that suggested that any jasq could turn someone into the state the olgrek-herder was in now. I shivered more, wanting to hide or curl up or somehow deny the hideous images the soft words of the lloruk had injected into my mind. I wished I could somehow unhear its voice. When Kelvar first selected me to become a sorceress I had been ecstatic at the thought of having a jasq. Yes, it had meant having to stay at a dragonlord's mansion for a few months while I trained, so that the dragons could ensure I had the right temperament for sorcery. Meaning that I was meek and obedient and wouldn't use my power against them. Despite that I had been overjoyed at my good fortune. Now... now it felt like a curse. Perhaps I would have been better not to have taken Wrack's jasq. The thought of being turned into a husk like Darhath...

I tried to shake myself out of my reverie. Our prisoner didn't know how a jasq was turned into a larisq, but he knew it wasn't easy to do. Maybe the lloruk responsible couldn't just reach out and twist mine. It would help if we could get out of their reach, though.

Korhus seemed to know a little about the carriaks and the skywire. I went and stood beside him. All our rescued prisoners were treating me as the leader of our group. I really wasn't sure what I made of that. I had been one of the commanders of the Firebirds, but that little group had been rather different to this situation. In the war, I had been a pilot, with some authority, but I was still obeying orders from Tolly, further up the rather ramshackle rebel chain of command. Here, I was making the decisions on my own. What I decided affected everyone in the group. If

I got it wrong, I would not be the only one to suffer. It was a sobering thought, and not one I wanted to dwell upon.

It had mildly intrigued me that they were turning to me, not Wrack, before I realised that of course none of them had met Wrack before. I hadn't bothered to introduce him at first, either, which had annoyed Wrack yet further. And I had no intention of handing over control to him. On the other hand, I didn't know what I *was* going to do as their apparent leader.

"Where does the skywire go?" I asked quietly.

"Luthvara" he answered unhelpfully.

"Next lloruk city?" Wrack hazarded, trying to elbow himself into the discussion. Korhus nodded.

"But before then it goes past those globes" I said firmly, pointing to the latest crop of spheres bobbing ahead of us.

"Ghisstai – creatures of gas that float, lifting the cables" he explained.

Hmm. "And beyond that, there is a spire?"

He nodded. "Probably. Or a tamed lantern tree. The lloruk use the high features to provide anchors and support for the skywire."

Wrack got his question in a second before I could ask. "So we could get down from here when we reach the spire?"

Korhus shrugged. "I don't know. Usually the carriaks go through tunnels dug right through the spires, probably two or three hundred feet up. If we did get out there I don't know how we'd get down."

I grinned wryly. Wrack knew I was good at climbing. "If we had a good amount of rope we could do it."

Wrack grimaced, glancing down at the sling on his arm. He could have flown down, if his arm was healed. But it wasn't. As it was he would find climbing difficult in the extreme.

I walked across to the lloruk standing at the prow. It hadn't moved since I had beaten it up. Now, as I approached it, it cringed. I looked at it levelly, and eventually it met my gaze.

"What are you going to do with me?" it asked sibilantly.

"I've no idea" I answered honestly. "I don't know what *we're* going to do, yet." I pointed ahead. We were coming up on the gas globes – ghisstai. As I watched, we shot beneath them. They were each at least twenty feet across, and there had to be six or seven of them.

I stared at the vast blimps above us. There were already yet another cluster visible further ahead along the skywire. Thoughts churned within my mind, ideas of cutting them loose and using them as flying craft to bring us gently to the ground. We would have to climb up onto the high keel of the carriak, cut them loose – assuming we had anything with an edge – and then find some way to hold on until they brought us to the ground. That is, if they weren't too buoyant. They might just take us further up into the sky, to hang in mid-air until we died of thirst or let go. Hmmm. Not such a good idea, after all.

The lloruk was still looking at me, eyes unblinking. Its pupils were narrow, vertically-slitted, and its tongue was flicking within its mouth. The creature was scared, despite its apparent calm. Good.

"Tell me what I want to know and I won't kill you." I wasn't sure if it relaxed at my words. "What will your people do to chase us?"

It shrugged but did not answer. Helpful. I tapped my foot meaningfully, and it flinched again before softly hissing a reply.

"They will send another carriak behind us, and they will send messages ahead."

I had already seen the pursuer on the wire behind us. Messages ahead? Somehow that didn't surprise me. Odds were we would meet another carriak heading towards us, boxing us in. I leaned over the side of the skyboat and looked back along our line of travel. I had somehow expected to taste salt in the breeze from the water below us, but there was no hint of it in the air. A mile or so away I could see a couple of sails – two small craft scudding over the water. Fishing boats, I suspected, each with a single triangular white sail.

"Is there any way down from the tunnel through the first rock spire?" I asked, dragging my attention back to my serpentine informant. It again shrugged unhelpfully. I glowered at it. "If you won't answer my questions I may have to change my mind about not throwing you over the side!"

The lloruk looked at me and quivered. I took a step towards it, menacingly, trying to seem as though I might actually murder it in cold blood. It stepped backwards slightly, and looked from me towards the others in the carriak, hoping for comfort. Wrack was beside me, now, adding his size and mean expression to mine.

"There is a way down at the second rock spire" the lloruk said haltingly. "There is a way-station which should have a stairway down."

"What about the first spire?" I asked.

The lloruk levelled its gaze at me, and looked at me evenly. "There may be a way down there, too."

"'May'?" asked Wrack frostily. "Either there is or there isn't."

"There is no waystation presently serving us there. But one may have been made." I glowered at it, wordlessly demanding that it explain. It obliged. "If it is there, it will not have been used since the construction of the tunnel and the chambers within the spire. It may well have become obstructed."

"Best chance we have" I said firmly. I turned back to the lloruk. "Show me how you control the carriak."

It pointed to the brass wheel. "Turning that regulates our speed."

I resisted the temptation to throttle it. "I know that, lizard-brain. What else?"

Beside the wheel were two levers, each of brass, set into the deck of our vessel, one set to move fore and aft, the other left and right. The lloruk pointed to the one on the left, set forward. "That will cause the carriak to slow."

A brake. Useful, but not in this situation. "And the other?"

"If the carriak comes to a junction in the skywire, that will decide if the carriak takes the left or right fork."

Simple and obvious. So much for Kelhene's alarm at lloruk mechanisms! The controls on this thing made my poor old tripe's cockpit look positively complicated.

I thanked the lloruk soberly. Sighting ahead, we were about to pass some more balloon-creatures. "Are those things really alive?" I asked curiously.

The lloruk looked at me evenly. "Yes" it answered simply. I briefly wondered about quizzing it further, but really I wasn't that interested in them.

On the other hand... "Can one of them lift an adult human?"

The lloruk looked at me up and down for a moment. "Yes" it repeated. "Eight

154

can support the weight of a fully-laden carriak. One would support you easily."

"Could it take me to the top of the Chasm?"

The lloruk shook its head decisively. "It would not wish to rise to the level of the clouds."

It had not struck me that the creature might have any will or desires of its own. It had been a nice dream. Oh, well. I stared ahead more carefully. The first spire was less than two miles ahead, I estimated. If my memory of the map was right, the second spire was very many miles beyond that. We didn't want to wait that long. I looked back again. The pursuing carriak seemed no closer. Our danger was a skyboat coming the other way, boxing us in. We needed to get off this boat as soon as we could. And then we had to think about what we were going to do about the larisqs.

I slowed our progress as we approached the first spire, the carriak labouring as it clawed its way up the rising cable. The incline was not steep, but it was enough to make the rumble of the skyboat's wheels even louder. Ahead of us the spire pointed its finger at the sky as it rose from the edge of the lake. Three lantern trees rose from a low island a couple of miles away, giving us bright illumination of the scenery. The coast looked bleak and unwelcoming, the vegetation low, scrubby and a mixture of orange, browns and even green rather than red. If we were to escape the skywire here, we would be in a grim part of the rift.

I collared Korhus. "Any idea what's round here?"

"Not a clue" he answered unhelpfully. "We're further south than I've ever been. All I know is that we're in lozaak terrain here."

Great. Another meaningless word. "Lozaak?"

"Lizard creatures. They roam the southern steppes."

I looked at him evenly. "And their view of humans?"

He shrugged. "Dinner or entertainment."

I grimaced. "And the lake?"

"Is big and deep and wet" Wrack growled beside me. I looked down at his arm, still nestling in its sling. He had never been fond of swimming. If he couldn't fly, he wouldn't want to be in a boat on the surface.

I ignored him and raised an eyebrow at Korhus. He shook his head mournfully. "There are all sorts of tales about creatures in the lake. Giant serpents and zharks."

"Sharks?" I queried.

"Zharks" he replied unhelpfully. "Big, savage fish, which eat people if they can."

I hated the Chasm. Even their sharks had to be awkward.

The skyboat plunged into shadow as it slid smoothly like a pin into a socket into the dark hole carved into the spire. The tunnel was almost circular, driven into the stone with no hint of any way down or any platform at which to dock the carriak. I turned the brass wheel, slowing us yet further.

Despite the pseudo-daylight outside, the tunnel was swiftly turning into a sojourn in deepest pitch. If there was a way down further through the curving shaft it would be quite invisible. I turned the wheel further, until we had almost halted, and yelled to ask my passengers if anyone had any means to create light. I received a plethora of responses, all of which translated as "no." I cursed quietly. The easy way to get a light source would be to dip into the magerealm for a second, draw a strand of fire out. Would there be pain again? There had been flares on the triplane, tools for pilots with no magic after the war. I would cheerfully have killed for one now. I gritted my teeth and slid into the other place.

The agony, this time, was unbearable. It felt as though my entire body was engulfed in raging fire, needles carrying the heat deeper into the core of my body. My vision was blurred and I couldn't stay on my feet. I slid moaning to the floor, my sight just crimson stars. I could hear Wrack saying something, and then other voices, but nothing made any sense. One of Wrack's muscular arms looped around under my arms and pulled me upright, but I still could see nothing. All I was aware of was the torture inflicting itself upon me via my jasq. My side was a mixture of broken glass and hot daggers. Was the pain easing? Like hell. Someone had asked me that question. I stumbled over my invective-filled response, the words tangling on my tongue.

The gloom of the tunnel was stygian after the agonising brilliance of the magerealm. The agony in my side was definitely fading, thank volg. I could see properly again. I roughly rubbed my knuckles over my eyes to get rid of the tears.

There was a jolt from beneath me. The carriak swayed to left and right, but the ever-present rumble of the wheels had stopped. Someone had braked us in the midst of the shaft through the spire.

I slowly tried to get to my feet, grateful for Wrack's arm around me. He was asking me how I was feeling, worrying about me. I shook my head. "We can't stay here" I growled. "The other carriak's on our tail. It'll hit us. We need to move on."

"Need to see if there's a way off this thing" Wrack answered. "We need light."

He was right. A second or two in the magerealm should be enough to get a strand of fire to show us what was in here.

But I couldn't. I didn't think I could bear that pain again. My side was still stabbing knives – there was just no way I was delving back into the magerealm again. Ever.

"Someone must have something we can use for light" I whispered again, before turning to look at Wrack steadily. He was grinning comfortingly.

"I'm likely to worry your friends" he murmured. Then, with a somewhat more serious tone, he added "And the lloruk will see me change."

My turn to grin wanly. "Let it see. Maybe it'll be a little more cooperative."

Wrack shook his head slightly. "Let the lloruk go, we lose my secret. Wanted to keep it as a trump card."

"Volg that!" I riposted elegantly. "If we can't get off this carriak, a trump card won't do us much good!"

He nodded. Without another word, he began to change.

My jasq – perhaps I should say *our* jasq – was hammering in my side like a racing aero-engine. This wasn't the agony of a few moments before, though it was roaring in my veins like bowling balls on wood. In the dim illumination from the end of the tunnel I could see Wrack's body stretching, the skin darkening as the scales crawled across his body. In this light they looked black, but I had no doubts about their true vibrant plum red colour. He had cast aside his sling and undone his harness, discarding it without shame or concern. The membranes were growing across between his arms and his body, his muzzle extending and his tail growing out from behind him. Horns around his head, the ridge along his spine, claws from both feet, his left arm spreading wide. If the carriak had been as full as I had originally feared, he would have crushed half the passengers as he grew into his full magnificence. His right wing, though, still seemed to be the mangled mess I had seen before. It had to be healing, but it seemed so slow and so weak. Without both wings he was not the dragon he used to be.

There were shouts and gasps of amazement from the people in the skyboat. Even in the dark of the tunnel it was clear that something extraordinary was happening. I leaned back against the rail, feeling ridiculously proud of my dragon, despite him being crippled.

Wrack turned his head, green eyes aglow. He growled, quietly for him, telling me to set the skyboat moving again. I concurred, and he opened his jaws, leaning over the side and breathing a stream of brilliant fire along the tunnel ahead of us, lighting it up so intensely that for a few moments it was painful to see, until my eyes adapted to the light.

The heavy cable ran above us, curving to the left with the tunnel, glittering in the dragon fire. Even as Wrack released his jet of fire and the tunnel plunged into darkness again I had seen what I needed to see. I dived forward and shoved the lever on the right out of its accustomed position whilst I spun the wheel back, before yanking on the other lever to slow our motion. We were only a few yards from a junction in the cable. To the left the skywire headed onwards, the cable glittering with the brightness of much traffic. To the right, though, the cable was black, and I had a strong suspicion that its colour indicated a deep lack of use. In the tunnel opening to the right I had fancied I had seen a plinth jutting from the edge of the tunnel – a way-station of some form?

If I was wrong, we might just hit a solid wall or rip the side out of the carriak. All the more reason to slow us down.

"More light, Wrack!" I demanded. He obliged – his draconian eyes had seen just as much as I had, and he directed his second blast of fire to show the right-hand tunnel clearly.

There was a platform, built out of the stone of the spire, and a dark opening to the side that led into the spire's heart. And beyond the platform the tunnel went – where? The darkness seemed total. I heaved on the brake, easing us to a grinding halt alongside the welcoming stone slab. If the tunnel did go further, we were still at risk of an oncoming skyboat.

Wrack was already scrambling onto the platform. I clambered ashore after him, to be followed hastily by most of our group. Wrack's second fire had faded, and it was becoming pitch dark again. I yelled at Wrack to brighten things up, and he obliged. A third blast of fire along the length of the stone ensured that there were no threats to us on its surface, and confirmed that the tunnel and the skywire came to a dead end a few yards beyond. We were in the skywire equivalent of the sidings that the steam locomotives of the surface railways used. And by all appearances, starting with the dust that Wrack was kicking up, this one had not been used for centuries. The place was dead and empty.

How stupid am I to think such a thing? I was relaxing, thinking that we might have found somewhere to hide for a time, when I realised that the platform was growing brighter. Cries of alarm from the Valley folk were enough to tell me where to look. Standing on the platform, like ghostly passengers, there were the glowing shapes of two lloruk.

Chapter Seventeen

Yet again I wished I had a sword. Both lloruk shone a pale, sickly green colour. I walked forward slowly, eyeing the nearer one. I could not make out its shape easily – its outline was blurred, like a torch seen through mist. It glowed brightly, lighting up most of the platform. And it didn't move. Everyone else was staying back. I could hear murmurs of alarm and confusion. Wrack was beside me, his dragon-form comforting in its bulk and power. If the lloruk attacked me, it would regret it. I could not work out how they had got here so fast. I glowered at the one nearest to me, waiting for it to respond.

It didn't. The other lloruk wasn't moving, either. They were as stationary as... as street-lamps. I glanced at Wrack – he looked puzzled. I leaned forward and prodded the ghost. My finger went right through it, and it shimmered like a flame in a gust of wind. I prodded it again, sweeping my arm through the glowing figure, and then laughed.

"Don't panic!" I said loudly. "They're just lights!"

Korhus was swearing caustically. "Scared the life out of me!" he added. Eldhor made a similar comment and swung his arm through the other figure, with equivalent results.

Wrack growled an oath. I lifted my eyebrows in surprise. He gestured at the plinth. "Those things shining, we'll be visible to the first carriak to get here!"

My turn to curse. Wrack was right, of course. I would have realised it myself had I not been worrying about the figures actually being lloruk. There had to be some way to extinguish them – whatever sorcery created the effect, the lloruk couldn't just leave them alight all the time, and they hadn't been illuminated when we got here.

"Everyone!" I yelled. It felt really strange to be taking control in this way, but someone had to make the decisions. I'd somehow got cast in the role. "Get into the tunnel! Get off the platform, and with luck the lights will go out!"

The platform became a bustle of motion like any busy railway station back on the surface. As the wary leaders moved into the opening, I saw the entrance begin to glow in the same stomach-churning green. I heard Veldhra yelling that there were various tunnels off the main passageway. Korhus responded that they should take the ramp leading downwards. Two of the men, I noticed belatedly, were escorting our lloruk, ensuring it did not get into mischief.

Wrack rested his clawed hand on my shoulder, and I jumped a mile. "Don't volging well *do* that to me!" I snapped.

"Time we both got off the platform, too" he growled, tongue licking from his muzzle. I gave another blistering reply, and stalked into the opening, pausing only to look back at the empty carriak. Were the two lloruk glowing less? Or was that just wishful thinking? There was another lloruk in the entranceway, standing in an alcove clearly carved for just that purpose. I stuck my tongue out at it as I walked past. Wrack, in dragon shape, was having to stoop to get into the passage. I was still glad to have him in that form – if we did face trouble down here, he was the only real weapon we had.

The lloruk on the platform were definitely dimmer. I grabbed Wrack's unbroken wing and dragged him towards the ramp leading down, away from the platform, pausing only when we were a good ten feet lower. The passageway behind us, after a few moments, was growing less bright; as I watched, the light faded more, until there was only the faintest green glow. I was holding my breath, waiting for it to go out. When it did, I heard Wrack's sigh of relief echo mine. Beyond it, there was only blackness on the platform.

Not a moment too soon, either. I could hear a distant rumble, the growl of carriak wheels in the cable. The pursuing lloruk were getting closer. If they saw the way-station... but the growl did not pause. After a few moments the growl was fading again, the pursuit heading out of the spire and beyond.

"They'll work out we must be here soon" I said softly.

Wrack chuckled deeply. "How do you reverse a carriak?" he asked. "Didn't see any controls in the stern."

I shook my head. "You didn't look carefully enough" I replied coolly. "They're there, all right."

"Volg." he replied. "So they'll be back looking for us pretty soon."

"Let them!" Korhus sounded remarkably cheerful as he came up the ramp towards us. "There's a passageway leading downwards. I think it goes all the way to the ground! Come and see!"

I needed no urging. I clattered down the ramp, wanting to see what was below.

At the foot of the dangerously smooth green stone ramp there was a large, open chamber, jade floor carpeted with ancient dust, with another opening leading on down. Our people were milling around, uncertain about what to do. I grabbed Kelhene and Korhus, told them to organise a couple of people to keep watch above, so that we'd have some warning if the lloruk found us. As for the rest of us...

"Everyone!" I yelled again. "Head further down! Odds are we'll have lloruk hunting us in the next two or three hours – we need to get out of this spire!"

Twenty minutes later I was more confident about getting away from our pursuit. There were a number of tunnels within the spire leading downwards. Off two levels there were more passages, leading to a host of chambers. One bonus – in one room Jandhri had whooped with glee, waving an ancient sword over his head. He had found a pitiful excuse for an armoury, but even three swords were better than none. To my chagrin, Jandhri, Borhun and (surprise, surprise) Wrack had appropriated the weapons before I got even close.

On the bottom level there was a heavy, round brass door. At first it wouldn't open, until Chelhik, who was one of our brighter sparks, worked out that it rolled sideways in a groove, rather than having a hinge. Chelhik was young, brash, over-confident, and was going to brag about solving the mystery for hours. Oh well. Once we managed to roll it to one side, we emerged from the base of the spire into the dim daylight. We were a good distance from a lantern tree, here. The spire was at the edge of the lake, and the beach looked grey and dismal, composed of gravel and chunks of stone, not at all the warm, sandy beaches I had liked to sunbathe on before the war. Not that there was any sun here, either, despite the ever-present, oppressive wet heat. The jungle at the edge of the beach looked fairly dense – as and when we did decide to head into the wilds, we should be able to hide reasonably easily. All we needed to do now was to decide where to go.

Kelhene, Wrack, Korhus and I stood in one of the chambers on the level above the door to the jungle. As a council of war it was a fairly quick discussion. Where to go, what to do? We had more than twenty people, no food, only a few weapons, and a lloruk prisoner. There would be graalur hunting us in short order. And we had nowhere to go.

"We've got to make for Jajruuk" Korhus said for the third time. I had gathered from the conversation that he had friends there, from when he had been a trader travelling across half the Chasm, long before he settled in Muranon. Kelhene had protested at the idea, saying that the city was too far and that the Eski were no friends of ours. On the other hand, she had no particularly good proposal of her own. Her answer – Tolgrail – was even further, right across the jungle to the north. I had listened patiently (well, relatively patiently) as they argued. I could see Wrack preparing to make his own views felt, and I intervened first.

"Kelhene, Tolgrail's just too far. Jajruuk may be some distance, too, but it's still closer. We can't stay here. Maybe we'll come up with something better as we travel."

Wrack interrupted me, wanting to take some part in making our decision. "Going to need food – jungle will be the best chance. Harvest as we march."

Korhus nodded again. "That fits with Jajruuk. The third alternative would be to head along the beach around the lake, hope to find one of the fisher villages."

I shook my head. "Jungle it is. We're too visible on the beach."

Kelhene shrugged, accepting the inevitable ungraciously. "I hate the jungle" she growled. "It's a lot more dangerous than the beach would be."

Korhus looked at her. "You think a cholooth coming out of the water isn't dangerous? Or a couple of tentacles from a lurking vursquid?"

"Better than a ruzdrool or a swarm of adjaliks" Kelhene retorted.

"You think so? A vursquid makes a ruzdrool look like a tabitha!"

"Like volg! You can get away from a vursquid by getting away from the water –

a ruzdrool can scramble over anything!"

Wrack's deep rumble of laughter broke through the argument like a bucket of warm water. "You finished swapping horrors?"

"What's so funny?"

I was grinning, too. Wrack's rare laugh is infectious. "You both are" I said. "Standing there describing monsters, each trying to top the other." They both glared at me, and I found myself grinning more. I struggled to stifle a yawn – I was relaxing, and I began to realise how tired I was. "We've made the decision. We need to get moving, so we can find somewhere to hole up and get some rest."

Unwillingly, Kelhene nodded agreement. Korhus half-smiled, ruefully.

I yawned again, and pulled myself to my feet out of the rather comfortable chair in the chamber. We'd set the others to searching the other rooms to see if there was anything of any use to us. One of the rooms was obviously a storehouse. The chamber we were in was some kind of bedroom, with a couple of surprisingly soft beds and a number of tables and chairs. There was also an alcove with a deep, water-filled depression in the floor that had to be a bath. Cruel temptation. I could have murdered happily for a soak in a tub. Somehow the water had seemed fresh and clear, and warm, too. If I'd thought we could have stayed here for long without detection I'd have taken advantage of it.

No such luck. We needed to move swiftly. "What about the lloruk?" I asked quietly.

"Kill it" was Kelhene's uncompromising response. Korhus was half-nodding, not quite so certain.

I shook my head. "It answered our questions. I told it I wouldn't kill it."

"Then I'll do it" Kelhene retorted.

"No" Wrack growled quietly. "Kill it in cold blood and you're no better than they are."

Korhus looked at him quizzically. "So we take it with us, having to watch it every step of the way?"

Wrack shrugged. "Leave it here. Lloruk know this is where we got to. It can't tell them anything they don't already know." I didn't point out that he was wrong about that – the lloruk knew that Wrack was a dragon. But I didn't want to kill it in cold blood, either. I kept quiet. Wrack paused, and eyed me for a moment. "Sometimes, treating an enemy leniently can be valuable." His expression shifted slightly. "Got to accept it doesn't always work, though."

"Depends on your definition of leniency" I snapped, before striding next door to make the arrangements.

The Iloruk looked at me with a faint air of surprise, its head swaying sideways on its long neck. In an odd way it reminded me of Wrack, in his dragon-form, moving his head to try to gauge his height better when in flight.

"Why are you letting me live?" it whispered. "I am not ungrateful, but I did not expect you to keep your word."

I shrugged. "I don't like lying to people. Even Iloruk." I looked at it fixedly. "But I don't like larisqs, either. If I meet your larisq-maker, I *will* kill it."

It inclined its head to me, and then tottered up the ramp towards the platform four levels above. I had little doubt that its people would find it soon. I watched it walk away, still slightly surprised how frail these master-sorcerers appeared in actuality. I didn't even know its name. It knew about Wrack... I just hoped I was not going to regret letting it go.

Two hours into the steaming jungle, and I was beginning to think I was seriously wrong to have chosen to head this way. It was (as far as I could work out) mid afternoon. I hadn't slept for more than thirty hours, and I was struggling to keep my eyes open. It was just as well that some of the Grihl Valleyers were in reasonable shape. I missed my flying jacket, buried outside Ilkadala. I wished there had been some way I could have recovered it. The slave-harness I was still clad in provided no protection against scratches from thorns or insect bites. The graalur boots I was wearing were frankly too big for me, and weren't suited for a long trek. Volg it, I was hungry, too! A number of our people were becoming quite adept at grabbing handfuls of berries and edible leaves as we marched, but the bounty they passed my way only seemed to remind my stomach how long it had been since we last had a real meal.

We had been climbing slowly and steadily, rising up from the level of the lake towards the wide plateau that was the site of the Eski clan lands. Korhus promised me that there were small towns and villages in the jungle this side of Jajruuk. So far, we'd seen no sign of anything hinting at intelligent life in the area, not even anything that could be blessed with the name 'road'. I had trails of sweat portraying quite complex artistic patterns all across my skin, punctuated by the red lines inflicted by sharp-edged vegetation and the red dots from sadistic buzzing things. Not that anyone else was any better off. Wrack, ahead of me, was struggling, his injured arm hampering him badly. We needed to take a break.

"Korhus!" I demanded. "Any idea where we can rest?"

He shrugged brusquely, not bothering to reply. I felt irritation welling up inside me like fermenting juices.

"Korhus! We have to take a break!"

He turned, angrily. "In the depths of the jungle? Don't be so stupid!"

It was hot, I was drenched in sweat, and I wanted to rest. I snapped. "Volging lafquass, Korhus, we need a squuming break!" I swung my hand at him, not quite in a fist, but enough to punctuate my feelings. He danced back, and there was a shout from behind us.

"Ruzdrool!"

I recognised the blue-skinned nightmare that had burst out from between the trees on its spindle-legs. Last time I had seen one, it had saved me from the graalur in the badlands. This one looked more intent on devouring one of us, small bat-wings flapping to draw its long neck up high. It reared over Eldhor like a praying mantis, its writhing, pointed tentacles pulling back before they struck down to carve into his flesh. He rolled sideways, desperately, and the creature's lunge scored mostly empty ground; only one violet tentacle slammed into Eldhor's arm. That was enough to pin him down, though – the monster reared back and prepared to stab him fatally. Instincts took over. Beside me, Wrack was starting to change, but it would be far too long before he could be in dragon form and able to breathe. I didn't have time to think about what I could do. I slid into the magerealm, snatched at a fireflow and flung it into the real world, letting the fire scorch into the ruzdrool.

It shrieked, the same steam-whistle howl I had heard before, staggering back. I had charred four of its tentacles, and it was shaking its head, as though blinded. Not that I could see any eyes in the twisted creature. Actually, I couldn't see much at all. I was gasping on the ground, another dose of the fire I had inflicted on the ruzdrool engulfing my side, my vision scarlet. The jasq was still hammering below my ribs, and then beside me I heard a deep breath, and then another tongue of flame lashed out. The ruzdrool didn't have a chance. My vision was clearing, sort of, and I saw the flower of Wrack's fire catch the brute squarely in the centre of its body, displayed cleanly as it reared back. It shrieked again, and crumpled to the floor of the jungle, twitching violently. Jandhri and Borhun were running forward, hacking at it with the swords, ensuring it had no chance of threatening us again.

I was still feeling awful. My head was hammering, my stomach wanting to rebel, my side felt like someone was using a red-hot iron on it. I tried to get to my feet, only to realise that I could barely walk.

"Come on, Sorrel!" Wrack was growling. "Get up! Not going to carry you!"

I looked at him. My eyes were full of tears of pain and despair. "I... can't" I whispered.

Wrack pulled my face round so I was facing him squarely. "Don't you volging well give up on me, Sorrel!" he snarled in sudden anger. "You never gave up before – so fight!"

I gritted my teeth, pulled myself to my feet. The pain was easing – a little. Anyway, Wrack was right. No way was I going to let him see me being weak. The pain was reducing. I was not going to wilt – I hoped.

Kelhene was tending to Eldhor, patching the nasty wound in his arm. I glanced at Korhus. "Is it poisonous?" I asked.

Wrack, beside me, murmured condescendingly "She means venomous." I gave him a venomous glare.

Korhus was shaking his head. "I don't think so" he answered. "It doesn't need to be. It can kill without it."

I took a deep breath, glared at Wrack again, and turned back to Korhus. "I actually *meant* poisonous" I said mendaciously. "Can we eat it?"

Wrack looked at me sidelong, trying to decide if I meant what I had said. Korhus was looking at the beast levelly. "I don't know" he answered calmly. "I've never known anyone try."

I sat down on the ground, and gestured at it widely. "Someone care to try butchering it? Maybe it's just because I'm ravenous, but the burned meat smell is making my mouth water."

I was lying – I still felt sick to the depths of my stomach – but I wasn't going to admit it.

It was over an hour before we got moving again. It would be dark pretty soon, which was worrying me, but on the other hand having a relatively full stomach helped enormously. Veldhra had found a stream, so we'd had fresh water. The ruzdrool was carved up by Helinhus, borrowing Borhun's sword. Helinhus had apparently worked for a time as a butcher. It was then roasted by Wrack, who had finally deigned to play some part in the task of feeding us, even though he clearly viewed such things as beneath him. Wrack had never been as bad as some of the other dragonlords for insisting on his status, but he still had an unconscious arrogance that assumed that making and cooking food was for lessers, not for him.

The ruzdrool had been quite filling, even though it actually tasted pretty foul. Meat eater, of course – never as edible as a herbivore. On the other hand, it was food, and the taste was only a very minor consideration. The bad news was that we'd created a certain amount of smoke, enough to be visible if someone was looking carefully, as well as attracting yet more volging insects. I swatted a couple more trying to have dinner out of me, and cursed again. We'd dumped the remains of the ruzdrool, apart from a small amount of meat that had been doled out before we set out again. Another meal's worth, anyway.

During the break, Jaldhor had scrambled up one of the trees, but he reported nothing he could see – he couldn't get high enough to see over the jungle canopy. We thought we were heading east, which should take us towards the human cities on the plain. I yet again cursed the lack of a sun to give compass bearings. If we were wrong, we could equally well be heading towards the other lloruk city,

Luthvara, which was north-west – albeit a long way off, but if we were that far off our bearing we would end up trekking right across this volging red jungle. Either that or we'd make Kelhene happy and reach Tolgrail or Daryan, to the north. There was a lantern tree not that far from us, and I had suggested making for that and climbing it. To my surprise, Korhus, Kelhene and Helinhus had all laughed at me, telling me that no one tried climbing lantern trees. Helinhus explained that the gigantic plants lived by focussing their light onto any creature that came too close, blasting the unfortunate victim to death so that its remains fed the tree's roots. Nothing claiming any wisdom scavenged within a couple of hundred yard radius of a lantern tree. Woe betide any traveller who did not spot the trunk as he forged his way through the dense, verdant jungle that surrounded it.

We needed somewhere to camp for the night. My sorcery and Wrack's fire had impressed our group immensely, but the power would do us no good at all if we couldn't see an opponent before it was upon us. Equally, I didn't want a fire burning brightly to lead any pursuers to us.

Chelhik solved the problem for us by tripping on a buried stone and tumbling into a hole. He shrieked as he fell, then called out in quite a different voice. "Hey! I found something!"

The chamber he had found was about forty feet across, and another example of Iloruk stonework. Once, there had been some buildings of the old race here. They had been abandoned millennia ago, and buried by the jungle. The stone that had ambushed our brash young explorer was one outcropping of the old settlement. The chamber below had probably been a cellar of some form, long sealed by the elements. Very recently a tree had fallen, ripping open the ground, leaving the pit that had swallowed Chelhik.

He was twenty feet down. Fortunately for him, his fall had been broken by a pile of earth which had once been the roof sealing the ruin. Our problem was how to get him out, or how to join him, a task not made easier by the unstable nature of the ground around the hole. A couple of lengths of red vine and a long branch were fortunately available and enough.

I scrambled down after Helinhus, and looked around in amazement. This was Iloruk work, but this was not the glowing crystal and glass of Ilkadala. This was carved stone, smooth and inset with strips of silvery metal. The chamber seemed bare, deserted, as though the Iloruk had stripped it clean before they abandoned it. Something about the glass-smooth stone reminded me of the shining walls of the living Iloruk city. Looking at this chamber, I had a strong suspicion that a thousand or more years ago there had been the same lambent fire illuminating this depth as now lit up Ilkadala. Aside from the lack of any glow, though, the centuries had been relatively kind; the patterns embedded in the walls had not weathered and the metal had not corroded. Nor, it seemed, had the void been filled by any enterprising creatures. The cellar was ours to use tonight.

Of course, it belatedly occurred to me that once we were ensconced within it we were trapped. If something blocked the entrance we would have nowhere to run. Nor would it be easy for the injured members of our group, Wrack primarily among them, to gain egress. On the other hand, it beat sleeping in the midst of the jungle, at the mercy of ruzdrools and adjaliks. I yelled up at everyone, and we set about bringing everyone down.

With all of us down in the chamber, apart from Dalhis and Veldhra on first watch, I walked around the group, ensuring I said something to everyone, patting the four younger children with us on the head, trying to make sure that we were all in good spirits. I even talked to Darhath, though that was pretty heart-breaking. He didn't reply or respond. Frankly, it was a miracle that we had got him this far. Fortunately, he took orders amenably, and could walk and scramble like anyone else. I was glad to walk away from him, trying not to think about what the Iloruk had told us as I went back to the place I had picked out for myself in the chamber.

It was only as I relaxed, having completed my round, that I realised just how much I did care about the Grihl Valley refugees. I had only been with them a few days, but I still saw them as my responsibility. I wanted more than anything to get them to safety. I only hoped that Jajruuk was it.

It felt very strange to feel the sense of duty to them. I had no reason to feel liable for their safety – and yet it felt good to be taking care of them. It gave me a sense of purpose. Looking at them, thinking about their well-being, gave me an odd mixture of alarm and pride. Fear that I might not be able to ensure their safety – satisfaction that I was doing the best I could. Not that there was much more I could do at present. We had set watches and now all we could do was settle down to rest.

Wrack, however, had other ideas. As I was trying to make myself relatively comfortable on the smooth, hard floor (relatively being a euphemism for 'not very'), he came and sprawled out alongside me. I turned my back, trying to drop a few hints. As usual, his thick hide was immune to such efforts at tactful rejection.

"Need to talk, Sorrel" he said quietly.

I allowed my back to answer eloquently.

"Keep ignoring me, and I'll find some way to get your attention" he murmured softly. Before I could offer some retort, I felt a hand slide down my spine and then sideways over my hip. I twisted over before he could let his fingers get anywhere really interesting. He was grinning widely, amused at my expression. If we hadn't been in company I'd have landed a punch on his jaw, or perhaps a kick somewhere lower. As it was, I didn't want to create a scene to attract everyone's attention. I simply snarled a sizzling oath in narynyl – the advantage of using the surface language was that no one down here would understand it. He grinned more, making it all the more difficult to restrain myself from thumping him.

"Do that again and I'll break your other arm" I hissed back.

He rested himself on his unbroken elbow and looked at me levelly.

"You've rescued your friends, Sorrel. Now we should be getting back to Sendaal."

"*We?*" I asked archly. "If I remember rightly, I told you I didn't want you following me!"

He shook his head. "You don't remember right. We said we'd climb the wall together once my arm was healed."

"And I said we needed somewhere to hole up until then" I retorted. "Your arm's not healed yet, Wrack." The thoughts tumbling through my mind were a worse tangle than a tabitha's wool collection. "And I'm not sure I want to climb with you. When we get to the surface... what then?"

For a moment, I thought Wrack was going to duck the question. His gaze dropped, his eyes growing shadowed. He started to turn away, then lifted his head back to look at me squarely, defiantly. "You cut my jasq out, Sorrel. Crippled me. Can't expect to get away with that without any come-back."

"You think you're going to make me your slave again, you can forget it!" My voice was growing louder as I began to storm at him. I saw heads turn and look in our direction. I shook my head warningly at Wrack. He scowled at me, but he kept his voice down as he responded.

"I can't let you go when you've got my jasq!"

"Why not?" I demanded in a harsh whisper. "Once you're back on the surface you can find out what it feels like to be a simple human like us!"

He slammed his fist against the floor in anger. "I'm not a human, Sorrel! I'm a dragon! Not going to let you take that away from me!"

"I was a sorceress, and you took that away from *me*!" I snapped back.

His expression grew even more angry. He opened his mouth to snarl at me... and Korhus sat down calmly beside us both.

"Mind if I watch you murdering each other?" he asked conversationally in veredraa. "Not much other entertainment down here."

For a moment I thought Wrack was going to lash out at him. Korhus could not have understood what we were saying – we had been using narynyl – but our tones must have been clear enough. Korhus' calm, unflustered expression as he faced Wrack's anger held my gaze, and I began to giggle. Korhus cracked a smile, too. I suspected that he was engineering the expression to try to quell Wrack's anger. It worked, fortunately. I saw the corner of Wrack's mouth twitch, and then he leaned back, his taut muscles loosening.

"Sorry, Korhus" he said quietly in his improving veredraa. I blinked, boggled at hearing Wrack apologise for anything. "Didn't mean to alarm you all. Sorrel and I have..."

"– business to sort out" I finished for him.

Korhus looked from me to Wrack, and then back at me. "I really hope you aren't planning to try to return to the surface" he said gently. Even if he couldn't understood our words, he had known what we were saying.

Wrack replied before I could say anything. "This isn't our land, Korhus. Don't belong here."

I didn't respond. I really wasn't sure what I was going to say. Korhus' expression showed his dismay more clearly than words. "You heard what that lloruk said" he answered. "Your help - " his attention was on me, rather than Wrack - " would give us a chance. Without you being able to get into the magerealm we can't do anything to deal with the larisqs."

I shivered. I had been trying to forget the soft words of the lloruk in the carriak. What it had known was that a lloruk mage, Ssathool, was responsible for the obscene creations. It had been trying to relearn old lloruk knowledge lost when the land fell and formed the Chasm. As we had now seen first-hand, there were ancient lloruk ruins throughout the rift, and in one of them Ssathool had discovered how to change jasqs, to pervert them into the obscenities it had named larisqs. Once embedded into a human – or a lloruk – it swiftly grew through the victim's body, its roots tangling around the nerves and spine, and through the brain. In so doing, it enveloped his will and his self-knowledge, turning him into a husk like Darhath. Worse still, if the lloruk was right, the larisq spread itself far deeper into the body than did a normal jasq. I intended to try carving out Darhath's larisq once we were somewhere safe, but I was not remotely optimistic that it would free him of its influence. How the larisqs functioned our lloruk had not known – but it had been very clear that the key to the larisqs lay in the magerealm. If the only cure lay outside the real world then Korhus was right – I was the only person who could do anything. No other human in the canyon had a jasq.

Wrack's face was bleak. He was looking at my face, almost reading my thoughts. "Not our fight" he said plaintively in narynyl.

I didn't say anything. I didn't need to. Korhus was looking between us uncertainly. I reached over to Wrack and squeezed his arm, just below where I had cut out his jasq. "You haven't felt it" I whispered, slipping into veredraa, letting Korhus know what I was saying. "Wrack, I've seen larisqs in the magerealm. They're hideous. Revolting. They need to be destroyed."

Korhus added "Anyway, I don't know how you'd get back to the surface. The lloruk constructed a barrier, millennia ago, to protect us from the horrors on the surface. Elves and other nightmares."

173

"Aren't any elves" Wrack growled. He tilted his head to one side. "And we came down without seeing any barrier."

Korhus shrugged. "I don't know enough to tell you any more. Only what the stories say."

Wrack shook his head decisively. "Volg that! Not letting some superstition prevent me heading up to the surface again!"

I shivered, not meeting Wrack's stern gaze. I was not going to agree with him – but I didn't want to argue with him. In a sense, Wrack was right – this wasn't our land. The reason for the raid on Wrack's mansion had not disappeared just because I had ended up down here. If we did get back topside, though, my possession of the jasq, and Wrack's demands upon me because of it, would make things much, much more complicated. I found myself wondering just what Tolly was going to say, too. He would be deeply, coldly angry with me – and telling him about gaining a jasq would cut no ice whatsoever. He had accepted the end of the war, and he would never have approved of the plans I and the other Firebirds had been hatching. Maybe I didn't want to return to the surface after all. And the larisqs did need dealing with – their foulness still tasted in my mouth when I thought about them.

"We need time to decide what we're going to do" I said cravenly, dodging the issue. "And I need to sleep – I'm really tired." Not a lie, but a very useful statement of the truth. Wrack knew I was hiding behind it, and opened his mouth to say so. I knew his expressions well enough that I could have quoted his pronouncement verbatim if he had been given a chance to speak.

Instead, though, Korhus spoke first, telling us both firmly to get some rest. Wrack glowered at him, and for a moment I thought he was going to argue. I saw his chest heave as he took a deep breath, and then he turned away, a growled good night hissed over his shoulder. Korhus nodded approvingly, as if we were errant children. I stuck my tongue out at him, and then at Wrack for good measure, before lying down, turning my back, and pretending to go to sleep.

My eventual dreams were a tangle of savage dragons, burning aeroplanes and bubbling larisqs.

Chapter Eighteen

I was stumbling along by the following afternoon. I had not slept well, despite being deeply tired, and we had not eaten much since leaving the hole in the ground. I don't think many of us were in much better shape. All around us was the deep jungle, every shade of scarlet leaves, flowers in a rainbow of colours, even a few green growths, and the dark trunks of trees like giant, clutching fingers. And eyes watching our passage, ranging from the tiny, glittering optics of insects up to the glowing yellow eyes of wild olgreks. What I finally decided was that there didn't seem to be any birds in the Chasm. The creatures I had seen flying had wings like Wrack's, membranes stretched tightly over fine bones. Not that the absence of avians was the main subject of my thoughts. We'd had to dodge another ruzdrool, and I'd been told there had been a swarm of adjaliks less than quarter of a mile to the east. One of our foragers, Belha, had been stung by a particularly nasty plant with a vicious spine. Her arm had swelled up – only swift action to try to get the venom out had saved her from needing amputation. She was just about able to walk, now, but she wasn't going to be doing anything else for a few days.

Kelhene reckoned we were another three days from the plain, assuming we were on track. We'd avoided a couple of lantern trees, and now we were making for a spire. Veldhra had spotted a skywire an hour ago, as it soared above us. Kelhene and Korhus, after some discussion, reckoned it was an old wire, probably one that had led to Ninthelya. Yet another lloruk city? Not really, to my pleased surprise. Two hundred years ago the human slaves in Ninthelya had rebelled, slain most of the graalur and the lloruk and driven the rest out. Now the city was a human enclave. It was over a month's travel on foot from where we now were. More worryingly, if the skywire was the road to Ninthelya, it suggested that we were well off course, much further north than we had intended.

If it wasn't a Ninthelya wire, then we were *really* lost.

Part of me imagined getting out of the jungle. Ninthelya might be over five hundred miles away, but if we could get ourselves a carriak we could get there in only a few days. A big if, of course – after the revolt in Ninthelya that skywire had been sealed off to prevent us humans misusing it. Using the skywire really wasn't very likely. More practically, though, there might be chambers in the spire that we were approaching like the ones in the spire we escaped. It might give us somewhere to rest for the night.

I gazed up at the spire, astonished again at the gigantic size of the finger of stone pointing at the clouds. Far above us the skywire was a line bisecting the sky. The jungle, bloody and livid, snarled around us. Ahead, Wrack and Eldhor were looking round the spire, seeking some way in. It was getting late – I was greatly heartened by their yell of triumph as they forced open the old, verdigrised door that must lead into the interior. I did not fancy another night in the jungle.

Not that the interior was very impressive. The tower where we left the carriak had contained smart, well-lit rooms with numerous stores and fabrications. This one was empty, battered, the chambers stripped and the smooth, glassy walls crumbling. No one had been here in decades, if not centuries, and the ruthless march of time had taken its toll. No lloruk-lights, which was less disturbing, but meant that without torches smoking out the chambers we were sitting in darkness. One room contained a stream of water which flowed apparently out of the wall. I was too tired to investigate, and ignored the minor but very welcome miracle. Food was a bigger problem – we had nothing left of the ruzdrool, (not to anyone's great regret, to be fair), and the few berries and fruits snatched from the jungle as we travelled had not been much help. We needed to send out a hunting party, but despite our hunger no one had the strength to volunteer. We slumped on the hard stone floor in a large chamber on the second floor, and we grumbled. Eldhor was the most vociferous, asking what chance we had in this savage jungle, unarmed and ill-equipped. Other voices rose in agreement or argument, until I finally got wearily to my feet and shouted at them all in a mixture of lloruk and veredraa. I can't remember what I said, now, but it contained a good selection of invective combined with a few orders. Eldhor was one of those I sent out to get some food.

Wrack was another, though it had taken a considerable degree of argument and shouting at him before he stormed out, complaining harshly that it was not his job. Three others got the job of finding more firewood to supplement the torches we had made on first arrival.

I stood in the communal chamber, directing my forces, bullying them into fixing up a fire and somewhere to skin whatever kill Eldhor and Wrack and the gang brought back, and feeling slightly guilty that I was not going hunting.

It took them almost two hours to return, and it was completely dark outside. I had posted Jandhri and Volhnik with torches to guide them back, and without the light from the flames they might well not have found us. Eldhor had a bad wound to his leg where a thorn vulch – some rather bloodthirsty breed of plant – had caught him unawares. It was bad, but it would heal. It would slow our progress, however. More welcome, though, they had a victim. The corpse was the size of a large dog, its skin covered in small plates, but Kelhene assured me it was a herbivore and was good eating. She was right, too. Once our kitchen complement had dug through its armour, they skinned it easily and the smell of roasting meat filled the spire, the first such odour it had experienced in a good few centuries, I suspected. Eldhor had even brought us back a collection of roots to boil alongside the beast – he had been seeking more when the vulch got him. We sat to a remarkably good meal, and humours improved greatly. To my surprise, I was being feted as the person responsible for everything. All I had done was give the orders. It felt good to have the adulation, though, if truth be told.

Afterwards, replete and exhausted, I set watches and crawled into a side room to collapse. I half-feared that Wrack would endeavour to come after me and badger me, so I had given him first watch. If he did have any plans, I was too far gone into slumber to be aware of them.

In the morning we got moving again. I had tried climbing higher in the spire, hoping to get a view over the red canopy of the jungle to get our bearings. No such luck – frustratingly, the way up was blocked by a substantial fall of stone, far too significant to dig through. No breakfast either, but the jungle locally turned out to be a good source of fruit, mostly tasty, some too tart to eat safely (as I discovered to my cost). I studied the landscape, gazing at the skywire above us. Even if the spire had not been very comfortable, it provided security in the raw jungle. I gave more orders to my little band, and we headed (as near as I could judge) due east, with the abandoned skywire high above us, trusting this might provide a solid benefit to us.

My hope proved valid. By late afternoon, we were nearing a second spire, the next support for the skywire. We had a little food, too, due to a lucky strike at a waterhole, where Kelhene had mugged a pair of vorodesqs (which looked more like small turquoise ruzdrools, with multiple legs and long tendrils from the heads, but which Kelhene confirmed were tasty). She had knocked them down with thrown stones, getting the first one before they knew she was there, and the second was stupid enough to run to one side, rather than away from her. I was well aware that she was a good shot with stones. Eldhor, despite his injury, had been doing his best to keep up, all the time indicating to the more agile members of the group where to find edible roots. All being well we ought to have the makings of a slim, but creditable meal.

I had been avoiding Wrack as we walked, unsure whether I wanted to talk to him. I'd ended up in Kelhene's company more than I had intended. I'd learned a certain amount about her background. She and Darhath had been lovers for some years in Muranon – she had been a glazier, and they had met when she'd been repairing a broken window at his stables. When the town fell to the graalur they had ended up in command of the exodus by default.

She was still keeping a tight rein on Darhath, but I knew that his vacant presence was damaging her morale badly.

I ended up admitting a little of my past with Wrack, explaining to her that the imposing dragon was not and was not going to be my lover. I still didn't particularly like Kelhene, but it helped to try to put what I was feeling into words... and she needed someone to talk to, to take her mind off the man only barely present with her. I was glad when we neared the next spire, and I had an excuse to wind up my exposition.

At first approach, the spire looked less welcoming. There was a gaping opening hacked into the rock, blocked by roughly-hewn chunks of timber. Wrack fingered the edges of the stone, and commented quietly that this was relatively recent work. Meaning in the last ten years, so it didn't necessarily give us cause for concern.

The base of the spire contained a single, large chamber, buttressed and pillared to keep the roof above us. Much of the heavy stone was poorly worked, but unlike our previous haven this one evidenced a soft pale blue light, apparently shining out of the few far older glassy sections of wall, which gave only just enough illumination to see by. At some stage this room had been used as some kind of stable. Straw was scattered over much of the floor, mixed with old, dry dung. A trough still contained fresh water. I eyed that warily – it looked unnaturally clean, considering the state of the stable. Had there been recent visitors?

While I was still worrying, Eldhor called out in triumph. "I've found the way up!"

Wrack reached Eldhor only a second before I did. The ramp led upwards, winding around through the wide base of the spire. A single glance showed the difference with the last spire. This one still looked in good shape, the sheen on the walls unblemished, light shimmering above us. I set out upwards, realising as I did so that Wrack had, in the same moment, done the same, wanting to take the lead. I grinned at him maliciously, and lengthened my stride to get ahead of him.

"Any justice, Sorrel, you'll walk into the traps first" he purred.

For a second I froze, before grinning again. "That's why I'm trying to get ahead" I said firmly. "I can't trust you to spot anything even if it's right under your snout."

He chuckled, but didn't argue. I slowed my pace, though, looking more warily in case there were traps left. I wished I had the nerve to slide into the magerealm, look for magical defences, but I couldn't bring myself to risk the pain.

At the top of the ramp there was a circular chamber, with numerous tunnels leading off, as well as another ramp heading further up. The layout was not dissimilar to the first spire, but this one was lit by glows from the smooth walls. That, at least, I was glad about – the lloruk-shaped lights in the first spire had been unpleasantly eerie, and I was relieved at their absence here. I glanced sidelong at Wrack. "Let everyone explore?" I said quietly.

He shrugged. "Why not?" he answered. There were more people coming up behind us. I turned as the chamber began to fill out.

"Scout around carefully" I said loudly. "If you find anything alarming, shout. Talhin, Jandhri, could you keep watch for the moment? Jeddhh, Eldhor, you take over from them in an hour, and pick two people to take over from you." To my mild amazement, the chosen victims simply nodded agreement, still not challenging my authority to give the orders. Talhin had been a stonemason in Muranon. Now he seemed content to play the soldier. He and Jandhri headed back down towards the entrance, and I saw Eldhor button-holing people. Wrack nodded slightly, almost approvingly. I straightened my shoulders, feeling mildly cross with myself that I was so pleased at his approval.

The chamber was already clearing as the rest of our motley gaggle of refugees began to delve into the spire's mysteries. Wrack nodded to me, and headed up the ramp to the next level. I followed automatically. The ramp led up to another junction, slick walls glowing softly, the floor marble-smooth and gleaming, with six passages leading off it, and rooms opening from each one. This was quite different from the spire where we had camped the night before – this place looked as though the lloruk had only just left. Wrack made his way into what looked like a surprisingly comfortable room, lit by a single glowing crystal. There was a wide, low bed and a table with depressions within it full of water. In a cavity under the table were a mound of soft, crumbly brown and ochre blocks – Wrack had already examined one, and held it out to me. "Dried food, I think" he said.

"There must have been someone here recently, Wrack" I said, worry sounding in my voice. "This tower is still in use."

"Don't think so" he replied. "Think about the spire where we left the carriak. Hadn't been used for centuries, but was still in good shape."

"Yes, but they were still using that skywire!"

"So?" he answered unhelpfully. "Depends if their magic was still working. Reckon in the last spire the magic had broken down, so it decayed. This one, their magics have survived."

"Enough to preserve their foods?"

Wrack shrugged. "How hungry are you?"

Ravenous, was the answer, now he unkindly reminded me of my stomach. I had no doubt that our group's cooks would be turning Kelhene's prey into a dependable meal, but I also knew how little meat there was on the vorodesqs. If this *was* edible... I took a handful of the chestnut and yellow lumps, determined to experiment. They didn't look very appetising. I dipped one in the nearest bowl – the lump swelled, and a savoury smell filled the air. Somehow, impossibly, it smelt like fresh food. I looked at it suspiciously. Could it be safe to eat? Lloruk magic, again, preserving it? My stomach growled, insisting that it smelt delicious. If I was going to die, I'd rather be poisoned than starve to death. I saluted Wrack, and took a bite. Not the best food I'd ever tasted, but palatable and filling. No hint of being a few hundred years old. I ate another couple of bites. My stomach told me this was a good idea, and I ate the rest. No immediate ill-effects, fortunately.

Wrack chuckled, watching me eat. "Thought I'd let you poison-test first" he commented, before following suit. I glared at him and concentrated on eating.

There was also a bathtub, which I was eyeing hungrily as I sated my need for sustenance. All right, so it was a depression in the floor full of warm water. What more do you need?

Actually, privacy. Did I dare undress in front of Wrack? During the long, fraught months as his slave I had expended a substantial amount of effort to avoid doing anything that he might perceive as an invitation. He had not made any secret of his interest in my body, and he had tried to persuade me to surrender to him more than once. I did not want to reawaken his intentions, assuming my current garb had not already done that. On the other hand, I really liked the idea of dunking myself thoroughly. I finished off the food and got to my feet. "I'm going to explore some more" I said firmly, and made for the door. I didn't need to look back to see what Wrack was doing – he had still been stuffing his face when I made my move. Dragons have big appetites.

Once into the corridor, I headed left, towards the next passageway. My hope was that there were a number of rooms like the one we had occupied, and that I could find another similar chamber far enough from Wrack for my safety.

The first room I tried was a store room of some variety. Bales, boxes, long tubes and odd globes. I poked some of them with interest. Lengths of cloth, pieces of worked metal, packets of the dry food. I picked out an iron bar, so that I had a makeshift weapon, and then I tried the next room, taking one chunk of loose cloth with me as a towel.

At first glance this was similar to the room Wrack had found. I only gave it one glance, though. The room was occupied – the red-haired woman and the tall, dark-haired young man who always seemed to be together were sharing the bath-tub. I blushed and backed out hastily, but I doubt that they noticed me at all.

I moved hastily into the room beyond. This was another living room like the previous one, but this was unoccupied. I glanced around briefly, and then went to the room beyond that. Not that I was embarrassed, you understand, but I didn't want to be next door to the lovers. It would have been helpful if these chambers had doors. Lockable ones. To prevent embarrassments... and also to keep out wandering predators, whether human or draconic.

I was going to have to make the most of this room. It was at the end of a corridor, and there looked to be no more openings beyond it. The layout was identical, and there was the same collection of food in the table cavity. And there was water, and it was steaming gently. How, I did not know. Nor care, at the moment. I had not realised until I peeled off my harness and slid into the water how much my body ached. I was covered with bruises and grazes, red marks and lumps. Not to mention accumulated grime. The water was going dark in moments. There was a cream oval that might be soap resting in a niche near the depression. It might just as well be more dried food, but I was going to make an assumption that the lloruk were not totally dissimilar in outlook to humans.

The oval lathered nicely, and turned the water even more dark and murky. I wished there was some way of emptying it and starting anew. Of course, I could just sneak into the next room and use the water there. I had a towel, and the odds were that I wouldn't be spotted by anyone. Probably.

Hmmm. Anyhow, the water had been clean and warm, despite the chamber not having been visited for decades. How could that be? The faint pulse in my side was the obvious answer. I pulled myself up out of the grimy water and turned to look at the murky scum. If this tub was being filled somehow from the magerealm then I ought to see a change pretty soon.

Sure enough, within moments of decamping from the warmth, the depression emptied. There was no opening in the structure – the water just swirled away into nothingness. I watched, trying to be patient, not wanting to reach for my towel and soak it.

Nothing happened. No new water. I scowled at it, willing the water to flow back into the space.

A soft cough at the doorway. I spun round and grabbed my towel. Wrack was standing, watching me, his eyes running up and down my body. I considered going for the iron bar, but instead I just pulled the towel around me and glared at him. "It isn't good manners to intrude when a lady is having a bath!"

He chuckled. "Not got any manners, you know. Where's this mythical lady?"

I stuck two fingers up at him. Beside me, there was a gurgle of water as the depression filled again, the water steaming, clearly very hot indeed. Too hot? I dipped a foot in, cautiously. Yes, considerably too hot! I waved my scalded toes to cool them down.

"Clever" Wrack murmured. "How did you make it refill?"

"It came out of the magerealm" I answered automatically. Wrack nodded as though that explained everything, still leaning nonchalantly against the doorpost. "Did you want something?" I added tartly, before realising that I was giving him a very easy opening.

To my surprise, he resisted the temptation. He was still in his leathers, and clearly hadn't yet availed himself of the opportunity to get cleaned up. "Wanted to make sure you were all right" he answered easily.

"I am" I snapped back. "Now, unless you've something useful to say, I want to go back to my bath."

"Too hot." Volg it, I hate it when Wrack is so calmly sensible.

"It'll cool down pretty soon" I replied shortly. Actually, I suspected it might be some time before it was bearable. I'd tried soaking in really hot water in Werintar one time, but that had been a matter of working up to it, adding hot water to a cooler bath gingerly. Going straight into this – I didn't want to be a boiled crab.

"You could share mine" Wrack murmured.

I actually relaxed slightly. I had been waiting for Wrack to try it on with me. Now he finally had, and I could respond. I shook my head firmly. "Not a chance, Wrack" I snarled. He looked almost surprised. I struggled to resist grinning at his affronted expression.

"Don't understand you, Sorrel" he growled, his deep, rich voice rumbling in his chest.

I bit back a couple of epithets, and just glowered at him. "Volg off, Wrack!" Crude, direct, but it avoided the need to say what I really felt about him. For a moment I thought he would storm in and try to grab me despite my words. I saw muscles tensing in his shoulders, in the set of his jaw. We faced each other for a moment that felt like a century - and then he turned on his heel and stalked off down the corridor. I released a breath I hadn't realised I was holding, and I sat down on the floor, pulling the towel tight around me, listening to him marching away. I was just waiting for the water to cool down, now.

I sat and stared at the water. I had really enjoyed soaking in the bath until Wrack turned up. Now... I didn't know whether I dared slide back into the warm embrace. I sat for long minutes, the towel wrapped tightly round me, before I finally returned to the water, still almost too hot to bear. I was going to have a soak in the clean water, wash my hair, make myself feel really clean for the first time in too many days. If Wrack wanted to come back and ogle me he did so at his own risk.

But it was not Wrack who appeared in the doorway.

Chapter Nineteen

I had almost dozed off when I heard the sound of feet. Boots, I realised. I opened my eyes blearily – the man standing in the doorway, grinning as he admired me, was not anyone I knew. He most definitely was not one of our group. He was tall, at least six feet, with short, fair hair and Chasm-pale skin. Good-looking, too. Very good-looking, I realised. His body was in proportion and well-made, wearing the same sort of kilt that seemed common throughout the deep land. He also had a sharp sword in one hand. He didn't look as surprised to see me as I was at his presence. I grabbed my towel and scrambled out of the water, only belatedly remembering the iron bar, which was, inevitably, out of reach. I suspected I was going to have to accept that my ablutions were over.

"Who the volg are you?" I snapped in what I hoped was comprehensible Veredraa.

"I was going to ask you the same question" he drawled. His voice wasn't as deep as Wrack's, but it had a pleasing timbre.

"After you" I said formally.

My discoverer executed a neat bow. "My name is Griffyn. Whom do I have the pleasure of addressing?"

"I'm Sorrel" I said firmly, not trying to match his theatrical speech.

He waited, expecting me to be more forthcoming. No way was I falling for that gambit. "What are you doing here?" I demanded instead.

He paused for a moment, and then calmly murmured "I and my compatriots happen to live here. What's your excuse?"

I took a step back. "You work for the Iloruk?"

His expression gave me his answer, even before he firmly denied any such position. "These chambers haven't been used for a long time" he added. "I'd thought everyone had forgotten they existed." His expression grew irritated. "It seems I was wrong." He pointed his sword at me. "What are you doing here?"

"Getting clean" I replied in an effort at wit. Not much of an effort, I have to accept.

His grimace suggested he was not amused. His sword didn't move away from me, either. "I take it you're in charge of this rabble."

It was a statement, not a question, but I nodded in agreement, before gesturing at his blade. "Do you have to point that at me?"

For a moment I thought he was going to say 'Yes', but instead he lowered the sword. I reached for my harness and my underwear. I glowered at him. "Turn around" I ordered.

"You expect me to let you thump me? Don't be ridiculous."

I turned my back pointedly. Over my shoulder, as I dressed, I asked "How many of you are there?"

There was a yell from down the corridor. We both broke into a run, bursting into the room at the far end together. There were three more strangers in here, swords pointed at Wrack. He was pointing his sword at them and was standing at bay, ready to strike. I shook my head in disbelief. I had managed to talk to my stranger. Wrack, of course, decided to fight.

"Wrack!" I bellowed. All heads turned, gratifyingly. I like being able to seize control. "Put the sword away! They're on our side!"

I hoped I was right about that. Still, any enemy of the Iloruk had to be a friend... didn't he?

Wrack lowered his sword. I was trying to get a handle on the quartet. Three men, one woman. All human, as far as I could tell (after all, it wasn't obvious what Wrack really was, either). My captor – no, my discoverer, I wanted to assume he was friendly - was probably the leader. The woman was fair haired, solidly built, rather plain, and was looking at Wrack warily. The other two... one was a mousy, slight type, who looked equally nervous. I mentally pegged him as a book-keeper. The last man was thinner than Griffyn, with straggly red hair and the edgy expression of someone always expecting to be scolded,. I wondered whether Griffyn or the woman was the one with a sharp tongue.

Other people were tumbling into the room with us, as more of my motley group of refugees came to the call. Griffyn was pointing his sword at Wrack again. I glared at him. After a few moments he lowered the blade, and the atmosphere grew more relaxed. I inclined my head in acknowledgement.

"This is Wrack" I explained unnecessarily. "That's Kelhene, Korhus, Jaldhor..." Wrack was evidently unhappy at the fact that I was the one doing the talking. Good. I liked making Wrack feel unimportant. "And your friends?"

Griffyn gestured widely, giving names. The woman was Darhia, the mousy bookish man Farrys, and the thin, harassed one was Kentyr. I used to think I was pretty good at remembering names, but I seemed to be meeting so many new faces that I was starting to get confused. I just hoped I could keep track of these. I nodded to Griffyn's people. Griffyn's disconcertingly blue eyes were on me. "I hope now you'll do me the courtesy of telling us who you are?"

I shrugged. As far as I was aware, we had nothing to hide. Well, not that much to hide, anyhow. I gestured to the chairs in Wrack's room, and we endeavoured to relax as I gave him a potted summary about the Grihl Valley, the graalur raid and the rescue from Ilkadala. I didn't bother to explain where Wrack and I came from, though, nor about my jasq. Afterwards, I fixed him with my eyes (not an unpleasant task, I would add). "So what's *your* story?" I asked.

Griffyn smiled, and bowed again. "I should have introduced myself properly" he said suavely. "I am Griffyn, the primary thorn in the side of the serpent-kind."

Korhus responded before I could think of a witty retort. "You're the gang who were killing lloruk" he said accusingly.

Griffyn's smile widened. "Precisely!" he said proudly. "My task is fighting back against them. I'm doing a very good job of hitting them where it hurts!"

Korhus wasn't amused. "The graalur say you're the main reason the lloruk are clobbering us."

Griffyn looked outraged at the implication. "Don't be ridiculous! I'm just used as an excuse for their desire to conquer!"

I interrupted the squabble before they could come to blows. "Where did you come from?" I asked. "I left guards on the door to the spire."

Griffyn chuckled. "I came down, not up. We were camped two levels above you. We use the skywire to get around."

I blinked. "You've got a carriak?"

All four of them were grinning, now, clearly proud of some secret, but Griffyn was shaking his head. "I can't really talk about that sort of thing until I know for certain I can trust you" he said calmly.

"What are you going to do with us?" asked Eldhor, a faint nervousness in his voice. This Griffyn obviously had quite a reputation. The question was what he had done to earn it.

Two hours talking did not give me a clear answer. Griffyn was charming, friendly, talkative – and told us virtually nothing. He and his little group of guerrillas had been lurking in the spire for some time, using it as a base for their activities against the Iloruk. Griffyn's gang had been raiding Iloruk outposts and outlying farms for over eight months. They were originally from Ninthelya, the Iloruk city that had rebelled. How they got to their targets he and his cohorts would not reveal. Nor would he tell us how they chose their objectives, or the intentions behind their efforts.

Griffyn was extremely handsome, in a lean, rakish fashion. There had been a hero in a number of Verin's trashier pulps – I couldn't for the life of me recall his name now – who had lived as an outlaw fighting back against a villainous dragonlord. Griffyn had rather the feel of that swashbuckling rogue, always getting himself into deep trouble but escaping by the skin of his teeth (and some rather improbable plots) in time to sweep the current damsel into his bed. Verin had dearly wanted to be him – Tornus, that had been the character's name. Verin didn't have the style or the charisma needed to be a dashing hero. Griffyn just might. I wasn't sure if that made me feel more or less comfortable about being part of his gang. Tornus had been too good to be true. In real life, anyone trying to emulate his deeds would end up dead in very short order.

What did become clear was that Griffyn loathed the Iloruk, and would do anything he could to attack them. Despite his charm, he was deeply suspicious of us, suspecting a plot or a conspiracy against him. By the time I finally gave up and told him I needed to sleep I had told our story three times, each time with more details as he probed my account, clearly looking for inconsistencies and lies. My people were equally unsure of him. Korhus did not disguise his dislike of the rebels, or his confidence that their actions were the cause of the lloruk offensive. Chelhik and Jandhri, on the other hand, were visibly elated at being in the presence of the hero (as they saw him). The views of the others fell somewhere between those extremes, with the majority tending to lean towards Korhus, apart from a couple of the women who were obviously smitten by Griffyn's good looks. Griffyn was sensing the mix of attitudes, and it only added to his edginess as he explored our description of what we had done. We had not come to any conclusions as to what he intended to do with us, or what our view of him amounted to.

As I walked back to the room I had chosen as mine, I found Kelhene alongside me.

"Do you trust him?" she asked bluntly.

I shrugged. "I don't know enough about him" I answered simply.

"Darhath had the same view as Korhus" she said quietly. "Griffyn pretty much single-handedly caused the lloruk to set the graalur to attack us."

I stopped and looked at her. "You really think so?"

"That's what the graalur said" she answered. "They kept telling us that if we handed him over, stopped harbouring him, the lloruk would stop their assault. The trouble was, we didn't know where he was hiding. No one did."

I grimaced. "That doesn't make things any easier" I replied. I was yawning, my eyes burning in my head. I bade Kelhene good night, and retreated. The room was the most comfortable accommodation I'd had the whole time I'd been in the Rift. I could understand why Griffyn had chosen the spire as his base. I had nothing to wear in bed, but I seldom did anyway. I pulled the sheet over my head, wishing I could stop the crystal glowing. Obligingly, as I settled down, it duly did. The lloruk magics were very clever.

Despite my fatigue, thoughts were churning in my head and I did not drift into slumber immediately. I was just settling down when I heard soft, careful footsteps as someone eased into the room, shrouded in the darkness. I sat up, trying to remember where I'd put the iron bar, and the crystal glowed helpfully.

Wrack was standing there, looking at me. His eyes were on mine, almost appealing. I had forgotten just how compelling his scrutiny could be. I held his gaze, letting him explain why he was creeping into my room.

"Wanted to... talk to you" he said unsteadily.

"Really?" I said drily. "You wanted to 'talk'?"

He sat on the corner of my bed. So close to me, I was intensely aware of his presence, his masculinity. I eased the sheet up round me. Not the best protection, but better than nothing.

"Yes" he said firmly. He paused, and I waited.

"Well?" I finally prompted.

"My arm will be fit enough for me to fly soon, Sorrel. Being near my jasq – healing faster."

"Good!" I said. I meant it, too. Seeing him crippled didn't amuse me. The jasq had felt warmer for the last few days – now I suspected I knew why.

"I want to make a bid for the surface" he said emphatically.

I looked away. His good hand caught my face, and he turned me to look at him. "There's nothing down here for you, Sorrel! This isn't our home!"

"I... haven't made up my mind what I want to do" I said lamely.

Wrack didn't give me a chance to say anything more coherent. He held my face and glared into my eyes. "You belong on the surface, Sorrel! We both do!"

And then he leant forward and kissed me, full on the mouth.

After an eternal moment, I reacted instinctively, shoving him away and scrambling to my feet, belatedly grabbing my sheet to provide some semblance of modesty. He grinned, gazing at me as I stood there.

"Try that again and I'll scream blue murder" I snarled.

He took a step closer, and shook his head in what almost looked like confusion. "Is my presence so horrible, Sorrel?" He reached out with his hand, resting it against the side of my cheek gently. It was a gesture he had used countless times when I had been his slave. He could be so harsh, so aggressive – but sometimes he could be calm, gentle, almost as though he cared for me.

"Do you want a straight answer?" I retorted.

His eyes hardened, the temper that bubbled to the surface so easily flaring up, engulfing the caring visage he had been wearing. I had seen his mood change like this so often at his mansion, and it usually presaged violence. "Try to be nice to you

– all I get is insults!" he snarled.

"Get out and you won't get any more insults!"

Wrack grabbed hold of my wrist. "You're still my slave, Sorrel!"

I tried to wrench myself free, but his grip was as strong as ever. He pulled me closer to him, his lips dangerously near mine. His voice was suddenly low and intense, and I was hotly aware of his nearness.

"What are you going to do now? Scream?" he asked fiercely.

Instead I kicked at him. He must have expected it, and twisted his body to prevent my foot hitting anything vital. At the same time he pulled at my sheet again, jerking it out of my grip. I snarled an obscenity and flung myself at him, clawing at him and trying to bite his face. He hadn't expected the sudden assault, and we toppled backwards onto the floor. He was underneath. He tried to save himself with his injured arm, and I heard him cry out in pain. Clobbering him hard was really satisfying. As he rolled out from under me, flinging me sideways, the crystal chose that instant to go out, and we were in darkness. I lashed out, guessing where he would be on the floor. There was a satisfying impact and another moan of pain. I had hoped to catch him between his legs, but it felt more like his thigh I had connected with. I kicked again, hard, hoping he'd move and leave himself vulnerable. Again I felt my foot strike his flesh, but this time he grabbed at my ankle. He only had one working hand – I kicked with the other foot at his elbow, hoping to cripple his uninjured arm. He gasped again, and wrenched my ankle upwards, slamming me back onto the floor with bruising force. I kicked again, aiming upwards, and there was another solid impact. His grip relaxed, and I scrambled back up onto the bed. The crystal lit, revealing his wan face as he sat there on the floor.

"You... didn't scream" he growled.

"Didn't need to" I said tartly. "You want to try that again?"

He chuckled. I could hear the edge of pain in his voice. I had hurt him. Good. "Tempting. You're worth fighting for."

I glared at him. "Next time I'll make sure you never touch anyone again."

He shrugged. "I tried to talk, Sorrel."

I turned my back on him, daring him to try it. He stood there for a few moments, and I could sense him running his eyes over my bare body. I waited, muscles tensed... and I heard him turn and walk out. I wasn't sure if I was relieved or disappointed. I turned over, watching after him. I could barely keep my eyes open, but it felt like a long time before I finally slept.

I was woken by shouts and pounding feet. By the time I was on my feet, I had Griffyn's sword pointing at my throat, his face wreathed in fury. "You volging squumer!" he was shouting. "You led them right here! Betraying your own kind to the lloruk!"

I had no doubt that he was about to stab me. His eyes were wide, bright with hatred. I had absolutely no idea what he was talking about, which didn't help. I didn't have time to ask questions – I flung myself backwards, feeling his blade scraping across my neck as he tried to execute me for whatever imagined crime I had committed. Only the speed of my reactions prevented the sharp weapon cutting my throat. I tumbled to the floor and scrambled backwards, trying to get further away from the homicidal maniac attempting to kill me.

The tower shook, the walls vibrating like a drum. My attempts to get up were sabotaged thoroughly by the impact. Fortunately, Griffyn tumbled over too, struggling to keep his footing.

"What's happening?" I yelled at him.

"Your volging friends are here!" he snarled, slicing the air in my general direction.

"My friends don't usually try to kill me!" I replied hotly.

"I'm not your friend!" he rasped in response.

The spire jolted again. I let the impact hurl me across the room, so that I could grab the iron bar from where I had dropped it the previous evening. As I felt the comforting shape of the metal in my hand I saw one of Griffyn's team – Farrys, I thought he was – at the doorway.

"Two scorturliqs!" he snapped. "And about fifty graalur!"

Griffyn turned, his attention momentarily distracted from spearing me. "How many lloruk?"

"One or two, no more!"

I finally had enough information to work out roughly what was going on, albeit that I had no idea what two scorturliqs were. "You need capable fighters, Griffyn!" I snapped. "I'm on your side, whatever you may think! Instead of fighting me, let's go get the lloruk!"

Obviously I'd got a pretty good handle on Griffyn already. He looked back at me for a moment, then nodded brusquely. He didn't say anything, just headed through the doorway and towards the ramp down. I grabbed my kilt and harness and followed, keeping a safe distance from him in case he changed his mind, pulling my clothes into place as I ran.

Chapter Twenty

Three graalur were hacking savagely at Talhin and Volhnik in the entrance to the spire. My two men were retreating, bloody scratches oozing scarlet as they fell back under the onslaught. Griffyn and I both leapt forward, weapons striking in tandem as we turned the tables on the attackers. My graalur fell to my second blow, his skull broken – Griffyn downed his a moment later. Volhnik shouted in triumph as he pushed the last graalur into the line of Talhin's blade, providing the stonemason with an easy target. I tossed my iron bar aside and seized one of the graalur swords.

The spire vibrated again, the deep boom of an impact against the structure shaking us to the bone. It felt like being inside a kicked kettle.

"What was that?" I demanded.

Griffyn glanced back at me as he scrambled through the door into the outside world. "One of the scorturliqs" was his helpful, clear response. I glowered at his back and followed.

The jungle was lit by the lantern trees. It could have been any time between dawn and early evening. I had no idea how long I had been asleep. Volg it, I wished there was an easy way to tell the time down here!

Not that the lack of a clock was high on my list of priorities. Looming over us, no more than forty feet away, was a gigantic monstrosity fully two hundred feet long and twenty feet high. It was the shape of a cigar, but with a multitude of legs sprouting from each side like oars from a galley. Each leg was twice the width of my thigh and stretched out fifteen feet to the side before bending almost back on itself and down to the ground, lifting the brute so that the lowest part of its body was more than an arm's length over my head. It looked like a dull purple spider stretched long and thin, with a dozen extra legs on each side of the extended body.

The head I could see very clearly, as it was looking down at me with four large, egg-shaped yellow eyes, mandibles in the jaw dripping some unpleasant creamy ichor. The creature reared up, and for a moment I thought it would strike down at me and bite with the jaws, which looked large enough to eat an aeroplane, let alone a pilot. Instead, though, it slammed its body forward, striking with its six front legs at the spire, causing the stonework to boom like a hollow tree hit with a mallet.

More graalur were swinging down on ropes from the sides of the brute; they must have been riding the creature. I realised the point of its assault on the spire – it had enabled some of the graalur to scramble off their mount onto the side of the spire where it had carved openings with the immense claws of its feet. The graalur were already inside our fortress, and we would soon be attacked from both sides.

Six graalur were bearing down on us now they had decamped from their monster. The scorturliq, having delivered its cargo, now looked down at us. I fancied I could see a lloruk still seated behind the head of the brute. I hacked at the leading graalur, only to find I was facing a far more competent example of the breed. She parried my first thrust with contemptuous ease and swung at me ruthlessly. Only dumb luck saved me – one of the graalur's companions, trying to get to Griffyn, slipped on a protruding tree root and bumped into my attacker, throwing off her blow. I took cruel advantage of the mishap to ensure the woman didn't menace me or anyone else again, catching her in her stomach and shoving the blade home. Griffyn downed the graalur whose mishap had saved me. See – doing a good deed doesn't give any just desserts.

As I wrenched the blade out of the body of my victim, I heard Volhnik cry out in agony. I turned, to see him slide to the ground, another graalur grinning at his victory. I snarled an obscenity and tried to go for him, but Talhin got there first. Griffyn shouted in alarm, and I flung myself sideways as another assailant did her best to eviscerate me. Unsuccessfully, fortunately for me. I returned the compliment with somewhat more success. I had forgotten the smell of this kind of conflict – blood, shit and sweat. I wiped some of that sweat from my left eye and turned. The scorturliq was at an impossible angle, a third of its body against the side of the spire as though it were planning to climb up it. The spire had to be four hundred feet high – it looked as though the brute stretched half way up it, more graalur scrambling into an opening broken into the side.

Griffyn had downed the last of our immediate opposition, but we knew that there would be more. A second scorturliq emerged from the jungle – I guessed it had been circling the tower, ensuring there was no other threat in the vicinity. It still had its complement of graalur on its back. We were badly outnumbered.

My jasq was pounding in my side. I clutched at myself, uncertain what I was feeling, hoping that it was not a sign of lloruk sorcery being used against us. There was a shout from one of the fresh openings in the side of the spire. A graalur tumbled towards the ground, hitting the side of the spire as she fell. She was dead before she crashed into a bush. Another figure was in the opening, sixty feet above us, deep red in colour, the hint of dark wings behind him. He stood there for a moment, dominating the scene, before a torrent of fire gushed down from him, coruscating over the back of the new scorturliq. There were screams and shouts from the graalur. Some leapt from the back of the monster, falling thirty feet to the ground below. Others were trying to beat out the orange flames. There were yells of surprised delight at the sudden change in our fortunes; I could see Griffyn staring upwards at the imposing figure, trying to work out what he was seeing. I grinned in amusement at his expression, and then dived sideways, grabbing him to pull him clear as a scortuliq's foot came out of nowhere to slam into the ground where we had been standing. My jasq was still thumping painfully below my ribs – I felt sure that it was lloruk work, not Wrack's change that was causing this new resonance.

I looked up, and felt the blood freeze in my veins despite the heat of the ground under us. Looming over us was the first scorturliq, its gigantic frame filling my vision as it wound itself around the spire and back to us. The lloruk atop it was looking down at me and at Griffyn as the vast jaws of its mount gaped like a doorway to oblivion. There was no doubt in my mind that its intentions were immediate and lethal. Griffyn was yelling something defiant and trying to squirm away, but there was no possible way that he could escape from the creature's bite. Above us I saw more yellow flame licking down to wreathe around the lloruk. My jasq was hammering in my side so loudly that I could not hear what Griffyn was shouting. The flames were having no effect whatsoever upon the lloruk, despite the fact that Wrack was expending every iota of fire upon it. The lloruk was using the elements within the magerealm to quell the heat somehow, turning Wrack's efforts into empty iridescence. The head of the scorturliq swung down towards us almost lazily; the brutish creature evidently enjoyed playing with its prey. Griffyn stabbed at it desperately as it came within a few feet of us, and it pulled back, emitting a hiss of foul-smelling vapour as it did so. The orange and yellow brilliance above us faded into the dull light of the Chasm, shadows rushing in as Wrack's efforts came to naught. I knew that I was about to die, devoured by a monstrous creature in the depths of a sunken world. I watched Griffyn driving his sword upwards in a hopeless frenzy. I was quite still, watching, taking no part as I waited for destruction. This was so vast, so far beyond anything I had imagined that I could not think of responding.

The jasq thumped in my side, the rhythm uneven as the lloruk guiding the brute worked new sorceries. When the scorturliq's jaws closed my agonies would cease.

Another blast of foetid air from the creature's mouth washed over me as it lunged down again, no longer afraid of Griffyn's sword. I stared at my death coming towards me, and half-choked in the foulness of its breath. I gasped and ducked, and the motion broke my paralysis. Yes, the monster was vast, its bulk greater than any living thing I had ever faced. Its hide looked like two inches of boiled purple leather, and Griffyn's blows had barely scratched it. But it was alive. And that meant it could be killed. Dying was going to hurt me far more than a few moments in the magerealm. I swept myself into the embrace of the brilliance and seized a length of fire. I had no idea where the creature's weak spots were, but the eyes seemed a good target. I flung the flame upwards towards where its eyes had been fixed upon us evilly a moment before. For good measure I hurled a torrent of water further up to where the lloruk had been seated upon its mount. The mage might be shielded against fire, but if so a gushing waterspout ought to catch it by surprise.

The pain hit me, but far less than it usually did – perhaps I was growing inured to it – and I slid out of the realm, tumbling to the ground. If my ploy had failed, I would be dead in moments, and the pain wouldn't matter anyway.

Above me, the scorturliq was twisting and turning. It was not screaming or shrieking, just hissing in the same tone as before, but acrid smoke was balled around the front of its face.. Griffyn was staring up at it in disbelief.

Something tumbled down towards us like a broken necklace, hitting the ground heavily. It stirred, clearly in pain. The scaled hide and the short, stubby arms of a wet lloruk twisted as it struggled to recover from its fall. It lifted its head, the tongue licking out through the narrow lips of the snake mouth. Around its head, incongruously, it was wearing jewelry, a tracery of silver inset with blue and yellow gems, held in shape by four curving ivory cylinders. I stared into the lloruk's indigo eyes, trying to read its expression.

Griffyn didn't bother to try. He stormed forward and hacked at it viciously with his sword, the blade carving a scarlet chasm into its neck. It cried out in startled pain, and he chopped again, decapitating the serpentman. The head hit the ground a few feet from me, still twitching, the jewelry shattering. The shining gems went dark. In my side, I felt my jasq quiver and subside, and a faint feeling of nausea clutched at my guts.

Above us, the scorturliq was throwing itself around in agony, the smoke rising from its head proving that its flesh was afire. It was still not screaming or crying out, but it was hissing like a punctured kettle. The smell of scorched meat was not even remotely appetising.

Yellow-orange light brightened above us for a moment, another tongue of fire lashing down from the opening where Wrack perched. The wash of flame was too much for the gigantic creature, and it turned, fleeing into the jungle, one of its forefeet slamming down into the ground only a foot from me. I rolled sideways instinctively, and two more of its legs dug into the scarlet grass where I had been a moment before. I heard Wrack's alarmed shout echo above me. Griffyn caught hold of me, hauling me further clear as the agonised creature blundered into the jungle, demolishing a wide pathway through the red vegetation.

"Are you all right?" he snapped. He didn't wait for my answer, though, already moving to intercept a graalur who was retreating in alarm. Griffyn ensured the soldier's worries ended, shoving his blade through the man's back mercilessly and twisting the blade. I wasn't going to argue – I didn't feel up to protesting.

Something dark, wings spread, slammed into the churned grass less than three feet from me. Griffyn whirled, blade extended to protect me. I was yelling at him to back off, that this was a friend. It would take too long to explain that the dark red figure, wings stretched wide, was actually Wrack. His head was turned towards me, the eyes wide and concerned. I grinned wanly. I could still feel the jasq beating slowly in my side, and the pain of the magerealm was still more than a memory. The dragon reached down, nuzzling me with his snout. Griffyn was beside me in a moment, pushing Wrack back from me. Wrack did not approve of this and bellowed at him to get away from me. I snarled an obscenity and tried to get up, only to realise that my legs were resembling soaked pasta. Both men tried to grab for me. Griffyn got there first – he had the advantage of arms instead of wings. Wrack growled something deep and surly, and I felt my jasq grumbling in my side as he changed back.

Griffyn was looking primarily at me, and asking again if I was all right, this time watching me as he waited for my reply. I nodded slowly, not sure that I could give a clear answer. It was not unpleasant being cradled in the arms of a very handsome man, and I didn't feel much like moving for a moment or two. I still felt like pasta, but just uncooked rather than soaked, now. Griffyn's eyes were no longer on me, though, and I turned my head, knowing what I would see. Wrack was reverting to his human form, the scales fading and his snout becoming more human. Griffyn looked astonished, and I grinned to myself. A few moments, and Wrack was his old self. Griffyn's eyes were wide, looking at him in disbelief.

"I'll take her" Wrack said firmly to him, reaching for me.

Griffyn shook his head. "What... what in blazes *are* you?" he hissed.

"A dragon. What did you think I was?"

Griffyn looked at him, weighing up his response. I could see the vein in his neck pulsing. Griffyn was clearly badly shaken at the sight of the transformation. Wrack did not give him an opportunity to protest, and effortlessly lifted me out of his arms, swinging me around. I was not putting up with this, however weak I felt. I struggled in his grasp, realising as I did so that I was not in any fit state to argue. He swept me towards the spire, Griffyn scrambling to keep up. Being held by two attractive men in one day - most women would have willingly been in my place. I wasn't so sure about it.

"I suppose you know you're nude?" Griffyn asked Wrack abruptly.

"Clothes are upstairs" Wrack replied shortly. As always, a state of undress did not trouble Wrack. Griffyn, on the other hand, was obviously somewhat uncertain about Wrack himself and his intentions.

Other people were clattering down the stairs to meet us. I again tried to get out of Wrack's grip, this time feeling strong enough to insist. He glowered at me, but as my protestations grew stronger he finally swung me onto my feet. I had a horrible feeling that I would wilt at his feet, but my legs were just about returning to working order, and I stood a little shakily beside him.

Darhia and Kentyr were reporting to Griffyn, eyes sidelong at Wrack as he stood unselfconsciously beside me. The graalur had been driven back. Wrack had roasted a lloruk, and the only other had fallen in front of us when I flamed the scorturliq. With the two lloruk down, the graalur had lost heart. One scorturliq - the one I had scorched - was dead in the jungle four hundred yards from us. The other had retreated with the surviving graalur. Only a handful had got away. The ones in the tower were all dead.

We had our own casualties. Aside from Volhnik, Borhun had been taken by surprise by the graalur who had entered the spire near the top. They had killed him before he could get his hands on a weapon. I swallowed, feeling a lump in my throat. I hadn't known the young man particularly well – I'd exchanged no more than a dozen words with him – but he had always been friendly and practical. Jaldhor was dead, too, the loser in a duel with two graalur in the entrance to the spire. Ulsdher and Belha were both injured, Belha seriously. A graalur sword had caught her below her ribs, and I was astonished that she was still alive; she had been injured before, and this second wound worried me intensely. Farrys was injured, too, a ragged gash to his arm causing him considerable pain.

I was surprised just how angry and upset I was about losing Volhnik, Borhun and Jaldhor, and how much worry I felt about Belha, particularly. They were my group, it struck me, and their pain hurt me, too. The battle strengthened my resolve – I was going to get them to safety.

Despite our losses, we had actually come through relatively unscathed. I suspected the graalur had been ordered to capture us rather than to kill us, or we would have had more casualties.

I slumped down into a relatively comfortable chair. Griffyn was looking at me, questions clearly bubbling on his tongue. Wrack had gone further up through the tower after seeing me settled. I sipped a glass of something red and strongly alcoholic that Kelhene had passed to me wordlessly. I had needed something to return some fire to my body.

Griffyn was perched on the arm of the chair opposite me like a worried falcon, waiting impatiently for me to submit to his questions. I lifted the glass to him in silent thanks for his forbearance, and quietly launched into our tale, telling him about the surface and the war with the dragons. By the time I was a quarter of the way through my bowdlerised account, Wrack had joined us, now dressed again. Griffyn had been watching my face intently as I talked – now his attentions went to Wrack, eyeing the man's muscled body.

"No scales in this form" Wrack said curtly after a few moments of the scrutiny.

Griffyn smiled a little uncomfortably. "I don't think you'll be surprised that we're curious about you. You must understand that it's natural for us to stare."

Wrack scowled but did not protest. I went on with the saga, describing the descent into the Chasm and the crash, skating over the cause edgily. Thus far, I had not admitted that Wrack had been one of the enemy. "I told you the rest of our story last night" I finished, rather weakly. I was feeling somewhat wan, and held out the glass towards Kelhene. She refilled it – the spirit wasn't brandy, but it was close enough to be welcome. She also handed me a plate of sweetbread liberally coated with something like marmalade. I devoured it hungrily whilst talking, realising as I did so that I hadn't had any breakfast. The marmalade was tart and tangy, tasting of some citrus fruit that I didn't recognise but which was very palatable.

"Can I ask the reason for the lloruk interest in you?" Griffyn queried as I ate.

I shrugged. "They realised I had a jasq" I said through a mouthful. "They didn't like that."

"Which is why they sent two scorturliqs after you" came Kentyr's growl from the side of the room. I looked round, to realise that virtually everyone was crammed into the chamber, listening to my account. I realised that even the Grihl Valley contingent had been hearing some of the story for the first time. I just nodded, trying to suppress pangs of guilt that I had brought this assault upon us all.

Griffyn clearly wasn't satisfied. "So why did you collapse after casting your magic?" he asked quietly.

"We all want to know that" Wrack muttered deeply. His face was shadowed, lines of worry across his forehead.

I shook my head. "I don't know. All I know is that sometimes when I go into the magerealm it hurts. A lot."

Griffyn paused, thinking about that. "I wonder if the lloruk suffer the same way?"

I shrugged again, licking a few traces of marmalade off my fingers. "I doubt it" I said, somewhat sourly.

"We need to find out what's happening to you, Sorrel" Wrack said. "Could be really serious."

"Tell me about it!" I said caustically. "I don't know how to find out. Odds are the only people who could tell us about what's happening to me is the lloruk!"

"I'll see what I can dig up" Griffyn said softly. "I've got quite a lot of books here."

"Books about magic?" Wrack asked sceptically.

Griffyn shrugged, and then leaned back. He had a glass of brandy now. Kelhene had been draining a barrel on one side of the room, and most people had a glass (or a clay mug, mostly) of the spirit. "We need to decide what we're going to do with you all."

"We can't stay here" Darhia muttered. "If some of those graalur get back to the lloruk, they'll send another force here. A bigger one."

"I expect nothing else. We'll move on" Griffyn replied calmly. "We've done that before."

"With all of us?" asked Kelhene pointedly.

The room slid into a melee of verbal barbs, thrusts and skirmishes. My head was spinning, either from fatigue or else the brandy was stronger than I had suspected. Farrys was holding forth about how extra warriors would improve the chances of their raids. Kentyr was pointing out that they were more likely to be spotted if their numbers were so much greater. Kelhene was protesting that she needed to get Darhath to somewhere he could be cared for. More than one of my people were protesting that they were not fighters. And Korhus was loudly proclaiming that he had no intention of aiding Griffyn's mad schemes of violence.

I bellowed for silence above the growing tumult, my voice cutting through the clamour. To my pleased surprise, the voices quelled.

"Griffyn!" I said firmly, "You and I need to talk through what is going to happen. Most of us are not fighters, and don't want to get involved in your operations. We need to get the majority of the Valley people to somewhere safe."

"Jajruuk" came a soft voice from one side. I glanced around to see Veldhra, her face set. "It's where we were heading anyhow. We need to get to Jajruuk. We have friends there."

I nodded at her words. "It's the best answer. We can't stay here in the jungle, and I need to get us to a human city where we can be secure and of use."

Slightly to my surprise, the majority of the people in the room seemed to be agreeing, even Griffyn's people. I caught Griffyn's eye, but he shook his head.

"I don't really think you want to go to Jajruuk" he said apologetically. "For a start, you're a long way off course." He shrugged. "Even if you weren't, I wouldn't recommend Jajruuk."

I raised my eyebrows. Wrack did the same, a single elegant eyebrow cocked in question. I really wanted to kill him for that, I was so envious.

Griffyn answered our unspoken question. "I'm pretty sure it's the next target for the Iloruk. It's only a matter of time before they attack it. The troops that hit your Grihl Valley – I think the Iloruk had been preparing a force against Jajruuk. If it were my choice, I'd make for Tolgrail."

I nodded acceptance of his advice before I glared at Kelhene, daring her to gloat. She didn't, much to my relief. "Can you guide us?" I asked Griffyn.

Griffyn nodded. "I'm sure we can. Kentyr, can you see the group to Tolgrail? Darhia, you'd better go too."

Kentyr was shaking his head. "You'll need both of us to shift everything if we're abandoning this spire. Where are you planning to go?"

Griffyn smiled confidently. "I talked about going to the Ship" he replied. I looked at him quizzically, but he did not explain the reference.

"That's a big move" Kentyr pointed out harshly.

"I'm assuming that Sorrel and Wrack are coming with me" he answered. I felt my eyes widen in surprise at his words. No way was I agreeing to that. I was going with my people to Tolgrail. "They can help me and Farrys get everything shifted" he added.

Before I could protest, Wrack was pushing forward, his face thunderous. Like me, he did not like being told what to do. I glared at him, responding before he could make himself heard. "We've got our own plans" I said sharply to Griffyn, making sure Wrack could hear my words. "I'm getting everyone to Tolgrail."

"I can't see there being anything for you personally in Tolgrail" Griffyn replied briskly. "My team can get your people to safety. You've no way to return to the surface. Here, with me, you two could make a difference."

"Here's not our place" Wrack replied before I could answer. "We *can* get back to the surface. Almost fit to fly."

True enough – he had been able to glide down from on high during the battle. His wing had to be almost in shape to carry him despite our tussle the previous night, always assuming the muscles were regaining their old strength. I smiled at Wrack, a little uncertainly. While we had been making our way through the jungle I had not had to make a decision about what I wanted to do next. Now... now I had to choose. A return to the surface, to a land ruled by the dragons, a serf or worse, dependant on Wrack's demands. Or remain down here and do... what? Once I got the Grihl Valleyers to Tolgrail, what would I do then? I looked at Griffyn. Join another hopeless rebellion against an oppressing lordship?

I got to my feet slowly and made my excuses, mendaciously claiming I was still worn down from the battle, before heading up the spire. I needed time to think.

I hadn't meant to go back to sleep. I had sat down on the bed. Thoughts were churning around in my head as though I had upturned a bucket of words and let the entire contents pour over me. It would have made as much sense as the way I was feeling.

When I did doze off, my dreams were a morass of old terrors. The destruction of Burundar. Being captured by Wrack, and paraded in front of his friends. Holnoris being executed at Allanti's whim. Shadrin, apologising and shuffling his feet as he recounted Starron's demand for an increase in production from the wool mill, knowing that it would mean impossibly long shifts. Clutching my mother's dress as Gallin was drafted into Starron's army. Watching Geller's aeroplane slam into the side of the cliff, screaming at the top of my voice and knowing it was too late. Sitting half-naked in Wrack's hall as his slave and hearing the confirmation that Malgarrin had surrendered.

I woke shivering, drenched in sweat, a half-scream strangled in my throat. I pulled the sheet around me tighter, looking around wildly for a moment as memory surged back into its wonted places. At least I had not had another visit from Wrack. I reached for the glass of brandy, but it was long since empty. There was probably more downstairs. I was already on my feet when I realised what I was doing. I liked to drink, but I had too much to think about to drown out my thoughts with alcohol. I walked down the ramp to the next floor, to where everyone had been gathered earlier. The chamber was all but empty.

Kelhene was fussing around Darhath, her face wan. Darhath was sitting quietly, eating food as she spooned it into his mouth. She glanced up at me.

"You all right?" she asked quietly. At my answering nod, she turned her attention back to her man.

"No change?" I asked equally quietly. She shrugged.

"Griffyn says there's no hope. That I'm better off putting a sword through him, giving him peace."

I shuddered, and went to hug the taller woman. She returned the embrace. Her eyes were glistening slightly. I squeezed her shoulder and looked at Darhath, hoping somehow to reach him.

Quarter of an hour of efforts did precisely nothing apart from dent Kelhene's emotions yet further. All my efforts, including a long kiss and a pretty savage slap to the face, brought nothing of Darhath back. It was as though I faced a scarecrow in Darhath's shape. I sat back, defeated and depressed.

"Can you cut it out of him?" Kelhene asked quietly, gesturing at the scar still visible on my arm.

I shivered, and shook my head. "If what the Iloruk told us is true, it'll be too far grown into him" I answered, an apologetic quaver in my voice. "Even if we cut the core out, there would be more left inside him. It isn't quite like the jasq I had. They grew it that way so it can't be removed again."

Kelhene sat back, staring at her blank-faced man with endless despair written across her features. "Are you even going to try?" she asked.

I shivered again. "Not yet. When we get to Tolgrail... then we'll try. But carving his flesh when he's about to need to trek through the jungle – not a good idea."

Kelhene turned away - I suspected she didn't want me to see the tears in her eyes.

"Where's everyone else?" I asked, casting around for anything to distract from the blank man in front of us.

"Spread out through the spire. Everyone's got their own space to rest and get ready for the journey." I looked at her with a degree of surprise – no one had consulted *me* about the arrangements. "Griffyn and Kentyr have been organising everything."

My expression must have spoken volumes. Kelhene looked vaguely embarrassed. "Griffyn said you were staying here, helping him and his people move to a new hideout." Her expression changed slightly. "I don't think he trusts the rest of us not to betray him to the lloruk."

"Would you?" I asked carefully.

She dropped her gaze. "I don't know" she finally admitted. Before I could comment she lifted her eyes to me again. "Are you coming with us? Sorrel, I know you don't like me, but... but we could really use your help." Her voice quivered slightly. "Without Darhath, we need someone who knows how to lead."

I rocked back mentally. Me, a leader? My immediate instinct was to deny it emphatically, but I paused before I said so. She was watching my face, seeing me thinking.

"Wrack wants me to go back with him to the surface" I said slowly.

Kelhene tilted her head to one side. "And do what?" she asked simply. "Be Wrack's slave again?"

I shivered, not wanting to think about her question. I had told her too much about events at Wrack's mansion. "When are you all leaving?" I asked.

"First light tomorrow. Get as far as we can. Darhia says we've got five days' journey to Tolgrail."

"What's Tolgrail like?" I asked lamely.

Kelhene shrugged. "I've only been there once, about six years ago. It's quite cosmopolitan, with visitors from most of the northern lands. There are mines in the hills near it, which was why it grew up." Her descriptions made it sound a bit like Varldren, north of Furulyeer, but without the furs. A walled city, with hard and often aggressive men and women who played hard and worked hard. A city where strangers were not uncommon, but had a tough time until they proved they were tough themselves. I ought to fit right in.

And do what? Once I'd got the Grihl Valleyers there, what was I going to do? I was a pilot – no way I was going down a mine, or breaking my back working in a field. And I disliked animals – I didn't think I'd be a success milking cows or ruzdrool or whatever the Chasm used as farm animals. And having a jasq wasn't going to do me any good if using it was going to kill me in agony. I still wondered if the jasq disliked being in the Chasm – maybe I ought to return to the surface, see if it still hurt there. I muttered something along those lines, and Kelhene's face fell.

"You're going home, then?"

Again I shook my head. "I don't know." I couldn't keep her gaze. "The chasm isn't my home. Perhaps I ought to go back to the surface."

As I spoke I was picturing the friends I had up there. Verin. Tolly. Shenli. Kemal. Volg it, I missed them all. I wished they were down here. At least on the surface I had a job. Yes, my thoughts jeered, flying mail between New Burundar and Werintar. Patrolling, watching for encroaching grathks? Occasionally detouring to fly to Trakomar. Was that really what I wanted to do? Sneaking out at night with the Firebirds, making plans or doing petty acts of destruction, always looking over our shoulders?

Or else I'd end up back at Wrack's mansion as his pet. Odds were that he'd demand I return there so that he had his jasq in easy reach. And if he insisted, the aerodrome would hand me over. We were allowed to fly as a privilege, under strict rules. The dragons were our lords and masters again, the whole of Sendaal back under their suzerainty.

I didn't want to return to being a slave.

Kelhene was watching me, almost visibly restraining herself from asking me what I was thinking. I smiled at her gratefully for her forbearance.

If I stayed down here, it would not be as a miner or a farmer or a menial of some form. On the surface, I had been a pilot, and I didn't know of any better task. In my heart of hearts I knew that fundamentally if I was to stay here it would be to fight. To strive against the brutalities and cruelties of the lloruk and the graalur.

Did I want to join a new conflict, a new struggle against another oppressor?

Could I bear to be on the losing side again? I shivered again. After the fall of Burundar I had thought I could not go on. Tolly had told me some guff about grief passing. He had lied – I still felt the same rage when I thought about what the dragons had done. Their treatment of us humans – the bloody arena games Mondi had staged, Rastor demanding the surrender of pretty girls for his bed, Allanti executing people who tried to leave her lands. So many abuses and cruelties. It had driven me to fight in the war – and to engage in the various actions I had been involved in with the Firebirds afterwards. It had led me to launch the raid on Wrack when we had stolen his jasq.

Another failure.

No. I now had his jasq. Was that a failure?

Only if I returned to the surface as his slave.

I gazed without seeing at the chamber I was in, feelings twisting within my head.

"You want to talk about it?" Kelhene said levelly.

I looked at her for a long moment. My thoughts had been tangled and unclear, but talking to her had brought a lot into perspective. I was relatively sure, now, that I knew what I was going to do. I quietly shook my head. "No need, Kelhene. I'm not going back to the surface. There are things I can do down here. Things that matter. I'm going to get us all to Tolgrail. And then I'm going to deal with the larisqs."

She reached out a hand and gripped it tightly. "Thank you" she whispered.

"Do I get a say in this?"

The growl from the doorway made me jump. I spun; Wrack was leaning against the door-jamb, face masked in shadow. I shivered, unable to stop myself feeling unnerved at his presence. I had only just made up my mind – I needed time to think it through, to explain how I felt to Wrack. I glared at him, and just shook my head bluntly. "No" I replied shortly. I was gratified at his expression of shocked outrage. He strode forward, lifting his arm as though to take hold of me. To my surprise Kelhene stepped into his path.

"You can go back to the surface if you like" she said tartly. "Leave Sorrel to do something useful."

Wrack stopped dead in his tracks at her challenge, and then looked past her at me. I thought he was going to shout, but his voice, when he finally responded, was dangerously soft.

"Going upstairs. Come and talk to me, if that's not beyond your intellect."

He stalked out, every inch affronted nobility. Yet again my feelings were churning in my head, drowning out any rational thought. Could I really make the decision to remain here without talking to him? Did I have that right? I did have his jasq, whatever way I looked at it. He could not change without me.

Kelhene was grinning broadly. "That told him!" she said brightly. I muttered something akin to thanks, and poured myself another brandy.

Sometimes it's easier not to think.

Chapter Twenty-One

Wrack didn't come looking for me. Instead, it was Griffyn who slid into the chair beside me. "I take it you want some lunch?" he asked. I nodded, and he passed me a plate of sandwiches.

We ate together, and he looked at me as I swallowed the last piece of bread. I hadn't had much more brandy, but I was aware that I was not cold sober.

"I'm really glad you're staying to help us against the lloruk" he said, as if it was settled.

I shook my head. "Not really, Griffyn. I'm going to get my friends to Tolgrail." He looked deeply, almost theatrically disappointed. I didn't give him a chance to try to talk me round. "What do you know about larisqs?"

He blanched at the name. "I know they're appallingly foul things" he hissed. "The lloruk designed them to make us... obedient." In his voice the word was a curse.

"Do you know how to destroy them?" I asked quietly.

Griffyn shook his head. "I've found a small number in glass cases occasionally. We go out of our way to smash them, but there are always more. Once someone's infected with one, there's nothing you can do. I think the kindest thing is to put the poor devil out of his misery."

"I promised Kelhene I'd do something about the larisqs" I said. "I want to find this lloruk called Ssathool. Maybe if we can deal with it, that'll stop the lloruk making more larisqs."

It sounded thin even as I said it, but it was the only approach I could think of to tackle the problem. To my surprise, Griffyn just nodded. "I don't recall a great deal about Ssathool" he said. I raised my eyebrows in mild surprise that he knew the name, and that irrepressible grin swept across his face. Griffyn liked being the centre of attention. He gestured towards the ramp leading upwards. Curious, I followed him up through the spire.

I hadn't been up to the top level until then. This was clearly where Griffyn and his fellows actually lived. In the first two rooms there were already signs that he and his group were starting to pack up their belongings – leather bags loaded with oddments, a couple of half-filled wooden boxes. The room he ushered me into, though, showed no signs of preparation to leave. This could have been Tolly's study at the Aerodrome – a large desk, bookshelves, some comfortable-looking chairs, even a cabinet with bottles and glasses on it. Griffyn paused and poured out two glasses of something, passing one to me. I was going to say I had already had enough, but thought better of it.

The contents were strong, more like jherrazh. I enjoyed its bite, ignoring the risks of mixing wine and spirits. I could cope with the hangover later. It wouldn't be the first. Griffyn was pulling books from the shelf, studying them carefully. I could see now that they were journals, each page covered with small, crabbed handwriting. If they were Griffyn's work – and every page looked to have the same scrawl – then he spent a lot of time writing things down.

The third journal seemed to be what he was looking for. "Ssathool?" he checked again with me. "Of Luthvara?"

I shrugged. "No idea – all I know is the name."

"A mage..." he mused. "I suspect this is our lloruk."

I leaned over to peer at the script. "What are these?"

"I try to keep tabs on all the major lloruk" he replied proudly. "I like to retain some idea of what they're doing and whereabouts they are. It makes choosing targets somewhat easier."

"How?" I asked bluntly. "How can you know what they're doing or who they are?"

Griffyn grinned again smugly. "I have spies. There are human slaves in the lloruk cities – a number of them investigate matters for me. They smuggle the information out and I write it up when I get it. It may be a few days or even weeks out of date, but it gives me some indication of what the lloruk are involved in."

I nodded, appreciating his organisation. "Then you can warn people if they're planning anything" I responded.

Griffyn's turn to shrug. "By the time I get the news, it's usually a little late. It's

211

more useful for me to work out how we can hurt the lloruk."

He studied the pages carefully. Over his shoulder he asked "I don't know if you want to call Wrack up, talk to him about this?"

I paused for a moment, then declined. "I'll tell him once we know what we're doing."

Griffyn turned slightly to look at me and then asked "Are you and Wrack..."

I shook my head vigorously and swallowed hard. "He's just a... a friend." As I said it I found myself wondering how to describe my feelings for Wrack. "Friend" wasn't even remotely close. On the other hand, it was probably the simplest description, in the circumstances. I didn't feel like trying to explain our relationship.

Griffyn looked pleased at my answer. "Good" he said immediately, and then coloured slightly, turning back to his journal. Well, well. I'd noticed his eyes on me. I wasn't going to complain if he found me interesting. I wasn't sure quite how much I found *him* interesting. There was no question that he was good looking. On the other hand, so was Wrack, perhaps more so than Griffyn, and that did not make me care for the dragonlord.

He tilted his head up from the journal he was perusing. "Luthvara" he said simply. "I think all the evidence points there. I hadn't realised before now that all the caravans we've raided containing larisqs being transported came from Luthvara."

"Once I've got us to Tolgrail, that's where I need to go" I said staunchly.

"You're more stupid than I took you for" Wrack's voice rumbled from the doorway. We both jumped. I hadn't heard him come into the room. I wondered edgily just how long he'd been lurking there.

"I don't follow you" Griffyn asked carefully.

"She can't use her magic" Wrack replied. "Wouldn't stand a chance without it. They're looking for you, Sorrel!"

I rounded on Wrack, letting a surge of annoyance drown out any feelings of guilt that might be crawling around in my stomach. "So you suggest instead that I should be sitting doing nothing?"

"Not your fight!" he snarled. "You've already fought one hopeless war, Sorrel. You want to join another?"

"It is not hopeless!" Griffyn snapped before I could open my mouth. "I have allies..." He stopped, and I guessed that he had revealed something he had not planned to talk about. Wrack, though, was more interested in me.

"Sorrel, it's not our war! You've no reason to join up with Griffyn and his band. We ought to go home!"

"And what happens then?" I asked tartly, dropping into narynyl – I didn't particularly want Griffyn understanding what I was saying. "I become your slave again?"

He paused for a moment, his gaze shifting away from my eyes. He didn't need to say a word; it was obvious what he intended. I didn't give him a chance to lie to me. I slid back into veredraa, and spoke quietly and firmly, letting him know that I was speaking for Griffyn's benefit, too.

"I'm not going back to the surface, Wrack. The war's over up there, but down here – maybe I can make a difference."

"Even if your magic is killing you?" he asked sombrely. "Not to mention destroying my jasq" he added.

"I might be able to do something about that" Griffyn said unexpectedly. He had a different book in front of him, and a quizzical expression. I glanced across at the text in front of him; the words seemed to writhe on the paper for a moment, and I shook my head. I hadn't realised how tired or how stressed I was. Griffyn was tapping the paper confidently. "I may well find something to help you here. It'll take me a few hours to check."

"Do we have that long? I thought you wanted to get out of here."

Griffyn shrugged. "All right, so when I get to the Ship I'll take some time to check."

Wrack clearly wasn't impressed. I rested a hand on his forearm, quelling his protests. "Wrack, we had no idea how to find out what's happening to me. Griffyn's information might be the best chance we've got."

Griffyn inclined his head graciously at my somewhat limited compliment.

Wrack had been looking around the study, eyeing up the multitude of books and ornaments.

"So how do you shift all this stuff? Take days to transport it all" Wrack growled

213

in a surly tone. I could understand the question – it would take a dozen journeys to carry half the contents of this room alone to a new home.

Griffyn was grinning again. "I don't think it'll take that long" he said mysteriously. "Come with me."

Two passages along, not far from the skywire platform, I realised I could smell something sharp. Almost acidic. I looked at Griffyn, but he was walking quickly and I had to stretch my pace to keep up. He had long legs. Nice arse, too.

He turned into a large room, and I stopped dead as I came through the door. Within the chamber, nestling between the pillars that supported the roof, were half a dozen gigantic spiders, long, stilt legs like broken masts supporting the small, shiny carapaces. No, not spiders, though my mistake was hardly surprising. They had ten legs, not eight. Their muzzles sprouted a small number of short fronds. Tentacles. I looked at them again, realising that in some way they were not dissimilar to the ruzdrools I had faced. Much smaller bodies, much longer legs, much less lethal tentacles, but still clearly related.

"What are those things?" Wrack voiced my thought exactly.

"Tuurgaaks" was the helpful answer. "We fought a ruzdrool that had just killed the parent – we collected the eggs and reared these."

"Why?" I asked pointedly. "You *like* nurturing man-eating monstrosities?"

Griffyn laughed. "They're herbivores. The ruzdrool eat them."

"And you ride them" Wrack rasped.

Griffyn nodded. I shrugged. "They're better than olgreks?"

"Oh, yes!" he replied, his voice stressing his pleasure at his pets. "I use them to carry us along the skywires."

I stared at him, across at Wrack, at the monstrosities – tuurgakks? - and then back at him. He obviously sensed my confusion.

"They can hang under the wires, each carrying one of us. The skywires can get us across the worst terrains in the world. We can go as fast as the lloruk do, and they have no idea how we do it." He pointed to the creatures. "I don't think anyone's ever tamed tuurgakks before. They're no good for anything else. But they make superb, fast steeds."

"Lloruk don't notice you swanning along on the skywires?" Wrack questioned.

"I tell you, that's the beauty of it" Griffyn enthused. "The tuurgakks are nocturnal. They can see in the dark. I use them to travel at night, when the lloruk aren't on the skywires, and when no one can see us."

"How do you get up and down?"

"The tuurgakks can climb any surface. They just walk down the side of a spire."

I stared at the brutes, trying to imagine riding one through the darkness as it climbed down a virtually perpendicular surface. "I wouldn't fancy that" I said tartly.

Griffyn cocked his head to one side. "I'd have thought flying your wooden... aeriplons, did I hear you right... would inure you to anything" he said with a slight edge in his voice. "I doubt my tuurgakks are more frightening."

Wrack cracked a smile, enjoying my discomforture. I shrugged, not quite sure how to respond. Griffyn held my gaze and said "I was hoping you'd be willing to handle a tuurgakk." His eyes shifted to Wrack. "Both of you" he added.

Now it was my turn to enjoy Wrack's surprise. "Why?" he asked bluntly.

"If I'm to clear this place before the lloruk return, I need your help."

"Why us?" I asked coolly. "There are a lot of people here at the moment."

Griffyn shook his head. "I can't trust any of them. You heard the way Korhus talks. When they get to Tolgrail, they'll tell people where I'm based. If word gets back to the lloruk, I'm finished."

"But you trust us not to talk?"

Griffyn looked at Wrack levelly. "Yes. I listened to what Sorrel said about your struggle on the surface. You know what it's like being under the boot of an oppressor. I need your help!"

I looked at Wrack and raised my eyebrows. Griffyn *hadn't* understood what I'd told him about the war on the surface. He hadn't realised that Wrack was one of the oppressors. I almost laughed at Wrack's expression. I wasn't sure how he would respond. Griffyn was right, after all. Fundamentally I was with him. The graalur and the lloruk were exactly the sort of monsters that I loathed and hated. No different to Wrack and his ilk.

No, the lloruk were worse – the larisqs were more foul even than some of the things Kabal and Mondi came up with. Wrack glanced at me, trying to read my expression, waiting for my answer.

I marshalled my words before I answered. "I've promised to get my people to Tolgrail, Griffyn. I can't just abandon them. Otherwise I'd probably help."

Griffyn grinned broadly, somewhat to my shock. "I don't think that'll be a problem" he answered. "They won't be ready to move for two days – they need to get into shape, recover from the injuries from the attack. That should us enough time to get everything shifted from here." He looked at me directly. "I'd suggest it's one way you can repay me for guiding you all to safety."

I'm not afraid of hard physical effort. I've spent many a long hour shifting barrels of fuel or carrying the crumpled remains of a downed triplane to a wagon. So in some ways the next two days weren't that bad – the tuurgaaks were tough, but they couldn't carry that vast a load, which meant I'd spend twenty minutes carrying crates to the tuurgaak stable, five minutes loading the beast up, and then a good hour and a half swaying beneath the skywire as the unreasonably strong creature swung its way across thirty miles of jungle to the Ship.

My first sight of the Ship from the skywire, half-visible through the jungle verdure, told me that Griffyn expected us to live in a rotting, dank, foul wreck. When we decamped from the wire, though, and trekked the quarter of a mile through the jungle to reach the Ship, I understood what Griffyn had discovered. Each time I saw it I wondered anew just how old the mammoth vessel might be. It lay, semi-submerged on the edge of a wide river of black water that cut its way through the dense scarlets of the jungle. The turgid water became thicker as the shore was neared, until the stretch of territory where the Ship lay was dense enough for it to be uncertain if it was water or mud. The Ship had been stranded there as the silt had gathered. I wondered, looking at it, if it had once sailed on the vast ancient oceans of the surface world, before the elf-lloruk war split the continents and dropped the land that now formed the base of the Chasm more than two miles into the earth. Even if the Ship was remotely water-worthy, I could conceive of no force that could uproot its two gigantic hulls from its resting place. Not that anyone would risk taking it into any depth of water. Gaping holes in the nearer hull admitted quantities of the river between the rank red weeds. Much of the breached hull was flooded. The upper decks were rotted and festooned with struggling growths that fought to find purchase on the superstructure. I could see no trace of masts, and any propellers had to be deeply submerged into the mud.

The black metal hulk was over two hundred and fifty feet long, and perhaps sixty feet wide. I hazarded a guess when I first studied it that it had at least three decks in each hull below the waterline – I was pleased to find I was absolutely right. Above the waterline the deck was wide and even, with two substantial cabins forming the superstructure. The one near the bow only had one more storey, and was only thirty feet long, though it spanned virtually the whole width of the vessel. There was then a long, empty section that I guessed was originally intended for cargo, before the two storeys of the rear superstructure, which ran from two-thirds of the way back along the hull right to the stern. The bridge was at the front of this structure, looking out along the length of the ship – the empty, shattered windows contained a wheel and other controls that would have sent commands to the heavy, powerful-looking engines that occupied a full third of each hull below decks. I wished we had more opportunity to explore – the engine chamber in the unbreached hull was extraordinary, with strange blue-steel cylinders and gear wheels, long cannisters of red glass and twisting bronze pipes that had to be the source of the craft's motive power that once had propelled the huge craft upon the water. Despite the vast age of the Ship, I saw no hint of rust or corrosion in those engines. I could see no sign of a furnace or combustion chamber, though there were tubes that might well be pistons. I wanted to try to fathom out how the engines drove the Ship, but there simply wasn't the time.

The rear superstructure, forged of the same dark, glossy metal as the hulls, was unbroken and whole. The bridge windows were shattered, but the remainder was unharmed. Within, there were a host of cabins and chambers, unstained by the centuries as they lurked behind closed metal hatches. One room I entered still had bedding on the bunk, curtains on the small, grime-covered window, and three dark bottles and two green glasses on the small table. A wooden chair stood awaiting an occupant on four sturdy legs. More surprisingly still, there seemed virtually no dust or cobwebs in any of the chambers.

Only when I felt the cream blanket on the bed did it sigh into ruin, turning to dust under my hand. The curtains did much the same, but the chair seemed more sturdy. The bottles were long since dry, and I decided that I did not care to try drinking from a glass that had to be more than two thousand years old.

The air within the Ship was stale, with no obvious odour, but still and dead. We swiftly discovered that there were tubes and channels within the walls and floors that would bring air in from the outside, but they were sealed by metal flaps. Once those were opened (and there were more than twenty scattered along the exterior of the superstructure, each of which had to be cleaned of mud and fungus, foliage and filth before this could be accomplished) the air began slowly to become sweeter.

I was grateful that there were no human bodies aboard the Ship. The decks bore a range of scattered animal remains hinting at death from natural causes (mostly being eaten by something larger – like I said, natural causes). Old bones and a few rotting carcasses. Our first task when the four of us got to the Ship was to clear enough of the decks of the debris so that we could get easy ingress and egress from the cabins. Not a pleasant job, as the deck was mostly thick with dirt and rotting vegetation. More than a dozen trees had somehow found purchase on the deck, and were too substantial to uproot.

The hatches themselves opened remarkably easily. Griffyn admitted that he had explored the Ship a few months ago, and had returned with oil to ease a number of sealed portals. The effort had been effective, and aided our explorations. In the distant past, the Ship must have been magnificent. Even now, sidling through the deserted corridors and opening forgotten doors it was not hard to imagine the vessel in its original glory.

We did not have much time to investigate, though. Griffyn and Farrys set a hard timetable to get their goods transferred from the spire to the Ship. For two days we did virtually nothing except transport the crates and boxes thirty easy miles along the skywire plus the backbreaking quarter of a mile from the skywire to the Ship.

The one mercy was that it did not give Wrack any opportunity to talk to me. I didn't know if I wanted to talk to him yet – I had made my choice, but I really had no clear idea where I stood with Wrack... or what he intended to do.

The operation also meant that I learned to master the tuurgaaks. The first few journeys were eerie in the extreme. I hadn't realised how strange a night sky could be without moons. Above me, black and all-enveloping, the roof of clouds blocked out any prospect of seeing either moon, let alone the stars. I'm not a keen astronomer, not like Kemal, but I was missing the black velvet sprinkled with diamonds that I was used to. I quickly became accustomed to the motion along the skywire as the tuurgakk's legs moved smoothly, almost mechanically, never more than two legs unattached at any time. The disturbing aspect was that the creature was, to my eyes at least, upside down, and I rode on his belly. Or her belly – I had no idea if the tuurgakk carrying me was male, female, or some other bizarre form of gender. The harnesses cinched onto the brutes had been put together with just this travel in mind, obviously. I still hadn't detected any mouth or nose or any apertures in its bulk. Come to think about it, I hadn't heard it making any noises either.

At first I hadn't been quite certain how I was supposed to control the brute. On our first journey Griffyn had promised that it would follow his mount. I had had no option but to hope he was right. The tuurgakk was singularly lacking in joystick, controls or brakes. By the return trip, though, I had learned to guide it by gentle tugs on the straps that formed the saddle. By the fifth trip I was entirely confident I could keep my mount under proper control. I got to the stage that with the world around me being scarlet black, and the only sounds the regular thump as each hooked foot found its grip on the wire and the hiss of the breeze around us, I found my eyes closing. I didn't fancy falling asleep – I had a strap holding me in place, but I wasn't confident that I would be secure without being able to keep a grip as need be. After a while, though, fatigue overcame me and I sagged in the saddle, only to waken a time later worrying that I had already gone past the Ship. I hadn't, but it taught me only to doze, half-aware, as the tuurgaak swung.

A good number of the packages we were shifting were books. Griffyn had a surprisingly large library. Some of the volumes were the product of crude printing, with large, ragged text in inks that varied in blackness. He told me that the eastern cities, Jajruuk and Maladzaal, were noted for their presses, and their books were carried by traders half-way across the Rift. Other books were journals that Griffyn had written himself, his small, neat script in even lines filling most of the paper. I peered at more than one of the books with interest and incomprehension – I could not read a single word. Even the alphabet was alien, a jagged, angular collection of symbols that were quite unlike the smooth, curved letters of the narynyl script I was used to. Nor was the writing akin to the cursive lloruk text. Being in such proximity to so many unreadable books was deeply frustrating to me. I resolved to get Griffyn to teach me how to read his writings.

Shifting Darhia's goods I came across a couple of jars of dry powder (all right, so I was being nosey). I made a guess and sniffed the stuff. The pungent odour brought a smile to my face – I couldn't believe that the women of the Chasm didn't have some variety of the herb we called Safety on the surface. I poured a little into a half glass of wine, and drank it, just as a precaution.

I was more surprised at the two crates of seed-pods, all of the same species, gnarled brown-green husks each the size of an apple but which smelt acrid and sour. I queried them with Griffyn – he shrugged, and said that growing crops was critical when hiding out. The seeds didn't seem at all wholesome, and I saw no evidence of any other seeds, or of any cultivation of crops at the spire. I filed it all away and didn't push it – I was not totally surprised to find that there were things Griffyn wasn't letting on about. The more I saw of our new ally, the more I began to wonder about him. I had no doubt that he was self-centred, and nearly as arrogant as Wrack. I also had growing doubts about his veracity. No, not entirely fair. I didn't think he was lying... but I was becoming more confident that there was an awful lot that he was not telling us. I looked at the seeds again. My suspicion was that the pods could be made into weapons, somehow – Griffyn did not strike me as the horticultural type.

We returned to the spire just as the lantern trees were reaching their full brilliance. I was relatively tired, and looking forward to a proper bed to sleep in, instead of the uncertain grip of a tuurgakk. Wrack looked worn, too, and I suspected he had found the work surprisingly wearing. Unlike us lesser mortals, he had always had slaves to do such hard labour. I didn't have much sympathy.

I made my way down the spire, expecting to find my people taking it easy, preparatory to our journey tomorrow. Even as I was coming down the curving ramp towards the main chamber, though, I could hear enough noise to assure me that something was going on. Shouts, calls and demands, questions and footfalls. By the time I had walked briskly into the circular chamber that had become our main gathering place, I was becoming sure – and deeply alarmed - that my group was in the throes of leaving.

Heads turned towards me as I stalked in. Korhus and Kelhene both grabbed my arm and pulled me forward, a chorus of comments from all sides about their being glad to see me and relieved that I was back. I was trying to make myself heard, demanding to know what was happening, when Kentyr's statement, bellowed through the confusion, impinged.

"What do you mean there are graalur coming?" I shouted over the tumult. "Everyone shut up!" I added for good measure.

"Just what I want to know!" Griffyn's voice cut into the subsiding cacophony.

Kentyr's voice held a slight quaver. "We got a message late last night. Some of the graalur that survived the attack – they've called for more soldiers. A force left Ilkadala last night."

Wrack's growl carved through the voices of concern. "How the volg can they know? For that matter, how do *you* know what happened at Ilkadala last night? Got to be more than sixty miles from here!"

Griffyn shrugged. "I suspect there's nearer a hundred miles" he said calmly. "We have spies in Ilkadala. They have... creatures... that can find their way to us, bringing messages."

Kentyr scowled. "Trouble is, the lloruk have the same kind of insects."

"How long have we got before they get here?" I demanded.

"Do they have scortuliqs?" Griffyn asked in response. Kentyr just nodded, evidently not to Griffyn's surprise. "I'd reckon three days, then."

"That's why I was getting the group moving" Kentyr explained. I realised that he was slightly nervous of his leader's reaction to his initiative, but Griffyn was nodding slowly. "We won't move as fast as the graalur force – we need to get some lead if we want to get clear of them."

Griffyn nodded again. "They'll find your trail – with this number you won't be able to cover it effectively. They'll follow. And they can move far faster than you can."

"You said about five days to Tolgrail from here" I said grimly. "How long will it take the graalur to do that journey on their scortuliqs?"

"Two, maybe three days."

"Be close, then" Wrack rumbled.

"So we get moving" I said firmly. "You were right to get it organised, Kentyr."

"We'll be ready to go in half an hour, I think" Kentyr replied, visibly pleased at my approbation.

"Wait a minute" said Griffyn quietly. "Sorrel, I need to talk to you and to Wrack." He gestured towards one of the side chambers. Farrys and Darhia were talking to Kelhene and Helinhus, while Korhus and Kentyr were directing the others to shift parcels and supplies. I looked at Griffyn as we ventured into a semblance of peace, out of the hubbub.

"What is it, Griffyn?"

"I need to clear the spire. The first of the graalur could be here in two days, even if the main force is behind them. Without your help..." His voice trailed off, but his meaning was clear.

Wrack shrugged and looked at me. Griffyn's eyes were on me, appealing silently. I took a step backwards, and lifted my hands uncertainly. "I need to look after my people, Griffyn! Get them to Tolgrail!"

"You need Kentyr to guide you to Tolgrail, or the odds are you'll get completely lost again. I can't send Kentyr on his own – he needs to have someone with him for the return journey. Going through the jungle alone is suicidal. So Darhia's going to have to go with him – Farrys, with his wounded arm, is no use. Which means I need you two to get the rest of the stuff to the Ship."

"Can't you send a tuurgakk to bring Kentyr back from Tolgrail?"

Griffyn shook his head. "There's no skywire within fifty miles of it."

"So how do we get to Tolgrail from the Ship, then?" I challenged.

Griffyn paused, and I saw his eyes drop, so that he was not looking directly at me any more. "Once everything's shifted, we can head through the jungle, take a different route to Tolgrail." He grinned suddenly, and I wondered if my doubts at his words were justified. "It'll be a bit of a trek, but the Ship is closer to Tolgrail than we are here."

"But my people need me!" I protested. I saw Wrack's eyebrows raise slightly at the term 'my', and felt my cheeks colour slightly.

"I need you, too" Griffyn said. Was that a hint of colour in his cheeks, too? "Without my help your people wouldn't have stood a chance. And I'm the only one fighting the Iloruk – without me, the Chasm is going to be over-run."

If I had had any doubts that Griffyn fancied himself, that speech would have driven them from me. On the other hand, though, he was right about the help he'd provided us. And I didn't want to see him tortured and slain by the Iloruk. In a lot of ways he and I were dangerously alike.

Wrack was standing to one side, waiting for me to make a decision. That surprised me – I wasn't used to Wrack letting someone else have control. I glanced at him and raised my eyebrows questioningly.

"Why should I say anything?" he growled. "You don't listen to me."

For a moment I felt my temper flare. Wrack, as usual, was being unreasonable. I glowered at him, but his comment didn't deserve a reply. I looked back at Griffyn. "My first responsibility is to the Grihl Valley people" I said slowly, the decision becoming clear. "If you can convince me they'll be all right, that they'll get to Tolgrail without me, then we'll stay and help."

The refugees were gathered in the chamber adjoining the entrance to the spire. The people from the Grihl Valley were about to move on. They were the nearest I had to friends down here... and they were leaving. I felt as though I was abandoning them. I had tried to explain, but I still felt like a traitor.

Korhus gripped my hand hard and hugged me, telling me to catch up with them as soon as I could. Kelhene echoed his words a little later, holding Darhath by the hand. He looked at me blankly, no spark of recognition or interest in his eyes. I hugged Kelhene, and she reciprocated. Considering how much we had disliked each other to start with, I was going to miss her dreadfully.

"Good luck" we both said, almost simultaneously. I hugged her again, and she moved to join the others.

A good many of the Grihl Valley people shook my hand or embraced and kissed me, wished me luck or wished that I was coming with them now. I stood back as they filed out with Darhia and Kentyr, aware that my eyes were getting misty. Wrack had had similar farewells, and I had watched him hugging Kelhene and a couple of the other women with some passion.

I realised Griffyn was standing beside me, watching my friends heading out. He squeezed my hand, wordlessly. I squeezed it back, but pulled away from him before the contact risked developing into anything further. I was growing very aware of how handsome Griffyn was, but I really wasn't sure how much I trusted him.

It took to the end of the second night after the Valley folk got moving to clear the spire completely. Much of what we were transporting was clothing, food, utensils and necessities, but some of our cargoes were more intriguing. A crate that buzzed and whined incessantly caused Wrack some discomfort – we both guessed before being told that within it were the messenger bugs that had warned us of the oncoming militia. Another small box was so heavy that I had serious difficulty lifting it – a peek inside revealed a substantial quantity of gold. Even here in the Chasm the yellow metal was highly valued, and was the basis of their currencies, just as it was on the surface. Some things go back even before the Elf-Lloruk war. Where Griffyn had obtained this clutch of ingots I didn't enquire. It was enough to know that it explained the quality of his furniture and the number of his books. I was glad he had spent some of the value – the box was difficult to carry even half-full. There were also a number of boxes containing a variety of weapons – swords and knives, crossbows and caltrops. Griffyn had a vicious accumulation of tools of war.

I had been avoiding Wrack, trying to stay out of his way as we worked. There was too much unspoken between us. Too much of our past lurking to torture us.

Farrys seemed to get on quite well with Wrack, mostly because they were both laconic types, I suspected. Instead I ended up in Griffyn's company by default.

Not that I minded that. Griffyn was attractive, and he could be entertaining when he was describing some of his previous escapades. His stories meant I was not thinking about how hard the effort was, making the task seem much easier. I had no doubt that Griffyn was not telling me everything about himself – in particular, he was always somewhat reticent about why he had launched his crusade against the lloruk – but he was pleasant company. He did not seem to have Wrack's intensity or dark moods, nor – quite – Wrack's arrogance. Not that he was without arrogance of his own – he had no doubts about what he was doing, or that he should use any means available to achieve the freedom of humanity in the Chasm from the lloruk. If that meant exterminating the lloruk, he would do it. Disturbingly black and white, Griffyn's outlook. I really didn't know what I made of his one-man crusade. I wasn't sure how much I could trust him. On the other hand, from what I had seen of the lloruk, and in view of my feelings about the larisqs, I had considerable sympathy with his objectives.

Our final farewell to Griffyn's spire was much later than Griffyn had wanted. The lantern trees were at full brilliance well before we reached the Ship, and we all felt dangerously exposed as the tuurgakks covered the last half dozen miles in bright daylight. It did not help that our beasts of burden were showing signs of exhaustion, too, so that their pace along the skywire was considerably slower. Fortunately, the journey was completed without detection, and the next few hours were occupied with sorting out the small army of crates and boxes that had been dumped unceremoniously into a large cabin. Farrys and Griffyn had the majority of the work; Wrack and I were relegated to stevedores, transporting items as directed as they unpacked into their new home.

By the afternoon we were all gathered in a chamber on the upper floor of the Ship. Above us a glass dome, intact despite the millennia that had passed since its construction, flooded the room with light. One of the other positive aspects of the Ship was that there were three lantern trees within five miles, meaning that the area wasn't too murky. We were slumped on pillows and cushions we had brought from the spire (between them a whole tuurgaak load, but essential due to the lack of any surviving cloth here). Griffyn had produced a couple of bottles of rather average wine, "rescued" from an occupied farm they had raided a few days before we had arrived, and we sat and toasted the new hideout. Griffyn and his gang had spotted the Ship a few months before, and had decided that it might provide a suitable place to lurk if they had to move. In some ways, I suspected he was quite glad to have moved here – the Ship was an extraordinary structure, and Griffyn enjoyed the idea that he was occupying something so magnificent, despite its faded grandeur. There was more than enough space for him, his people, and his books, with a large stable for the tuurgaaks, all within the rear superstructure.

As I sipped the wine, I was aware that Wrack was gazing at me, his expression masked. I could almost read his thoughts. We had finished the big move – where were we to go from here? He wanted to return to the surface. He intended to compel me to go with him. His wing was pretty much healed, and I had seen him flexing his arm experimentally. During the morning I had felt my jasq pounding suddenly, and I had known, instinctively, that he had changed into his draconic shape. I had not seen him take to the air, but I was confident that he was ready to fly.

Perhaps Griffyn was better at reading people than I had given him credit for. He leaned back lazily and lifted his glass to me, before saying quietly "I may have found out a way to stop your sorcery hurting you, Sorrel."

Both Wrack and I were all ears instantly.

"You've found out something about jasqs?" I queried, trying to keep the note of hope out of my voice.

"I'm not sure" he answered. His voice definitely did have a note of optimism in it. "I came across something I was told a few months ago." He lowered his voice conspiratorially. "It's why I record everything. I never know when some snippet of material could be important." I resisted the strong impulse to puncture his pomposity. Griffyn might be all too full of himself, but he could be useful, too. I suspected I would like him more if he was a little less self-important, though. "Someone in Luthvara said that the lloruk need a head-dress to be able to work magic outside their cities."

Memory flooded through me of the jewelry the lloruk with the scortuliq had been wearing. Other images impinged, too, the strange structures at the farm and in the tower. Silver tracery and ivory tusks. I straightened up in my chair excitedly, and described the things I had seen. Griffyn was nodding enthusiastically as I spoke. Only Wrack was grim and unimpressed.

"So why should one of these tiaras help *you*?"

I glared at him, and then, as thoughts surged through my mind, replied in a more moderate tone than I had intended. "I could use my sorcery without pain in Ilkadala. And in the farm. And there were the large structures in both. The head-dress was a small version of it. It makes sense, Wrack!"

His expression indicated that he did not believe me. I ignored him pointedly and looked at Griffyn, who seemed far more enthusiastic about the idea. "It means I need to get hold of one of these tiaras" I said firmly, ignoring Wrack's scepticism.

Griffyn shrugged elaborately, and I narrowed my eyes. He was almost too laid back, too casual. I wasn't entirely surprised when he said he might have an idea in that direction. I leaned back and looked at him archly, and waited for the other shoe to drop.

Chapter Twenty-Two

I lay on my back and gazed up at the curtain of cloud hanging over me, seeming close enough that I could reach up and sweep it aside. I should be so lucky. I was heartily tired of a grey, starless, sunless sky. The ground under me was warm. That I could learn to live with – it made sprawling like this rather pleasant. The soft red grass smelt a little like hay. After a night clinging to a tuurgakk as we swung through the darkness I was glad to be able to relax, at least for a while. I was just disappointed that the light in which I was bathed was from a couple of lantern trees, not the sun. In this costume I could have got a good suntan. Oh, well.

Wrack was slumped twenty feet away, Farrys stretched out between us. I wasn't sorry about that – it meant the dragonlord couldn't come and hassle me, and after the last two days I really wasn't sure I wanted his attentions. Well beyond them both, in a secluded hollow, our force of tuurgakks were resting after their exertions getting us here.

The trouble was that my thoughts started churning. Daylight hours always seemed to crawl past like snails with arthritis. I found myself thinking through the events of the last couple of days, and wondering if I had made the right decisions.

I had been right to wait for the second shoe to drop. Griffyn had told us that a group of his people were planning a raid on a tsergiaad tower. His grandiose claim that his little band were the only ones fighting the lloruk was, after all, a little misleading. He organised and manipulated a number of groups of rebels who struck at the lloruk under his direction. They would scout out a target, report back to him, and he would then sweep in with weapons and tools to equip them. He would lead them in the raid, and then afterwards (reading between the lines) he would take the credit.

To be fair, if I could believe what he told us, it was the planning and preparation that made sure the teams won, and Griffyn led the assaults from the front, not shirking the dangers.

And now he wanted us to join in, trusting that we would find a headdress for me there afterwards. He had leaned forward, looking at us with military passion. "Your help could make all the difference!" he had said. "A tsergiaad tower isn't an easy target. There are three lloruk there, and I'm pretty sure they're working on weapons to use against us. Not larisqs, but other obscenities. I could really use your help."

The trouble is, I'm not immune to flattery, particularly from a handsome man. He would have had all of his quartet on the mission if Kentyr and Darhia hadn't been on their way to Tolgrail for me. Wrack had muttered something about that, about the fact that Griffyn continued to play on it, but I still felt obligated.

"How far away is it?" I had asked.

"I reckon it's around a hundred miles" he had replied. I had sighed at that, imagining the trek through the jungles, but he added "And it's on a skywire, so we can take the tuurgakks."

Wrack was again shaking his head. "Not our fight, Sorrel" he grumbled.

Griffyn had looked at me levelly, keen pale blue eyes pleading. "I'm asking you for only two days." He ran a finger along the violet lines on a map – I guessed they showed the skywires. "There's a cave we've used before as a place to lurk, to break the journey." Griffyn looked at me levelly. "Please help me."

All rational logic had said I should refuse. Deadly, lethal danger, for a fight that was not mine. And it meant I would be even longer getting to Tolgrail. I said as much, and Griffyn unfurled his map, showing that the target was about seventy miles from Tolgrail, and beyond the jungle. The journey from there to Tolgrail would be considerably easier than from here. It also put off the time when I would have to make a decision about whether I stayed here in the Chasm. When I got to Tolgrail, I would have to make a choice, and I still didn't really know what I wanted to do. Yes, I was being indecisive.

"All right" I eventually conceded, the prospect of delaying the inevitable confrontation with Wrack about our futures being a significant reason for my decision. "I'll come on this raid with you. But we need to get a message to Korhus and the others, so that they know I've not abandoned them."

"I can do that" Griffyn answered immediately. He looked smugly pleased that I was going along with his proposal, and then he glanced at Wrack. "You don't have to come if you don't want to, Wrack."

"Don't be stupid" he had growled in response. "It's *my* jasq she's risking."

The tuurgakks had seemed indefatigable, maintaining their pace for hour after hour through the stygian darkness as we headed towards the target for the raid. I could not even see Griffyn ahead of me, or Wrack or Farrys behind me. Whenever we reached a spire Griffyn would halt us for a time, and he and Farrys would feed the brutes large, thick leaves and pour out a dark fluid which they sucked up with one of their tentacles. Twice, if not three times, we passed places where the skywires divided. Griffyn was confidant about our route, directing the tuurgaaks one way or other at each junction without hesitation. It was only after I had seen a lantern tree glowing, and a second growing brighter, that Griffyn led us down the side of the next spire. I half-expected him to sneak into the spire chambers, but he commented quietly that it was too risky, that this spire was in use by the lloruk. Instead, we went about half a mile into the rich scarlet jungle, leading the tuurgakks, which were finally showing signs of tiredness. Griffyn clearly knew this area – he led us straight to a heavy clump of viciously bethorned orange bushes. When he shoved them aside, not without difficulty, he revealed a gaping hole in the side of the hill. He had stayed here before, and there was already a makeshift stable for the tuurgakks.

"Isn't there a danger of something taking over your hideout?" I queried.

Griffyn shrugged. "If something did I'd have to drive it out" he said simply.

There were even supplies stashed in a wooden box in the corner of the cave. "I use this as a regular stopping place for us" he explained. "I've got a number of similar hideouts."

I'm not used to sleeping by day. I'd dozed during our journey, and I ended up feeling dangerously wakeful. The rough straw pallets were surprisingly soft and comfortable, but I simply wasn't tired. Griffyn was unwilling to let us venture out of the cave during daylight, but there was more than enough light to keep me awake in here. I sat and scrawled a grid in the thin grey dust on the floor of the cave and tried to play Vraan, using stones for the counters. Needless to say, I couldn't get a single game to go out. Some people call Vraan "Patience", because you need perfect patience to keep trying. After less than an hour I kicked the grid into a tangle of chaos and stalked off. Griffyn and Farrys were both snoring gently. I considered kicking Griffyn, too. Wrack had got to his feet before I could kick *him*, and nodded at me.

"Can't sleep either" he had said quietly.

I hadn't bothered replying – why state the obvious? - and just shrugged.

"Sorrel" he said quietly "I'm nearly fit to fly."

"Good" I said warmly. I looked at him sidelong. "What are you going to do?"

He smiled slightly, edgily. He was speaking in narynyl, obviously ensuring that our companions, if either was awake, could not understand his words. His focus was upon me alone. "Won't be able to change back when I reach the surface. Need to bring you up, too."

"You can't carry me that far" I said warily. I wouldn't put it past him to try. Odds were he'd drop me before we got half way up, particularly as his wing wasn't going to be in such good shape. He needed to exercise the muscles, get the wing working properly even before he tried to fly out. I started to say so, but he was shaking his head.

"I know I can't carry you" he growled. I could tell what an effort it had been to admit such an inability. Dragonlords don't like admitting there's anything they can't do.

"So you can't fly out" I had said quietly.

Wrack grinned. A wide smile on Wrack's face is a rarity, lighting up his face. He can actually be very handsome when he smiled, and I had felt myself melt towards him – a little. Thinking back now, I remembered seeing him smile like that sometimes before the war, when I was learning my sorcery at his mansion, under his supervision. If he had smiled like that when he invited me to his bed, I might have accepted. I shivered, despite the warmth, wondering just what would have happened if I had done. Which side I would have been on in the war. No – I could never have sided with the dragons. I knew too much about what his kind did. That was why I had refused him then.

This time, his smile had been evidence that he had a plan of some kind. I had raised my eyebrows, knowing him well enough that I didn't need to ask.

"I take a message" he said. "Fly to your aerodrome. You've got more two-seater aeroplanes. One of your people flies down with me, lands, picks you up, and we all fly out!"

Considering it was one of Wrack's ideas, it was a remarkably good scheme. I thought it through, thinking about the problems. "You need me to write the note. Tolly won't fly a tripe into the Canyon without being sure it'll work." I had mulled the idea some more. "We'll need a four seater for safety. One of the big Molgaru transports, loaded with fuel to make sure we can all get back."

One of the pre-war aeroplanes would have been a better choice. When I first learned to fly, we hadn't had to worry about fuel. I had been one of the original sorcerer-pilots, using the realm to draw water and fire into the boiler of the engine. The early aeroplanes were primitive, the engines desperately inefficient – without a mage to drive them, they had no chance of flying.

Since the war, the engineers managed to fuel 'planes with liquid coal, or similar oils – the range was drastically limited, and the new breed of aircraft could carry only a fraction of the weight that our old crates could, if they were to travel any distance. But I doubted that there were any of the original engines left. Whatever aeroplane came down into the Chasm would need a lot of fuel.

"Not going to be a problem, surely" Wrack replied.

I shook my head, then paused in recognition of the difficulties. "A Molgaru twin-prop needs a big, smooth field to land on. Preferably a proper runway. We'll need to find something suitable."

"What about those flying boats?" Wrack queried. "Lake be a better place to land?"

Volging lafquas, had been my immediate mental response. He really had been on good form. I should have thought of that myself. To be fair, he'd been thinking about this for hours, if not days. "How are you planning to carry the message?"

"Something slung round my neck."

I had nodded slowly. "It ought to work." I looked at him coldly. "But you're assuming I want to go back to the surface."

"Had this argument before" he snapped. "This is not our place, Sorrel!" He looked at me levelly. "Your friends are safely on their way to Tolgrail. Don't owe them anything more. Griffyn's been moved to his Ship. Nothing else down here you need to do. You don't need to be on this raid." I'd seen that look on his face before. He was preparing what he hoped would be a devastating, unanswerable proclamation. "Don't you want to be able to fly again?"

I had taken two deep breaths. He had hit home again. He was right, of course. I looked him straight in the eye, marshalling my own unstoppable riposte. "All very well, Wrack, but when I was your slave the last thing you'd let me do was fly. Why should I expect that to change if we return to your mansion?"

He snarled in frustration. "That was during the war, Sorrel! You were flying fighter 'planes, trying to kill me and my kind! No way you could be allowed back into control of an aeroplane!"

I was on my feet, angry in response. "And that's somehow going to change, now, Wrack? I'm a sorceress again! Your people won't let me into an aeroplane – I might try to burn one of them out of the sky again!"

Wrack was equally angry, glowering at me with eyes that blazed like a magerealm fireflow. "What did you expect, Sorrel? Your vicious rebellion killed fifteen of us!"

Griffyn had stirred at that. I had tried to quieten my voice, but I had been fuming. "We were trying to get away from you lafquassing volgs, Wrack! That's why we used the aeroplanes – to keep you monsters at bay!"

Wrack's voice had been low and dangerously soft. "How many of your people died in your volging rebellion, Sorrel? A thousand? Fifteen hundred? More? *We* didn't kill our subjects – so who caused the greatest bloodshed?"

I spun round and snarled at him "Don't kid yourself, Wrack! Of course you murdered us! Serfs who didn't obey their lord got starved out or occasionally toasted by dragonfire! A family who refused to surrender a pretty daughter to some dragonlord's lusts might be executed or just barbecued! Just disobeying a dragon was usually enough to lead to punishment or execution! And if a village angered a dragonlord the whole area might be laid waste!"

"Weren't all like that" he snapped back. "All right, so a few overstepped the boundaries, but most of us treated you well – and so you attacked us!"

"A few? A few? I could name a dozen, Wrack, out of the forty lords. One in three? You call that a few?"

His hand clawed at my arm, pulling me to face him. "Name them, then!"

For a moment I had thought my mind had gone blank – I couldn't name a single dragonlord. Impossible. I blinked, and then the names had flooded through my thoughts again. "Starron. Ember. Troth. Mondi. Castell." A pause as I tried to think of the others. "Rastor. Allanti," I glared at Wrack hard. "Not to mention Kabal."

"Still gloating about Kabal, then?" he hissed.

I looked at him levelly, trying to gauge his temper. I shouldn't have mentioned Kabal, but the temptation had been too great. "You deny that he was a lafquass of the first order, then, Wrack?"

A sharp intake of breath. If he had been in dragon form, he would have breathed at me. I watched for him to start to change, but he had maintained enough self control not to. "Won't speak ill of the dead, Sorrel."

"You won't. I will!" I retorted. "He enjoyed bullying, torturing and destroying. His treatment of the people of Werintar caused the revolt in the dragonlands. And you know it!"

"And you killed him" he replied hotly. "Blew him out of the sky with your sorcery. Ripped his wings to shreds and burned him so badly that he had no chance."

"He deserved everything he got!" I growled. "He and those like him made us live in terror, Wrack! Always afraid that death might come from the sky at any time! Do you blame us for deciding that enough was enough?"

"You killed a dragonlord, Sorrel! One of fifteen lords who died during the revolt!"

"You said it, Wrack. Fifteen of you. More than a thousand of us!"

"But we are so few! Six of the dead were female!"

"Some of your women were worse than the menfolk" I rasped. "Ask yourself about the arena games Mondi played."

"Those were convicted criminals" he answered. I had heard the hesitation in his voice, and closed in for the kill.

"Convicted of what, Wrack? Stealing food because they were hungry? Refusing to work in her factories? Breaking a curfew or travelling without a permit? That means they should die horribly?"

"Not talking to you in this mood, Sorrel" he had snarled. He turned his back on me firmly.

Looking back at it now, I know I should have dropped it. The trouble was, I so seldom had the chance to pour out my anguish and frustration. Volg it, we should have won! I had grabbed Wrack by the shoulders and turned him to face me. "Don't turn your back on me, Wrack! You know what I'm saying is right!"

He lashed out with his uninjured arm. Typical Wrack. Push him too hard and he resorted to violence. Trouble was, he was faster than I was. The blow connected, catching the side of my face with the flat of his hand, sending me tumbling to the floor of the cave. He flung himself at me, snarling in anger. I struggled sideways, twisting so that his full weight did not pin me down. On the other side of the cave I heard Griffyn and Farrys shouting at us. I ignored them and kicked at Wrack's injured arm viciously. He tried to evade the blow – for once, I was faster, and caught him squarely. He cried out in pain and I grabbed at his throat, slamming his head against the hard, rough floor of the cave, hard. I saw his eyes water and glaze, and I held his head down, my fingers tight on his throat.

"Now you'll listen to me, Wrack!"

He tried to gesture, indicating behind me. No way was I falling for that. "You had no love for Kabal! He was your rival!" I was going to berate him with his glee at seeing Kabal fall, when someone grabbed me from behind. Griffyn, of course. Volg it, Wrack had been telling the truth when he gestured behind me. I tried to struggle but the rebel was strong and had a firm grip on my arms, hauling me away from Wrack. Farrys was grabbing at Wrack – he was braver than I thought – to ensure the dragon did not try to continue the fight.

"What the squum is going on?" Griffyn demanded in veredraa. "I thought you two were friends."

Wrack laughed coldly, answering in the same tongue. "Why'd you think that?" He was rubbing his arm. I hadn't done him any serious damage, but he was going to have a good collection of bruises in due course. All right, so I would have some, too, but it had been worth it.

"If I let go of you, are you going to attack him again?" Griffyn asked me.

I thought about it, letting Wrack know I was not instantly ending hostilities. I leaned back into Griffyn's grip, feeling his warm body against mine. He took a sudden, unsteady breath, and I realised that he was rather enjoying the contact, too. I made sure Wrack could see that I was pressed against Griffyn. His eyes narrowed, making his face even more snakelike. He didn't immediately say anything, but his eyes lifted so that he was looking at Griffyn. "No" I said eventually. "Fun though it was."

Wrack shook his head in disgust. "You want to stay down here, Sorrel?" he demanded.

"I've got a job to do down here" I had snapped back. I looked into Wrack's eyes. "And I don't want to be your slave again, Wrack. Not now, not when – if – we get back to the surface. Not ever." I pulled myself out of Griffyn's grasp and walked towards Wrack again. Farrys tried to step between us while Griffyn muttered something obscene and strode after me, but Wrack was shaking his head. He opened his mouth as if to say something, then closed it again. He stalked towards the entrance to the cave. Before he pushed his way through the bushes he had looked back over his shoulder.

"Need some fresh air – away from *her*. Be back later. Maybe."

He was gone. Griffyn gestured at Farrys – the other man had paused for a moment, irresolute, but at a second motion he followed Wrack out.

Griffyn had taken my arm, making sure I didn't storm after him. "What's he going to..."

"He won't go to the lloruk" I said quietly. "His gripe's with me, not you."

"Did I really hear you say that you were his slave?" Griffyn mused, a question in his voice.

I had sat down on one of the mattresses and shrugged. "He and I were on opposite sides in our war. His side won."

"I'd assumed he was a renegade, on your side against his own people. You escaped from him, and he chased you down here?"

236

"Something like that" I said uncomfortably.

"I hope you don't regret being here" he said softly. He had perched himself on the side of my mattress. I was very aware of his presence close to me, of the heat of his body. He was very handsome, and his body was almost as fit and strong as Wrack's. I was still angry with Wrack. He didn't own me, whatever he thought. I had had lovers over the years. In the early days of the war I had known that I could die at any time – it had made me more eager to make the most of every moment of life that I had. That same awareness had gripped me again. I had turned towards Griffyn, and smiled at him.

"No. I don't."

I had reached up to him and kissed him hard. Griffyn didn't need any more encouragement.

The harness I was wearing came apart with only a couple of tugs on the buckles. His, I had quickly worked out, was equally easy to remove. Griffyn had made no demur as I rolled him onto his back and straddled him. I had wanted to be in control.

We had both thoroughly enjoyed what followed. It was only afterwards that I had begun to wonder what I had done.

Wrack had not returned by the time I had disentangled myself from Griffyn. Half of my thoughts had been rehearsing justifications for what I had just done, running imaginary conversations through my mind as I explained to Wrack that I had every right to take a lover. Griffyn was still relaxed on the mattress, looking smug and comfortable, a cat after devouring the canary. Hmmm. I wasn't sure I liked that metaphor. I had slid my harness around me and tightened the clasps, and tossed Griffyn's costume to him, bending over to kiss him as I did so. He smiled at me, and I relaxed slightly. I always felt slightly uncomfortable emotionally after bedding a man for the first time – a mixture of uncertainty and embarrassment. I had smiled back, and gently told him to get dressed. Maybe it was weak of me, but I hadn't wanted Wrack coming back and seeing us obviously together. I suspected he would know what we had done. Volg it, I had no reason to care what Wrack thought! I wasn't his property!

I had explored the stores in the cave, and poured us both out some of the wine. I didn't want us to sit in silence, and so I asked Griffyn about the target we were heading for.

By the time he had finished describing the tsergiaad tower, I was relaxing on the mattress, much more comfortable than I had been. A sound by the entrance had announced Wrack's presence. He glowered at us sourly as Farrys hurried in after him, and he walked over to the stores. He poured himself some wine as well, and picked up a handful of dried meat. "Don't let me interrupt you" he growled in his fast improving veredraa. "Carry on."

"I haven't much else to say" Griffyn replied. "We'll get moving as soon as it gets dark. Another couple of hours."

"Good" was all Wrack had to say. I couldn't meet his eyes when he looked towards me. He walked out towards the entrance again, and then looked back at me. "Sorrel?" he had asked. Almost pleadingly, I realised. I hadn't been sure if I was still angry with him, so I had slowly got to my feet.

"Wrack?"

He gestured towards the outside world. I hadn't really wanted to go with him, but it was easier to agree than to argue. I slowly followed him into the light of the lantern tree that stood less than a mile away, shining towards our cave.

Wrack had walked twenty paces away from the entrance. His face was shadowed, and he had not met my eyes. "Sorrel" he said again, his voice rumbling in his chest.

"Well?" I had asked, not knowing what else I could say.

"I can't let you go" he said simply, slipping back into narynyl. "You ensured that when you took my jasq."

I looked at him levelly. "The only reason you need me is to become a dragon" I said slowly, emphatically. "We humans have to live with one form for our entire lives. Perhaps it's time for you to find out what it's like to be human."

I had rehearsed the statement in my head. Saying it to Wrack, though, it

238

sounded pretty lame.

He had grabbed my shoulders. "Why the volg should I, Sorrel?" he snarled. "I'm a dragon, not a mere human! I like being able to fly!" He shook me roughly. "You did this to yourself when you stole my jasq! If you don't like being with me that's just too bad!"

"What choice did we have, Wrack?" I snapped back, shrugging off his grip upon me. "After you... after you won, after you crushed our revolt, you and your friends carved the jasqs out of all of the mages who survived the war. Without a single jasq we had no way of getting any new ones!"

He had looked at me coldly. "Without magic you couldn't attack us again. No more stupid revolts. No more needless bloodshed! There were... incidents... after your people surrendered. Raids on the dragons. Wanton acts of destruction and robbery." He glared at me suspiciously, emerald eyes impaling me, and I tried to keep my face expressionless. "We had to ensure it ended."

"Magic isn't just for war, Wrack! We needed mages for other things, too!"

"Like volg, Sorrel!" He had reached for me again, wanting to hold me so that he could shout into my face as he had done so many times before. "You and your violent friends were only interested in fighting us!"

Trouble was, he was right about that. I blanched, then looked him in the eyes again, trying to be strong, holding his upper arms so that we were even. "If you and your kind treated us decently we wouldn't need to!"

He had let go of me so suddenly I almost tumbled over. "Sorrel" he rasped. For a moment I thought there was a catch in his voice, almost a sob. "We changed. We did learn from what happened." He paused. Thinking back over it, rolling the argument around in my thoughts, I suspected he had actually been uncertain about what he was going to say. "You were right" he went on. For a second time I had almost fallen over. Wrack, admitting I was right? "Some of us were monsters. Sorrel. We did treat some of you appallingly." He looked at me, pleading again. "Your revolt made us stop and think. The worst offenders... you were right about Starron and Ember and the others. We made rules so that they can't be like that again."

I had looked at him blankly. Now I was pretty sure I must have looked completely dumb for a moment. "You made rules?" I said stupidly. "Binding the dragonlords?"

"Yes!" he said firmly. "Tried to learn from our mistakes." He took my hand, and looked me in the eyes. "Sorrel, *I* was the one who drew up those rules. Forced the rest of us to accept them."

I hadn't been able to meet his gaze, then. I pulled my hand out of his grip and walked away a few paces. I heard him walking after me, but I did not look back. I was trying to make sense of what he was saying. Trying to decide if I believed him. I still wasn't certain if I did.

I had turned and looked at him again. He stood, balanced on both feet, facing me squarely. Wrack had never actually lied to me. If he said something was so, the odds were it was. Of course, he was pretty good at not saying the whole truth or being misleading.

"Wrack, why didn't you tell us about those rules? We went on trying to fight because we thought nothing had changed!"

He had looked thunderstruck at my question, almost as startled as I had been. "Why should we tell you humans about our decisions, Sorrel? Demeaning enough we had to bind ourselves without crawling to you and telling you our shame!"

I sighed, and shook my head. "We needed to know! How can we be sure you'll follow these rules? How can we feel secure if we don't know they exist?"

Wrack had been growing angry again, and my heart had sank. I didn't want him to be angry at me!

"Sorrel, you humans should do as you are told, not make demands or expect to be treated as equals!"

I turned away. My own anger had been bubbling within me. For a moment, just a brief instant, I had thought his attitude had actually changed. Stupid, Sorrel. Stupid. Of course he hadn't changed. He still thought of us all – and me in particular – as slaves. I had spun round and shouted back at him "Maybe you need to find out what it's like to be human, Wrack!"

"Why should I?" he snarled. "You are coming back with me, Sorrel! Not letting you cripple me again!"

I opened my mouth for the obvious retort when Griffyn shouted at us both.

"Will you two shut up!"

We had both turned, astonished at the sharp intervention. Wrack opened his mouth to shout back, but Griffyn got in first. "I reckon if there's a graalur patrol within a mile of us it'll be round our necks in minutes!"

I closed my mouth, realising that my cheeks were bright pink. Wrack looked from me to Griffyn and then back to me.

"I'm sorry" I said softly. "It... we..."

Wrack was in less apologetic mood. He stalked past Griffyn, not quite pushing him aside. He clearly did know what we had done. "Maybe I'd prefer the graalur and the lloruk to you" he snarled, and walked away up the hill. Griffyn looked helplessly between us, and then shook his head despairingly. He had reached out his arm to me, but I had just shaken my head. I was too mixed up inside to want to complicate things further. I turned away and walked slowly back towards the skywire, needing to think.

Griffyn followed. He spoke my name, quietly, and I turned slowly.

"Do you want us to get moving, Sorrel?" he asked. "I could write a note, just leave Wrack here – we could pick him up on the way back?"

It was tempting. I thought about it quite hard. But Wrack would be even more angry. I wasn't sure I wanted to burn my boats where Wrack was concerned. I had shaken my head again. Griffyn looked disappointed, but, for a mercy, did not argue. Now, I was sure that for once I had actually made the right decision.

Two hours later, safely enveloped in the darkness, all four of us were on the move again, swinging beneath the skywire as the tuurgakks carried us towards Olotha, our target. Wrack had stalked back, but we had spoken less than a dozen words since he returned. Strapped onto the insectile body of the tuurgakk I had had more time to think, but I had still not reached any conclusions. I had been exhausted, worn out by the emotional ups and downs. Griffyn had told me I was fairly secure on the back of the tuurgakk – I had checked the straps were tight, and tried to sleep.

My dreams had been a morass of angry, overbearing dragons, falling aeroplanes, fire and swords, and too many men. Now, lying waiting on the grass, my waking thoughts were little better. It didn't help that I was worrying about Kelhene, Darhath and the others from the Grihl Valley. They were trekking through the jungle towards Tolgrail from the south. We had gone much further along the wire, travelling east as well as north, and once we had finished this task we would trek west on foot until we reached the city. I just hoped everyone was all right.

It was a relief when Griffyn crept back towards us, a small cluster of other figures on his tail. The tuurgakks had delivered us not far from a village, controlled by graalur overseers – Griffyn had told us he could call on a quarter of the adults of the settlements, slaves all, who would sneak out just before dusk to become our assault force.

The tuurgakks had carried two crates of weapons, mostly swords, to arm our little force. There were eight people who had joined Griffyn. I chatted briefly to Norghar and Lerhis, two of the older raiders. They told me about fighting in the last war when the lloruk had assailed Nintheyla, unsuccessfully, but they had been captured. I had no doubts that both had lost friends and family in the conflict, and both expressed their desire to hit back now they had the chance. Wrack had been cornered by a woman from the village called Veldhini. I decided that I was pleased about that – it kept him away from me. Anyhow, Veldhini wasn't Wrack's type. Too solidly built. I found out later that she was over fifty, too, and far too old for him.

Griffyn hissed at everyone to move in. When Griffyn told me and Wrack about the object of the raid, the plan he'd drawn had shown a circle at the centre. I'd expected the tower to be some fairytale structure, all pointed roofs and marble walls. Instead, it looked more like a pile of narrow aeroplane tyres, each smaller than the one below, built out of some granular material that made it look pockmarked. Around the outside three minarets rose, weirdly like the spires on the Neraldan temples in Bernuur. Graalur guards watched from two of them, their boredom visible. I could see a pinprick of red light at the mouth of the nearer guard, a trickle of smoke above him being dispersed by the breeze.

I lay on my stomach, inching forward cautiously, peering at the structure looming through the gloom of evening. Two lantern trees had already gone out – the third was dimming visibly. Griffyn leaned over and squeezed my hand. I smiled at him and squeezed back, before glancing sideways, a spasm of utterly irrational guilt making me look over to where Wrack was lying, twenty feet from us. He was not looking towards me, and I felt a burst of relief. I mentally kicked myself. Wrack had no right to interfere in my life. In what I wanted to do.

Now Norghar was creeping towards the tsergiaad tower. Everyone seemed to know what tsergiaads were except me and Wrack. When I'd dared to ask, Lerhis had growled something about insect-people, and that the lloruk had taken the tower from them.

Norghar had been given a crossbow, and seemed thoroughly competent with it. Griffyn had asked me if I could use my magic against the watch-graalur. I'd demurred, pointing out that even if it didn't cripple me, a sufficient blast of fire to fry a graalur was likely to draw attention. He hadn't seemed troubled about my refusal.

Another of the raiders – I didn't know her name – was heading round the other side with our other crossbow. I didn't give much for the chances of the two graalur on watch duties. I watched from our hiding place at the edge of the cultivated land. The tower stood on a rise overlooking the slave-village quarter of a mile from it. Graalur – just dark red dots – were patrolling outside the stockade, unsuccessfully (though we hoped they didn't know it) ensuring the slaves did not try to escape. The round pyramid of the tower dominated the fields around it.

Norghar was in position. Moments later the woman raised a hand slightly, confirming she was ready. I drew in my breath, willing them to shoot straight. Beside me Griffyn hissed in excitement, his face drawn in a half-smile, half-scowl. The light was draining away fast, leaving the fields drenched in shadow. Much longer, and our sharpshooters would not be able to see their targets. Griffyn hissed again, a pale cloth lifted for a moment in the signal… and I heard the double clunk as both crossbows loosed.

Both graalur gasped and slumped down within their respective towers. Griffyn chortled something obscene under his breath, and he was on his feet and running towards the tower. I was only a pace behind him, and Wrack was alongside me. Two hundred yards to the main entrance of the tower. I'm obviously fitter than Griffyn – I reached the door before he did. Bad move – as I did so, it opened, and a graalur wandered out as though he was going to pick flowers. My sword took him in the throat, and he died with a look of surprised annoyance on his face. Griffyn snapped some approbatory comment and was through the door and into the entrance hall.

The benefit of this being a tsergiaad tower was that they were all built on the same basic layout – Griffyn had sketched the interior, and we all had our allotted targets. Mine was a first floor chamber, reached by following a spiralling ramp that led off the entrance hall. Griffyn had already put down the graalur in the hall by the time I was onto the spiral. A bell began to clang above us. I heard Wrack's muffled curse, but I was heading up the ramp without a pause. The blood was pounding in my veins as I took short, sharp breaths. Everything seemed sharper, every sound a little louder than normally. I hadn't felt this since the raid on Wrack's mansion with Merik. It felt like a century ago.

I burst into the upper level, slamming through the poor quality wooden door the lloruk had built in place of the tsergiaad bead curtains that Griffyn had told us about. The wood splintered noisily. Within, a slavegirl was crouched, holding a tray. The lloruk she had been serving was on its feet, a short crystal staff in its left hand. The lloruk turned to confront me, blue robe swirling around it, as I skidded on the polished wooden floor. It pointed the crystal towards me. Even without slipping into the magerealm I knew that it was engaging in sorcery. Sometimes violence *is* the best policy. I slammed bodily into the serpentman, knocking it backwards, before hacking hard with the sword. The blade caught the creature in the side of the neck, but it was already twisting to evade the blow, and the glancing impact only cut a little way into it. I was spattered with a sprinkling of its blood, but it was still moving. It struck like its small cousins, trying to sink its fangs into my shoulder. My turn to evade. I ducked desperately, dropping almost to my knees, and punching with my left hand. Volg it, I should have brought a shield! Its scaly skin felt like padded leather, giving enough to absorb the strength of my blow. It was trying to bring the crystal rod to bear – I chopped at its arm, catching it squarely this time. The slavegirl was screaming; her cries increased in pitch and volume as I cut through scales, sinew, and bone. The blow was jarring, but I sliced through the creature's thin arm cleanly. More blood. As I crippled it, something caught the side of my thigh hard, and I realised that the lloruk had swung its tail around to try to knock me off balance. It worked, and I stumbled against the low couch upon which the lloruk had presumably been reclining. The lloruk was hissing in pain, clutching the stump of the wounded arm with its other hand. I struggled to my feet as it tried to face me. The crystal staff was on the floor, inert and useless. Now the lloruk was relying on physical means of attack. It grabbed a fallen goblet from the floor in its right hand, and flung it at me. I ducked, and it shattered noisily against the far wall. The lloruk took the opportunity to run for the other door out of the room, its robe just shreds of torn blue silk. I staggered after it, realising that my thigh was stinging from the impact with its tail.

Through the door, and into another chamber. Lerhis was supposed to be dealing with this room. He was locked in combat with a graalur, hands around each other's throats. I wondered briefly what had become of their swords. The lloruk ignored them, struggling to reach a red wooden box on a shelf. This room was obviously used as a library – there were books on shelves and also strange-looking sculptures on plinths. The box had been on a shelf – the lloruk flung it to the floor as I got close enough to hack at it, and orange dust spilled out. I instinctively held my breath and hacked again at the wound on its neck.

Lerhis scrambled backwards, away from the graalur as it crumpled to the ground, a dagger embedded in its armpit. I yelled at him to be careful but he was already stumbling into the dust. He gasped in alarm, and his face went violet. I leaped away, shouting for help. The lloruk, despite the latest wound I had inflicted, slithered sideways towards the next door. The problem with the tsergiaad tower was that every room was interconnected. I reached for Lerhis – he turned burning, bulging eyes to me, his expression agony. His voice was a husk, dry and struggling. "Stay back! No cure…"

He slid to his knees, blotches in darker hues breaking out on his skin. I backed away, horrified, needing to help, but knowing that all I could do would be to share his pain. He gasped for breath, and then slumped forward onto his face. I

245

swallowed an oath, and turned to pursue his killer.

In the room beyond a structure dominated the scratched parquet floor. Four curving tusks rose, angling together to a point at the centre. Around them a tracery of crystals. If I had had time, I would have crowed with delight. I did not have time to study it. There was a dead graalur on the floor, a victim of Veldhini's sword. Now she was striking at the lloruk as it tried to loop away from her. It turned back towards me, and blanched, recognising the fury in my eyes. I didn't give it any chance to react – I cut deep into its neck, trying to take its head off. Dark blood poured from the wound, but I hadn't got the strength to do the damage I had wanted to achieve. The blow was bad, possibly fatal – but unfortunately not yet. It swung back and then tried to ram its fangs into me – I pitched sideways, letting it miss me by the thickness of a piece of card, and forced my sword between its lips, so that the fangs bit onto metal. Behind me, I heard Veldhini snarl a battle-cry and chop down hard. The lloruk's head was flung backwards by the impact, spattering us both with drops of gore, and the serpentman dropped, whipping like a severed steel hawser. I jumped back and watched it twist and writhe for a few moments.

"You all right?" Veldhini whispered as our hearts slowed.

I shook my head. "It killed Lerhis" I muttered. "Some kind of poison – you can't go in there."

Veldhini looked at me in shock. "Poison?"

I told her what I had seen. She shivered. "Medus extract. Murderous swine!"

From below, there was a shouted question. I ran to the next door, to be met by one of the men I didn't know. We both spoke together. "You all right?"

I almost laughed, the tension beginning to seep out of me. I went back to the door that led to Lerhis, and closed it gently, before looking for something to mark it. The man was lifting his sword, intending to hack at the strange lloruk structure.

"No!" I snapped. "Leave that! I want to look at it!"

"It's lloruk magic" he replied blankly. "We always destroy it."

"I want to confirm what it does" I answered hotly.

"I take it you're all right?" came a new voice. Wrack was at the far door, blood on his sword, too, but the question had come from Griffyn, a foot behind him. At my nod, Griffyn was casting around, looking at the people in the chamber.

"Where's Lerhis?" Griffyn asked. I shook my head and gestured at the door, not able to speak. Veldhini growled something bitter about Medus extract, and Griffyn paled. He ran back to the door he had come through, and yelled something down the stairs, warning everyone about the room.

"There was a girl in the room beyond" I suddenly chattered, the picture of her slipping into my thoughts. I grabbed my sword and headed past Griffyn, pushing between him and Wrack to hasten right round the spiral. If the girl walked in… I lengthened my stride, only realising after a few paces that the additional footfalls were the sounds of pursuit, rather than echoes off the grainy stone walls. Wrack was matching my stride, wordless as he followed.

A full circle of the tower brought me to the door I had originally burst through. The lloruk's staff was still lying on the floor. The slave was hunkered down in one corner, half-hidden behind a wooden table. Beyond, through the far door I could see a tracery of orange dust spread across the floor. Amidst it lay Lerhis, his skin a pattern of violet veins. I swore under my breath and made my way to the door, walking gingerly so that no breath of air disturbed the lethal concoction. I eased the wooden panel closed, sealing off the poisoned room, and then shoved a stiff wooden lloruk chair in front of the door so that no one could walk through accidentally. I felt the tension seeping out of my veins. The battle was over.

I took a few slow, deep breaths, and straightened my shoulders. We had dealt with the lloruk, and the tower was ours. Griffyn had achieved his objective. I had come here to find out if we were right about the pain I had been suffering. I had no reason to wait. I took a deep breath, not giving myself time to prevaricate, and I slid into the magerealm.

Chapter Twenty-three

The spiced roast meat tasted delicious. Veldhini was an excellent cook. Her kitchen was small and neat, well-organised and with an eclectic collection of utensils. The solid iron range, black and looming in the corner, was red-hot, as Wrack had discovered to his cost and Farrys' amusement. The source of the heat was simple, old-fashioned peat, carved from the ground nearby and burning slowly in the bottom of the ironware. Veldhini had told Wrack that it was always hot – the range took weeks to get to full temperature, but little maintenance to keep it there.

I swigged a second mug of wine. It felt quite wrong to be drinking the surprisingly good beverage out of crude earthen cups. But, it didn't seem to interfere with the taste. Wrack was demolishing his third mug, and seemed a little more cheerful as a result.

It had taken us nearly an hour dodging guards to sneak into Veldhini's house in the village. Farrys had told us we were being dangerously unwise, and that we ought to head back to the Ship without delay. Frankly, I agreed with him intellectually, but the prospect of good food and soft beds had overridden any common sense. Riding the tuurgakks was not painful, but I wasn't going to pass up some comfort if we had the chance.

We had spent more than two hours in the tower after the assault. Griffyn and his people had been looting the chambers, finding valuables and weapons that the slaves could keep hidden in the village or which he could take with him back to the Ship. Meanwhile I had delved into the magerealm. I had shouted with joy when I first slid into the blaze of colour, much to the alarm of the others. There had been no pain, and I was sure it was a result of the tusked structure in the tower. The magerealm had been its usual psychedelic self, with flowing streams of liquid, semi-solid blocks of earth, pathways of air and fire, but beyond it, only barely visible, I had realised there was a shimmer of violet and green, almost like a dome around us. I realised that I had seen the realm looking a little like this before, both in the Iloruk

248

farm and in Ilkadala, but I had not had time to look at it then. More importantly, as far as I was concerned, my jasq was not trying to cripple me.

It had not been difficult to confirm that the dome nestling around us had its centre at the four-tusked edifice in the upper chamber. The edge of the dome was not solid, but the effect of the tusks seemed to fade out about sixty feet from it. A little experimentation told me that as I neared the edge of the dome my jasq began to quaver in my side, the pain increasing. Without any doubt, the structure within the tower was keeping something at bay. Unfortunately, it was far too large to carry it with us. It had taken me over an hour to find a box in one of the rooms downstairs that contained two coronets, like the one the Iloruk who raided Griffyn's spire had been wearing. With that crowning me, I had walked out into the darkness beyond the tower, and slid back into the realm. Wrack had been beside me, his hand on my shoulder in case the agony returned.

It hadn't. The coronet was holding back the dark miasmal influence that caused the pain and nausea I had suffered before. I might not know what caused it, but while I wore the coronet, or had it within a couple of feet of me, I was safe from it. Around me I had the same shimmer of emerald and amethyst that formed the much larger dome in the tower.

I had expected to go straight back to the Ship, but Griffyn had told us it was too far through the night to get back to our half-way camp before daybreak. Hence our decision to invade the village. I sipped the white wine and decided it definitely had been worth the risk. Wrack had had some good wines in his cellar, collected from across half the world. Vintages from Jehannush and Naarlbruch, jherrazh from Justarin, even some bottles of ghamani sparkling wine. At the moment this tasted as good as any of them. I had a shrewd suspicion that the glow of success had more to do with the wine's allure than its actual quality. Wrack's expression suggested I was right. He was always more of a snob where wine was concerned.

Most of our assault team had returned to their own homes, before their absence could be missed. Griffyn had collected the weaponry from them, but in return had handed out a clutch of the green pods for them to plant in due course in out-of-the-way spots. I had quietly asked what they were, but Griffyn had just smiled mysteriously and said they would make life more difficult for the lloruk. So much for him being horticultural – I had guessed they were actually some kind of weapon.

No one expected the graalur to find out about the raid until morning, by which time they ought to assume we were long gone. The tsurgakks were tethered well away from the tower – it would be considerable bad luck if they were discovered. For once we ought to be able to relax and take it easy in comfort for a day, before getting moving tonight.

I can be dumb sometimes. Even thinking something like that is enough to put a jinx on it.

There was a sudden knock on the front door. My alcoholic glow faded swiftly as alarm ate the benefit of the wine. Griffyn was on his feet, reaching for his sword. Veldhini gestured at us savagely to be silent, and then walked warily to the entrance to the house.

"Who's there?"

"Veldhini? It's Norghar. Can I come in?"

Veldhini cautiously undid the door, and drew Norghar into the house. When he had left the tower he had been going home. Now he was dripping with sweat which plastered down his long, rather lank fair hair. Either he had run all the way, or he was scared by something. Or perhaps both.

"Veldhini, Griffyn, there are graalur!" he said breathlessly. He had a long, rather coarse face, not helped by being clean shaven. "There's a big force camped to the north of the village!"

Griffyn was on his feet, alarm all over his face. "Are you telling me they've discovered the raid on the tower? They're hunting us?"

Norghar was shaking his head. "I sent Berryk back to check the tower." He added "I told him to be careful. But the graalur were here before we attacked. One of the villagers saw them arrive and setting up camp before dark. They're on a forced march, heading east." Norghar looked at Griffyn levelly. "Tolgrail."

Griffyn's expression twisted through surprise, dismay and then anger. Veldhini, beside him, had become ashen, despair cutting through her stoic countenance. I felt my own face pale, as I realised what Norghar was saying. An army. Probably the one I saw at the lloruk's farm. And they were intent on capturing or destroying the city my friends would be at. A grisly image slid behind my eyes, Kelhene and Darhath and the others, dead in the ruins, jubilant graalur gloating as the city burned. I felt quick anger flaring within me.

Griffyn shook his head. "Why Tolgrail?" he demanded of the air. The air didn't answer, of course. "I expected them to make for Jajruuk if they were going to strike at any more human cities!" His voice expressed his frustration that the enemy were not doing as they were supposed to. "It makes no sense to me at all!"

Farrys was shivering. "How many graalur, Norg?"

"At least three thousand, perhaps more."

"Lloruk?" Griffyn asked. Norghar shook his head, but seemed uncertain. "Artillery?" Griffyn pressed.

"They had a lot of carts. I think they've got snarqs, too."

Veldhini and Griffyn looked at each other. "That's an assault force" Griffyn growled. Veldhini nodded, her expression bleak.

"What do we do?"

Griffyn sat for long moments, gazing into space. I was holding my breath, hoping he would pull some rabbit out of the hat and come up with a solution.

"I can't tackle a force like that" he said quietly. No rabbits. I swore under my breath as he added "There's nothing we can do."

"But Tolgrail!" Veldhini wailed.

My voice joined with hers. "We've got to do something, Griffyn! My friends are heading for Tolgrail – and your people, too!"

Norghar grimaced. "You think the graalur can take Tolgrail?"

Griffyn and Veldhini's grim silence was more eloquent than any answer could have been. Wrack growled under his breath something obscene about graalur soldiers.

"Can we get to Tolgrail before them?" I asked, trying to look for answers.

"I can't see how. The graalur will be between us and them."

"Use the skywire" Wrack demanded. "Go right over their heads."

Now it was Farrys and Veldhini who were shaking their heads. "The skywire heads to Luthvara, to the north-west. It'd take us in the wrong direction. We need to go east."

"How far is Tolgrail from here?" I asked.

"About ninety miles" Veldhini answered. Hmmm. I narrowed my eyes and glanced across at Griffyn. He had told me seventy. A simple mistake? Deliberately trying to make it more palatable to aid him? If it had been a falsehood, he had lied without a pause or a moment's thought. Not that I had time to worry about his veracity just at the moment, but I filed it away for later consideration.

"The graalur are camped about a mile beyond the village" Norghar added helpfully. "They're on the old ridge road." That might have been helpful if I had known the area.

"So what we can we do to stop them?" I asked bluntly.

Griffyn shook his head. "We can't" he said grimly. "There's nothing we can do against a graalur force of that size, backed with lloruk sorcery."

I couldn't believe what I was hearing. Cold despair was creeping up on me, despite the heat in the Chasm, and I couldn't get the corpse-faces of my friends out of my mind. "Griffyn, you're talking about a human city being threatened by the graalur and the lloruk! You can't just sit on your hands and do nothing!"

Griffyn turned on me, his expression hard. "I'm not taking the risk of us dying hopelessly trying to help them."

Veldhini and Norghar did not look happy at that response. I looked at Wrack sidelong. I hoped, against all the odds, that he would back us up on this. He had seemed dismayed at the idea of leaving the city to face the enemy without any warning. I did not know if he would actually take a stance on it, though. My hope was that his evident dislike of Griffyn would tip the balance in our favour.

Wrack looked back at me. Sometimes I think he can read my mind. He held my gaze for a moment, and then turned away. He then looked back over his shoulder at me and said, quietly in narynyl "Better try some more feminine wiles, Sorrel."

For a moment I was tempted to hit him. Griffyn had heard his muttered aside, and turned towards me enquiringly. I glared at Wrack, and then extended my glare to encompass both men.

"So you'd let a city fall to the graalur just because you're too scared to help them?" Norghar snapped.

Griffyn picked up his mug and drained it before resting it on the polished wooden table. His eyes were dangerously fiery when he lifted his head to face us. "There's nothing I can do!"

"And you've no clever tricks to get us past the graalur, get us to the city in time to fight?" I demanded.

Griffyn put down his cup with a heavy click as it hit the table. For a moment I thought he had cracked the pottery. He shook his head. "Don't you think if I could get there I would?" he demanded.

Wrack quietly, evenly, murmured "No."

Griffyn's fist flew, catching Wrack squarely on the chin. The bigger man stumbled backwards, even Wrack's fast reflexes caught by surprise by the sudden blow. Griffyn flung himself after Wrack, more blows hammering against his shoulder and arm as Wrack tried to block the violence. Veldhini and I were both shouting at them, demanding that they stop fighting. I was storming forward, intending to grab Griffyn, when Wrack turned. He slammed his own blow into Griffyn's face, neatly driving the blow past Griffyn's belated effort to block the punch.

Now it was Griffyn's turn to tumble backwards, Wrack let him recover, before striding towards him, fists clenched. I felt a chill in my spine at Wrack's expression. I had seen him lose his temper and lash out at Starron once. The other dragonlord had visited the mansion, shortly after he had razed Burundar to the ground. The town had been defenceless, its small flight of biplanes demolished by saboteurs organised by Troth. Starron's raid on the town had killed over four hundred people, nearly a quarter of all the human casualties, most of them non-combatants. It had broken the rebellion's morale, and the war had been over within two more weeks. Before the humans had surrendered, though, Wrack and Starron had fought savagely, both fuelled by drink after a supposedly friendly meal. Wrack had been furious about Starron's actions. He had worn a similar expression then.

Wrack moved like a snake, pausing before striking savagely. Griffyn had backed away, hunching low and lifting his hands to block Wrack's blows – as Wrack struck, he weaved sideways and lashed out himself. Neither man connected, and they both moved to prepare to strike again. Both men were supremely fit, sweating in the heat of the Canyon, Griffyn breathing heavily. I could see the tension in Wrack's muscles as he readied a blow. Griffyn was balanced on his toes, a cat tensed to pounce.

I could have stood and watched both men with considerable pleasure, if they had not been trying to kill each other, and had I not been worrying about Tolgrail. As it was, I stormed between them, trying to stop myself cringing. If they decided to strike as I moved, I would get pulverised. "Stop it, both of you!" Not the most original words, but they ought to work. I hoped.

Griffyn stepped back slightly. Wrack, though, just glowered at me. "Stay out of this, Sorrel" he growled.

I put my hands on my hips and glowered back at him. "Or what? You'll hit me, too?"

"Think I wouldn't?"

I was sweating now. I knew very well that Wrack was not afraid to hit me. The dragonlords did not have any delusions of chivalry towards women. He knew I could give as good as I got, too. I raised my fists and held his eyes. "Try it and see what happens to you" I said softly.

For a moment I thought he would. Behind me, though, Veldhini and Norghar were squawking protests. Wrack slowly stood back, lowering his hands.

"Well?" I asked. "Enough, or do I have to start hitting you both?"

Veldhini muttered something about me being no better than the males.

Griffyn cracked a smile at that, Wrack was still hard-faced, anger burning in his eyes. I looked at him again, trying to read his thoughts. I knew he was raging at me for sleeping with Griffyn. He still thought of me as his property. I put my hands on the table and looked at him levelly. "Well?" I asked again.

Wrack opened his mouth... and there was a thunder on the door, heavy fists hammering. Deep, graalur voices demanded to know what was going on. Volging lafquass! Our two idiot men had been heard!

I looked around wildly. Veldhini and Norghar looked equally terrified. Griffyn gestured at Wrack to head upstairs into the low room under the roof. Wrack, though, had other ideas. He walked to the door and wrenched it open. Three surprised graalur stood outside, two male, one female, all startled at the sudden apparition before them. Instead of swords, they had pain-rods, red gems glowing balefully. Wrack grabbed the first one by the wrist so that he couldn't use the weapon, and hauled, hard, pulling the graalur into the main room. Off-balance, the graalur tumbled to the floor, his rod skittering across the smooth tiles. We couldn't let the graalur get away and raise the alarm – I dived forward instinctively, landing a punch on the jaw of the second graalur, taking him by surprise. Wrack grabbed the woman in a headlock – I heard a sudden, unpleasant crunch, and saw the graalur's head twisted round. Wrack dropped her body contemptuously. Within the house, Griffyn and Norghar were struggling with the graalur Wrack had yanked inside. I concentrated on my graalur. He had staggered backwards from my blow. I scrambled into the darkness outside the house and lashed out with my booted foot, catching the graalur in the stomach. He tried to swipe at me with his pain-rod, the glowing red crystal winking at me malevolently. I swung sideways, letting it whistle past my shoulder, and then I kicked again, catching him in the leg. He stumbled to the ground, still trying to hit me with his rod. I kicked him in the head, hard. He jerked backwards and sprawled across the grass beside the path like a broken puppet. I turned. The graalur in the house was dead – Griffyn was pulling a sword out of his stomach. Veldhini was spluttering in dismay. I could understand that. I had no doubt that if anyone found out that the graalur had been ambushed here, she would have to flee. As it was, if the graalur were anything like the dragonlords, the disappearance of three guards might well bring about savage reprisals against the villagers.

I looked at the one I had knocked out. The other two were dead. I couldn't leave my one alive. Volg it, I really did not like killing people! Even graalur! In a fight, it didn't feel so bad... but in cold blood?

Wrack walked forward. He had a knife in his hand. He nodded at me, ushering me out of the way. I shook my head. "My responsibility" I said quietly. I took the knife and knelt down. The graalur was out, cold. I had kicked him pretty hard. I bent down, clenched my teeth, and before I could think about what I was doing I cut his throat quickly and cleanly. Hot, dark blood flooded out. I gagged at the smell, and turned away swiftly. I could no longer count the number of people I had killed, but cold-blooded murder like this... I didn't want to think about it. A nasty corner of my mind tried to remind me of a job I had done with the Firebirds, where a guard had been killed equally cold-bloodedly. I kicked the memory in the head but it didn't go away.

Wrack picked up the body. The red grass drank the blood quickly. I hoped that nothing would show by daylight.

Back inside, Veldhini looked stunned at the sudden, lethal violence. Wrack and Griffyn were already stripping the bodies, both men asking about the best place to dump them. Norghar said something about a deep sinkhole on the south side of the village, near the olgrek stables. Veldhini was pale with shock, spluttering about her home. I went over to Veldhini and put an arm around her shoulders.

"We'll make sure the bodies aren't found, Veldhini" I said quietly. "There'll be nothing to suggest they were ever here."

"What reprisals if they disappear?" Wrack asked. I glanced at him levelly. He also remembered what the dragonlords would do.

But Veldhini was shaking her head, her panic subsiding. "The graalur kill each other occasionally, and sometimes desert afterwards. If they disappear the slavemaster won't know for certain what happened. She'll ask questions and search the place – so long as she doesn't find anything, she probably won't do too much." She didn't look too certain of the prospect.

I shook my head grimly. "We'd better shift the bodies."

What little remained of the rest of the night was spent carting the three corpses through the gloom, and dropping them down the deep shaft Norghar showed us. Veldhini was confident that there would be no excavation or investigation down there – it was a remnant from building works which had been abandoned months before, when a torrential storm had revealed an underground stream that made the ground unstable. We dropped a considerable amount of soil down, too, to cover the bodies. The nearest lantern tree was beginning to shine as we slipped back into Veldhini's house. Fortunately, it seemed our three graalur had been the only guards on patrol inside the stockade.

We sat in the kitchen. All of us stank of sweat, blood and bodies. I needed a bath so badly I could have killed for it.

Well, no, not really. Maimed for it, maybe.

"What are we going to do now?" I asked heavily.

"We go back to the tuurgakks" Griffyn replied. "When I get back to the Ship we can think about plans from there."

"And Tolgrail?" I whispered.

Griffyn dropped his gaze.

My heart was ice in my chest. I felt like screaming at Griffyn in rage. So full of himself, yet utterly useless when we needed action. Volg it, I cared about the Grihl Valley people! I felt... responsible for them. I'd never really felt such an obligation before, and in some ways I really didn't know why I felt so strongly. But they had trusted me. They had headed to Tolgrail, because I had agreed that they would be safe there. And now they faced assault, slavery and death. And I was helpless to do anything. I really, really didn't like feeling so useless. The room was silent, the city's name hanging in the air like an epitaph.

To my surprise, Wrack shattered the icy silence. "Norghar said about three thousand graalur troops, plus cart-borne weapons, and a couple of flying creatures. And maybe some lloruk." Wrack wasn't one for long speeches. He had clearly been thinking about this with some care. "Not a big force to attack a city, Griffyn. Especially if it has decent walls."

His voice was accusatory. Griffyn shook his head. "They've got sorcery. The accounts I've heard talk of lloruk raining fire down inside the walls, or bringing the walls crashing down with floods of water in the foundations. We've no way of stopping them, Wrack." His voice was grim.

I looked at Wrack. He was looking back at me, for once with both eyebrows raised. "Fire from the magerealm?" he questioned.

"And water into the foundations to wash them away" I concurred, beginning to see what he was saying.

"Where are their mages when they do this?" Wrack demanded.

Griffyn looked blank. "If I remember rightly, a long way from the walls" he replied. "When Belgran was taken the lloruk were well beyond bow-shot. There was no way the defenders could hit them."

I began to smile, an imp of hope kindling inside me, melting the ice that had frozen me before. "If you could stop their sorcery, could Tolgrail be held?"

Griffyn cocked his head to one side. "I think it's one hell of an 'if', but yes, probably."

"Which only leaves one question" I said quietly. "How do we get me to Tolgrail before the enemy attack?"

Veldhini, with some acerbity, demanded to know what I was on about.

"Sorcery" I replied. "I told you about the magerealm. That's what the lloruk are using."

"Sorrel can stop them" Wrack explained. "In our war, that sort of long range magic was easy to block."

I gestured at my coronet. "With this I can use my sorcery. Give the lloruk a very nasty surprise."

Griffyn looked at me appraisingly, but then shook his head. "I told you, the graalur are between us and Tolgrail. There's no way to get us there in time."

I turned at looked at Wrack. "How fully recovered are you?" I asked.

He shrugged, surprised. "Arm is healed. Should be able to fly."

"Enough to carry me past the enemy troops?"

Wrack paused, uncertain. I blinked. Wrack had changed since coming down here. On the surface I had never seen him doubt his own abilities. I waited. "Don't know" he said simply. "Not flown in quite a time – don't know how much strength I have in my wings."

"What are you talking about?" Veldhini demanded.

It was Griffyn who replied. "Wrack can turn into a dragon."

Wrack just glared. "Don't 'turn into' a dragon. I *am* a dragon."

Veldhini looked him up and down, slowly, appraisingly. "Really" she said coolly.

I went and stood next to him. "He can take either human or dragon form. Both shapes are still him."

"But would you be able to carry us?" Griffyn asked.

"Not carry *you*, Griffyn" I said firmly. "Carry *me*."

258

"Might be able to carry Sorrel" Wrack agreed. "No way I could carry you, Griffyn."

Griffyn's face was a mixture of frustration and relief. Frankly, if I had been Griffyn I wouldn't have wanted to take the opportunity of being carried by Wrack. Wrack was quite capable of getting to a decent altitude and then dropping him. Accidentally, of course.

"You'd need to fly all the way to get there before the graalur do" Norghar growled. "They move fast. They'll be at the gorge by tonight, and at Tolgrail in three days."

Farrys muttered something about hitting the graalur before they got to Tolgrail. Wrack shook his head firmly. "Attacking a ground force from the air is suicidal! May well burn down a good number of them, a couple of dozen or more. If they have bows or javelins they'll bring *me* down, too!"

I nodded in bleak agreement. "Wrack's fire's only effective at very short ranges." I explained.

Wrack glared at me. "Your human troops got extremely good at bringing down dragons who attacked them on the ground." His voice softened, almost into a veiled apology. "That's why Starron and his friends took to hitting civilians. It was... *safer* for them."

I turned away, not wanting to look at him.

Griffyn looked at us both. "Can you stop the graalur getting to Tolgrail?" he asked evenly.

Wrack shrugged. "Not by a frontal attack, no."

Veldhini was on her feet, face suffused with excitement. "The bridge at Heldriss!" she said loudly.

We all turned to look at her. She looked back at us as though she was making sense. "What about it?" I demanded.

"If Wrack's a real dragon and can breathe fire, he can burn the bridge at Heldriss! Then the graalur can't get over the gorge!"

I looked at Griffyn, my eyebrows raised. Veldhini spoke before Griffyn could. "The bridge is guarded. There's a small group of graalur there."

"How small?" Wrack questioned.

"I'd guess three dozen or so" Griffyn answered. "And the bridge is wooden. Don't get me wrong - it's substantial. It's the main thoroughfare. The graalur guard it to ensure we humans don't launch an assault on them."

"Can't the people at Tolgrail destroy it when they see the graalur coming?"

Veldhini shook her head. "The graalur control the lands on both sides of the gorge."

"I doubt it would stop them forever" Griffyn said after a pause. "But it'll slow them down. Give Tolgrail a chance to be ready."

"And for us to get there and prepare for them" I added excitedly. "How soon will the graalur be at this bridge?" I asked, trying to work out where this bridge must be.

"By tonight" Norghar answered readily.

I looked at Wrack. If we were going to do this, there would be no time to delay. It would mean he would have to fly by daylight, visible to anyone who looked for him. And he would have to carry me all the way.

Chapter Twenty-Four

Veldhini was supposed to be at work. She had run to the next house to tell her neighbour to tell the farm-master that she was sick, and that Norghar was looking after her. The village had been in the grip of the graalur for long enough that the overseers were more accommodating about human frailties. The neighbour suspected that Veldhini just wanted to spend time with Norghar. I could guess the rumours that might fly from that little story. So much the better – if the villagers were speculating about Veldhini's love-life, they would not be linking her absence with rebels and enemies of the lloruk.

I was not surprised that she wanted to stay and see what was going to happen. Anyhow, we could use her assistance. We crept out of the village soon after the lantern trees had brightened, getting through the disguised break in the stockade that the rebels had made weeks before. Most of the graalur had already accompanied the villagers to work in the fields, or had escorted the few privileged individuals who had specific professions, like the village's sole hivemaster. As we crept near them we could hear the buldyik hives buzzing, their inmates extruding the strong, slightly sticky fibres that made good string and rope. No one saw us pass. Veldhini told us which field was being left fallow, so that there would be no one there to see us. The brilliant red hedgerows provided enough cover so that we would not be overlooked.

Wrack shrugged off his harness, unashamed at standing nude in front of us all. I realised I was holding my breath as he began to change. Our jasq was thundering under my ribs, as excited as I was about his transformation. His skin was growing more ruddy, the rough shapes of the scales emerging. His face and his neck were lengthening. He lifted his arms in triumph, skin unfurling into place beneath them like unfolding petals. The horns slowly grew into ivory daggers atop his head. His legs were clawed, his body already much larger than his human form. He turned, his glittering yellow-green eyes sweeping over us, pausing for a moment as he gazed at me. Was that a smile on the long, muzzled jaw? His arms looked firm and steady, lifting the wings in exultation.

He stretched out a wing towards me, gesturing with it as though it was still his hand. I walked forward. He opened his mouth and roared. I flinched instinctively, an atavistic terror chilling me as he roared his triumph, flame crackling at the corners of his lips.

"Hold on, Sorrel!" he growled.

"Don't you want to fly alone first, Wrack?" I said, trying not to let my voice tremble. Volg it, I never could get used to how imposing he was in this shape. "Test your wings?"

The great head shook from side to side. "Can't carry you now, won't be able to after a few hours of travel. Come here."

I tucked his harness into mine – he would probably want it when we landed. Then I slid my left arm around his neck, above his wings. He lifted a clawed foot, the knee coming under my backside, almost like a seat. I could turn my head to the right and look ahead, sitting sideways against him. I let my other hand clutch onto his leg. It felt precarious, to say the least. If it got particularly gusty, I could turn against him and put my other arm around his neck, too. When he first snatched me from the ground by the side of my crashed triplane he had flown with me dangled beneath him, clutched in both his big claws. Neither elegant nor comfortable... and hard work for him. He had managed to get me behind his lines, but I had virtually worn him to a shred in the process.

Not that he was put off by that. Weeks later we had had one of our shouting matches in his mansion. A typically stupid clash of words, but I had responded to his assertion that I could do anything there that I could do as a free woman by saying I could not fly. He had hauled me out, onto the flat roof of the mansion, and simply demanded that I hold on tightly. Not difficult to obey when the alternative is a very long drop. His knee gave me a little support, but it still felt pretty insecure.

I'd suggested riding him from behind, like a piggy-back. His derision at that idea had been clear – I would have fouled his wings. According to Wrack, that flight, and the three or four that followed, had been for fun. If clinging onto a flying reptile with a two hundred foot drop below counts as fun. Wrack enjoyed it. He had wanted me to know what it felt like to fly without a noisy engine roaring at me, without spars of wood, lengths of wire and sheets of canvas all around. I hadn't been impressed then. Now it was the only choice we had.

I gripped tightly. As we soared into the air, I wondered again to myself why Wrack was keen to take action. This wasn't his fight. I wanted to help Kelhene and the others, protect them from the coming assault. Wrack, on the other hand, I suspected was more interested in scoring points against Griffyn. Whatever the motive, it had worked.

I watched the ground shrink as his wings beat the air into submission. We were already fifty feet up. I could feel his hearts pounding in his chest, the muscles moving inside his scaled hide. There were sudden shouts from a neighbouring crimson field – some of the villagers had seen us ascending, a winged demon and its priestess. We had told Veldhini and Griffyn to move as soon as we were airborne. Their faces as Wrack had changed had been a picture of astonishment and awe. I knew how they felt. I hoped they had moved – the graalur guards were sure to investigate, to find out where this apparition had sprung from.

Wrack was flying smoothly, seemingly effortlessly. I knew better – I could smell his sweat and feel the muscles straining to lift me. I'm not that big, but my weight is not negligible. We had twenty miles to go to the gorge – there was no chance that Wrack could fly us that far. A couple of miles or so at a stretch was all we could hope for. That ought to be enough to get us past the graalur force once we found it.

And it was glorious to be flying again. Even if I was having to cling onto Wrack for dear life. There were worse people I could be hugging tightly, I have to admit. And if truth be told, I *had* come to enjoy flying with Wrack. I liked having an engine in front of me – it gave me a sense of security in the air – but this almost silent conquest of the air was extraordinary. I was still startled by the size of Wrack's wings. When he was fully transformed his wing fingers extended more than fifteen feet on each side, wide sweeps of membrane filling the sky on each side of us.

As we lifted into the daylit sky I gazed down at the crimson tapestry below us. Heights don't scare me. Falling does, but so long as I kept a good grip, and kept my bum on Wrack's thigh, I was pretty secure. Always assuming he did not weaken and stop beating those wings. The low thud at each stroke of the wings was comforting.

He was already swooping downwards, now, the wings held out stiffly, air surging over the curved surfaces. All my pilot's instincts wanted to press the pedals for the ailerons, adjust our angle of descent, but Wrack wasn't made that way. I still preferred my triplane. We lifted slightly to take us over a plum-coloured hedge, and he beat his wings faster as he brought us down towards the ground. He had picked a smooth stretch of russet grass on the ridge overlooking the outermost field of the village. We had only flown half a mile, and Wrack was dripping with sweat, his hearts pounding so hard that I could almost hear them as well as feeling them throbbing against my cheek. We swept downwards, and I flung my feet sideways, releasing my grip as we swooped parallel to the ground. The side of my feet hit the ground and I fell cleanly, the impact slamming into the side of my calves and my thighs as I let my legs absorb the force of the landing. Wrack hit the grass a few feet from me, his clawed feet slamming into the ground. Without my weight, landing was easy for him. I got up slowly, and walked over to him. I was confident I wouldn't even have any bruises from landing – I had done it enough times to know how to avoid hitting the ground too hard.

Wrack was gasping, slumping to the orange turf. He was changing already, reverting to his human shape, his scales merging into smooth skin, his muzzle and his horns retreating. I tossed his clothes to him. He pulled the kilt around his waist and then lay back on the ground, stretching. He looked exhausted. I shivered. Twelve months ago I was sure he could have flown that distance with me without breaking a sweat. He ought to be able to get us past the graalur army in the air, but if we wanted to slow the force down then we had to catch up with them before they reached the bridge. They were too far away if we couldn't make up some distance by flying.

We lay and rested for a few minutes. We both knew that we needed to get moving, and I finally pulled myself to my feet and prompted Wrack. He glowered at me, but did not argue. We began to walk steadily north-east. At least we had managed to reach the ridge. No slope to climb, just an even pace through the long orange grass waving gently in the breeze. There ought to be a road somewhere ahead – then we would be able to pick up the pace.

The rough sketch-plan Veldhini had drafted gave us a relatively good picture of where we needed to go. Griffyn had told us that the guard commander at Tolgrail was called Berindyl, and that she was pompous, a stickler for rules and protocol, and quite insufferable. The person we needed to talk to, assuming we could get to him, was Lendalyn, the Chancellor. We would have to get past Berindyl and her troops to achieve that. Wrack and I had grinned at each other at that. Having wings would make getting past the guards considerably easier.

The first target, though, was the bridge. It would not be easy to torch. Wrack's fire was hot, but the wood was seasoned and solid, and would not catch light instantly. I just hoped his assault from the sky would take the guards by surprise.

We found the road after quarter of an hour. It was smooth, pale grey stone, apparently seamless, embedded into the top of the ridge. We had been walking briskly along it for nearly two hours when Wrack stopped suddenly, and I walked into the back of him. He nodded ahead. "Any ideas?" he asked quietly.

I peered in the direction he was indicating. From up here, on the ridge, we had a good view out over the local area. A cool breeze was welcome, too. To the right of us there was deep, raw jungle filling a wide valley. To the left the fields of another human village were spread out, tiny figures toiling in the fields as graalur overseers lounged, occasionally looking up at us on the ridge, far enough distant to be unrecognisable. In some ways, apart from the scarlet colour, it was not greatly different to the fields of Burannil or Salveyn. Lantern trees loomed over the jungle and on a grey atoll of rock emerging from the fields. Ahead of us, in a gully alongside the smooth grey roadway there was a disc, black as coal, perhaps thirty feet across and four feet thick that rested in the dry ditch like a giant child's carelessly dropped plate. It was tilted at perhaps ten degrees from the level. If we kept walking we would go right past the plate. I looked at it suspiciously. The air was shimmering over it, just like a hot runway with the sun on it. I fancied that there was a hint of steam rising from it.

"Ever seen anything like it?" I asked carefully.

Wrack paused, and then shook his head. The disc was about two hundred yards ahead of us. Curiosity was enough for us to climb down the slope twenty feet to it, studying it warily. The surface was smooth, but there were signs of weathering. This had been here for a good many years. I looked at it carefully, taking in how the grass grew around it, and revised my guess. It might well have been here for centuries. There were markings engraved into it, but they made no sense to me. Wrack was peering at them, too. He knelt down and then he gently reached out and put his finger onto the disc.

"Ouch! Volging lafquass!" he snarled, scrambling to his feet, and sucked his finger fervently. "Volging thing's red hot!"

"How?" I asked blankly. I was kicking myself. There was no sun, here. The warmth came out of the ground. The black disc couldn't have been shimmering the air because of the sun's rays.

Wrack was shaking his head. "Some more lloruk madness" he growled angrily. I took hold of his hand. He had a small blister on his finger – nothing like as serious as his oaths and furious face would suggest. I demonstrated considerable strength of will and resisted the temptation to make fun of him. "Haven't time to wonder about lloruk strangenesses" he said shortly, and turned to walk on past it.

"Wait a minute" I said quietly. He raised an eyebrow at him. I didn't reply – I just put the coronet on and slid into the magerealm, trying not to be nervous this time. It wasn't going to hurt, I told myself firmly.

I tried vainly to blink as my eyes watered from the brilliance of the radiance. It was the first time I had braved the realm since the tsergiaad tower. I wasn't quite sure whether it would seem different, now. There was a fireflow only a few feet from me, and around it there was a obelisk of black diamonds, directing the flow so that it swept over the glittering amethyst that had to be the disc. It had a substantial presence here in the magerealm, more solid and defined than anything had any right to be. I studied it, revelling in the chance to enjoy the magerealm's wonders without pain. I also noted, as I admired the realm, the green haze around me. I was beginning to think that it was not a dome of green, but that the realm beyond my little globe of safety was full of a vile green emanation. What caused it I had no idea.

Wrack put an arm around my shoulder. "What can you see?" he asked.

"Some kind of lloruk structure. Old, I suspect. A fireflow to make it hot. A permanent structure in the realm" I answered, a little of my wonder at the lloruk engineering seeping into my voice. "It's red hot" I said slowly, thinking about it. "Wrack, any idea how near we are to the edge of the lloruk-controlled lands?"

"Other side of the gorge" he growled. That was still anything up to twenty miles ahead of us. I slid back out of the magerealm and eyed Wrack.

"The graalur are still ahead of us" I said carefully.

Wrack nodded, knowing what I was going to say. He said it first. "Need to fly" he said bluntly. "I know."

I grinned. "So we use this lloruk thing." I held his gaze. "Thermals."

For a moment his expression was blank, and then he began to smile in response. He shrugged off his harness as we climbed back up the slope. I gazed around. The nearest graalur were a good half mile away – odds were they wouldn't be able to see what we were doing. And we needed to get moving. We had been forcing a punishing pace on foot, but I was not confident that we would reach the bridge before the graalur.

I grabbed Wrack's harness as he transformed, and slid one arm around his neck again, sitting sideways on his proffered knee. He beat his wings and leaped off the ridge, falling for a moment before his wings caught the air. Heavy claps of sound demonstrated the ferocity of his wing movements – and suddenly the air was stifling. He had brought us around and directly over the disc, and the heat was unbearable. Every lungful of air seemed to sear at me. He was gasping, too, but he was circling, staying in the baking heat from below us as it rose. I struggled to breathe, but I did not argue. Any pilot can tell you the benefit of a thermal. A column of hot air rises; let the wings catch the rising air, and an aeroplane can gain a thousand feet of altitude or more within a minute for virtually no effort. This hot air was extraordinary, far better than a typical thermal, and the potential lift from it was impressive. Wrack was holding his wings spread, letting us spiral upwards. The air was still hot, but we were already way above the disc, and the danger now was that we slid sideways out of the cylinder of rising air.

I gazed around, comparing the ground spread out below me with the sketch-map I had studied. We were approaching the thousand feet mark already, and I could see for miles. A few miles behind I could make out a dark cone on the ground that had to be the tsergiaad tower. I was disappointed that we could still see it. To my right I could dimly see the walls of the Canyon rising towards the permanent grey ceiling of cloud. Directly below us I could see an impossibly-thin grey line, wiggling slightly like a piece of string laid over the ground, which had to be our road. It cut through the myriad shades of red that were the farmland. Lantern trees loomed from the ground, among the tallest objects in my field of view. Scattered clusters of dots – they had to be buildings, too big to be people. Four villages on one side of the road, at least six on the other, each surrounded by an orange, red and yellow patchwork of fields of crops, interspersed with the darker crimson, evenly spaced blots of orchards. And ahead... I peered forward, wanting to believe that I could see a hint of a black gash in the ground that was the gorge.

We were still climbing. The ground was almost too distant below to make out details any more, just a lush blanket of numerous reds more than two thousand feet down. Above us the hard grey firmament looked ever closer, almost near enough to touch. I tightened my grip slightly on Wrack. Cool air was blowing across us, allowing us to breathe more freely. The thermal was almost gone, fading, and Wrack was starting to beat his wings again, tumbling us out of the thinning column of hot air and gliding north-east. Now my body was the worst source of drag for him, destroying his aerodynamic shape. Without me, he could glide to the distant, still-invisible bridge in under an hour. With me, it would take twice that much time and three times the effort. I hoped I was worth it.

Within ten minutes I could tell that he was tiring again. The precision of his wing beats was faltering, and he was not holding the curve of the wings so accurately. We had also lost more than three quarters of the altitude the thermal had given us. I was about to tell him to land, when he suddenly cried out in delight. While we were flying I had little chance of talking to him – the rush of air past us flung our voices to the four corners of the sky. I gazed ahead, and then matched his yell of triumph. There, on the road below us, less than a mile ahead, were the graalur.

A dark mass, a river of dark red marbles rolling down an uneven surface, suddenly became a sea of heads. Some of them were carrying spears that poked up out of the flowing throng. To the vanguard there were mounted figures on olgreks. And swooping over their ranks there were a pair of snarqs. I punched Wrack's leg, trying to draw his attention to them. "Climb!" I was yelling. "Get into the sun!" I started to add, fighter pilot's instincts kicking in, before remembering that there was no sun, no single bright enough light source to hide within. If one of the snarqs saw Wrack, encumbered as he was... I was still worrying about what might happen, when it did. One of the snarqs twisted in the air, and then began to beat steadily towards us, both heads writhing in contemplation of this interesting target. I felt Wrack judder, and knew he had seen the snarq.

He was already dropping like a stone, and I began to yell at him again before I realised what he was doing. Carrying me he had no chance of evading the brute. I shut up and got ready for a rough landing, jamming the coronet onto my head hastily so I had my magic but also had my hands free, hoping that the graalur were concentrating on what was ahead of them.

They weren't.

Chapter Twenty-Five

Six graalur soldiers, bringing up the rear of the force. They had probably been taking a breather, and they were quarter of a mile behind their friends. They saw us tumble out of the sky and threw aside their smoke-cylinders, reaching for their swords. Wrack swooped down beside the road towards the first open patch of grass. I realised he wasn't even going to touch the ground, and I flung myself free of him, rolling into a landing as he swept back into the air. He was already tired, I knew, but he was turning to face the oncoming snarq. I wasn't sure if he had seen the graalur, but the snarq was already swooping towards him – he didn't have time to worry about me.

To my horror, as I tumbled across the ground the coronet slid off my forehead, and spun away. I yelled in alarm, but it had hit a stone and bounced into the undergrowth like a stone skimming off water, ending up twenty feet from where I came to rest.

I didn't have time to retrieve it. The graalur were bundling towards me, swords drawn, grinning manically. I drew my sword and backed away warily, sizing up the opposition. Four male, two female. One of the males was already snarling something about taking me alive. Two of the other males had grinned at the suggestion enthusiastically. I suppose it meant I wasn't in immediate lethal danger. On the other hand, I really, *really* didn't want to be the plaything of these thugs.

They were spreading around me. I glanced around briefly to judge what I had to work with. We were on a sward of long red grass alongside the road, sloping slightly away from it. The patch was only a couple of dozen feet across, and then there was a drop as the slope steepened. How steep, I couldn't tell. I hoped and prayed that the coronet hadn't gone over the edge. There were bushes and large-leafed plants further along, bounding the further edge of my grass. No dependable cover, nowhere to run. And they were up slope from me, pinning me between them and the drop. Not good, Sorrel.

I briefly considered the magerealm. The coronet was too far from me to give me any succour. I could, if there was a fireflow handy, probably torch two of them. But I would be left gasping in pain, and easy meat for the other four who would probably be angry by then. I glanced towards where the coronet had disappeared. Three of the graalur were already between me and it – no chance of getting to it. Forget that, Sorrel, concentrate on dealing with the situation.

They were grinning, knowing I was boxed in and thoroughly outnumbered. "Drop the sword" one of the males growled. "Nasty sharp thing. You might hurt yourself with it."

One of the others laughed at the supposed wit. The larger brute wasn't so amused, possibly because she had a modicum of intellect, or else just didn't have a sense of humour at all. I shrugged, looking the talker full in the eye, all the time moving slightly to the left, towards the slighter graalur at the edge of their line. I was in trouble, no doubt about that. No way I was letting them take me without a fight, though. I glared at the talker. "Don't worry about me. I'm surprised anyone let *you* out with a toothpick, let alone a blade."

The larger female grinned broadly at that. Maybe she did have a sense of humour. The subject of my jibe snarled in anger, and lunged, striking at my sword-arm. I barrelled sideways, flinging myself at the slight graalur, catching him – I hoped – off guard.

For once luck was with me. He had had his sword lowered as he chuckled at his comrade's annoyance, and I hammered into him before he had a chance to raise his guard. A square left hook to his face and a knee in his stomach as I went past, not bothering to try to stab him with my sword. I didn't care about killing these – though I wouldn't be upset about doing so. All I wanted to do was to get clear.

There was a sudden roar of flame in the sky above me. I couldn't stop myself glancing up, despite the fact that I still had five graalur yelling for my blood. Wrack was wheeling, one wing visibly singed by the snarq's acid. I couldn't see the snarq, and I didn't have time to look for it. Fortunately, the graalur had been equally startled by the sudden noise and brilliance in the sky, and I hadn't lost my lead. I ran up onto the road, and then pounded at full speed away from the army ahead. Five graalur were in hot pursuit – obviously I had downed the slight one. Good.

Instead of impossible odds against me, I was down to merely hopeless odds. An improvement!

I was running between trees, now, unable to see what was happening in the sky. I had to trust that Wrack could deal with a snarq on his own. Nasty thoughts slid through my mind about whether the other snarq would come to assist its comrade. No time to think about this – I couldn't keep up this pace forever. I had to act. My hope was that my pace would have split up the graalur, if only by a fraction.

I spun around, stopping dead, and hacked wildly with my sword. The leading graalur – the one who had done all the talking, I realised – was only feet behind me. He flung up his sword desperately to parry my swing, but a moment too slow – my sword caught his arm just below the shoulder, and carved through meat and bone. He screamed in agony. Odds were he was out of the fight. I'd been aiming for his neck, which would have been more certain. More importantly, it would have been easier to wrench my sword out of his neck. I yanked hard, almost tumbling backwards. The graalur was spraying blood from the severed arteries, trying to hold the half-severed limb in place. Two of his comrades were upon me, though, and one – the woman who had laughed before – was carving at *my* neck. I flung myself sideways and let her tangle with the other graalur who had caught up. He was too close beside her, as he tried to reach me, to avoid being caught by the flat of her sword. Accidents will happen. Usually that sort of thing happens to me – the Silver Elf had to be smiling at me today. I took to my heels again. Two down. I had no doubt that the talker was out of the equation now. His mates would be angry with me, though. Even if they kept me alive, I was not going to come out of this well if I was caught.

I tried the same trick a second time. There were three on my tail, now. One of the women – I didn't know or care which one – was tending talker. The other three graalur were waiting for me to spin, and the one I went for parried me with contemptuous ease. They spread out round me, making sure I couldn't run again. This was looking bad. I was still under the spreading branches of trees, too – no chance of Wrack sweeping overhead and toasting them.

The taller of the male graalur was gesturing with his sword, waving it around wildly. The female in the middle was watching me levelly – I suspected that of my three opponents she was the most dangerous, particularly as the other male was too busy laughing at his friend's gesticulations to be concentrating. There was a low branch over me, high enough to need a jump to catch it. Escape into the trees? Not much chance of that succeeding. They would move faster below me. The taller male made a tentative lunge, enough to be worrying without being a real strike. The woman's eyes narrowed – any moment now she was going to launch a serious assault. I drew back my sword, remembering a trick I'd seen used effectively during the defence of Teldrinton. The soldier who'd tried it had brought down a dragonlord's lieutenant, killing him outright. Of course, the soldier had died moments later. The trick was pure madness, but sometimes risks are the only effective answer. I held the woman's eyes, then briefly glanced sideways at the laughing hyena. She for an instant followed my gaze, knowing I was too far to reach her before she could recover – and I threw the sword point-first. The heavy blade caught her squarely where I had been aiming, in the soft, vulnerable flesh of the throat. Blood spurted from the wound. I wasn't sure if I'd achieved a lethal blow, but I could dream. Of course, it had left me weaponless. I leapt before the other two could work out what was going on, and grabbed the branch with both hands, swinging swiftly. The taller male tried to lift his sword to hack at me, but I was moving too fast – I released my grip, and my foot hit him in the face squarely as I landed on top of him. He went down, stunned, and I wrenched his sword from his hand, driving it into his chest as I rolled away. He coughed and died.

The female graalur was down, too, my sword on the ground beside her as she bled heavily. I had hit the jugular, which had been my hope. One left.

Pounding feet from behind told me I was being over-optimistic. The female who had been tending talker had abandoned her efforts to save him. Now I suspected she wanted revenge. And behind her was the slighter one I had knocked out, back in the game. Three to one. Still – considerably better than the odds I started with.

I hauled the sword out of the graalur I had just killed and turned, parrying laughing boy as he endeavoured to spit me. No more laughter, and it didn't look much like he was aiming to capture me any more. Perhaps things were looking up. I backed away as the three formed a semi-circle with me as the focus. No more jokes or jibes – I'd gained a bit of respect, anyhow.

Two of them came at me, the female jabbing with the point of her sword, laughing hyena hacking low and savagely. I dodged sideways, trying to get the swipe to connect with the female's sword while I struck fast at my first assailant. He parried me cleanly, forcing me back, and the other two neatly avoided each other. So much for that plan. They wouldn't fall for the branch trick either. They were being wary, cautious of my skill. I suppose I should have been flattered. I took another pace backwards, stepping round the body of the dead female and almost standing on my own sword. I swayed sideways, trying to avoid tripping on the blade, and a lethal lunge missed as the living female struck savagely. She was over-extended, my sudden motion sideways throwing off her blow – I lunged back, catching her cleanly in the side. The blade went deep and I twisted savagely – no time for genteel duelling, this was her or me. She screamed in her final agony – I wrenched the blade out, but by now laughing boy had cut at me, his blade catching my left forearm. It hurt like volg, and I screamed in pain, too, afraid he had actually cut through the bone. He hadn't, fortunately, more by luck than any skill of mine. I was bleeding heavily, but I only faced two, now. Both flung themselves at me, hacking brutally as they sought to finish me. I was weakening fast, despite the jasq burning red hot at my waist. I managed to block their first efforts, but the ferocity of their onslaught had driven me back. I stumbled, and tumbled backwards onto my backside, jarring me and knocking the wind out of me. I kept a tight grip on my sword and shook my head – I had sweat in my left eye. One of them was fast – he lashed out, the flat of his sword slamming against the side of my head. The edge cut into me slightly, and I felt blood oozing from the cut, but he was no longer trying to kill me. I was stunned by the blow, though, unable to recover, and the other pointed his blade at my stomach. I froze, surprised they had not just killed me immediately, before realising they were both ogling me in traditional graalur fashion. I glanced down – the straps of my harness no longer covered any significant part of me above my waist. That was the danger of exertions in this sort of garb.

"Let go of the sword" snapped the one with the blade at my stomach in accented veredraa. "Cooperate. Maybe you'll enjoy it!"

The other graalur laughed at the supposed humour.

"Cooperate with you?" I retorted in the same tongue. "I'd rather mate with a ruzdrool."

I had no doubt that once they had both satisfied their lusts with me they would kill me anyway, probably slowly and painfully. On the other hand, if I didn't obey, odds were that I would die instantly. I didn't want to die at all. I let go of the sword, let it clang onto the smooth grey stone of the road, and I slumped back. I was still bleeding heavily – I clamped my hand over the wound in my arm, trying to slow the damage. It was healing already – the jasq was hard at work trying to keep me alive. I lay back and played half-dead (which wasn't difficult, I have to say).

One of the two undid the buckle at my waist and pulled the harness off me. They weren't planning to waste any time, evidently. The other removed his loincloth. Their intent was as much vengeance for their fallen comrades as lust. The sword was still at my stomach, the graalur inscribing small circles as the blade ran over my skin like a lover's kiss. The other graalur snarled at his friend to get out of the way, and the sword was withdrawn. The graalur standing over me shoved at my left thigh with his foot, spread-eagling me. I opened my eyes, and kicked, hard. At this angle I could drive my foot right up between his legs – he gave a strangled half-squeal and clutched at himself. I rolled sideways, taking his legs out from under him, and leapt to my feet, grabbing the sword from where it had been lying beside me. The other graalur had put down his sword as he undid his own clothing. Stupid of him. Not a mistake he would make again. I rammed my weapon into his stomach and twisted the blade. My hand was sticky with my own blood, and the wound in my arm was pumping out gore again, but I didn't have time to worry about it. The one I had kicked was still gargling, but was trying to pick up his sword from the ground. I hacked at his neck, putting him out of his pain permanently with the second blow.

Six dead graalur. A lot of blood on the road. I felt weak and light-headed, and realised there was still blood trickling from the cut on my cheek. I put down the sword once I was confident there were no more graalur approaching, and applied my hand as a bandage to the more serious wound. I reached down and picked up one of the discarded loincloths. Not the bandage of choice, but I didn't have much else available. I hoped I wouldn't catch some unpleasant graalur disease from it as I tied it tightly into place – not an easy task. Have you ever tried bandaging your own arm?

I was collecting my sword when I heard feet padding on stone. Someone was jogging towards me. I turned, lifting my blade to defend myself. Wrack was heading along the highway, back in human form. Nude, of course – I wondered what I'd done with his harness in the excitement. I'd dropped it somewhere. Admittedly, I was in the same state, but at least my harness was nearby. Wrack was favouring one arm again, and my heart sank.

"You all right?" We both spoke simultaneously.

I shrugged, answering first. "Nothing serious – it'll heal. What happened to your arm?"

Wrack duplicated my gesture. "Acid burn. Snarq was faster than I expected. Only damaged the membrane. You know how quickly that heals."

That I did. The first time we had duelled, during the war, Wrack had been cocky and self-confident, victor of half a dozen aerial duels. I was a better pilot and sorceress than he expected, and I caught one wing squarely. I had chased him most of the way back to his lines. If Troth hadn't intervened I might have downed him. He had been back in the air within three days. I knew that very well, because he had sought me out. It had been the first of our inconclusive dogfights. We had clashed half a dozen times before he finally brought me down.

But three days would be far too long. "Can you fly?" I asked anxiously.

Wrack dropped his gaze. "Yes" he said, somewhat to my surprise. "Not that bad."

"Then what?" I demanded.

"Don't know if I can carry you" he said quietly. "Not got so much wing surface. Can get myself aloft, but carrying your weight? Don't know."

I looked at him bleakly. "How far are we from the gorge?" I asked as I picked up my clothing and donned it again. I walked back, making for where the coronet had fallen.

"Five miles" he answered. "Graalur are still on the march. Be there in an hour and a half." He bobbed his head in answer to my unspoken question. "Can be there in fifteen minutes or less. Could see the bridge from the air."

"Did the graalur see you?" I asked then. "The snarqs?"

"Downed the one that came after me. Dead. Other didn't get involved – didn't see me, or they didn't want to risk losing both." He looked at my kills. "You?"

"Rearguard. They wanted some fun. I wasn't in the mood."

For a moment I thought Wrack was going to respond. 'You never are' seemed the most likely retort, but he bit back the comment and just shrugged.

"Need to take out the bridge" he said simply. "Be back soon."

He jogged back to the edge of the trees, before transforming. I watched him change, still rapt in awe as he took on his draconic form. The red dragon beat his wings, and soared into the air. His left wing had a nasty hole in it, blistered around the edges, and he was noticeably less agile than usual. I sighed, and began delving into the undergrowth, hoping against hope that I could find the coronet, and that it would be intact.

Chapter Twenty-Six

I watched the fires flickering below me, and wondered again what had become of Wrack. It was almost fully dark, now, and the campfires were burning brightly. From where I was perched in my tree overlooking the stretch of land adjoining the gorge, the plateau looked like a sea of candles. At each tiny flame there were a dozen or more graalur. Some were sleeping, but most were carousing, demolishing barrels of ale from the wagons that had accompanied their march, or enjoying the presence of members of the opposite sex. Graalur had no taboos about coupling in public – at the nearest campfires I could see pairs or groups of graalur engaged in aggressive copulation. The women were as enthusiastic as the men.

Beyond the graalur camp the gorge lay like a knife-cut into the land, eighty or ninety feet across, and probably a good proportion of that in depth. An impossible barrier, now. The remains of the bridge were still smouldering, glowing embers rising from the charred remnants of the structure. Wrack had arrived just before the army, and the bridge no longer provided any form of thoroughfare.

I had got to the ridge looking down over the valley just as Wrack struck. Below me, well over a mile ahead, I had seen a red cross sweeping through the air like a vengeful dagger, striking down towards the bridge as the graalur began to traverse it. A flicker of red-orange flame had lashed out. I was too far away to hear the shouts and screams, but I saw the sky around the swooping figure darken as a hail of bolts and spears momentarily filled the air with black death. Wrack rose sharply, pulling out of the dive fast enough that the cloud of lethal shafts missed easily. He turned, and I had winced, knowing how much strain he was inflicting on his wings by the sudden twist in the sky. Another gout of flame, and smoke began to soar after him. The graalur were in disarray, enough of the troops wanting to get off the bridge to throw all the force into mayhem. Wrack came around again, but this time missiles rose with more accuracy, and he jinked hastily as they swept far too close to his wings. A third lash of fire, and the bridge was burning properly. A few of the graalur tried to extinguish the growing conflagration, but the rest were exercising discretion and retreating.

And then Wrack had vanished. I had cried out in alarm for a moment, before I realised that he had dived straight down, into the gorge, under the bridge. It was an insanely dangerous manoeuvre, with every risk that he would catch his wings on the side of the gorge or slam into the underside of the bridge, but it meant that he could blast the bridge from below with a blossom of fire that licked around the sides of the structure, ensuring its final doom. A few of the graalur, realising what the demonic figure had done, rushed to the side of the bridge and slung spears over the edge, but Wrack was already streaking up from the far side, riding the hot smoke into the sky again. He swung sideways, and I had imagined I could hear his roar of triumph, even at the distance I had been from the gorge. And then he vanished away into the tower of smoke that was engulfing the scene. I had watched for long moments, waiting for him to reappear, but there had been no further sign of him. The graalur had been in chaos, fury and soundless shouts signifying anger and impotent rage.

Wrack had been magnificent, his speed and power reminding me of our duels in the skies of the surface lands. I had enjoyed our duels, even though he had been trying to kill me, and vice versa. It had been a game... until it ended.

Barely visible in the spreading darkness on the far side of the gap, a human merchant with a string of olgreks was already heading away from the ruined route. I had no doubt that he would report to Tolgrail when he got back there, assuming, logically, that the city had been his point of origin. At the pace he could achieve, though, it would be three days before he returned there. He had seen the graalur, and was doubtless very relieved now that the bridge was gone.

Where Wrack had disappeared to, I had no idea. I had followed in the footsteps of the graalur until I reached their encampment, and I had scrambled into the cover of this dull red copse urgently as they milled around, stumped by the absence of the bridge. The common troops weren't desperately upset by the loss of the thoroughfare – soldiers of any complexion are quite happy to have an excuse to do nothing for a time. I suspected their officers were less happy at the turn of events.

I had hoped that Wrack would have swooped back to join me before it became dark, but I had seen no sign of him. Now I lurked, nestled in the crook of a gnarled branch as I waited for him.

The lloruk who had been leading the graalur were in the village that nestled beside the gorge. A few privileged graalur were in the inn with the lloruk. The village's human slaves were serving the senior officers. I shivered at that thought. In the morning the enemy would have to decide how to cross the gorge. Building a bridge would not be an easy task, but I suspected that with the aid of lloruk sorcery it would not be insurmountable. Once a new crossing was in place they would recommence their advance. We had to be over the gorge before then, en route to Tolgrail, or we had no chance of getting there before them. Without Wrack that was a hopeless dream.

Not for remotely the first time I thought about Wrack. I hated him. That was something I knew fundamentally. The fun and games had ended when he had flamed me out of the sky, then snatched me from the wreckage of my triplane and dragged me to his mansion. He had sliced the jasq out of my flesh and drowned it in acid, and once I had healed enough he had paraded me in front of the other dragonlords as a slave, an abject thing, to be beaten and abused and humiliated. Not a respected prisoner, but cheap scum to be pushed around and treated as a figure of fun. Of course I hated him.

But down here he was the person I knew best. I needed him. He needed me.

I could feel my nails digging into my palms, my hands clenched, as thoughts churned through my head. I hated Wrack... but I couldn't take my eyes off him when he was with me. Before the war, when I had been training at the mansion, I had been attracted to him. Seeing him again, now, I was finding it very hard to deny that I still was.

What made me hate him was that he had made me his slave. I had thought he respected me – I was the pilot who came closest, on three occasions, to bringing him down. That final aerial battle still haunted me. It had been nine days after I killed Kabal. I had found Wrack in the air over Werin Fastness. The duel that followed had been the most intense I had ever fought. I had been within inches of burning him down more than once – if I had been a second faster with my fireflows I would have got him. He had taken insane risks, even after I caught his tail with one flow. Despite the pain from that injury he had come around again, pulling incredibly tight turns and banking so that he lost hundreds of feet in moments. If he had not been able to pull out of those dives he would have hit the ground at fatal speed. He had been a dragon possessed.

And yet he had visibly been trying to take me alive. He could, twice, have flamed me. He didn't. He went for the triplane, and it took him three flamestrikes to do so much damage that I could no longer stay in the air. If I had been as driven as he had been I would have got him before then. If I had hated him then the way I did afterwards I think I would have nailed him. It had been so close.

I had managed to bring the wreck down behind our lines. He had swept down and snatched me.

I didn't try to break free after he got me into the air – I didn't particularly want to fall to my death. I had expected a modicum of respect and decent treatment. I found myself wondering, now, how unhappy I had been when he seized me. I had assumed that he would treat me well, wine me and dine me and court me as an honoured guest as much as a prisoner. Instead, he carved out my jasq, and then humiliated me, parading me as his helpless, semi-clad slave before his visiting dragonlord comrades.

I wished I knew what had become of him.

I shivered, despite the warmth of the air, and clutched the tree, glad of the rough, comforting texture of the bark.

I had time to kill while I waited for Wrack. It gave me a chance to think. Not something I'm desperately good at, I might add. Something down here was causing me agony. Fortunately, I now had the coronet – I can't tell you how much relief I felt when I found the lloruk creation, intact and hooked over a twig in the scarlet bushes just over the slope. I still didn't know why the Chasm was so inimical to sorcery – I had no idea what caused the faint green miasma that I saw in the magerealm. It was one mystery that alarmed me. And then there were the larisqs. They were foul, hideous things. Were they somehow connected to the poison in the magerealm down here? I couldn't think how they could be. The larisqs were jasqs, but jasqs that had been twisted and corrupted so that they spread through the whole body. I really, really wanted to do something about them.

And I was the only person down here with a jasq, apart from the lloruk. The nearest people I had to friends were at Tolgrail, assuming that they had reached the city by now. I wished I knew how their trek through the jungle had gone. The lloruk wanted me badly, that much was clear. The march on Tolgrail made no real sense strategically – were the lloruk really so alarmed about my jasq that they would attack a city to get me? The trouble was, I suspected that they were.

Which left the critical question. Did I want to stay down here? I was the only human with a jasq in the Chasm. I would also be the only human with a jasq on the surface. If we were going to fight back against the dragonlords then the humans needed me up there. The Firebirds had been depending on our raid on Wrack's mansion. With one jasq I could get more, rebuild the mage contingent. Give us a fighting chance again against the dragons.

Wrack said they had imposed rules on themselves, so the atrocities of the old order wouldn't happen again. Could I believe him? He didn't lie to me. But he was down here, with me. If he wasn't on the surface to enforce the new dragon laws? My thoughts churned around in circles. There were other dragonlords who were relatively decent. Wrack was one of the most powerful. If I returned to the surface, what would I be?

What did I want?

I hugged myself and lurked in the shadow of the tree, my thoughts increasingly jumbled.

I was wakened by the feel of my jasq thundering in my side. I grabbed at the tree, for a moment thinking I was going to tumble down before I realised I was sprawled on the ground. I staggered to my feet, and swayed alarmingly until I regained my balance. I looked out to see what had become of the graalur. The camp was quietening – more than half of the brutes were asleep, but the sentries were still wary. Most of the campfires were still burning, and in their dim radiance I saw a dark shape moving. It was coming from the side of the clump of trees away from the graalur. I retreated behind the trunk of my tree as I gripped my sword warily, just in case I was wrong and the figure there was another wandering graalur, instead of Wrack. I could already feel that he was close, the connection stretching between us.

The sudden drumbeat of my jasq had ceased as quickly as it had started. I had been right in my guess, though – it had heralded Wrack's transformation. He stood at the edge of the copse, peering inwards. I hissed a greeting, and his head turned. I crept past the dark tree-trunks to his side, and handed him his harness with a grin. He was, of course, quite nude, and typically unflustered at his state.

"What kept you?" I whispered as he slid his clothing around him.

"Too many graalur. Too many fires – didn't want them to see me landing" he replied, equally softly. "Didn't think I'd be popular."

I nodded in agreement. "How's the wing?"

He shrugged. "Painful. Give it a while. It'll heal."

"We need to get to Tolgrail" I said.

He smiled. "Did some scouting. There's a rope bridge across the gorge about a mile further on. Bet the locals use it to avoid paying the toll on the main bridge."

I leaned over and hugged him. He looked at me with some surprise. I looked down, not holding his gaze. I really didn't know why I had done it, but it had felt right.

"We'd better get there before the graalur find it" I said hastily, to cover my discomfort. Wrack nodded, and gestured to show me the direction.

His estimate of a mile was woefully inaccurate. It was at least double that, or felt that way, before we found it. Not that our journey was helped by the darkness. Volg it, I really, really missed the moons! There was absolutely no light at all once we were away from the graalur campfires. We stumbled desperately onwards for less than quarter of a mile, pretty much feeling our way through the velvet, cloying darkness, before I gave up and slid into the magerealm, first making sure the coronet was securely on my forehead. A fireflow flickered in the real world for a few moments, long enough for me to spot a fallen branch from the trees that had been mugging us at virtually every step. A second blast of fire gave us a reasonably serviceable torch. I was so pleased to be able to use the magerealm without pain! I just hoped we were far enough from the camp that no graalur would notice the flicker of light.

Two more chunks of wood had burned down before we reached the bridge. Not that bridge was quite the term I would have used. Three ropes, one to walk on, two to hold. Not even as impressive as the structure across the gorge at the Grihl Valley. It looked old and worn. I took a deep breath, and strode out over it, not pausing to give Wrack a chance to say anything.

The gorge was more than fifty feet deep, with dark water growling and grumbling below us. Without any moonlight this was difficult in the extreme. Wrack was holding up our latest excuse for a lantern, giving me such light as there was. Odds were that any alert graalur in the vicinity would come running. I was hoping we were actually far enough away to be well clear of any observers, alert or otherwise. We'd pushed through more than one stand of trees, and the gorge had twisted a couple of times, so I felt reasonably safe from pursuit. Anyway, odds were that by the time the pursuit reached us I would be a mangled heap of bloody flesh and broken bones at the foot of the gorge. This clutch of strings gave bridges a bad name.

It was swaying as I eased across. I didn't want to take too long. At least when Wrack came over he would be able to fly if it broke, assuming he could change before he hit the bottom of the gorge. He was, as usual, more comfortable walking in human form – whatever he might claim about draconic superiority, on the ground a human was far more agile and walked more easily than any dragon. In the air... well, then I might have to think about it.

The far side of the gorge was very welcome. It was a meadow, soft orange grass rising to my shoulders. It hadn't been cut in months. Good hay going to waste. I ignored this evidence of poor husbandry and watched Wrack struggle across. It was harder for him than it had been for me – he was heavier, burlier, far more likely to come to a sticky end when the bridge gave up the ghost, and he had not dared bring the torch over. All I could do was watch his silhouette against the dying flame where he had left the torch dug into the ground.

Against all logic, the bridge didn't disintegrate. Wrack scrambled into the long grass, sneezed vigorously, and hugged me. I didn't protest, and we inched away from the edge.

"Can't leave it there" he said quietly, lifting his sword.

"Volging right we can't" I said warmly. "That bridge is a menace to life and limb. Sooner it's dismantled the safer everyone will be!"

Wrack chuckled, and sliced through the cables. The lowest one took two hacks before it parted, belying its apparent age. I didn't think the lack of a crossing would stop the graalur for long, but it would slow them up.

We were both exhausted. We got a few hundred yards from the remains of the rope bridge, and then simply collapsed, flattening a nest in the long grass. Wrack sneezed a few more times, but fatigue overcame any allergy he had, and he began to snore gently. I was not far behind him, curled up against his back. Neither of us were keeping watch, and anyone could have seized us or run us through.

Fortune sometimes favours the immensely stupid. It did this time. I woke much later, feeling relatively comfortable with the world. Wrack was still dozing. The weather was dry, the field bright from the two nearest lantern trees. The air was still, and as yet there was no indication of graalur movement this side of the gorge. I seized the opportunity to kick Wrack in the ribs – only relatively gently – and told him to get up and get moving. He growled at me, but I ignored him. I wished aloud for a plate of breakfast, preferably toast and marmalade and quelis juice. The Silver Elf didn't oblige, much to my disappointment but not much to my surprise. Wrack told me to shut up about food. I stuck my tongue out at him.

"You up to flying?" I asked.

He felt his arm. I was never quite sure how much he could tell about his draconic form from his human shape. He shook his head. "Not and carry you" he said bluntly.

I shrugged. "We'll have to walk, then" I said firmly.

Wrack didn't say anything, and did so eloquently. I cracked a smile. I had forgotten just how surly he could be first thing in the morning. He needed a cup of caff. Not a chance of that down here. No wonder he was in a bad mood. I benefited from the stimulant in the morning, too, but I wasn't as addicted to it as he was. I got to my feet, judging our heading towards Tolgrail, and paused in mild alarm.

Looking ahead, there was another human settlement a few hundred yards from us. In the deep night, with only a torch for illumination, it might as well have been on the surface. Now we could see it easily. My assumption was that this was a farm of some sort. My fear, as I looked towards it, was that there were graalur here.

I could already see three people hard at work. I wasn't quite sure how far into the morning we had slept, but these three were well past the stage of breakfast. One was weeding a vegetable patch that ran along the side of one of the buildings. Another was feeding a sty full of young vergiiks, all squealing and getting unnecessarily excited. The third... she was walking towards us, calling out in veredraa. Something about not trampling the crop.

I made my way towards her warily, trying not to trample down the hay any further. A few minutes' grovelling and bland mis-statements were enough to mollify her, helped by the fact that Wrack was actually doing his best to be charming. When he tries, he can be. Most women respond to his strong face and well-made figure. With the growth of beard now on his face he looked positively dangerous, which just made him more attractive. We ended up in the kitchen of the farmhouse, demolishing a fresh breakfast. Toast! With butter and rather a palatable orange jam – I had no idea what fruit it was made from, and was mildly disappointed that it lacked the bite of marmalade, but it was still delicious. Vergiik milk and a rasher of bacon. Quite glorious, particularly because it was so unutterably normal. I would have wolfed an egg if they had any, but there seemed to be no birds in the Canyon, wild or domesticated. Never mind. I could live without an egg, and the bacon and fried bread complemented the toast perfectly.

As we finished, Wrack very gingerly asked the lady – her name was Trinyi – if she had caff. She looked blank, the narynyl word meaning nothing to her. He described it, dark hot liquid from brown beans. I expected no joy, but she nodded at the stove with a sudden smile of comprehension. Within a couple of minutes, there was a taste in the air that was familiar. She poured out three small cups of dark, hot liquid, and I took a cautious sip. Not quite the caff of the surface, but pleasingly close. I took another sip, and glanced across to see Wrack looking at his cup in unalloyed pleasure. Trinyi glanced at me.

"Another man who can't live without fulvraan in the morning?" she asked. I nodded with a grin, and she chuckled, pouring out another cup of the hot, dark stimulant for each of us.

It felt really cruel, after she had fed us so well, to tell her that there were graalur coming. We spent more than half an hour telling her what was going on, warning her and then telling the story again to her man and the other tenants of the farm. Their faces were grim and alarmed as we finally got moving again. Trinyi said they would take cover when the force got too close, and they would try to hide their livestock. Running, heading for Tolgrail, wasn't an option – they would not abandon their farm. They had lived with the graalur border only a few miles away for years – they had plans and hiding places for this situation, but it was clear that they had never imagined it would actually happen. All we could do was to wish them good luck.

By the time we set out along the road to which Trinyi had directed us it was already late morning. Despite that, we had slept thoroughly and eaten well, and we made good time. By mid afternoon I reckoned we had made twenty miles.

"Two more days like this and we'll reach Tolgrail" I said conversationally. We had been walking in virtual silence, concentrating on keeping moving. To our left there was a relatively dense cluster of trees masking sight of the gorge. To our right the land rose in a smooth, majestic sweep towards the distant peaks which rose more than half way towards the sky. They were the highest mountains I had seen in the Canyon – only the lantern trees and the stone spires came close to their magnitude.

"Another hour and I'll take to the air again, see what's ahead of us" Wrack replied absently. He had already made one short flight, confirming that the graalur were working on building a bridge behind us and might be across by nightfall. We had gained a day on them. Ahead, he had seen Tolgrail as a distant smudge on the horizon. He had not been able to see any graalur approaching from the other direction, but I had little doubt that they could be at Tolgrail before Wrack could actually see them. He seemed distant, though, at the moment, as though deep in thought.

We had walked for another quarter of an hour before he broke the silence again.

"Sorrel?" he said quietly. "Assuming we can stop these graalur and save Tolgrail, what then?"

I had been half-expecting the question for much of the day. Walking along in companionable silence had been surprisingly pleasant. I had been able to ignore nasty memories from our mutual past. I had been afraid he would spoil it.

I tried to stop myself snapping as I answered. I had been thinking about my words for quite a time, imagining what we might say to each other. "If I come back to the surface... with you... you'll try and turn me into your slave again. You'll be the grand lord, and I'll be human scum. At least down here we're equals."

"Equals?" he snarled. He opened his mouth to challenge my words, and then closed his mouth again, his lips tight and his spine stiff. For a few moments he remained silent. I realised that I was holding my breath. "Nothing for us down here" he finally said. "We need to head home, Sorrel! Down here we're just wanderers with no status, with nothing!"

"That's what I'd be on the surface, Wrack! Your possession! No status – nothing!"

He stopped and turned to face me. "Doesn't have to be that way, Sorrel" he said intensely. "You could stay with me without being my slave."

I laughed bitterly. "Oh yes. I should believe that?"

He looked into my eyes. "Yes."

I shook my head, breaking the twin glints that tried to hold me fast. I started walking again, not trying to answer him.

"Sorrel!" he snapped. "Stop! Talk to me, volg it!"

"You never seemed that interested in talking at the mansion" I replied grimly.

True enough. I'd been a slave, albeit one he favoured. But he didn't talk to me or explain things. Just orders and demands, or the occasional shouted arguments when I dared to stand up to him I scowled at him, old wounds reopening as I thought about the way he had treated me.

"Nor were you" he growled back. "My efforts to talk usually got swearwords and sullen silences."

I glowered at him. "The first thing you did when you captured me was to carve out my jasq. You treated me like a whipped animal in front of your dragonlord friends. You expected gratitude?"

For a moment I thought he was going to lash out at me. He took two swift steps towards me, and I clenched my fists, ready to strike back if he tried it. He saw my motion, and paused. He was alarmed at me? He stared at me, his mouth tight. "Look who's talking, Sorrel." He tapped the scar on his uninjured arm meaningfully.

"The technical term is revenge" I snapped.

"Revenge for what? For saving your life?" he retorted.

I stared at him blankly. "What?" I asked. Not the smartest response, but for once he had caught me by surprise. "You saved my life? When?"

His turn to show surprise. "When I captured you, of course."

This was turning into a contest to see which of us could look more confused. I locked my eyes onto his, waiting for him to explain, letting my expression confirm that I was baffled.

He looked equally confused. "Sorrel, after you killed Kabal the dragonlords wanted you *dead*!" he said, as though that explained everything. "Flying in pairs or groups, to make sure they downed you."

"So?" I riposted with extraordinary wit. "And that was news?"

He snarled an obscenity. "Why I gave up trying to talk to you, girl! You don't listen! Don't think!" He started to walk away.

I surged towards him and grabbed his arm, yanking him round and making him face me. "Don't you volging walk away from me, Wrack! Explain it, then! Make me understand!"

He stared back at me. "You're saying you didn't know why I... why you had to be my slave?"

"Because you enjoyed lording it over me! You *liked* me being your helpless prisoner!"

289

He dropped his eyes. Whatever his excuses, I knew I was right. He *had* enjoyed being the master. I shoved him away and began to walk again.

"Yes." A single word, soft, almost too quiet to hear. I stopped dead and turned round. He was standing, facing me, arms by his sides. An utterly relaxed pose – except that I could see every line of tension in every muscle. Guilt and shame in his face, despite his desperate effort to be impassive. He had enjoyed the fact that I had been his abject slave – and he was ashamed of that fact. Guilty about how he had treated me. And I could see that his guilt was tearing him apart inside.

I slowly walked back to him. I knew Wrack better than I wanted to admit. I knew just how much that single syllable had cost him. Somehow I knew how much he was afraid of my response. I could break him. His fear, his guilt – I could tear him apart, shred his emotions with a few well-chosen words, a snarl of invective. This was my chance to express all the bitterness bottled up inside me from those long, tangled months. I had dreamed of *really* hurting Wrack – somehow, impossibly, I could sense that I finally had the chance to do it.

Chapter Twenty-Seven

I stared at Wrack for long, echoing seconds. He stood still, silent, waiting for me to rip out his throat with my invective.

And I couldn't. The anger was still there, churning in the depths of my soul, but I needed to know. It was more important than anything in the world that I found out what had been going on in his mind. I replied to his monosyllable with one of my own.

"Why?"

He looked at me and took a deep, shuddering breath. "Why did I enjoy it, or why was it necessary?"

I grinned harshly. "Both."

"Sadist" he said quietly. I went on grinning, though I knew the smile did not reach my eyes. He dropped his gaze, and went and sat down on the orange grass beside the road. We didn't have time to waste – but this was too important for me to state the obvious. I needed to understand. I went and sat opposite him, looking at him coldly. I resisted the temptation to make some obvious comment about him being a sadist too.

After a few moments' silence, he finally spoke.

"You were always so confident, so sure of yourself." He lifted his eyes to mine. "You knew I wanted you. I knew there were other men... As my slave... no one else could have you. Had you to myself. Thought that... after a time... you would..."

"Wrack, I'd said no. Remember?"

I could see the memory in his face. The rebellion had been months in the future, no obvious warning that it would come. Kelvar had given me the jasq, and I had been practising sorcery at Wrack's mansion. All new mages were vetted by one or other of the dragonlords, observed during training to ensure we were "suitable". I had realised after a few days that Wrack had regularly been watching me at work, his eyes exploring my shape. I had half-expected to be propositioned – no, be fair, I had more than half expected that Wrack would demand that I go to his bed. I knew what Troth, the local lord where I grew up, was like. I hadn't served Troth's lust personally, but I knew a number of girls who did, and I knew Troth's attitude. When Wrack finally put a hand on my shoulder and invited me to spend the night with him I had pointedly refused. His expression then had been extraordinary – hurt surprise, dismay, shock, a soupçon of injured pride – and I had braced myself for trouble. He had snarled something about me being ungrateful and not knowing my place, but he hadn't tried to force me, then, or when I was his slave.

"I remember" he said unnecessarily. He held my gaze. "Wanted you to change your mind."

"And you thought humiliating me... cutting out my jasq... beating me in front of your friends... would... would..." I choked into silence, unable to put what I was feeling into words.

"Told you that" he snapped impatiently. "Only way to save your life."

I glared at him. His expression said volumes – he thought he had said more than enough. I waited, eyes fastened onto him like fish-hooks.

"Dragonlords wanted you dead. You brought down Kabal – one of the three senior lords! They had to bring you down. You were a figurehead for the rebellion!" Dimly I was starting to see where this was going. I wasn't sure I wanted to. "They expected you to die. I captured you instead." He took a slow breath. "As a mage you were far too dangerous. Had to stop you having magic." He rubbed the scar on his own arm. "I know what I put you through, Sorrel. If I hadn't, the other dragonlords would have insisted you were executed." He looked at me, emerald eyes wide with the need to make himself understood. "What I learned from you also saved the lives of the other mages who survived the rebellion. The other dragonlords would not accept humans with magic. They lost their jasqs, yes, but they kept their lives. And so did you!"

"And that justified the way you treated me?" I said quietly. The trouble was, I suspected it did.

Wrack put my ill-formed thoughts into crisp words. "Dragonlords hated you. Wanted you to be executed bloodily." He held my gaze, knowing that now he had me on his leash. "Had to show them you were being punished. That you were suffering for what you did. If I hadn't, you would have died."

I dropped my eyes. The first three weeks after he captured me he had treated me appallingly. There had been other dragonlords at the mansion almost daily, ogling me and enjoying my misery and impotent rage. After that... in the weeks that followed, Wrack's actions had changed. His treatment of me had mellowed. I had been too stubborn and too angry to register it. The trouble was, Wrack *had* enjoyed having me at his beck and call; my anger at that had blinded me to anything else. I had always known Wrack was possessive.

There was still something unsaid between us. I really didn't know if I wanted to ask him why. I knew now what he would say. I didn't know if I believed it. More critically, I didn't know how I felt about it.

Wrack didn't wait for me to ask. "Couldn't let that happen" he said quietly.

I didn't want to sit there meekly, letting him profess his feelings like some love-lorn poet. I knew him better than that. Wrack did not talk easily – I don't think I had ever heard him give such a long speech. I got to my feet and walked to him. He stood, his usual graceful movements somehow lacking as I faced him. I stuck out my index finger and prodded him in the chest.

"Why the *volg* didn't you tell me what you were doing, Wrack?" I knew my voice wasn't entirely steady, and I spoke louder to try to drown out the quaver. "You didn't give me any hint of what you were thinking. I can't read your mind!"

"I credited you with a little intelligence" he snapped back, his own voice raised in response. "Why do you think so many of the others came to visit after I captured you?"

"I assumed you wanted to gloat – to show me off!" I shoved him roughly. "You certainly seemed to enjoy that!"

Wrack shoved back, equally roughly, and I stumbled on uneven ground. As I struggled to keep myself upright he kept coming, shoving me again. "What did you expect?" he growled. "Had to make it look good."

I drove my right heel into the ground, holding me upright, trying to keep my balance. Wrack was standing very close to me. His face was only a few inches from mine. I could have leaned forward slightly and kissed him. He could easily kiss me.

He opened his mouth as if he was going to say something more.

I looked past him, and then I grabbed him and flung him to the ground with all the strength I had. He tumbled to the grass like a shocked scarecrow, astonished at my sudden violence. I threw myself on top of him and pushed his head against the ground. I was yelling something about keeping down as a shape with pale silver-blue scales soared overhead, the vast shadow surging over the grass. The snarq was only a few feet above us. If I hadn't grabbed Wrack it could have bitten his head off. Globs of acid slammed into the ground where we had been standing moments before. We both rolled in different directions. A blob of acid smacked into the ground only a foot from my outstretched arm, and droplets stung my bare skin. Wrack was still moving, trying to transform into his draconic form, but the snarq was coming round again, both heads focussing on us as we lay in full view, easy targets. I dived into the brilliance of the magerealm. I didn't have time to think. I snatched at a coil of fire nestling in a bed of deep black diamonds and flung it out of the realm, trying to judge where the snarq would be. Mages on the ground never judged how fast a dragon was flying – they invariably flung their flames directly at the enemy, and the bolt of fire would pass harmlessly behind it. My pilot skills meant that I could judge it far better. This time was no exception – my gout of orange flame caught the snarq squarely, and it shrieked like a burst steam pipe. It spat more acid – the trouble was, it didn't have to worry about *my* speed. I threw myself sideways, terrified that I was too slow. The greenish fluid sprayed across my shoulders and I felt it clawing into my back, scorching my bare flesh. I screamed in agony. There hadn't been any discomfort in the magerealm this time – the coronet was doing its job superbly. It wasn't fair that I was feeling pain now!

There was a roar of rage and alarm from above me. I ducked my head into the grass as another shape swooped through the air. Wrack, all dragon now, fiercely pursuing our assailant, driving the creature away from where I lay. Another ball of fire put a brief sun in the sky. The snarq was already wounded from my strike – now Wrack beat his wings fast and hard as he swung onto the tails of the twin-headed creature. I had seen him fly like that before, and I had no doubt as to the outcome of this duel. I dragged myself into the magerealm again, seizing a crystal-blue torrent and dragging it through into reality. The gush of water poured over my poor, tortured back, easing the pain. It had only been a couple of seconds since the acid hit me, but it had felt like a tenth of an eternity. I rolled onto my back, rubbing my sore skin across the orange grass to try to get rid of the last of the acid. Above me, dark red scales glittered in the lantern-tree light as Wrack wheeled across the sky. The two winged figures spiralled around each other, red twisting against blue, each trying to get a clear sight of the enemy. Wrack was weaving in tight turns – the pressure on his wings had to be cruelly painful, but he was pushing himself to the limits, curling round so that he swung out of his turn directly behind the snarq. It was only a few yards ahead of him, both heads angling in different directions as it tried to shake off the dragon's vengeful pursuit. Wrack breathed again, but the snarq had rolled, letting the blast of crimson flame sear harmlessly above it. It turned one head and spat, but Wrack was already climbing, evading the spittle easily as he swung into line with the snarq. I watched how gracefully Wrack spiraled and coiled in the sky. I had only seen him fly like this, driving himself to the edge of endurance, once before, in the final aerial duet when he brought me down. It was as though he wanted to express his contorted feelings in the way he flew. The winged beast suddenly folded its wings, plunging downwards to try to throw Wrack off its tail. Wrack copied the motion, plummeting towards the ground, gaining on the snarq, falling at a terrifying speed. He drew back his head, and I saw his lungs expand. His jaws opened, and another gush of fire licked forth. Wrack instantly spread his wings wide, his tremendous wingspan catching the air with a clap like thunder, halting his dive as the flames caught the snarq squarely. It was already badly burned, and the fire tore into its wing membranes. It screamed again, unable to pull out of its dive, slamming into the ground with a crunch of sundering bones and ripping skin. It squirmed and twitched on the ground forty yards from me. It had been trying to plunge into the gorge, but it had been too slow. It raised one head for a moment, turning to look towards me, but the green eyes were glazing, dulling. The neck could no longer support the dying creature's undamaged head, and it slid to the ground and lay still. I felt no pity or remorse for the brute's death – this was war. If it had spat even a fraction more accurately, my heart and lungs would have been seared by its acid, rather than just the skin on my back.

I don't think of myself as particularly vain, but I desperately hoped that my jasq would heal me cleanly. I didn't want my back to be scarred.

Wrack swooped down and spread his wings, landing cleanly a few feet from me.

"You all right?" he growled.

I nodded. "It got a bit close" I said quietly.

"I saw" he replied. "Thought it had got you." He was changing as he spoke, his scales fading and his body subsiding into his human guise. Only when he was fully human did he kneel beside me. "Let me see your back."

I reluctantly rolled over. His fingers ran over my skin gingerly, exploring the pattern of burns across my back. "How bad is it?" I asked.

"It'll heal" he said, after a few moments. "May leave a few marks, but could have been far worse."

I turned over... and Wrack's arms slid around me. He held me tightly, pulling me against his warm body. I could smell a hint of the caustic acid from the snarq about him, mingled with his sweat. I clutched at him in response, instinctively holding him. He bent down and his lips fastened on mine, kissing me hard and insistently. This wasn't a gentle, romantic kiss – this was desperate, full of need and ferocity. He had thought the snarq had got me. I responded to his embrace without reservation – it had been far closer than I wanted to admit even to myself.

We clung together for long minutes, before Wrack finally relaxed his grip on me. I held him for a few moments' longer, before I slowly slid out of his arms. He looked at me levelly, but he didn't say anything. I wasn't sure what to say, either. I got to my feet, still a little unsteady, and reached down to take his hand. "We need to get moving" I said, trying not to let my voice quake. "We need to give Tolgrail as much warning as possible."

Wrack nodded wordlessly. He reached for his harness, discarded in the amber grass when he had transformed. I watched him dress. I had been very aware just how nude he had been just then... just how little I was wearing, too.

He said nothing more as we headed along the road again. I was not sure if I was relieved or dismayed at our mutual reticence to speak.

I had almost plucked up the courage to reopen our conversation when the lantern tree a mile to our right began to dim. I realised that the sky was a darker shade of grey. "Night's falling, Wrack" I said unnecessarily. "We need to find somewhere to camp."

"Assumed we'd find another settlement before nightfall" Wrack said, an odd mixture of regret and pleasure in his voice. I wondered at his tone, before common sense told me what he was thinking. I shivered, and realised that I didn't know if it was from fear or anticipation. Perhaps a bit of both.

As the landscape slid into velvet darkness, we scrambled off the road, down to a hollow shaded by trees. No hint of human life here – this was wild, unmastered land. All we needed to fear were creatures of the wilderness... and each other.

The trees were ancient and half-dead, only a smattering of dull red leaves protruding from the grey branches. By the time we had explored the hollow and confirmed that a couple of paralyser plants were the worst we needed to beware, the darkness had swallowed everything. As ever, the Chasm was almost uncomfortably warm – a fire seemed an unnecessary risk.

We lay on the soft orange grass, far enough apart that we would not roll over into each other accidentally. The small amount of food we had brought from the cottage did not assuage my hunger. There was a stream near where we rested, but I would have preferred wine.

I had had time to think as we had walked. Time to ponder my own feelings, and to put Wrack's words into the context of what I remembered from my time as his slave. His intensity... the way he treated me in that first bitter fortnight... how his attitude to me had altered, subtly but critically over the following months. I lay on my stomach in the darkness, waiting for Wrack to speak.

"Sorrel." His voice was soft, caution underlying his tone. "Can't leave it hanging like this. Need to talk."

I didn't want to talk. I crawled towards his voice through the still darkness.

"Sorrel!" he said again, only a foot away from me, now. I realised that I was smiling like an idiot.

"No" I said firmly, though not much louder. "We don't need to, Wrack. Not any longer."

I leaned over him, feeling the heat of his body and I ran my hand across his chest, identifying where he lay. I much preferred this with enough light to see what I was doing, but in the circumstances I would have to improvise. He twisted under my touch, and I leant down to where his mouth ought to be. I was close enough –

my lips silenced whatever he intended to say.

His hands reached for me, ran over my body. He realised very quickly that I had already slipped off my harness. My fingers undid the buckles on his while my mouth kept him quiet. His hands held me, pinning me to him, incidentally making undressing him considerably harder. I didn't complain. His touch on me was like soft, cool fire. I had always known, even if I hadn't admitted it to myself, how strongly attracted to him I was. The touch of his lips, the feel of him against me, aroused me intensely.

I made sure he was excited, too. Not that I had any difficulty doing so. I tried to hold him on his back and come over on top – he gripped me tighter and rolled us both over so that I was beneath him. I gasped, the pain of my sore back forcing a protest from me. To my surprise, Wrack hissed in sympathy. He changed his hold on me and rolled us back so that I was on top again. I ran my hands down his chest, moving my hips into the right place. He slid between my thighs and pushed upwards, entering me with fierce passion. My vision blurred as I at last had him inside me, strong and vigorous, sparking lightning across all of my body. I clutched at him, moving against him, helping him thrust into me deeper. His hands held my hips, pulling me down onto him, not that I needed any encouragement. My hands slid across his chest, over his shoulders, and I leaned forward and fastened my mouth onto his. A glorious pressure was growing through my stomach and below, and I held him tightly as his movements grew faster. I was barely aware that his pleasure was nearing its peak – I was too busy devouring his face and clutching at his shoulders. It felt as though light exploded within me, drenching me in a shuddering pleasure that left me shaking, collapsing onto him, too weak for a moment to move. Under me I felt Wrack gasp and cry out in his own pleasure, his eyes holding mine as we clung together, both relaxing in our shared release.

I lay, holding him. This felt more right than anything in the last seven years. Even in the virtual darkness I could see the gleam of his teeth - he too had an uncharacteristic smile on his face, and I kissed him gently. He smiled more. I slid my hands and my lips down over his body, encouraging him to further exertions – we had been divided by incomprehension and misplaced anger for far too long, and I intended to ensure we made up for lost time.

Chapter Twenty-Eight

Later – quite a lot later – we were lying holding each other. I was sated, physically and emotionally. I was relatively sure that Wrack was, too. He nuzzled my neck and murmured something, too soft for me to be sure of what he had said. I suspected it was something as clichéd as "I love you". I squeezed him slightly, not needing to answer. He had taken a considerable risk to keep me alive after the dragonlords had decreed my death. If the idiot had told me what he was doing... I wondered again what would have happened. Would I have struggled so hard to escape his mansion, to get back to my friends? Would I have been so keen that *he* should be the dragonlord we targeted to gain a new jasq and regain sorcery for the humans?

Would we have ended up here in the Chasm?

My thoughts were interrupted by a sudden, blinding flash, turning everything white for an instant before plunging us into even deeper darkness. Moments later there was a deep, rolling rumble that seemed to grind on for minutes, sounding right inside my ribcage as it echoed around us. Something slammed into my back, so hard that I thought it was a hailstone. Another, and I felt this one trickle off me. I could barely hear Wrack's oath as the rain began to spatter us, driving through the inadequate defence of the scant number of leaves above us.

I remembered the storm I had evaded at the graalur-controlled farm. It seemed like years ago, now. If this was as bad... "Wrack!" I bellowed. "We need to find cover!"

I was trying to think what I had seen as we had been walking. The rain was already pummelling us, hammering against my bare skin. I had no idea where I had left my harness.

"Isn't any!" Wrack howled in my ear. "Shelter under me!" His voice was changing as he shouted, and I knew that he was taking his dragon form. He roared fire at the sky, whether in defiance or because he thought it would clear the air above us for a moment I did not know. He might be a magnificent dragon, but his body was not much more resilient than mine. The storm could pound us both into bruised and bloody pulp. I slid into the magerealm, one hand instinctively going to ensure that the coronet was in place. The pain was absent. I could remain within the realm as long as I needed to for what I intended. The relief felt glorious, despite the pain of the rain already hammering at us. I half-expected to see the rain as solid rods of blue here.

Nothing of the sort. In the hissing silence of the magerealm I grabbed some of the glittering black diamonds of earth and heaved them above us, weaving the patterns together into a crude bowl above our heads, supported by pillars of blackness. It might not last forever, but it would hold for long enough... assuming I could pull it through.

I had never worked in such a fashion on the surface. Magerealm structures did not last – that was a truism. Their realm shape would be washed or burned away in minutes, or else the flows would sweep them into oblivion. On the other hand, down here I had seen structures forged in the realm by the lloruk that seemed somehow to have permanent strength. Which simply proved that the lloruk were tricksy types who knew things we mere humans (and dragons) didn't. I slid out of the realm and yelled at Wrack to furl his wings and get down. I delved into the realm, seized the bowl I had forged and heaved with all my strength to wrench it into the real world.

It felt as though I was trying to pull an unwilling bull across muddy ground. My muscles were screaming blue murder, and I could feel my grip on the magerealm weakening as the jasq struggled to achieve what I was demanding. I had to succeed. I could feel my strength failing – I hoped I had done enough.

I slid out of the magerealm. Wrack was letting a few trickles of flame gush from his nostrils so that he could see what was happening. I looked up, to see that half the bowl was over us, creaking as it threatened to collapse without two of the pillars I had so painstakingly constructed. I shrieked in frustration, but I didn't have time to think about it as the rain hammered the bowl. It tilted alarmingly, threatening to crush us under the weight of crudely sculpted sandstone. I dived back into the brilliant, blinding colours and motion and grabbed the rest, standing looking idiotic like abandoned skittles. I yanked again – this was far easier, and it slid into the real world just as the bowl tumbled forward. Wrack had shoved his folded wings upwards, pushing at the bowl as he reached up to try to keep it from becoming our tomb. The pillars were half-in, half-out of its structure. There was an dull thud as two chunks of matter tried to coexist, and splinters of stone flew outwards in a bruising hail, as if trying to show the rain how to be really destructive. Both Wrack and I cried out as the fragments slammed into our bodies like handfuls of flung gravel.

But the bowl was not tumbling any further. It was gripped, canted at a strange angle like a clumsily-worn hat perched on the broken pillars. The rain was drumming on its surface, but beneath it we were sheltered.

By blind fortune none of the chips had hit anything vital – they could so easily have taken out an eye. They had peppered our skins – Wrack's scales had been some protection, but in the thin light from the wisps of fire from Wrack's nostrils I looked like someone had fired a spray of bruise-purple paint over me.

Wrack held me, licking with a long draconic tongue as he tried to soothe the sore pockmarks across my back. I shook my head and I almost laughed, despite the host of stinging pains across most of one side of me, where the stones had connected.

"I'm all right, Wrack. Nothing went too deep. The jasq is healing me already."

"What the volg happened?" he demanded. I did my best to explain, all the while being very aware of his tongue sliding over the patchwork of marks across me. The jasq was warm, almost too hot in my side as it struggled to undo the latest damage I had done to myself. I had been very proud of my body. I strongly suspected, now, that I would have scars across it when all these injuries healed.

I heard a soft rasping cough as Wrack breathed another candleflame of fire. In the darkness, all I could see were his eyes reflecting the flames as they flared infernally around his muzzle. He turned his long head, inspected my handiwork, confirming that it was holding the rain from us for the present, but that it was already growing less solid, the magerealm earth evaporating back into the place from which it had been dragged. All we could do was to hope that it would last until the rain let up.

By morning the stone was all but gone, just a few slivers left to remind us of its presence. The rain had stopped well before the stone had melted away. Around us the landscape had been flattened into submission by the savage precipitation, but already the crimson plants were starting to recover, pushing upwards to take on their original shapes or sprouting new red leaves to replace those hammered off the trees.

It took me a few minutes to find my harness and get dressed. I was ravenous – my exertions during the night had left me starving and weak. Wrack, on the other hand, was looking in better humour than he had demonstrated since we came to the Chasm. I suspected that our earlier activities had a lot to do with that.

The road should lead us to Tolgrail. I took hold of Wrack's hand and headed us towards it... and, with luck, towards something resembling breakfast.

We had been walking for half an hour. We had assuaged our thirst from a spring that was flowing towards the gorge – cool, clean water that had been deeply refreshing. The trouble was, it left me even more hungry. The storm had left the vegetation battered and broken – it seemed as though we were walking through one of the war-shattered fields I had traversed on the surface during the rebellion, made worse by the ground being the colour of blood.

The first farm we reached seemed deserted, a dark hulk of a house set back from the road and an echoing barn without fodder or animals. I looked across at Wrack and grimaced. He shrugged.

I was feeling decidedly wan. I thought I had slept well, but I felt drained, unsteady on my feet. It would have been like being drunk if it felt good. It didn't, of course. Wrack looked at me worriedly, and slid his arm around my shoulders. He led me towards the looming building and tried the door. It opened easily. The place was empty, the sound of the door reverberating as we peered into the dim interior. We were looking into the kitchen – all the signs suggested that it had been abandoned not long ago.

"They've been warned of the graalur" Wrack said softly. A loud voice in the silent kitchen would have felt like an intrusion.

"Did they take all the food?" I asked glumly. I slid into one of the rather nicely carved dark wood chairs that stood round the heavy table. Wrack glanced at me again and began to open cupboards and peer into pots on shelves.

"Not everything" he said after a couple of moments. I grunted something that was meant to be relief. He worked for a few minutes. I heard a sizzle of something frying, before he slid a plate under my nose, followed by a fine earthenware mug of liquid. The plate smelt wonderful – he hadn't bothered to give me any cutlery, and I was far too hungry to worry. I hadn't had a proper meal since breakfast yesterday. This wasn't toast, unfortunately – I particularly liked toast and marmalade for breakfast – but it was piping hot meat and fried fruit. I nearly burned my fingers trying to juggle it to my mouth before Wrack passed me a fork with a serrated side. I carved into the bacon and wolfed it down. I was vaguely surprised that Wrack knew how to cook – I had assumed he left such duties to his slaves. Wrack wordlessly took my plate before I could finish off the fruit – he had been at work at the hot griddle, and now added another rasher and some mushrooms to the meal. The liquid was fruit juice, rather stale, but still very drinkable.

"Aren't you eating?" I managed to ask as I swallowed another mouthful. Wrack turned and grinned, and slid into the chair beside me. He too had a substantial plate of food. I devoured the rest of my bounty before reaching across and spearing one of the mushrooms he had fried for himself. He growled a protest as I stole the loot. I smiled at him, and his mild irritation soothed. He slid his plate closer to me, and we demolished the remainder of his food between us.

I felt far more human, much more my old self. I leaned over and kissed Wrack on the cheek before I got to my feet. "We need to get moving."

"You look better for some food" he replied. I concurred, and we headed back onto the road. I was feeling more relaxed, happier with life than I had felt in a good many months. I had my sorcery back, and I had Wrack. All I needed now was an aeroplane to make my happiness complete. Oh, well. Two out of three was pretty good.

Within two more hours we had passed a dozen farms. All were deserted, the fields empty of people to tend the crops, the livestock missing or, in a couple of grisly places, slaughtered and the carcasses burned. Nothing was being left that the graalur could use. I commented to Wrack that the farmers obviously didn't think the graalur would harvest the bounty in the fields. Wrack just looked at me as though I was being stupid.

Another hour trekking eastwards, and we were no longer alone. On the road there were clusters of worried, laden men and women, together with wailing or frightened children. Wagons hauled by unwilling olgreks tried to manoeuvre around handcarts and pack animals. Ahead of us we could see the city. Heavy, grey-green walls stretched, stern and forbidding, to each side of us, wide, low towers squatting at intervals like crouching stone giants. Around the walls, a forest of shacks of a variety of shades of red wood leaned or slumped against the stonework or against each other. As we drew closer, I could see that the buzz of activity around the structures. People with bundles were struggling to carry their meagre belongings through the wide open west gate. Carts and laden olgreks were moving slowly through the worried crowds seeking to retreat into the dubious protection of the basalt defences. More people, mostly heavily laden, were heading towards the city, the stragglers from the deserted farms and communities we had already passed. The noise of worried people grew louder as we neared the main gate, a hubbub of shouts and demands for children not to wander, requests to get out of the way in varying levels of politeness, and protests at imagined or real trespasses. I realised with dismay that it might well take some hours before we could negotiate the tumult at the gate.

Troops were visible in bright blue capes, shepherding the ingress and trying to maintain semblances of order, as well as investigating any arrivals who looked at all suspect. I had no doubt that we would come into that category. The ground to each side of the roadway before the gate was swiftly turning to mud – they had had the same rain we had suffered, and the constant surge of people across the ground was creating a morass. I did not fancy wading through the treacly black ooze, and said so to Wrack. He nodded in agreement. We had an advantage over the people struggling to get into the city – wings.

It did not seem sensible that Wrack changed too near the gate. There were figures visible atop the defences watching the events below. We retreated around away from the western gate, only to realise that we were nearing a major road that ran towards Tolgrail from the south. It too was thronged with refugees from the oncoming graalur force, mobbing the south gate in similar fashion to the western portal.

"Two gates?" Wrack growled. "Didn't want to make the city easy to defend, did they?"

I ignored his words – something about a cluster of the figures nearing the gate looked familiar. I let out a whoop of delight, and started running headlong towards the bedraggled wanderers. Heads turned as I yelled at them, and half a dozen faces lit up with smiles. Wrack, behind me, grumbled something incoherent. I ignored him and flung my arms around Kelhene, hugging her, before doing the same with Korhus and Helinhus. Kentyr and Darhia both smiled at us, too, Kentyr looking around for his leader and asking if Griffyn was all right. He relaxed at my affirmative, and at my brief explanation for his absence. Other Grihl Valleyers were gathering around us, demanding to hear my news and asking about the coronet firmly nestled on my head. I had bound some of my hair around it during the walk from the bridge, to ensure that I didn't lose it again. As and when I ever planned to brush my hair again I would regret it, but since I hadn't had a chance to make proper use of a hairbrush the whole time I had been down here I suspected that the coronet's presence would be the least of my tribulations.

A babble of exchanged stories and minor anecdotes, mixed with repetitions about the pleasure of meeting up again, told me that the Valley-folks' journey had been relatively uneventful. They had had minor brushes with a couple of relatively savage local denizens, both of which had been driven off without significant injury. Chelhik insisted on showing me the bandaged gash to his arm, suffered when an adjalik bit him. His excited description left me none the wiser about adjaliks.

The group had trekked through the jungle for three days, arriving only an hour before we had, and had been joining the throng seeking the uncertain shelter of the city. The news of the graalur advance had brought everyone who lived within a dozen miles of the city to seek safety. Tolgrail was going to be very crowded for a while.

"Any word of when the graalur will get here?" I asked quietly.

Kelhene shrugged. "Anything from an hour to a week, depending who you ask. The latest news is that they've been held up at a bridge."

Wrack actually cracked a smile, and I grinned broadly. Our account of the events at the gorge drew something of an audience, and I realised that it was not just the Grihl Valley people listening. I wasn't sure how much the story made sense – our people knew about Wrack, but to everyone else it had to sound like fiction.

I belatedly wondered how Kelhene and the others got across the gorge, only to discover that the river ran to the east of the city, blocking our path, but nowhere near the route from the south-west that the Valley-folk had followed. We had crossed the gorge originally on the way to the tsergiaad tower via a skywire; the others had simply stayed on the other side throughout.

We mingled with our group as they waited patiently to reach the south gate. I wondered aloud what our reception within would be like. An ageing woman from a neighbouring group scowled, and answered me.

"If you're fit to fight, they'll find you something sharp and put you on a wall somewhere. Otherwise they'll shove you into an empty building with no food and leave you to rot."

"Better than being in the hands of the graalur" someone else responded. The discussion broke down into a chatter of worry and speculation. Wrack touched my arm and leaned down to murmur at my ear "Hopeless, Sorrel. If you want us to be any use we need to get to the guard commander."

I nodded. I had been thinking in similar vein – but I really didn't want to abandon my friends again. I half-spluttered some comment to that effect, but Kelhene was at my elbow. She turned me to face her. "Sorrel" she snapped, with a vestige of her old acerbity. "The most valuable thing you can do to help us is to beat the graalur. Make sure they don't take the city. Queuing here isn't doing any good at all."

"What about all of you?" I demanded hotly. "I'm not leaving you to... to..."

"To be refugees like everyone else?" she asked tartly. "That's what we are,

Sorrel. I'd love to demand special treatment for us, but we're in the same position as everyone locally. *You* can make a difference – so volging well go and do so!"

I grinned despite myself at hearing Kelhene using the narynyl expletive, and nodded in reluctant acquiescence. Wrack was nodding, too – being down here, amongst the plebs, had to be torture for him. A corner of my thoughts murmured that it would do him good to see how the less fortunate lived, but my feelings for Wrack had warmed greatly in the last day or so, and I quelled the vicious streak and told it to pipe down.

I looked up at the forbidding walls. Wrack smiled. "Move away from the crowd to change?" he suggested. I nodded. If he caused a panic when he transformed, it could hurt a lot of people – including my friends. I gestured off the road. There were stone buildings only a few hundred yards from the road, already abandoned. The nearest looked like a workshop, and as we approached I realised I could smell the rank odour of tanning. A leather-workers, outside the city to prevent its stench overpowering the citizenry. It provided a good place to shelter as Wrack shrugged off his harness and transformed. I watched in pure pleasure as his shape changed, our jasq thundering its chorus of welcome in my side.

The dragon loomed over me, and extended a leg delicately. I gripped Wrack around his scaly neck and settled myself onto his thigh, and the vast wings clapped behind us, the ground lurching away as we climbed. I could see the valley folk pointing up, identifying us. There were shouts of surprise and also alarm from other people around the gate. On the walls, more shouts, and a single arrow sped past us, missing widely but still giving me palpitations.

"Hold your fire!" I bellowed in my best parade-ground voice. "We're here to help you against the graalur and the lloruk!"

More shouts, interrogatory but unclear through the churning air. I nudged Wrack – we had picked out one tower as our intended landing stage, and now we swooped towards it. "Not too fast" I growled at Wrack. "Don't make them think you're attacking!"

"With a pretty woman on my knee? What kind of attack could they think it was?" he rasped, a chuckle in his voice. I grinned too. The soldiers atop the tower were scattering, crossbows and spears in evidence but not yet deployed. Wrack circled once, and then dropped slowly, his wings angled so they held the air. I yelled again that we were on their side, and my feet slammed into the weathered wooden decking that formed the roof. Soldiers in blue capes stood around us, spears nervously jutting towards us. I looked around for someone with some hint of authority, and eventually decided that a well-built man with slightly more gold on his harness had to be the best choice.

"Wrack and I are here to help you against the lloruk" I said impressively.

The man stared at me in disbelief. Beside me, Wrack transformed again, back into human form. I handed him his harness, and he pulled it around himself. I could hear the sound of jaws hitting the ground, and struggled to stop myself laughing.

More heads appeared, a ladder up to the tower disgorging half a dozen more people. At their head was an older woman, hair mostly white, her face lined with worry and a sour expression. Her garb was almost substantial, marked with gilt curlicues and an ornate headdress that would be of far less value in a fight than the helmets her soldiers wore. I took a wild stab in the dark. "Are you Commander Berindyl?"

A moment's consternation on the worn face. "How do you know my name?"

"A friend of mine told me to ask for you. He said you were in charge of the guard."

"Who are you?" she asked again.

I gave her our names, and told her I was a sorceress and that Wrack was a dragon. She looked disbelieving, and started to demand to know more, accusing us of being servants of the lloruk. Beside me Wrack was pacing back and forth, his irritation becoming visible. I put my hand on his shoulder, but he had already taken a breath and snarled loudly "If we were your enemy, your gates would be charred ruins and you would be tumbled amidst the rubble of your walls. We're the best hope you've got of defeating the coming attack. Now show us some courtesy before Sorrel gets angry!"

I struggled to keep a straight face as the commander blanched, before she nodded obediently and we were ushered into the city.

Our dramatic arrival on top of the tower was enough to persuade the top brass in Tolgrail to listen to us seriously. An hour took us from the green-grey stone of the walls to a slightly more prepossessing edifice jutting from what I assumed was the main square. Three storeys, pillars in front supporting a wide porch, the ground floor well-cut stone blocks, the remainder red wood beams and white-painted plaster. Inside we had an ageing blue carpet and an imposing sweep of stairs up to a spacious council chamber and a dozen people in varying styles of garb. Names, introductions, handshakes and doubting questions. I barely kept a grip on the identities of half the people in the room; the rest blurred into polite oblivion.

Griffyn's description of Berindyl had been remarkably accurate. Within half an hour of sitting down at the wide ashwood table in the meeting room I wanted nothing more than to puncture the white-haired woman's pomposity, preferably with a fist. Lendalyn, the thin, rather querulous Chancellor, not to mention the remainder of the council, seemed to be bowing to Berindyl's military knowledge. Unfortunately, her concept of tactics was to lurk behind Tolgrail's walls ("cower" was the word Wrack quietly murmured) and hope the graalur would go away. The two lieutenants she had brought with her to the conference seemed unable to argue with her – the older of the two, Trelyar, seemed even more monosyllabic than Wrack, and I suspected his highly buffed harness was an indication that all he knew was spit and polish. The younger of the two, Fordyral, was far more keen to take the fight to the enemy – he had fair, curly hair, a wild glint in his eye, and a hot-headed streak onto which Berindyl made a point of pouring gallons of metaphorical cold water. I sympathised with his growing frustration – I too was almost at the stage of chewing the smart blue carpet under our feet. The idea of venturing out in sorties seemed to fill the older woman with dread. All she wanted to do was lurk and keep her head down. "The walls are strong" was Berindyl's watchword.

"Walls are *not* strong" Wrack finally growled, drowning her platitudes with his deep voice. He had been virtually silent until now, letting me do the talking. Now he chose to make his presence felt. "*One* lloruk sorceror could bring down your stonework in minutes. Been told they have half a dozen!"

"We can't fight sorcery!" Berindyl retorted. "Our best hope is that we can shoot the lloruk with spears or arrows before they get close enough to do any damage!"

"Fat chance!" I snapped. "They won't be that stupid! They'll have graalur around them shielding them from anything you can throw!"

"Are you saying it's hopeless, then?" boomed one of the representatives of the city merchants, a large woman whose name I had completely forgotten. She was standing in front of one of the large glass windows that overlooked the square, her expansive figure blocking out a significant amount of light from the nearest lantern tree. Fordyral bridled at the suggestion, and I felt Wrack draw breath to snarl an oath. I got to my feet, too, and firmly told her not to be so defeatist.

"So what do you suggest, sorceress?" asked Lendalyn quietly, cutting through my expostulations. I felt a gush of relief that the thin councillor was finally making a sensible contribution to the discussion. I wasn't a great tactician, frankly, but I had survived a siege before, and I had a better feel for what the city faced than anyone except Wrack. It felt quite unnerving to be the centre of attention. I leaned forward, hands on the grey ashwood, hoping I knew what I was doing, and began to outline what we needed to do.

Chapter Twenty-Nine

I had only been involved in one magical sortie on the ground, during the fall of Trakomar. I had been one of the defenders, trying to block the dragonlords' magic from bringing down our defences and slaughtering our fighters. It had been a very grim episode, and when our defences had failed I had only just got out of the town alive. I had learned a lot about using magic for warfare in the process. I had had no regrets about taking to the skies for all my remaining battles. The idea of battling a squad of lloruk filled me with some dread. I had to act as though I was confident, but I was terrified that I did not have enough skill or ability to block one lloruk mage, let alone six. And I knew that I would tire quickly. It was far too many months since I had used the realm for any length of time. Fifteen minutes there and I would be weak. An hour would probably leave me unconscious. The strongest hope I had was that the lloruk would not be expecting any opposition on their own territory. If I could hit them fast and hard, baffle their efforts, that would give time for the human defenders to hit the graalur... and time to use the weapon we had that the lloruk might not be expecting.

Our strategies depended on the mages being in no more than two places. If they were spread evenly amongst the attackers we would be in real trouble. Wrack was a good tactician, far better than Berindyl. He intervened as I tried to talk about what we should do – within a few minutes I sat back and let him take over. Lendalyn and the Councillors were clearly impressed by him, whereas the Guard Commander obviously felt threatened. Good. She deserved to feel inferior.

We talked for over three hours, arguing over details and revisiting options. More than once I found myself struggling to understand what Lendalyn was saying – he had quite a pronounced accent, and I was realising that I was not as good at speaking veredraa as I had thought.

I didn't like what I was hearing, much of the time. Retreat was not an option – there were numerous cities beyond Tolgrail, in the wide plains north of the mountains, any and all of which might take in fleeing refugees. The problem was that we couldn't get through the pass between the two major peaks before the graalur caught up with us. In the narrow gorge a fleeing group might hold them off, particularly with the aid of the fastness at the narrowest point, an ancient stone stronghold built there expressly to hold the pass – but in the open lands before the gap they could cut us to pieces in short order. The scouts had confirmed that the graalur were only hours away – there simply was insufficient time to get everyone away and abandon the city.

Not that we particularly wanted to retreat. Tolgrail was a well-made city, with fine, imposing buildings and a substantial cluster of businesses within the walls. No one wanted to abandon everything that had been built here to the graalur.

I walked through the narrow streets with Wrack, gazing up at the tall wood and stone buildings around me with some envy. This was as good a town as Werintar, or Malgarrin before it surrendered. In happier days I could imagine the streets bustling with traders and shoppers, children charging between people's legs in incomprehensible games, and tabithas prowling at the edges looking for mice to eat or people to fuss over them.

Not that it was like that now. All the faces I saw were full of troubles, the extra influx of people a burden on the residents, and no one had any confidence in our chances of holding off the oncoming assault. The children were being kept indoors, and any tabithas had sensibly gone to ground. We had finally left the meeting with reasonable arrangements in place – the Commander had bowed to the dual pressures from us and the Chancellor, and submitted to our defence plan. I just hoped it would work.

"Toll Street" Wrack growled at me, indicating a turning on our left, and I glanced around in surprise. There was a signboard with the local script prominently displayed.

"How do you know?" I asked. "Are you telling me you can read veredraan?"

Wrack shook his head. "Got the Chancellor to draw me a sketch of the streets. Didn't want to get lost finding your friends."

Sometimes Wrack's efforts at being efficient can be really irritating. I stalked across the reasonably smooth cobbles, looking for the empty art shop we had been told the Grihl Valley contingent were occupying. Sure enough, three doors along, I saw a sign of a paintbrush, and moments later I saw Eldhor open the bright green wooden door.

I had missed my charges badly. Friends. People I cared about. I hugged half a dozen men and women, told two of the children that the jungle trek had made them grow, threatened (with a big grin) to feed the third to a ruzdrool when she got under my feet, and talked to most of the Valley-folk, trying to reassure them that we had a fighting chance against the oncoming Iloruk forces. Even Wrack seemed to care about the group, his imposing figure permanently at the centre of clusters of admirers. Everyone was safe at the moment; even Belha, who had suffered more than one significant injury while I had been responsible for the group, seemed to be recovering well. Seeing them all in good shape gave me a vast improvement to my morale.

I spent a few minutes talking to Darhia and Kentyr. They had heard from Griffyn, courtesy of one of the buzzing insects. Supposedly he was on his way to Tolgrail, but I was not entirely surprised when Darhia said that it would be a few days before he reached us... and the graalur would be here first. I was getting more of a feel for our freedom fighter. He was happy to lead assaults where the odds were firmly in his favour, but I didn't think he had much taste for more real threats. Kentyr told me Griffyn had found out that his old spire had been invaded and searched thoroughly. I was glad he had escaped, but I really didn't trust him. Darhia and Kentyr had already arranged that they would stay with the Grihl Valley-folk until Griffyn did get here, and in the meantime would help Tolgrail against the oncoming army.

The reunion with my friends also had a grimmer purpose. I stood in a small white plaster-walled bedroom above the art shop, looked down at Darhath, and shivered. I had an extremely sharp knife, lots of bandages, and some dark memories. I knew what I was about to do to Darhath, and what he would feel. By the look of Wrack's expression, his feelings were not much different. Kelhene looked at me wanly. We had told our friends what was coming, and what we had planned. Half the Valley-folk intended to be on the walls, adding to the strength of the defending force. It meant we could not spare anyone to watch over Darhath. By unspoken agreement we would try this now, in the slim hope of freeing Darhath from the thrall of the larisq.

Eldhor had managed to get hold of a small bottle of strong spirits, quite how I didn't intend to ask. I could have done with a swig from the bottle myself, but Darhath would need it far more. I nodded at Wrack and Talhin. The two men took a tight grip on Darhath's arms, holding him still, stretched out over the wood-framed bed. Kelhene was facing him, holding his attention, crooning to him to try to keep him calm. In his mouth was a strip of leather, and he was biting upon it at Kelhene's command. I took a firmer grip on the knife, bent to his arm, trying not to gag at the nearness of the larisq, and I began to cut.

I don't want to think about the next quarter of an hour. Suffice it to say that the task was grim and bloody. I wished I had acid to destroy the foul thing that I carved from Darhath's flesh. I had to settle for burning it in the small brass stove at the back of the shop.

I also wished that I could have removed everything from Darhath's body, but within five minutes of Darhath's first scream I had known the task was hopeless. Fine purple strings emerged from every square inch of the foul purple slime, extending into Darhath's body. I could cut them, and hope that without the central mass they would have little effect upon him, but there was no doubt that they had grown into much of his skin. When I had first leaned close to him I had seen faint violet traceries under the skin of his chest. Carving those out would almost certainly have been fatal in moments. I did everything that I could... but I feared, as I worked to sew the savage wound closed, both my arms scarlet, my body spattered with warm blood, that it would not be enough.

Darhath had fainted, mercifully, before I had finished. Once I had excised the larisq, I slid into the magerealm. I had studied Darhath for only a moment in the realm before I began my task. That brief sojourn into sorcery had left me nauseous. The mere presence of the larisq was enough. And my coronet did not protect me from this revulsion one jot.

Darhath's wound was far worse than Wrack's – or mine, come to think about it. An ordinary jasq doesn't invade its host; it nestles just under the skin, growing to fill the original gash, but does not take over the person it inhabits. Larisqs... spread. They grow aggressively, like a cancer, if Darhath's was anything to go by. Burning it, despite the foul stench of it scorching, felt like a cleansing.

I sat and talked to Kelhene and Korhus, waiting for Darhath to recover, wondering how he would be when he wakened. I learned quite a lot about the local area. I had no doubt, now, that this assault on Tolgrail was, in the main if not entirely, intended to capture me. It made no other sense. There were far more obvious targets for the graalur if they wanted to conquer the human lands. Tolgrail lay between two other cities, Daryan and Falnaul. An occupying force would be permanently at risk of assault from two flanks. There was a far easier route through the mountains to get to the plains cities beyond. And Jajruuk, to the south, was isolated now the lloruk had struck into the Eski lands.

I sipped a cup of fulvraan. Not quite like caff, but very palatable as an alternative. Chelhik was telling me something about the task he'd been allotted. For some reason, Berindyl wanted a squad in the main square, as though the graalur could appear out of nowhere in the open area. Chelhik was talking worriedly about vorulgaqs and how to drive a spear between the plates of their armour when Darhath groaned.

I'm not sure if I moved quite as fast as Kelhene, but we were both beside him where he lay upon the rough off-white blanket before he had opened his eyes. He looked up at us blankly.

"Kelhene?" he asked slowly. The blonde woman bit back a sob and hugged him desperately. I realised that I was in tears, too, and reached out to grip his spare hand.

His eyes were vague, unfocussed, and he was in considerable pain. I wished we had had some more of the spirits we had plied him with before – a hangover would be the least of his concerns. He knew who we were! He was speaking and thinking for himself! Even if I had not removed all of the larisq from his body, I had broken the hold the foul thing had exerted over him.

It took well over an hour to try to explain to him what had happened, and by the end of that hour my elation had subsided. Darhath was not the dull-eyed automaton that he had been for days – but he was not the keen-eyed leader the Grihl Valley people had followed before. A spark, a presence had faded. And I had a horrible suspicion that the larisq's influence could return as the fibres still within him regrew. I knew how good a jasq could be at repairing damage to its host – repairing itself ought to be a doddle. I couldn't bring myself to tell Kelhene what I feared. It was almost a relief when a runner hammered on the door of the shop, sent by the Chancellor expressly to find me and Wrack.

Her expression gave her message before she even opened her mouth. The enemy force was upon us.

Chapter Thirty

Lines of marching graalur like dusky red snakes slithering around the walls. Three snarqs beating their wings heavily above their masters. And far back, well outside any possible missile range, two small clusters of indistinct figures. Lloruk. Around each was a squad of graalur, heavyset and heavily weaponed. I looked sidelong at Wrack.

"Lots of crossbows" he said grimly.

The tower we were standing atop of was at the south-east corner of the city. It gave us a spectacular view of the force preparing to launch itself at us. The only significant question was whether they would attack us before nightfall, under cover of the dark, or bright and early in the morning. My suspicion was in the midst of the night, once we had waited for long enough to get agitated, but while they still had night to shroud them. It depended on how tired the graalur were after their march.

"How many?" asked Berindyl quietly.

For a moment I thought she was asking me, but then a soldier on the far side of the tower ventured an opinion well into four figures. Not so far off, in my estimation. "They're making camp" she added.

The graalur were all round the city, ensuring there could be no escape from the siege. A few tents were slowly, tiredly taking shape, but most of the enemy were happy to collapse onto the grass. Camp-fires were being lit, sergeants bellowing orders, the common troops endeavouring to ignore them as much as possible. All armies are the same.

I looked across at Berindyl. "What time is it now?"

"About fifth segue."

Volg it! While I had been in the Grihl Valley I had been introduced to the Chasm's concept of measuring time, but I still had to think hard to translate it into surface time. There were eight segues in the day, four transits at night. Fifth segue

317

was about three in the afternoon. Another five, maybe six hours until full dark.

"Second transit" Wrack said before I could work it out. "That's when they'll hit. Middle of the night."

"In the dark?" Berindyl queried.

"Why not?" I said grimly. "Trust me – the lloruk will be able to give the graalur light."

Lendalyn had found us a chamber with a soft bed. Perhaps more important, there was a polished wooden bathtub in the adjoining room. I beat Wrack to it without much difficulty. He scowled as I submerged myself. I grinned at him wickedly, and his scowl lessened. Unfortunately, it wasn't large enough for him to join me. He didn't let me loll in the warm water for long – after five minutes, he hauled me out (with much entertainment for both of us) before he doused himself. I didn't let him have long in the water either before I dragged him (without any struggle whatsoever) to our bed.

We both knew that the graalur would attack, and that we would be in the thick of the conflict. Neither of us said that we might die, but the threat of the conflict to come spurred both of us to greater passion. By the time we slid into sleep, tangled together on top of the sheets, we were both satiated and exhausted.

I don't know how much time passed before we were woken by the clangour of the heavy bronze bells that topped each of the towers. All I know was that it hadn't been long enough. I kissed Wrack swiftly before pulling on what passed for my clothing and bolting for the top of the tower we were in. Breakfast? Not a chance.

The sky was burning red and gold, three columns of fire searing the clouds, rising from the two edges of the main graalur force and from behind the midst of their mass. We need not have worried about the graalur assaulting us under the cover of darkness. What I could not see was the lloruk. I peered into the massed forces of graalur, looking for well-defended knots of figures, but I couldn't spot them yet. I glanced sidelong at Wrack wordlessly.

"As we feared" he murmured, his hand squeezing mine. "Can't do anything until we know where they all are."

I returned the pressure on his fingers, and smiled at him encouragingly. "I'll draw them out – make sure we know where to find them."

Shouts rose from the south gate. The vast majority of the graalur force were at the southern walls. Scaling ladders were already lifting in two dozen places, defenders waiting with poles and swords to fend them off. At the gate, a heavy battering ram was slamming against the thick timber, the steady impacts like a heartbeat measuring out the life of the city.

So far, aside from the pillars of flame illuminating the walls I could see no signs of lloruk sorcery. I squeezed Wrack's hand and slid into the magerealm.

The brightness of the realm was barely worse than the flaming sky of the real world. I tried to blink, but then looked around. The columns of fire were clearly visible in this environ. Not far from each was a minuscule stick-figure of gold and blue diamonds and spines. Two were moving across the strange, brilliant landscape towards each other. The third vanished as I watched, and I realised that it had withdrawn from the magerealm. I narrowed my eyes against the blaze, knowing that what I was seeing was two of the lloruk sorcerers, their figures foreshortened by the distance. Between us was a panoply of magerealm features – a pool of quicksilver, numerous fireflows, a couple of smoky air towers and more than enough chunks of emerald and black earths, undulating slowly. The lloruk seemed so far away – it did not seem possible that they do anything to the city from that distance, but I knew better. Frustratingly, there was no way that I could affect them from here. It felt oddly familiar to be so far up. The last time I had been high up within the realm I had had an aeroplane around me, only the engine visible in front. I peered into the brilliance, wishing I could see the others.

Berindyl seemed relatively confident that if we could stop the lloruk, she could hold out against the graalur. We had discussed our strategy. Now, I slid out of the realm and gripped Wrack on the shoulder. He lifted his hand to squeeze mine, and then he stood back and transformed.

The fires in the sky were just starting to fade, now, the lloruk mages no longer feeding the illumination. I judged it would be at least an hour before the columns had burned out of the real world completely. We had torches all along the walls, so that even when the lloruk fire was gone we would see the oncoming hordes. In the flickering yellow illumination Wrack's change seemed even more phantasmagorical than usual. Everyone around us was watching him as his scales glittered in the magefire. He nodded at me once. We both knew what we needed to do, and we no longer needed words between us. He spread his vast, dark wings, and then he launched himself into the sky.

I looked around for the snarqs. One was in the air above the gate, harrying the defenders. A hail of spears and crossbow bolts seemed to be having no effect upon it whatsoever. Another, however, was already down; a lucky missile had taken it in one throat, and now it was choking and struggling on the ground, five graalur vainly attempting to tend the grievous wound. Even as I watched, it twisted its uninjured head sideways and snapped its jaws closed on one of the graalur surgeons, its pain and anger quelling any comprehension of their efforts. Good. That left no more than a couple at most to threaten Wrack. He was gliding smoothly over the besieging forces, relatively high, a ghost in the darkness. The clouds were reflecting back the fires of the siege – if anyone looked up, they would see him silhouetted against the red-lit sky. I just had to hope no one had any reason to gaze up at the heavens.

I could see one more snarq, drifting in similar manner towards the east wall. As I spotted it I saw it spitting acid at the top of one of the towers. Screams and commotion cut dimly through the general shouts of the assault.

A dozen scaling ladders had lifted to that stretch of wall, and now graalur were climbing swiftly, showers of arrows and other missiles, and the ever-present threat of the snarq, keeping the defenders on the walls from flinging them off. I slid back into the magerealm for a moment, gauging what I had to work with, before emerging again to get a clear picture of my targets. Wrack's widespread wings would carry him high over the conflict, looking for victims, but it would take time before he would be in position to strike decisively. For the moment the crux of the conflict lay with me.

My first target was the snarq, brilliantly illuminated by the nearest column of fire, its pale blue wings gleaming in the orange glow. It swept around, preparing to strike again at the defenders atop the east wall. Just a little closer... it beat its wings once more before dropping fast, both sets of jaws opening with malignant intent. I slid into the realm and snatched at the earth-flow I had tagged a few moments before. I did not want to alert the lloruk to my activities for the moment – a flicker of fire from nowhere would be obvious to even the most stupid sorcerer. Solid, night-black rock, on the other hand... The snarq swept forward, and I tugged the flow. With a sickening crunch the snarq dropped like a bat with a brick on its back, tumbling forty feet to slam into the ground amidst a force of startled or just plain squashed graalur. The solid chunk of basalt that had emerged out of nowhere to mug the flying beast would have dissolved back into the realm by the time the lantern-trees began to glow. I grinned, and looked for more mischief.

Without the snarq to strike from above, the graalur on the east wall were not having a good time of it. The defenders had been heartened by the sudden, unexpected accident that had befallen the menace. The graalur were falling back, too many tumbling from their siege ladders for the effort to succeed.

The main stretch of the south wall was holding firm, experienced Tolgrail soldiers bolstering the civilians as they flung anything solid down onto the unfortunate graalur below, the only real threat coming from the graalur arrows. So far not a single ladder's climbers had reached the central walls.

Over on the south-west side, however, a different story was developing. The graalur had been clambering in five places, and in two they had topped the wall. Now there were savage, short and bloody duels with the defenders, giving time for more ladders to give access to the invaders. Lieutenant Trelyar was overseeing the forces there – somehow, I wasn't totally surprised that they were in trouble. I snarled in anger, and dropped a couple of large chunks of flint onto the climbing graalur. Shrieks and sounds of tumbling objects drifted faintly to my ears. The duellists I could not hope to aid – my efforts tended to be far too drastic to inflict them near my friends. I just had to hope the west wall contingent could drive back the graalur if they had no more assailants to worry about. Berindyl was marshalling reserves to go to the west wall's aid. I slid back into the realm and caught a column of turbulent yellow smoke. Air flows were notoriously difficult to manipulate –

Kelvar, when he was teaching me sorcery, had advised me not even to think about playing with air. Being me, I'd spent the next month experimenting secretly, and nearly blew myself away. Tonight, though, my escapades from my murky past might be of value. I twisted my spindles through the yellow smoke, weaving it into my own being, before I swept the tornado across the ground near the yellow-green mist that was the wall. There were satisfying yells and confusion, all six ladders toppling sideways and depositing their cargoes atop their comrades. Now all I could do was leave the defenders to cope with their existing troubles.

A sudden hiss caught my attention. Something vast was moving out of the darkness towards the south wall, figures atop the purple hide sprouting weapons as they prepared to strike. Wide legs were slamming into the ground as the scorturliq crept unsubtly through its allies towards us. I stared at the approaching nightmare in disbelief. We had not seen a single one in daylight – my first thought was that the lloruk must have kept this one hidden, way back from the city, as their secret weapon. It was only as the monstrosity stalked toward me that I belatedly wondered if the scorturliq was part of the brigade that had trailed the Grihl Valley-folk from Griffyn's spire. Odds were it had only just arrived to bolster the graalur force. I decided I preferred my original theory – more graalur as well did not sound good. I stared at the yellow eggs it had for eyes, remembering how the one at the spire had loomed over me, my stomach suddenly leaden again. This time I was on the wall looking down at it. No way was I letting it climb the side of the city. I suspected the largest rock I could hope to pull from the realm was unlikely to stop something that size. I had to reveal my true colours.

Behind me there were sudden screams of alarm - I spun round, looking over the back of the tower into the centre of town. Torches were being brandished in the market square. I remembered blaspheming at Berindyl's insistence at leaving people on duty there. For once, the Guard Commander had been right. The large cobbles of the square were shivering, boiling up as something broke through from under the ground. A large indigo head burst out from under the stones, and then a second emerged alongside it. Heavy black claws, each the size of an olgrek's head, were tearing at the ground as the creature hauled itself out from the tunnel it had dug for itself. It was related to the snarq – two wide, flat heads, short, stubby arms and legs, and a vicious pair of bites. The defenders were falling back in alarm, yelling for help, and then I saw a second part of the market-place begin to quake. I glanced over my shoulder at the scortuliq – it would be at the wall in short order. But the defenders in the square – I couldn't leave Chelhik and the others to the emerging monsters. Another armour-plated form was scrabbling its way out of the ground.

More stone from the realm – I was depleting the earth-flows dramatically. I just hoped they would hold up for the rest of the conflict. Even the realm is not inexhaustible. A large chunk of limestone hit the first of the creatures squarely from twenty feet up, and it dropped back into its hole, its armour no help against my missile.

The wall shuddered behind me, and I spun back to face the scortuliq as it reared up, close enough to smell the acrid odour it was emitting. Volg it, the lafquassing squum was fast – it had reached the wall in seconds, far sooner than I had anticipated. I stared into its unblinking yellow eyes, feeling the same terror I had experienced at the spire. Around me shouts and screams told me that I was not alone in my panic. The scorturliq was just too volging big!

I realised I was shouting something obscene at its uncomprehending maw. I dived back into the realm, and seized the largest fireflow within reach. The scorturliq at the spire had had a lloruk guiding it, and a protection around it against Wrack's fire. If this one had the same, it would eat me whole before I had a chance to try anything else.

I could see no hint of the gold and blue diamonds – I had to hope this one had a graalur in command. The fireflow swept towards the scorturliq's realm presence – barely more than a tracery of gigantic lime-green spheres melded together – and I dived out of the realm, and jumped sideways across the roof of the tower, fire blazing ahead of me. The scorturliq had struck forward, the fire I had doused it with wreathing its head as it moved. Now it reared back in pain, trying to escape the agony. Both graalur upon its neck were squealing, too, one tumbling from his perch into the darkness forty feet below, the other clinging on desperately to the burning harness around the creature's neck.

The scorturliq jerked its head sideways, trying to rid itself of the fire consuming its eyes. The second graalur cried out and spun away into the night, as the monster thrashed its body around. Beneath its feet there were more screams and a stampede amidst the graalur, seeking to escape its throes of agony. Its feet slammed into the wall, carving deep gashes in the hard stonework. I felt the tower lurch beneath my feet, and grasped the peril that the creature presented. Another hasty surge into the realm, more fire, this time aimed with – I hoped – some skill to drive the scorturliq away from the city.

If the lloruk sorcerers were even remotely alert they had to be aware of me now. My second blast of fire flared to the left of the scorturliq's head – it hissed again, the smell of burning flesh unpleasant in the extreme, and it twisted away, turning from the threatening fire, and incidentally away from the wall, towards the comforting darkness. I had not killed it, but it was blind and in pain and no longer interested in demolition duties.

I gazed out from the top of the tower for a few seconds before remembering the drama in the market-place. A hasty glance behind me convinced me that my friends were capable of handling the one remaining miner – the shiny indigo carapace was holed in half a dozen places, ichor oozing between the armour plates. It was already limping, injured, and surrounded. There were three people down, too, though – I shivered, hoping my people were not among the casualties.

I had worries of my own to contend with. I slid back into my battleground. The realm was alive with motion. In the brief moments I had been back in the real world, the lloruk had finally become active. I could finally see six wire sculptures of blue and gold diamonds, clustered almost at the edge of visibility. To my dismay, but not really to my surprise, I could see that they were more than capable of extending their influence as far as the city. The dark walls were barely discernible in the realm as glittering, indistinct lines of yellow and green, just the edges showing. Under the east tower there were new patterns of orange and silver moving in tumultuous vortices. Somehow the lloruk were dragging a waterflow through into the real world, to wash away the support upon which the tower relied. There was no way that I could have worked at such a distance. Fortunately, I didn't have to - the tower was far closer to me, within my reach. I reached with the blue spindles that were my arms, stretching out towards the first vortex. In the magerealm there was no need to balance. I could reach across and grip the waterflow, flinging it bodily back towards the lloruk so that as they wrenched it into reality it surged into the mud outside the wall. I could not see what it had done to the mass of graalur preparing to launch themselves into the expected breach, but I had no doubt that they would not be happy. Graalur aren't noted for their love of bathing. My heart bled for them.

The distant shapes that were the lloruk were turning, seeking me. They now knew I was here, and I had their full attention. Not so good. A fireflow blasted towards where I stood – volg it, they were fast! They were far better in this realm than I was. I took the only easy escape from the sparkling red flow – I pulled back into the real world just as the flame licked around me. I felt myself singe, but I was already back in the relative darkness of reality. The fireflow could not harm me if we were in different universes. Not that it would save me for long – they would doubtless shove the fire into the real world and immolate everyone atop my tower. I yelled a warning to the soldiers manning the tower with me to get clear.

I didn't dare return to the realm here – I had no doubt that there would still be fire flaming through the spot where I would appear. My jasq should not let me go through into danger (there had been a lot of speculation for decades as to whether jasqs could think, somehow), but I didn't intend to risk it. Instead, I made for the ladder down to the wall below the tower. I ought to be able to reach the next tower in a couple of minutes. I strained my eyes in the real world darkness. How had I thought that the siege was brightly lit? After the realm, it seemed like deep gloom.

I went down the ladder too fast, scorching the skin off my palms. As I reached the wall, orange light crackled at the top of the tower I had just vacated. I heard a scream of agony, and swore in anger, pausing for a few moments to look back. At least one of the troops up there had not retreated in time. I looked around, wishing I could tackle the lloruk from here, but I needed height to be able to see... and I needed to pick somewhere that would not breach the wall if the lloruk struck back at it. The next tower carried a dozen troops with a ballista. I paused for a moment to check the market-place – the surviving intruder was no longer surviving. Good. I scrambled up to the top, wondering where Wrack had got to.

A moment before I reached the top of the ladder, more fire ripped across the roof of the tower. Men were screaming in pain, and I felt my eyebrows singe and my hair crisp. My momentary pause, out of concern for my friends, had saved my life. There had to be a moral in that somewhere, but at the moment I had more important things to contemplate. I leaped back down, and realised there was more light across the city. The tower on the other side of my first tower was on fire, too – the lloruk had guessed that I would make for one or other of the adjacent towers, and had blasted both to ensure they got me.

Further along the wall there were shouts of alarm. I peered through the smoke wreathing the walls now. A scaling ladder was against the stonework, and now a gang of graalur were at the top of the wall. The defenders here were not soldiers – they were refugees, pressed into service and painfully inadequate as militia. They waved their sickles and pitchforks and tried to hold off the onslaught, but the graalur were experienced and far more savage. One of the five assailants fell, but the other four were holding the top of the wall, the few surviving humans falling back in disarray. I snarled. If I used sorcery, the lloruk would know exactly where I was and everyone on the wall would die.

Where the volg was Wrack? The incursion on the wall would finish us in short order if the graalur forces flinging up scaling ladders with gay abandon extended their foothold. I slid into the realm again. The fireflow atop the first tower was only a few yards from the graalur. I dragged it sideways and pulled it into reality, and let it blast the top of the wall clear of graalur. Shrieks and shouts of pain and terror – some of the brutes leapt from the top of the wall, tumbling down inside or outside the walls. Others burned where they stood. I gritted my teeth, sweeping the fire to ensure there were no survivors, scorching the scaling ladders to send the graalur climbing them to the ground in smoking agony.

From within the realm I could sense the attention of the lloruk. They could see me, and I was the focus of their wrath. I dived out of the realm again and tried to decide where to run, yelling at the people atop the wall to get clear. When the lloruk hit this wall, everyone here would die, the same way I had just slaughtered the graalur. I was already heading for the nearest ladder down to the city street below the wall – I had very little doubt that the next lloruk response would be devastating.

Something wheeled above me, and two soft, soughing coughs told me of my peril. I flung myself sideways as the final snarq dived towards me, acid scouring the stonework where I had stood a moment before, and scorching the ladder I had been making for. It sagged and tumbled to the cobbles below, the acid devouring the wooden framework in moments. I was trapped on top of the wall with a lethal flyer right above me, and a lloruk assault already overdue.

I still to this day don't know why the lloruk didn't flame-strike me. I can only assume that they didn't want to risk burning down their snarq. It was the last surviving flyer, and perhaps they granted it more value than it deserved. If I had been in their shoes I'd have blasted me without compunction, and let the wingbeast take its chances. Perhaps one of the lloruk had a sentimental attachment to the brute. All I know is that I lay there, looking up at the snarq as it came round for another strike. I tried to dive into the realm, but my jasq shivered in my side, telling me that the magerealm was deeply unhealthy just at this moment.

The snarq beat its wings hard, hovering only twenty yards from me, eyes fixed on mine, and it opened its jaws to spit – and then jerked backwards, a crossbow bolt in the left-hand throat, two more slamming into its underside. Fordyral, the hotheaded lieutenant, yelled at me in triumph, his crossbow discharged in his hand, as the snarq plummeted to the ground within the walls, the troops on the ground gleefully leaping in to skewer it.

I struggled to my feet. The jasq was still telling me that the realm was lethal. I was yelling at Fordyral to get clear, and flung myself along the wall, knowing that with the snarq gone the lloruk would delay their devastation no longer.

And then more fire blossomed, well away from the walls, out amidst the attackers. A gorgeous fountain of yellow-orange that rippled and clung to the tiny, dark figures that cried out within it and fell into the black ground and invisibility. Some were the hulking, heavy-set shapes of the graalur – others were the thin, sinuous forms of lloruk. Above, illuminated by the fire he had lit, the dark wings of the dragon soared and wheeled, coming round to send a second torrent of flame down onto the enemy below. I had held their attention for long enough to ensure that Wrack could strike unexpectedly and blast all of them. We had hoped the sorcerers would gather together, working as a team, coordinating their efforts and directing the graalur. They had worked out as the battle commenced that I could not threaten them at a distance – and they had reverted to their usual approach, staying together, well back from the battlefield, at the mercy of a silent dragon.

There was consternation among the graalur. The destruction of the lloruk had been seen by a good number of the troops, and they fell back, crying out in dismay. Another tongue of fire lashed out, and a scorturliq, menacing the eastern wall, reared up and hissed in agony before bolting for the darkness. Wrack turned smoothly, fully-visible against the sky. He had flown up a long way, and then out into the darkness, so that he could glide in without being detected. I yelled in jubilance, triumph mingling with relief at the sudden reversal of fortune. In the distance Berindyl was shouting orders, her strident voice cutting through the tumult. The soldiers on the walls, their confidence boosted by the graalur dismay, launched new volleys of missiles into the milling besiegers. On the west wall a graalur contingent had been making inroads into the defence, holding a thirty foot section of wall as they waited for reinforcements. The sudden loss of their lords and masters convinced the thugs that retreat was the best policy, and they scrambled back onto their ladders, abandoning the stonework they had fought so hard to achieve. Trelyar's people were shouting out their relief at the withdrawal.

I looked back into the market-place. A small group of figures were there, their assailants gone. I just hoped my people were all right.

Wrack turned again in the air, and swept back towards our walls. I grinned and slid into the magerealm. No trace of the fireflows the lloruk had directed at me, or of the spindles and crystals that had indicated the presence of the lloruk only a few moments before.

I caught a fireflow of my own and flung it through into the real world, blasting the graalur by the gate. The ram had fallen silent at the destruction of the lloruk; now it fell to the ground as the burning graalur scattered, screaming in pain. I seized a handy flow of water and flung that against the squads near the west wall, washing them back. Less lethal, but just as devastating.

The graalur were falling back, retreating from the walls in disarray. They had lost their commanders and their expectation of success, and they were turning and running. I pulled out of the realm, realising as I did so just how exhausted I felt, and watched them abandoning the attack, the prospect of magic being used against them more than enough to turn their morale into porridge. The soldiers on the walls were whooping with delight, the hail of artillery from the towers almost ceasing as they realised that the assault was over. I didn't know if the siege would be abandoned now, or if they were just falling back to regroup later, but we had struck them a heavy blow. There were a significant number of still, dark bodies on the abandoned grounds. I slid back into the magerealm, planning to encourage them to retreat further with another rush of water.

I looked around for a suitable cerulean flow. In the sky, just turning, there were a cluster of purple veins, stretching out from a central core of blue diamonds. I grinned, watching Wrack soaring over the panicked graalur. The army was retreating in disarray like drops of water fizzing on a hot skillet. Wrack poured another blast of fire to hasten their embarrassed retreat, before soaring back to sweep into a neat landing on the tower. Close to, I could see numerous gashes and tears in his wings, and two small patches that looked suspiciously like acid burns on his hide. But the battle was over. The lloruk were gone, and the graalur in full retreat. The jasq beat a counterpoint to the retreat as Wrack transformed, his skin losing the scales and the horns, his body shrinking to his human shape. I reached out as the change completed and hugged him. I had plans for more substantial celebrations with him later, but unlike the graalur I did not fancy such activities in public. He held me and kissed me, leaving me in no doubts that he had very similar plans. A wide smile was lighting up his face.

I kissed him back. Around us, other men and women were clutching each other and yelling their triumph and their relief. The feeling of glory at the success was buoying me up, a better feeling that I had had for a long time.

A heavy hand slammed against my shoulder-blades, and I staggered, gasping at the impact. The columns of fire were still blazing; in their light, I could see Fordyral, his face lit up with a bigger smile than I had seen for months. He hauled me out of Wrack's grip and hugged me, babbling something about the victory. I could sense Wrack's glower, but I could feel a mirroring grin on my face, too, and I squeezed Fordyral, and then two other soldiers in turn, neither of whom I could name. One of the female soldiers was clutching at Wrack, and I took hold of my dragon before anyone else endeavoured to inveigle him away from me. We were stranded on the wall for a good five minutes before someone on the ground below thought to find us a ladder to replace the one the snarq had destroyed. Fordyral struggled, with some considerable difficulty, to order a couple of men to stay and keep half an eye on the retreating graalur, to ensure they didn't somehow regroup, but none of us thought there was any risk of that tonight. The reversal of their fortunes, and the sudden, awe-inspiring appearance of Wrack in his dragon form, had been more than enough to crush any desires the graalur had to fling themselves at our walls.

The streets were thronged with Tolgrailers and refugees alike, bottles and tankards appearing as if by sorcery, barrels that had been dragged into hiding earlier in the day being hauled into the market square or onto the widest streets so that everyone, men, women and even children could slake their thirst and celebrate. The tumult of shouts of jubilation were lessening now, but yells of happiness were still echoing off the stone and plaster walls as combatants were confirmed to have survived the fight.

In a few places I saw still, silent, sometimes sobbing figures. We had not had the battle all our own way, and there had been casualties. Good men and women... wives, fathers, husbands, daughters, mothers and sons lost to the hatred of the lloruk. Most of those grieving had friends and family offering what empty comfort they could. I took hold of a bottle someone thrust into my hand, and gulped a mouthful of the strong, sweet wine within.

Wrack caught hold of me and hugged me close. "Without us, there'd've been a lot more lost" he whispered, and snagged the bottle from my fingers as I smiled a little wanly at him. I was making my way towards the market square. I needed to know if my people were all right.

The square was thronged with elated men and women, crowing their delight at the change in fortunes. Torches and a few of the glowstones I had seen elsewhere added to the illumination from the fading columns of fire, so the square was lit brightly. To my astonishment, as we walked into the square there was a sudden burst of cheering, and the crowd turned as if pulled by wires to gather around us. I heard a dozen people yelling my name, and a similar number calling Wrack's. I realised that my eyes were misting over – I wasn't used to bursting into tears, but I was seriously at risk of doing so. We were suddenly surrounded, hands reaching for us and shouts of delight at our presence.

To one side I saw half a dozen figures I recognised. I yelled at Kelhene and Korhus, and half the Grihl Valley contingent shoved their way through the surrounding mob to reach us.

"Are all of you all right?" I tried to shout over the tumult. There was no way Kelhene could have heard me over the cacophony of cries, but she just raised her hand, thumb pointing upwards. She gestured at Chelhik – his leg was heavily bandaged, and he was limping badly, but he had a broad smile. Darhia had a somewhat more wan grin – one of the mining creatures had obviously caught her across the side of the head, but she was alive, and the three deep weals were no longer bleeding. Two more of my contingent were bloodied but unbowed – Dalhis and Ulsdher – but they were all in one piece, alive and well. I yelled my own relief and happiness, and Wrack grabbed me and pulled me into his embrace again, his mouth silencing my whoops.

It was more than an hour and another bottle of wine before I could hear myself think. The celebration was going to go on until the lantern-trees burst into light, or perhaps later, but already people were slipping away from the main throngs. I had been kissed, hugged, groped and danced with by – so it felt – half the men in the square. I had managed to find everyone from the Grihl Valley – even Darhath had seized me and held me.

My people were all in pretty good shape – even Korhus was in good humour. They had acquitted themselves well against their aggressors, with the help from me, of course. They had earned their presence in Tolgrail, and I could see that they had forged new friendships in the fire of the battle. They would be welcome here in the city, now. Talhin had already been told he had a job working on repairs to the walls, and Belha was making herself popular as a skilful cook. It might take others of my charges a little longer to find new niches into which to fit, but they would do it. I was still worried about Darhath, but the Tolgrailers would find a place for him and for Kelhene. It felt strange that I might no longer have to worry about their safety. I had hugged Kelhene tightly, and did the same with Korhus and Chelhik, warning the latter not to let his hands wander while Wrack was watching him. Even Darhath seemed to understand that the threat to the city was over (for the moment, at least), and I enjoyed hugging him.

I finally made my way back to Wrack and dragged him away from the current woman embracing him. He had been grinning broadly, his face warm with a relaxed, open smile. I looked at Wrack with the lessening tumult around us and smiled at him. "Feels good, doesn't it?" I said. "Doing something to win against the bad guys?"

He shut me up passionately. We were near the edge of the square, across from the council chamber. For the first time since the graalur retreated, no one seemed to be paying the two of us any particular attention. I took hold of Wrack's arm, and eased him into one of the side streets, out of the clamour. I wasn't sure which way led to the chamber the city had provided us with, but I wanted to get Wrack into private and celebrate our survival.

In the doorway of a bakery, in a degree of shadow, I took hold of Wrack again and kissed him fiercely. When we finally broke apart, I was short of breath. I tried to drag him off, but instead he gripped me tightly and looked down at me. "Staying down here, aren't you?" he murmured, barely loud enough to hear over the distant, unmusical effort at singing that had just enveloped the square.

I hadn't wanted to spoil the mood with concerns about the future. I tried to kiss him again, to silence the question, but he held me at arm's length, looking into my eyes, the question hanging between us. He didn't ask again – he didn't need to. I looked into his viridian eyes, recognising his need for an answer. I paused, taking a slow, unsteady breath, trying to marshal my words, before I finally nodded in response.

"There's work to do down here" I added softly. "I promised Kelhene I'd deal with the larisqs." I looked at him. "It matters, Wrack. It needs to be done."

He tightened his arms around me, his face close to mine. In the shadow of the doorway, only his intent eyes were really visible.

"You're a volging idiot, Sorrel" he growled. I shivered, not wanting to spoil the moment with the bitter argument I was afraid was coming. "Getting yourself caught up in something that wasn't our fight before."

I didn't want to fight with Wrack. I so wanted him to understand what I was feeling. I stared into his eyes, trying to work out how to explain the need that I had... the need for a purpose. Down here, I could make a difference. Volg it, the lafquass ought to have some perception of my feelings... and of my feelings for him.

I could feel his fingers digging into my arms as he gripped me. "It is my fight now" I said softly. "I want it to be *our* fight."

Wrack's grip tightened around me, and he held my gaze, his eyes brilliant emerald. "Volging fool" he rasped. "Taking on the lloruk – you're an idiot!" I opened my mouth to snarl an answer, but he fastened his mouth on mine, ensuring he didn't let me get a word in edgeways. When he had finished kissing me hard he murmured "Can't leave you alone down here, can I? No knowing *what* trouble you'd get into without me here with you."

I opened my mouth to argue. It came naturally to argue with Wrack. But then I closed my mouth and looked up into his eyes, a stupid grin spreading across my face as I realised what he was saying. I almost began to say something deeply wet and emotional that I would have regretted bitterly, but fortunately my tongue was tangled for long enough for common sense to strangle such inanities stillborn. Instead, I just looked into his eyes, snuggled against him, and whispered "You do realise you're still a very poor substitute for a triplane?"

ABOUT THE AUTHOR

Peter Vialls drove his parents mad when a child with his constant demands for books to read. Now nearly fifty he still drives people mad, mostly by his writing. Crimes against literature include a Doctor Who stageplay, The Empress of Othernow, which received considerable acclaim; various articles and rolegaming scenarios in White Dwarf magazine and other publications; sections in a Dragonlance module; and various short stories. When not torturing his word-processor he is a practising solicitor in Cambridgeshire. He is married with two teenage graalur.

21999187R00180

Made in the USA
Charleston, SC
10 September 2013